Albert Harkness, John Henderson, John Seath

Exercises in Latin Prose

Albert Harkness, John Henderson, John Seath

Exercises in Latin Prose

ISBN/EAN: 9783337371012

Printed in Europe, USA, Canada, Australia, Japan

Cover: Foto ©Andreas Hilbeck / pixelio.de

More available books at **www.hansebooks.com**

Classical Text-Book Series.

EXERCISES IN LATIN PROSE

A COMPANION TO

HARKNESS'S LATIN GRAMMAR.

FOR THE USE OF

INTERMEDIATE AND UNIVERSITY CLASSES

BY

JOHN SEATH, B.A.

HEAD MASTER, ST. CATHARINES COLLEGIATE INSTITUTE,

AND

JOHN HENDERSON, M.A.

CLASSICAL MASTER, ST. CATHARINES COLLEGIATE INSTITUTE.

Toronto:
COPP, CLARK & CO., 9 FRONT STREET WEST.
1881.

PREFACE.

The object of this volume is to furnish candidates for University Matriculation and the High School Intermediate Examination, with a suitable manual, and to assist the teacher of Latin in economizing his time. The Authors are of the opinion that Grammar and Composition are best taught when they are taught together, and that a good deal of labor is unnecessarily spent in committing to memory one set of rules in the text-book on Grammar and another in that on Composition. They have, consequently, omitted introductory remarks to the exercises in Part I. and explanatory comments in Part II., and refer simply to the paragraphs in Harkness's Latin Grammar, which paragraphs the pupil is supposed to have studied thoroughly before attempting to write the exercises based thereon. He will also find it to his advantage to memorize many of the quotations introduced in Harkness's Syntax to illustrate the different rules.

It was at first intended to merely adapt Mr. BELCHER's " Short Exercises " to the Latin Grammar ; but when the work had been proceeded with for some time, it was found impossible to do this satisfactorily owing to the want of a Vocabulary for Part II., and of suitable exercises on the Syntax of the Verb in Part I. The first part of this volume has, therefore, been wholly rewritten, Part I. of the " Short Exercises " being incorporated in those on the Syntax of the Noun and Adjective. The exercises have also been made gradually more difficult, as an introduction to independent composition.

The Vocabulary is intended to supply little more than the Latin for the English word, and is supplemented by foot-notes to the exercises, in which the common idioms of English and Latin are contrasted. As the work is in-

tended as a class-book, the Authors have avoided giving
too much help, and a good deal has been left to the intelligence of the pupil and the judgment of the teacher.

Part II. requires little comment. The exercises in it
consist of translations from the best Latin Prose authors,
and an effort has been made to adhere as closely as
possible to the Latin without an undue sacrifice of the
English. As in Part I., the exercises are graduated in
difficulty, and the idioms of the languages more and more
contrasted. It is hoped that it will save the teacher the
time now lost in dictating exercises in the class.

The Grammar Papers, which have been selected from
Mr. BELCHER's sets, and those of London, Toronto, and
other Universities, with additions based on Harkness's
Grammar, will be found useful by those who have not
access to the sources whence they have been taken.

Before beginning the study of this volume, the pupil
should have completed Harkness's Introductory Latin
Book and made some progress in the Latin Reader and
Grammar, to the latter of which this "Composition" is
intended to serve as a Companion. Many of the later
exercises in both Parts are too difficult for the ordinary
Intermediate candidate ; but, while the first thirty-nine of
Part I. and the first fifty of Part II. are especially de-
signed for this class of pupils, further progress may be
easily secured, now that their examination is held but
once a year.

Any suggestions from teachers for the improvement of
the exercises will be thankfully received by the Authors,
who will be gratified if this venture of theirs prove as
useful to their fellow-teachers as they anticipate it will in
their own classes.

St. Catharines, January, 1881.

CONTENTS.

PART I.*

I.

NOMINATIVE: ACCUSATIVE WITH INFINITIVE.

(362-369, 375 & 545)[1].

1. It was said that Servius, the general, had crossed the river with his army.[2]

2. Who said that the general with his cavalry was crossing[3] the river?

3. They saw all the horses swim across the river in the morning.

4. The robbers had heard that all the horses were hidden in the neighbouring wood.

5. It is believed, O Servius, that the robbers in this thick wood have been made prisoners.

6. Caius having been declared an exile said that he had seen horses and men in the wood.

7. He had heard that there were robbers in the woods who did not start on their journey.

8. I feel that danger is at hand : they say robbers are hidden in the trees.

9. All of us (say: "we all") know that teachers who are diligent, daily learn wisdom.

10. It is clear that pupils learn a great deal from[4] wise teachers.

11. He thinks a teacher who teaches faithfully, is chiefly teaching himself.

12. They say that flowers can feel pain ; but experience, the best instructress, denies this.

---

[1] The references are to the paragraphs in Harkness' Latin Grammar.

[2] As the Romans preferred the personal to the impersonal construction, this may be put in the following form also :—" Servius, the general, was said to have," &c.

[3] When in a sentence introduced by *that* the notion expressed by the verb is represented as not over before the time of the notion expressed by the principal verb, the past tense must be translated by the *present* infinitive. If over before the time of the principal verb, it is to be translated by the *perfect* infinitive.   [4] "from " = *ab* or *apud*.

* Before beginning the Exercises the student should become familiar with the rules for the Arrangement of Words and Clauses (592--602). Paragraphs 603—606 should be taken up when required.

1

13. Quintus had read that all the flowers in the garden feel pain.

14. All flowers cannot feel pain, but it is clear that this flower feels it.

15. I think that my horse, which is everything (say: "all things") to me, is in the field.

16. They would have seen that there are ten horses in this field.

II.

ACCUSATIVE WITH INFINITIVE.

(371, 375 & 545.)

1. We hear that you have caught fish in the lake.

2. Do you think that your friend has dreamt a wonderful dream?

3. We hope to catch[1] a good many fish in the river to-day.

4. I have heard that there are excellent fish in the pond which is near your house.

5. Titus has promised to go with us: (but) he says that his friends stand round him in tears.

6. They would have undertaken to finish the business by-themselves.

7. You were in the habit of saying[2] that a business well begun is well ended.

8. You used to say that men desire to command others.

9. Have you heard that a new book has been sent to you by a friend[3] who laughs at Fortune?

10. We have promised to give him a book.

11. The ancient Germans are said to have gone across the river Rhine.

12. Tacitus says that the Germans valued the advice of women.

13. They used to say that women speak with prophetic voice.

---

[1] After verbs signifying "to hope, to promise or to undertake," the Eng. pres. inf. is translated into Latin by the fut. inf., with its subject expressed in the accusative, thus:—

"He hopes *to come*" becomes in Latin
"Sperat *se venturum*."

[2] 469, II.   [3] See 414, 5.

14. It is declared that the Germans never despised the answers of women.
15. All the ancient nations considered women holy.
16. Tacitus has recorded that women were always esteemed by the Germans.

III.

TWO ACCUSATIVES.

I.—*Of the same person or thing.*

(372 & 373).

1. He thought himself a very clever, useful, and industrious man.[1]
2. Why did he, who had been chosen king, not render himself both useful and industrious?
3. The Romans chose Marius consul for the seventh time.
4. They had made Cæsar consul on account of his victories.
5. Both the Greeks and the Romans used to think themselves powerful.
6. We have made thee a goddess, and have placed thee in heaven.
7. We have called you our father on account of your kindness.
8. The consul Cicero thought Catiline a wicked man.
9. Having set out they saluted Marius (as) consul.
10. Who said that he had made Fortune a goddess?
11. She has been made a goddess by both the rich and the poor.
12. To create Marius consul was a dangerous (thing[2]).
13. You had considered yourself industrious and good.
14. No one thought Marius a good man although they made him consul.
15. He may think[2] you good : he does not think you happy.
16. No one was made happy by Sulla, although by him many were made rich.

---

[1] When three coordinate words come together, we may use *et* so as to connect each with the preceding, or attach *que* to the last, or leave out all the conjunctions, but not put *et* before the last only. 587, 6.　[2] 438, 3.

IV.

TWO ACCUSATIVES.

II.—*Of different persons or things.*

(374 & 376).

1. My father taught me letters, although he concealed his reason from me.
2. His mother would have taught him music.
3. Why did not his mother conceal her[1] design from him?
4. It is very difficult to teach some people to be wise.
5. Socrates, the wise man, had taught many people (say : "many men ") many things.
6. The master teaches all of us letters very carefully.
7. Achilles was admonished of these things.
8. When were you asking peace from the Gauls who live in the Province?
9. Verres asked a price from parents for the burial of their children.
10. The soldiers kept on asking[2] their general for money for this reason.
11. It is not easy to ask (one's) friend for money.
12. Do not[3] ask your brother for the book, because he has not read it himself.
13. He thought that Balbus had led his army across the Rhine.
14. He has been taught the Arts by his father.
15. Let us beseech God for our daily bread.
16. He doubled the original number of the Senate, and called (those) of the elder families, the ancient Senators : and them[4] (say : "whom") he asked first for their opinion.

---

[1] Use *suus* for *his, her,* and *their,* when they stand for the same person as the subject of the verb. In the same way use the proper case of *sui* for *him, her,* &c. In the case above, if *her* refer to *mother,* use *suus;* otherwise, use the proper case of *is.* Of course, when the reference is obvious, *his, her,* &c., may be omitted in translating into Latin.—448 and 449.

[2] 269, II. [3] 584, 1. [4] 453.

V.

REVIEW EXERCISE.

(362—376).

1. I, an enemy, said that I hoped to slay an enemy.
2. Socrates, who is considered a wise man, called himself a citizen and inhabitant of the whole world.
3. They have concealed their crimes from their father Hannibal.
4. It is very difficult to conceal (one's) faults from a friend, who proves himself to be a true friend.
5. His brother always denied that he (himself) was clever.
6. He said[1] he could not come to-morrow on account of the return of his brother, who had lived a wicked life.
7. Ovid, the poet, thought himself a great man, and says that his verses are excellent.
8. All of us thought Titus a clever general.
9. Fabius, who had been created consul, showed himself an example of patience.
10. Go on, O son Caius ; I hope that you will conceal nothing from me, who am your father.
11. Cæsar said that he always used to conceal his plans from his generals.
12. Hannibal has promised to attack the enemy.
13. The enemy have said that they will resist the attack, although the general has turned out wonderful.
14. It has been said that History is a good instructress.
15. He used to think that his brother was a very clever man.
16. It would have been told Hannibal that his cavalry were on the march.

---

[1] Whenever the words *said* . . *not* occur, translate them by the proper tense of *negare*, if they are supposed to be used in answer to a question ; otherwise use *dixit — non*.

VI.

ACCUSATIVE.

Duration of Time and Extent of Space.

(378).

1. Troy was besieged for ten years by the Greeks under the leadership of Agamemnon.[1]
2. The Greeks were besieging Troy, a fine city, for ten years.
3. Not many cities have been besieged for fifteen years.
4. His father was six feet high ; his brother was taller than his father.[2]
5. He, who is six feet high, and therefore a taller man than I am, says that the Arabians have slender swords, *each four*[3] cubits long.
6. We saw yesterday a house fifty-five feet high and eighty feet broad.
7. This house was built twenty-five years ago.[4]
8. Cæsar led his forces three miles away from the Forum.
9. The army marched, by forced marches, one hundred and fifty-eight miles to his camp, where they asked him for corn.
10. Cæsar's gardens are on the other side of the Tiber, and are twelve miles from Ostia.
11. I have walked to-day twenty-two miles : which[5] is a long journey.
12. The town of Saguntum, situated nearly a mile from the sea, was by far the most wealthy of the Spanish towns.[6]
13. Ten years ago a wall which stood here was twenty feet high and one thousand feet long.
14. This wall is said to have been built by the Romans 1800[7] years ago.
15. It was built by Julius Agricola, who lived many years in Britain.
16. Cæsar's camp was pitched three miles from the camp of Ariovistus.

---

[1] 431.   [2] 417, 1.   [3] Use distributive numeral.   [4] See also 427.   [5] 445, 7.
[6] 396, ILL   [7] See Grammar, p. 56, note 3.

VII.

ACCUSATIVE OF LIMIT AND SPECIFICATION, &c.

(379, 380 & 381.)

1. I am-going-to-start[1] for Rome at once.
2. My brother and I[2] went to the city of Rome yesterday.
3. Blind that I am! Marcellus sent the boy to the army at Capua (say: "to the army to Capua"), which was encamped at[3] a distance of two miles.
4. In the name of the Gods! did you receive a message from Marcellus, the great general.
5. He told us that he was setting out for Capua, a city of Italy, and that there[4] are three roads to Mutina.
6. His brother and I walked ten miles yesterday, and went to York.
7. Capua, a city of Italy, is distant ninety miles from Rome.
8. It was announced to Marcellus that the Carthaginians had at this time set out in the direction of Syracuse.
9. Why did the Carthaginians set out for Syracuse?
10. They were not at all moved because the army of the Romans had encamped close to the walls of the town.
11. O holy Jupiter! did he wish to go home to Rome with me yesterday?
12. He said that he had wished to go into the city with my brother.
13. Cæsar marched with his whole army to the town of Marseilles and besieged the inhabitants.
14. They are all going with your father into a country where the inhabitants live chiefly on milk and flesh.
15. Where are you going? Wretched that I am! I am going to Delos as-fast-as-I-can.
16. It is pleasant to return home after hard labour.

---

[1] 470.   [2] 463, II., 1.   [3] 378.   [4] The English expletive is omitted in Latin.

VIII.

DATIVE WITH VERBS.

(383, 384 & 385.)

1. He told Labienus that Cæsar's army is near the river which[1] is called the Rhine.
2. Show me, my friend, the book of which you spoke.
3. Believe me, I have narrated to you everything that was done at Cicero's house.
4. It was announced to the multitude that the two Consuls had been killed by the enemy who had surrounded the city with a wall forty feet high.
5. "Show us," cried they, "the road : we will destroy that city or die for our country."
6. He persuades his friends that life is the end of all things.
7. To prove to an ignorant man that he knows nothing is most difficult.[2]
8. Caius proved to the citizens that they knew nothing; they, therefore, devoted themselves to labour and obeyed his commands.
9. The Athenians hated Socrates because he had proved to them that they knew nothing.
10. To persuade a man that he is ignorant is difficult : all of us think highly[3] of ourselves.
11. It is easy to persuade anyone that he is clever, but to do this does not benefit him.
12. "I have explained to my friends," he said, "the whole circumstance."
13. To fight for liberty has always been considered by the ancients to be the road to Honour.
14. It has often been told you that the temple of Jupiter is situated on a hill four hundred feet high.
15. These things have been explained to Cæsar to be for the most part[4] false.
16. He kept me ignorant of the money which had been entrusted to him by Cicero, the orator. O, immortal gods ! how blind avarice renders men !

---

[1] 445, 4.   [2] 438, 3.   [3] 402, III., 1.   [4] 380, 2.

IX.

DATIVE WITH VERBS.

(Continued).

1. They gave the general as a present—a helmet, a shield, and two spears : he pitched his camp near the city of Syracuse.
2. Cæsar, to whom they had given these things, had set out for Marseilles.
3. Give me back my legions, Varus, which thou hast lost.
4. I entrust to you, my friends, these children : tell your son that I am starting for Cumae, a most delightful place.
5. Marcellus had already given his helmet and shield to his slave who is called Achilles.
6. This benevolent woman gave money to the wretched man, who, being severely wounded, died after a few hours.
7. They left him one of his children,[1] a little girl, called Julia.
8. The money which I received from you, has been most useful to me.
9. I shall leave you a great coat, a hat, and a stick, with which set out for Sardinia.
10. The children, to whom the apples were given, have gone away. When are you going into the country with your sister ?
11. He turned out to be the son of the Consul, and lived ten days after his father's return from Spain.
12. This little boy has entrusted me with the money.
13. Bread was given to the people by the benevolent women, all[2] of whom had promised to assist him.
14. We shall all walk to London to-morrow, where we shall remain for eight days.
15. All men naturally (say: "by nature") are anxious for liberty, and hate the condition of slavery.
16. "Render," it has been said, "unto Cæsar the things which are Cæsar's.

---

[1] 396, III., 2, 2) ; also *ex* with ablative. [2] Cf. the idiom in *all of us.*

X.

DATIVE WITH VERBS, &c.

(Continued).

1. Marcellus says that he can not satisfy himself.
2. It is much easier to put a check on oneself than on any-one else (say: "any other person").
3. The Romans, a very proud nation, consulted for their own interests.
4. Help, citizens, a poor man, whose house has been de-stroyed !
5. I have learned to help the unfortunate, because I have been unfortunate myself.
6. He is not unacquainted with misfortune, and helps the wretched.
7. It is very difficult to help an obstinate man.
8. Help had been rendered to Labienus in a great strait.
9. "Bring me a horse," he exclaimed, "the enemy are at hand."
10. They had brought the general a horse and a sword.
11. Baculus had been sent forward to Labienus, who was holding the top of the hill.
12. Thou wilt send his brother to the king, who is now in the camp of Cæsar.
13. The sheep did harm to themselves in the midst of the thick trees.
14. It is hurtful to sheep not to have a careful shepherd.
15. The wolf said to the lamb, "For a long time you have done me harm."
16. The lamb replied to the wolf, "Wolf! I have never done you harm."

XI.

REVIEW EXERCISE.

(378—385).

1. The house of the spider did no good to the flies, which were anxious for his friendship.
2. No one wishes to help this obstinate man, because he does not put a check on his anger.

3. The brothers Sosii are booksellers, and are very useful to all of us.

4. The slaves, to whom the masters were giving money, went away from Rome yesterday.

5. You will return to your brother these five minæ.

6. He sent a messenger to Marseilles, when Cæsar was besieging the town.

7. We shall all walk to London to-morrow, where we shall remain for eight days.

8. Cicero sends his compliments to you, and your brother.

9. Tullia had told us that her brother, and all our friends are well.

10. He promised to kill certain animals that live for a few days.

11. London, the capital of Britain, is distant from York two hundred miles.

12. Tell them that many dangers surround them, although the town is distant nearly fifteen miles from Carthage.

13. The learned Cicero [1] informs us that he is a very learned man.

14. I am able to assist you, my friend, for my house is large.

15. The flies listened to the spider with much pleasure. [2]

16. Cæsar plunders and burns the town, gives the booty to the soldiers, leads his army across the river, and reaches the territory of the enemy.

XII.

REVIEW EXERCISE.

1. The army had been seen by the messenger, who said that cavalry were now crossing the river.

2. The general sent word to the brave general Brutus that he had marched forty miles.

3. Cæsar asked Labienus for help. "I have," said he, "no cavalry with me." [3]

4. The camp was pitched on the top [4] of a hill, and surrounded [5] by a ditch two hundred feet long.

---

[1] Lat. idiom often *Cicero, the learned man.*   [2] 414.   [3] 434, 5.   [4] 441, 6.
[5] This may also be translated according to 579.

5. They told the king that for forty years they had resisted the foe.

6. "Give us," cried the multitude, "bread or money."

7. Marcellus, the general of the Romans, made Publius master of the cavalry.

8. I am going to-morrow to Syracuse, a very beautiful city, situated in a fine country.

9. It is related that the spider said to the fly that his house was large.

10. The people of-Rome [1] made Marius Consul, after a great victory.

11. They have all gone into the country, where they will remain fifteen days.

12. He says that he and his father have lived in Spain for ninety years.

13. I had asked the learned [2] Publius his opinion about the circumstance that occurred on the top of the hill.

14. Publius, whose opinion he would have asked, is a most learned man.

15. We make Wealth, Fortune, Health, gods; for they tempt mankind.

16. I shall help his brother, who has set out to Rome with my son.

XIII.

DATIVE WITH VERBS.

(Continued.)

1. The queen commands her servants, who at once obey her.

2. They all cry out with one voice that they will harm no one.

3. Obey your parents; help the wretched; do good to all.

4. They serve a hard slavery to Metellus the Consul.

5. Regulus is reported to have said, "I will obey myself rather than you."

6. Happy is the man who is-lord of himself: he can consult for the interests of others.

7. Money is to Horatius a servant, [3] to Seneca a master. [3]

8. Ten slaves obeyed Horatius, a kind-hearted man.

---

[1] 441, 5   [2] See p. 11, note 1.   [3] Use *servire* and *imperare*.

9. We have all listened[1] to our passions, whose sway is destructive.

10. They have asked me my opinion. I reply, "Be your own masters.

11. I am opposed to your plans, which seem to me to be bad.

12. The wise master gave orders[2] to his servants that the letter should be brought.[3]

13. Certain animals are by nature obedient to man, and some men are the servants of (say : "serve") others.

14. Julius Agricola served Cæsar and became himself a great general.

15. It was reported that you commanded these undertakings, O foolish Consul !

16. Cicero is said not to have been lord-of himself, though he wished others to put a check on themselves.

XIV.

DATIVE WITH COMPOUNDS, &c.

(386, 387, 389 & 390).

1. The Consul, who had the name of his father, conferred benefits on his soldiers.

2. The slave did a kindness to his master, Lucilius the Prætor, who was present with his friends.

3. It is very pleasant to do a kindness to Lucilius, who is himself a very kind man.

4. Do not revile Lucilius ; he has been most kind to all your brothers.

5. The Germans will resist the general of the Romans whose name is Varus.

6. We have resisted your plans, for avarice is an evil (say : "for an evil") to men.

7. I have a very kind-hearted father and a most loving mother ; they[4] are now a care to me.

8. I am opposed to the plans of Cæsar, which seem to me to be injurious.

---

1 " listen " = obedire.   2 Use jubeo.   3 551, II.   4 See 439, 2, 1.

9. Let us help the Germans, who are now very bravely resisting[1] the legions of Varus. Their general has left four cohorts for the defence of the city.

10. The troops were opposed to Cæsar's plans : "Let us," said they, "resist the foe."

11. These grapes are good ; we will carry them to our sister at Naples,[2] who is setting out for Tenedos.

12. Bad wine will do harm even to a bad man : good wine often to a good man.

13. He has sent wine as a present to his father, who has started for Britain.

14. The legions of Varus were sent as a defence to the camp pitched near the Rhine.

15. The friendship of the spider is for the most part not very useful to the fly.

16. These things are of use to the soldiers who come to the assistance of the Athenians.

XV.

DATIVE WITH ADJECTIVES AND DERIVATIVES.

(391 & 392).

1. It is pleasant to us to go to the country in the summer.[3]

2. Every one believes that obedience to the laws is true wisdom.

3. Regulus was more acceptable to the people than to the Senate.

4. Sulla, the dictator, is most bitterly-hostile to Marius the exile.

5. We have received a present most acceptable to all of us.

6. Let us go to Baiæ, a delightful place, close to the sea.

7. The prudent Labienus was most fitted for command.

8. It is a very wise (thing) to be one's own master : to be anyone's slave is foreign to our nature.

9. Servitude to greed is considered by all of us a very great evil.

10. He has gone to Athens, a dangerous city for its own citizens.

---

[1] The English relative clause may frequently be translated into Latin by a participial phrase. Here *who are resisting* may be so translated.

[2] See Exercise VII., 3.   [3] 426.

11. What is grateful to one man is bitter to another.
12. They have told me that you are not conscious to your-self of faults.
13. We shall tell him that he is very like Achilles.
14. Gellius is hateful to all of you ; to whom did he ever do any good?
15. The Romans have been for ten years bitterly-hostile to Varus, who had ordered his soldiers to build a wall twenty feet high.
16. He is unfortunate, and is no match for Achilles, who excels Hector in valour.

XVI.

DATIVE WITH ADJECTIVES AND DERIVATIVES.

(Continued).

1. His son has been most useful to Cæsar, who has set out for Gaul, where he will lead his forces across the river.
2. He had thought that no one was so useful to himself as himself.
3. The defeat of Varus is a most disgraceful circumstance for the Romans.
4. Give us what is most useful to us : teach us to be wise.
5. What is most pleasant is not always the most accept-able even to a good man.
6. The Sicilians were exasperated against Verres, that most base man, whom you bespatter with praises.
7. Verres and Varus are two names, most hateful to all good citizens.
8. This circumstance has turned out (to be) most advanta-geous for my father.
9. Caius Cæsar, with all his army, marched to the assist-ance of the Province of Gaul.
10. It is disgraceful to a Roman to oppose the plans of the Senate.
11. Horace has a good word for all, and has been very kind to me.
12. Horace went to Baiæ, a place most grateful to him.
13. It is agreeable to nature to live honourably.

14. He told me that the boy's name was not Caius, although he was called after the name of his father.

15. But that which was attributed to me as a crime, not only was not a fault: it was (even) a most noble deed.

16. Horatius has declared that death is common to every age and every clime.

XVII.

REVIEW EXERCISE.

(384—392).

1. All of us know that death is common to all, and hateful to some.

2. Marcellus used to be present at every danger: he was often an assistance to his friends.

3. Who was a match for Achilles, but (say: "unless") Hector.

4. I am a friend to his plans, which are acceptable to the Senate.

5. They have declared that money is a most dangerous[1] (thing) for a very poor man.

6. Govern your tongue when you are angry:[2] put a check upon yourself.

7. You will never be able to repay by words his kindness to you all.

8. Of whom did Gellius, who was called after his father's name, ever say a good word?

9. My horse, that animal most useful to man, is more useful to me than to my sister.

10. The Greeks besieged Troy for ten years, to which city they were bitterly-hostile.

11. I have done nothing disagreeable to you, I hope: a deed injurious to you would be very disagreeable to me.

12. When Regulus returned to Carthage, he (say: "Regulus having returned," &c.), served a hard slavery to the Carthaginians.

13. Gellius used to speak ill of everybody, even of his own father.

14. The wisest men have always governed their tongues carefully.

---

     [1] 438, 4.   [2] 578, I.

15. The City of Rome built on seven hills, ruled the nations of the world for many years.

16. He who now goes from the-country-of-the-Veneti (*Veneti*) to Naples crosses the Apennine mountains.

XVIII.

GENITIVE, SUBJECTIVE, OBJECTIVE AND PARTITIVE.

(395 & 396.)

1. My father's opinion was asked by his brother Horace.

2. Let us see this man's horse, which he says is a good (one).

3. We have all learnt that the walls of the city are very high.

4. As much[1] rise as the Nile undergoes, so much[1] hope is there for the harvest.

5. Near Capua I saw Hannibal's camp, which was very large.

6. They have sent a quick messenger to my friend Cecilia's husband and sister, the former[2] of whom is twenty-four years old (say: "has been born twenty-four years").

7. The tomb of Metellus is close to Rome, a city of Italy, where the most opulent of all men live.

8. Hector's (wife) Andromache, after his death, married a king. Which of you doubts this?

9. They saw Hector's (wife) Andromache holding[3] her son by the hand.

10. Sulla's (son) Faustus left Rome three days ago, and the house became a disgrace to its owner (or "master").

11. All the country is divided into five parts, one of which the enemy inhabit.

12. Cicero's letters to Atticus are read by many people.

13. Let us go to Rome to-morrow, where my son's wife has been left by one of the consuls.

14. It is a long journey to London, but I have finished it in one day.

15. Varus was conquered more by the prudence than by the valour of the Germans.

16. The Senate asked Sulla his opinion concerning the war which was being carried on by the Samnites.

---

1 " as much " — " so much " = *Quantum — tantum.*

2 450, 2.   3 Use the participle. " They saw that Hector's (wife) held," &c., would require *held* to be in the infinitive.

2

XIX.

GENITIVE OF CHACTERISTIC, OF SPECI-
FICATION, &c.

(396, IV. & V., 397 & 398.)

1. The enemy had used[1] spears of very great length against the defenders of the temple of Jupiter.

2. They all declared that Atilius, the son of Atticus, was a man of wonderful valour, although only thirty years old.[2]

3. Atilius, son of Atticus, was born in Italy, and is (a man) of fifty years (of age), and one of the noblest of the Romans.

4. By forced marches, they finished a journey of fifty miles to-day.

5. He said that he had built a wall of forty feet for his own advantage.

6. We have ascended a hill of great height, near the river Rhone.

7. There are two approaches from Syria into Cilicia, each[3] of which on account of its narrowness can be blocked up by a small body of troops.

8. The Romans are said to have been men of very wonderful courage.   Which of you says that they are not brave?

9. Cicero is consul, and we do not fear Catiline, a man of disgraceful life : to compare the life of the former with (that)[4] of the latter would be disgraceful.

10. Horatius thought Baiæ a place of delightful climate.

11. The ancient Germans, men of the greatest courage, used to live on milk and flesh.

12. When he had finished a journey of five miles he declared that he was tired and that he would return to the land of Italy.

13. It is better to have a friend of great virtue, than of great wealth.

14. With an army of twenty thousand men, the general of the Germans attacked the town, the inhabitants of which threw themselves in tears at his lieutenant's feet.

---

[1] 419, 1.   [2] 578, IV.   [3] 459, 2.
[4] In Latin leave out *that* when it stands for a word mentioned before, putting in its governed genitive

15. The fortifications of Alesia were of great height, and wonderful strength ; but they were taken by storm by Cæsar in his Gallic wars.

16. Augustus had clear and brilliant eyes, in which he wished it to be thought that there was something of divine vigor.

XX.

GENITIVE WITH ADJECTIVES ; PREDICATE GENITIVE.

(399, 401 & 402, I. & II.).

1. It is the characteristic of a father, who is anxious for praise, to do good to his children.

2. It is the duty of good children, who are desirous of praise, to obey their parents.

3. To help the poor and miserable is the mark of a good man who is full of dutiful affection towards the Gods.

4. He says that it is his son's duty to help himself ; it is that of a kind father to consult for his son's interests.

5. It is the office of a king to govern ; of a general to command; of a soldier to obey.

6. He concealed his opinion from me, but being greedy of knowledge I said to him, "O friend, entrust yourself to me."

7. He set out for the country with all his friends two days ago.

8. He said he considered it the duty of a Christian to help the poor.

9. Let us all learn that it is a Christian's duty to succour the wretched when they asked help (say : "asking," &c.).[1]

10. It is the duty of a soldier to conquer or die : for the brave man death has no terrors.

11. It is Cæsar's duty to command his troops ; it is the soldier's duty to obey Cæsar.

12. It is the duty of every good man to obey the laws of God, even when they put a check upon his desires.

---

[1] 578, 1.

13. Courage is the mark of a soldier, justice of a judge, prudence of a general : the wise man is fond of duty.

14. It was the function of Cicero, the Consul and orator, to make speeches full of eloquence.

15. It is the mark of a crafty man to conceal his crimes even from his friends.

16. It will be Cæsar the general's duty to attack to-day the camp of Ariovistus, who is second to no man of his age.

XXI.

GENITIVE OF PRICE, &c.

(402, III., 403 & 404.)

1. I value at a high price this horse which your brother gave me eight years ago.

2. This horse is valued more highly because your father gave it to me as a present.

3. Courage has been valued little because it is the enemy's.

4. It seems to be characteristic of the inhabitants to build on a very high hill houses of very great value.

5. No one thinks that[1] of your opinion.

6. Caius valued the opinions and orations of Caius very highly, although other people (say : ''others'') did not care a straw[2] for them.

7. Metellus bought a horse of a white colour, and this thing (say : "which") those who were mindful of the past took in good part.[3]

8. My name is Caius ; my horse belongs to me ; and I have three children.

9. He said he would not return to the country, and that it was your duty to return to the island of Tenedos.

10. They sold your brother's slaves at a higher price than I value them at.

11. They are anxious for wisdom, but they think little of those who fear for themselves.

12. He fought bravely for his country and surrounded the city with a wall eighteen feet high.

13. The bravest of all the Greeks did not care that for the general who had sent soldiers for the defence of the camp.

---

[1] ''that'' = *hujus*.   [2] ''straw'' = *floccus*.   [3] 402, 3.

14. It seems to be the mark of a man to give help to the wretched.
15. They were distant two days' journey from a ditch twelve feet deep.
16. A crown of great value was sent by the master by a slave to my house, but I would not (say: "I was unwilling") accept it.

XXII.

REVIEW EXERCISE.

(399—404.)

1. It is the duty of every brave man to resist the foe ; of a Christian to do good to all.
2. It is said by very many of the wisest men that horses of a white color are not useful to all of us.
3. Let us say that the legions of Varus were conquered by the Germans, a people who are anxious for praise.
4. What can be pleasanter than to have a son of beautiful countenance and admirable disposition ?
5. We have all said that it is not your duty to help all his friends.
6. My father's horse has finished to-day a journey of fifty-two miles.
7. O wretched woman ! we have always thought much of your daughter.
8. Give me that man's book that says that the spider's web is not very fatal to flies.
9. They declare that it is not Cæsar's duty to surround with a wall twenty feet high the top of the hill where the camp is pitched.
10. We all say that Cecilia's son Atticus is a boy of beautiful countenance.
11. Hear, ye people of Rome, that the city has been surrounded with a deep ditch.
12. He did not care a straw for the general who was a match for the bravest of the Gauls.
13. He married a woman of great beauty : she married a man of great courage.
14. Caius concealed from me for ten days the disgraceful defeat near Syracuse.

15. He promised me that the boy would be called Atticus, but I learned afterwards that the boy's name was Caius.

16. Crassus set out for the territory of the Gauls : then indeed the barbarians began to pitch their camp in the middle of the plain.

XXIII.

GENITIVE WITH VERBS.

(406—410.)

1. Which of you, having been accused by the orator, in many eloquent orations, of very heavy crimes, fled from Italy ?

2. His daughter's companions were found guilty of many crimes, chiefly of theft.

3. It is the interest of all of us that there should[1] be plenty of corn.

4. Metellus has always thought iron of more value than gold.

5. Found guilty of treachery, he said he was innocent of the charge.

6. Boys easily conceal from parents who trust them, the crimes they have committed.

7. To die on account of (one's) crimes is dreadful ; but for an innocent man to be accused of crime is more dreadful.

8. Let them pity the condition of those accused of wickedness. What does it matter to us?

9. It concerns you greatly that he should return to the country to-morrow.

10. Gold was not valued highly by the most warlike nations of the Germans ; because they were not greedy of pleasure.

11. He sent soldiers as an assistance to the general who needed aid, whose interest it especially was that his soldiers should be men of renowned courage.

---

[1] *Should* in a subordinate clause introduced by *that* is to be translated by the infinitive, unless it denote duty or a future event. What is the force of " should " in 9 and 11 of this exercise ?

12. Virtue needs no defenders ; vice very seldom has them.
13. "Let us forget," said he, "our accusers ; we will then declare ourselves innocent of the crimes."
14. It concerns us that the Consul's two sons are about to go to Capua.
15. I am tired of the daughter of Metellus who was found guilty of bribery. You, however, remind me'of my duty.
16. Cecilia's husband, Gellius, never said a good word of any one, although he was often sorry for his faults.

XXIV.

GENITIVE WITH VERBS AND WITH ADVERBS: REVIEW.

(400—411).

1. The Romans, whose interest it was that there should be two consuls in Italy, were disgusted at Varus.
2. Having become masters of the house, we always considered his book about war to be of small value.
3. "With an army of twenty thousand men," said he, "I would attack Cæsar himself, whose interest it will be to stand high in the favor of his soldiers."
4. The wolf said to the lamb, "I used to have a very high opinion of your father ; accordingly I am about to eat you."
5. He reminded me that they had said that they did not care a straw for a man in extreme need (say : "needy of all things ").
6. I am ashamed of my purpose: I repent of my folly : pardon me, my son.
7. Being asked his opinion, he said that the King's army was near the banks of the river, and that the general's daughter was in command of the soldiers of the left wing.
8. They finished a journey of fifty-two miles in two days on the day before that day.
9. Being accused of theft, your brother declared to his daughters that he would rather[1] die than be found guilty.

[1] Use malo.

10. Have you heard that the son of Metellus has been condemned to death ?

11. The day after that day he obtained possession of a man of the name of Caius, but he freed him from blame.

12. The punishment of theft among the Romans is very heavy : it is your duty to consult for the interests of your sons.

13. The city is mine, and it is my duty to watch over the citizens : it is yours to remind me of that.

14. Nothing was more dreadful than the punishment of treachery : I am therefore sorry for my folly.

15. The more learned of the two young men remembers the past with sorrow. Both were condemned on the charge of bribery.

16. Brutus, a boy nine years of age, sold his father's weapons ten days ago. We were sorry, my brother and I, that he had been guilty of so great a crime.

XXV.

ABLATIVE OF CAUSE, MANNER AND MEANS.

(414).

1. By means of the tenth legion Cæsar conquered Britain, an island situated near Gaul.

2. To die of old age is, perhaps, the most honourable death.

3. Lucilius died of old age, and was buried outside the city.

4. Pale with rage, the general cried out to the soldiers, " Kill him."

5. The brothers, desirous of a revolution, said that they were disgusted with their lot.

6. Exhausted by old age and hunger the poor man died.

7. He said that his father had not died of grief for his son.

8. I am pleased at your arrival, my friend Pompey.

9. All say that Cæsar was not pleased with the leaders of the tenth legion, which had its winter-quarters in Gaul.

10. Because he was exhausted [1] by many grievous wounds, Baculus regretted the disgraceful cowardice of Varus.

11. All the women and children of that town died of hunger ; though a cohort had gone as a guard for them.

---

12. M. Atilius, who had set out with a large army, sent word to Servilius, who lives with Balbus, that his horse had been killed by a dart.

13. Cicero, rejoicing at the prudence of his friend, went home, where he lived with him and his children.

14. Three hundred of the brave men have fallen ; two hundred are exhausted with wounds. Pity, ye Romans, the lot of the army.

15. Let us die for our king ; it is better to perish by the sword than to perish in silence of hunger.

16. These letters have been written[1] by my own hand, and have been sent by a slave to the city of York.

XXVI.

ABLATIVE OF PRICE : ABLATIVE WITH COMPARATIVES,* &c.

(416, 417 & 418).

1. They thought Caius a better bookseller than Labienus ; because he bought his book from the Sosii for ten drachmas.

2. This wall is a foot higher than that one which is near the river.

3. The river Rhone is more rapid than the river Rhine.

4. A more eloquent man than Cicero said that, clad in his cloak, the Consul ascended the hill.

5. Nothing, he declared, is more amiable than virtue.

6. Do you think that Manlius was selling corn at four asses a bushel ?

7. The Romans used to say that this victory had cost us much blood and many wounds.

8. These grapes are very sweet, they are far sweeter than those which were bought for an ass.

9. Caius was more hostile to Servius than Servius to Caius : the latter was disgusted with his life : the former repented of his folly.

---

[1] Where in English we use two principal verbs, the Latins generally turned one into a participial phrase qualifying the common subject. Here translate, "These letters having been," &c., "have been sent," &c. 579.

* In doing this exercise express comparison in two ways. Read also 402, III., 2, 2).

10. Do you think that he whose name was Cicero was a wiser man than Antonius?

11. What is stronger than a lion, what sweeter than honey?

12. Crœsus was richer than Lucullus, who is said to have been for more than two years the richest man among the Romans.

13. He promised to show me the horse he had sold for a hundred drachmas.

14. On the twelfth day of next month I, (who am) without prudence, shall be richer than my father, although he is a man of very great prudence.

15. In the name of the Gods, which of his brothers is called Metellus?

16. When more than thirty years old[1], he lived in Africa with you for two years.

XXVII.

ABLATIVE OF DIFFERENCE: ABLATIVE IN SPECIAL CONSTRUCTIONS.

(418 & 419.)

1. Relying on their valour, the Germans two days ago crossed a river called the Rhine, which is several feet deeper than the Rhone.

2. The ancient Germans used many weapons, but chiefly darts and shields.

3. I shall discharge my duties as propraetor in the island of Sicily, where I need no defenders.

4. He has enjoyed his victory, and will remain near Capua for more than a year.

5. Hannibal having attacked the Romans the day before, took possession of Capua.

6. Cæsar relates that the Nervii, a nation of great valour, made no use of horses. He preceded me three days by forced marches into the country of the Veneti.

7. What is the need of words, if we have no money?

8. They declared that he was a man worthy of friendship.

9. Hannibal used to say that a coward was unworthy of life.

---

[1] Say: "having been born more," &c.

10. Endowed with valour, and relying on his troops, Marcellus attacked the foe.

11. · Content with few things, and trusting his friends, he enjoys his life.

12. What can be more wretched than not to be able to enjoy life ?

13. The crafty spider feeds on flies, which his net catches : it is my duty to catch the spider : it is his interest to catch the flies.

14. To the poor man there is need of money, to the rich man, of health.

15. Use counsel rather than money, and money rather than arms.

16. To use advantages well, he said, is a very difficult thing : we need your aid.

XXVIII.

LOCATIVE, ABLATIVE AND GENITIVE.[1]

(420—424).

1. Julius Agricola set out from Marseilles to Rome, in which place he had many friends of noble rank.

2. My father and mother, who are very old, live at home at Cumæ.

3. Horatius the poet used to live at Baiæ in Italy.

4. Some are at Miletus, some at Anxur, others at Tibur.

5. The general, imputing this to them as idleness, said that the bodies of the young men would be more healthy in service than at home.

6. When twenty-four years of age, we shall go away from York to the country.

7. Whence and whither Catius? I have just returned to the city from the country.

8. It is a long journey from London to York, but I have finished the journey to my satisfaction.[2]

9. Cæsar marched from Nismes to Lyons, from Lyons to Alesia, from Alesia to Rheims.

10. Cicero, the orator, dwelt at Athens many months.

---

[1] Read carefully 423, 2.   [2] "to my satisfaction" = *ex mea sententia*.

11. Some praise Rhodes, others Mitylene, but I prefer to live at Rome, in which place I can be of service to my friends.

12. Expelled from Corinth, he used to teach little boys music at Athens.

13. Marcellus having set out during the summer with all his forces pitched his camp in the middle of a plain three miles broad.

14. She sat on the ground, and cried out : "I am wretched because my husband is disgusted with the folly of my daughters."

15. His father and mother set out from Africa for Italy, where one of the consuls died fighting bravely for his country.

16. Having been conquered by the people relying on the tribunes, all the soldiers marched from Rome to near Baiæ.

XXIX.

ABLATIVE OF SOURCE AND SEPARATION, OF TIME, AND CHARACTERISTIC.

(425—428).

1. (Though) born of humble parents, he became consul at the City of Rome once in seven years (each seventh year).

2. O thou, born of Jove, we ask thee this one thing.

3. The very illustrious Horatius was born at Venusia in Apulia, of very humble parents.

4. We have seen a man to-day who, (though) born in an obscure station, has said that he will some day or other[1] become general of the army.[2]

5. (Though) descended from the equestrian rank, one of them, named Caius, is Consul, the other, named Brutus, will be Consul.

6. O child of a goddess ! in the next six days Verres, a man of wonderful greediness, will go as proprætor to the Island of Sicily.

7. Verres we will call, with your permission, in reality greedy of wealth.

---

[1] "some day or other" = *aliquando*.   [2] Use *præsum*.

8. Four years since, Verres was hateful to the Sicilians, whom he oppressed in a wonderful way through his great greediness.

9. Five years after he had returned, he became proprætor by violence and treachery.

10. Caius lived many years before Brutus, though the former was a man of more renowned courage than any[1] of the sons of the latter.

11. I heard this, two years after his return, from my father, who had, after his death, a statue made of bronze.

12. She was a woman of great filial love; for from her own breast she nourished her very aged[2] father for very many days.

13. He warded off with great violence the attack of the learned Cicero.

14. He lived with his father and mother at Athens, a convenient city, many years before Cicero.

15. Twice a day and about the middle of the night, in time of war, he went as a guard to the Consul.

16. I have declared that the ancient Germans, men of pre-eminent valour, fight with great bravery on the top of the hills near their towns.

XXX.

ABLATIVE OF SPECIFICATION AND ABLATIVE ABSOLUTE.

1. The two consuls being killed, the Roman troops marched to a town of Latium.

2. When the journey was ended, he undertook to go to Brundusium, a city in Italy.

3. Which finished, our friend left the city, lame in one foot.

4. When the fly had been caught, the spider ate him with very great violence.

5. When his opinion was asked, he gave no answer, although to reckon money by weight is not always the custom of our own time.

6. The battle being ended, our troops ascended the hill where it is said that flowers of beautiful colours are wont to grow.

7. When the camp was pitched, Cæsar who was consul in name but king in reality, sent forward the centurions.

---

[1] 457, 458.　[2] " very aged " = *admodum senex*.

8. Under the leadership of Cæsar, we conquered the whole of Gaul, which consists of three parts.

9. In my judgment, your clever counsels will not be acceptable to the people of Rome.

10. O daughter! more beautiful than thy beautiful mother! in the consulship of Plancus, this which we are now drinking was new wine.

11. At the conclusion of peace, the whole army returned home, clad in the skins of beasts.

12. When the battle was ended, the general attacked the enemy's camp, saying "Let us go home together; we have made a journey by the same road."

13. When my house at Baiæ is built, I shall dwell in it the whole year.

14. At the shutting of the gates, our brave troops left the walls; they used to say that nothing is more disgraceful than dishonour.

15. When Cicero's letter was finished, he sent it to Atticus, who had declared that he would write a letter with his own hand.

16. In the judgment of Atticus, the letters of Cicero which he had written to the Senate at Rome, were shorter than is usual.[1]

17. When Cicero was consul, he preserved Rome from a very great danger, but his rashness afterwards cost him his life.

18. Under the leadership of Boduognatus, the enemy attacked the camp, situated on the top of a hill which is fifty feet higher than the town which is six miles distant.

19. At the end of the battle, many, exhausted by wounds, died: death is easier to bear than dishonour.

20. Ovid, in my opinion a most excellent poet, was sent to Tomi, when Augustus was Emperor.

XXXI.

REVIEW EXERCISE.

1. The slave had done a kindness to his master Cicero, who afterwards bestowed upon him his freedom.

2. All of us have resisted the Germans, and their leader Ariovistus.

3. Nothing can be more acceptable to a poor man than money.

---

[1] 417, 6.

4. Gellius is a hateful man ; he never says any good of any one.
5. His plans are good and most acceptable to the Senate.
6. Have you heard that his brother is very useful to the king ?
7. These things have turned out to be most advantageous to all of the Germans.
8. By means of his legions Cæsar conquered the Gauls, a very warlike nation.
9. The king, pale with rage, cried out to his soldier, "Let him be killed."
10. The ancient Germans, men of great bodies, did not pity their enemies.
11. I think that the most pleasant death is to die of old age.
12. At Rome we like the very pleasant City of Naples, at Naples we like the very beautiful City of Rome.
13. They sent a message from Naples to Hannibal at Capua.
14. The messenger arrived on the same day at Naples, whither he had gone to help (say : "as a help to") his sister.
15. Naples is a more delightful city than Rome ; Rome is larger than Naples.
16. Horace, in the summer, used to go to Baiæ, a more delightful place than Rome : in the former city he dwelt many years.

XXXII.
REVIEW EXERCISE.

1. Cæsar's soldiers defended with much valour, against the Nervii, his camp, which he had pitched on the top of a hill and fortified (say : "which pitched on, &c., he had, &c."—579) with five castles and a ditch ten feet deep.
2. This soldier is braver than that one, and Cæsar has praised him for his valour.
3. All of us hope that Cæsar, relying on his valour, will conquer the Nervii, although they are fighting for their country.
4. The Nervii, coming by night, attacked Cæsar's soldiers when they were not expecting them.
5. Having defeated the Nervii, Cæsar followed them many miles with his horse at full speed.

6. Cæsar, having followed the Nervii many miles, slew a large number of them although they attempted (say: "attempting") to resist him.

7. They have seen the king with his army near the banks of the Rhone, whither he had gone to aid (say: "as aid to") the Germans.

8. When the king was dead, the ambassador was killed by the order of Metellus, the Triumvir.

9. Let us use wise counsel rather than arms in this matter: let us pity their misery.

10. They have declared that they will use violence when the business is finished.

11. Relying on his courage, he attacked the lion and slew him.

12. The lion was slain by the brave soldier with his sword three days afterwards.

13. We have taught you that counsel is better than violence: we prefer the former to the latter.

14. The young prefer to use violence, the old, counsel: the former are disgusted with counsels, the latter weary of violence.

15. He has returned from the country near Capua, where he presented your father and Caius's daughters with their freedom.

16. By reckoning the years of the Kings, it may[1] be discovered that Pythagoras first reached Italy nearly one hundred and forty years after the death of Numa.

XXXIV.

CASES WITH PREPOSITIONS.[2]

(432—437).

1. In the presence of my parents I wrote a letter to my friend who had come with Hannibal into Italy.

2. In Germany they say that at Gabii they like Anxur, at Anxur Gabii.

3. In front of the camp which he had surrounded with a ditch, about the middle of the night, he placed the bravest soldiers he had (say "the soldiers whom he had the bravest"). [3]

---

[1] "may" is here = *possum.*

[2] For the Latin prepositions, the student is referred to the lists and examples in paragraphs 432—437.   [3] 453, 5.

4. At the foot of the mountain he was slain with swords with the greatest violence by the cavalry, who afterwards, through fear, betook themselves in the direction of the city.

5. What have you done with the bread (which you) brought back under your toga?

6. To enjoy life there is need of money, health and friends: I will, however, gladly[1] write on this subject to you after a few days.

7. Born of humble parents, he condemned to death Fabius, who had been pardoned by the people.

8. He reminds the soldiers of their ancient valour; but they are ashamed of his cowardice.

9. We have departed from the island of Delos on account of the death of our mother.

10. On this side of the river and in the direction of the mountain, where it is my interest to plant them, many very beautiful trees grow.

11. He departed from life five days before the calends of March.

12. At a distance from the camp he fought on horseback without his father's knowledge and without the general's permission.

13. He was unworthy of life, and died within the walls of the city in the twenty-third year of his age, when Cicero was consul.

14. When all other things were lost, many of his friends lived contentedly on bread, milk and eggs.

15. Valour is a fine (thing); but it is wise (say "the part of a wise man") to fear for oneself.

16. For Claudius to fight for his country is surprising: it is to the advantage of cowards to desist from battle.

XXXV.

AGREEMENT OF ADJECTIVES.

(438—444).

1. He belongs to that class (say: "is of that number") who have ever been accounted sacred.

2. The heads of the conspiracy were flogged and beheaded without the permission of the consul.

---

[1] 443.

3. The intellect, soul, prudence and opinions of a state reside in the laws.

4. The chief post and the supreme command were handed over to a man only twenty-one years old.

5. At Rome there is a temple which by the Romans is called that of Janus; and when this is shut (say "which having been shut") we know that peace has been made.

6. The fourth and the fifth legion came to Rome from Sardinia four days after, when Hirtius and Pansa were consuls.

7. When you are returning from Athens, my brother and sister will carry these letters to the propraetor, who says that wars and victories are not for the most part accidental.

8. All of you are sorry for the past, and think that cares and sorrows cost most men many tears.

9. What is more foolish than a fly, which the spider easily catches by means of nets?

10. The consuls when sober, and the Roman fleet having attacked the enemy towards evening, and endeavoured to detain them during the first part of the night, undertook to be of service to the first and second cohorts.

11. He first promised to do as great a pleasure as possible to Caius and Junius Brutus, whom he had been the first to forget.[1]

12. Spain was the last of the Roman provinces to be thoroughly subdued, though many brave generals hoped to conquer the inhabitants.

13. They defended the walls as bravely as possible, some with darts, others with stones.

14. O, son of Jove! with thee as leader we have no need of friends: we do not fear misfortune.

5. Peace, which benefits all things, is often far more pleasant than honorable; sometimes it is pleasant rather than honorable.[2]

16. Near[3] the temple of Jupiter the brother and sister to-day, or at the furthest to-morrow, will cheerfully entrust themselves to the too rash daughters of the Consul of Rome.

---

　　　[1] 442, 1.　　　　[2] 444, 2.　　　　[3] 397, 1.

XXXVI.

PRONOUNS—PERSONAL, POSSESSIVE, AND DEMON-STRATIVE—AND LICET, AND OPORTET.

(445—452).

1. A letter was brought to-day from Naples, and when I read it (say: "which having been read"), I was the one[1] who called out, "I must go to Carthage at once."

2. All of us must oppose the men and women who have attacked the building[2] we call home.

3. I shall have[3] to send the swiftest messenger to Rome, which is the capital of Italy.

4. Some think that all of us should practise virtue, a thing that all good men do.

5. There are many things I may do (say: "which it is permitted me to do") which you will think it better not to do.

6. What pleases you indeed, my friend, the same pleases me; wherefore ask for what you will.

7. Those friends of yours as they ought (say: "that which they ought"), value highly this life of mine, though I am a boy of only fourteen years of age.

8. No one can say that he is a coward even if they say he is not prudent.

9. The well-known Caius, who lived in the country just four years, says that the mind itself feels that it is moved by its own power.

10. What he had done was afflicting to his friends who, though they love one another, give every one his due (say: "his own").

11. Both Hannibal and Scipio were present; the former is now in your city, the latter in that of the enemy.

12. That man is not valued at a straw; he is the same at Anxur as he has always been at Athens.

13. The King had said that nothing could be more acceptable to him than the courage of his own soldiers who are such as they ought to be.

14. Relying on their own powers they have begun an under-taking—and that too a very great one—of which they will repent in a few days.

---

[1] "One" = is. [2] Supply in Latin an omitted relative. [3] Use *oportet.*

15. It is the duty of every man of true courage to make use of his own powers, and that too both at Rome and in the country.

16. That friend of his died just five days ago, surrounded by his own and his brother's children, and asserting that nothing is useful which is not also (say : " which the same is not ") honorable.

XXXVII.

PRONOUNS—RELATIVE, INTERROGATIVE, AND INDEFINITE.

(453—459).

1. All of your friends will have to think that you cannot pay Lucilius the money ; and of this they will be ashamed.

2. I like[1] to go in the summer to Baiæ, for it is a very pleasant place, and my Horace is there at present.

3. I am tired of my consulship ; let me go home to Cumæ, where live the most faithful friends I have. He is miserable who neither loves anyone nor is loved by anyone.

4. Listeners (say : "those who listen ") will seldom hear good of themselves.

5. What kind of man was he that told you he had sent his first book to his father at Anxur, which is six miles distant?

6. Lucilius may, with your permission, do what he likes : but anyone can see that he does many things others ought not to do.

7. A certain orator says that no one may leave the camp to-day, and that all the bravest men think it dis-graceful to any Roman to oppose the plans of the general.

8. Do you think that there is anyone who ought to think of, not only what he likes to do, but what he may do ?

9. Anything will please Marcellus, who, such is his folly, has written a very long letter to the senate about his victories.

10. The more one teaches, the more one learns, and that too, though it is very difficult to teach oneself.

---

[1] Use *libet*.

11. Some are fond of money, others of fame; but all are anxious for happiness.

12. They asked him his opinion, some in one way and some in another.

13. Both Brutus and Caius were condemned; the one was found guilty of theft, the other of bribery.

14. Certain persons think that some are slaves[1] of glory, others of avarice.

15. The most beautiful woman I have ever seen, for the most part obeys her husband.

16. I indeed think that that learning of yours is useful to every man—even to those who are naturally (say : "by nature") clever.

XXXVIII.

VERBS: AGREEMENT WITH SUBJECT, TENSES OF THE INDICATIVE, &c.

(460—473).

1. The multitude who were distant from Rome a two day's journey were slain very quickly with the greatest possible[2] cruelty.

2. The general with his lieutenants is taken; the former is scourged; the latter are beheaded. Ah, wretched men !

3. Each of them (say: "they each") leads out his forces, and four thousand of the enemy are killed.

4. Volsinii, a town of Italy, was destroyed by the Romans, who had for many years carried on war with its inhabitants.

5. They make the time a day longer,[3] saying that nothing but peace is desired.

6. Neither the camp nor the general was seen by the soldiers, although they had made a stand for more than an hour on the top of a hill a thousand feet high.

7. The senate and the Roman people are believed to have undertaken to satisfy the ambassadors.

8. Caius and I[4] say that the boy's name is not Hannibal, though he is called so by his parents.

---

[1] Use *servire*.   [2] 444,3.   [3] 418.

[4] Note that in the Latin order the pron. of the 1st person precedes that of the 2nd, and that of the 2nd that of the 3rd, or a noun.

9. Having set out from Athens five days before his arrival, you and I need not revile him on account of the taking of the city (say : "city taken").

10. While they were returning home to the country, Athens, the city of the Athenians, was burned by Xerxes.

11. It would be better for us to perish (say : "we will perish better") utterly than to conceal this from our father.

12. When I come[1] to Baiæ, I am pleased to see my friend Cicero.

13. You ask me for news ; I have no news ; I have already replied to all your letters ; when I have reached Rome, I will write to you again.

14. Thebes, which is the capital of Bœotia, is a very fine city.

15. Our parents, as[2] they ought, gladly love their children, even when they resist them (say : "resisting them").

16. Relying on the citizens, he sent his lieutenant to help (say : "as a help to") the praetor, whose soldiers had been accused of cowardice.

XXXIX.

REVIEW EXERCISE AND SPECIAL USES OF THE INDICATIVE.

(474).

1. I do not think that of his opinion ; he spoke more quickly than he should have done[3] and values his own opinion too-highly.

2. In the presence of his parents he says that he is not ashamed of his most disgraceful cowardice.

3. On the other side of the river, and near the temple of Juno, he was slain by the soldiers of the general, although he gave them as a present the finest horse he had.

4. Word was brought (say : "it was announced") to Rome that Cæsar had crossed the river two days after the general's departure, and was approaching the city by forced marches with a band of the bravest of his troops.

---

[1] 471, II., 3.   [2] 445, 7.   [3] 475, 4.

5. There is a pleasant garden near my house, in which Cecilia used to sing those songs we all think so much of.

6. Horace's poems and slaves were sent on the first of July[1] to my brother at Baiæ, by his friend Metellus, who also presents his compliments to your father and daughters.

.7. Britain, an island placed in the midst of the ocean, at a distance from Gaul, is surrounded by a tempestuous sea. The inhabitants of this island are said to be most skilful sailors.

8. It would be[2] difficult to enumerate the causes of the war with-the-Gauls ; many men, women and children perished of hunger during the winter.

9. When Plancus was consul, all of us, both boys and girls, were young and happy ; but now, thirty years after, although it is my interest to be happy, I am tired of life.

10. London is not only the capital of Britain, but also, I had almost said,[3] of the whole world. Like that ancient city which was called the mistress of the world it is built on a few hills.

11. It is said that the Romans once fortified London with a wall, ditch and castles, and that nearly two thousand years ago it was a most delightful city.

12. Cæsar and his army crossed the Thames at a place (which is) twenty-eight miles from London, and, having conquered the Britons in a few days, marched as quickly as possible towards their capital.

13. He is a man of admirable valour, but I am sorry you have made him general, because his prudence is not equal to his valour, nor his wisdom, I might almost say, to his prudence.

14. You and I will take care[4] and write to our friends ; it would be better[5] for us to return home to Athens on the twenty-fourth of June.

15. While they were rejoicing at his misfortunes,[6] he married, at Naples, the woman who had married Caius at Baiæ.

16. When a young man, Cæsar was sent by the senate, who thought a great deal of his valour, to Spain, where he remained one year and robbed the Spaniards of their wealth with great greediness. After his return he was made consul, with Pompey and Crassus as colleagues.[7] These three were called the Triumvirs.

---

[1] 703.   [2] 475, 4.   [3] 471, II., 2.   [4] 470, 1.   [5] 470, 3.[6] 467, 4.   [7] 431.

XL.

POTENTIAL SUBJUNCTIVE.

(485, 486)[1].

1. I should think that after the conquest of the Germans the general will be [2] tired of service.

2. I am-inclined-to-think Caius a very bad man ; he may [3] be a good man, but I should not trust him.

3. You would have thought better of them when they set out (say : "them setting out") for Gaul on the 7th of October, ten days before the taking of the city.

4. Cecilia declares that her husband has left Marseilles in tears, and that he says he is disgusted with the country when he returns to the city.

5. Who would have given him money every time he asked for it? Should [4] we yield to his folly ? Are-we-to-listen-to his terms ?

6. Though he prove to the citizens that they are ignorant of justice, I shall devote myself to labour and obey his commands.

7. I shall return to my dear home on the 10th of August, or whenever the circumstances require.

8. Perhaps you believe that it is an easy matter (say : "easy") to persuade a man that he is ignorant. You may [4] think so (if you like).

9. My brother might [4] (say: "would be able,") help me, if he would [6] ; my father and sister might [4] return to-morrow, but I-am-inclined-to-hope that the former will walk home by-himself.

10. Who would have valued the opinions and speeches of Cicero so highly as himself (did) ?

11. Which of you would have thought that Varus, the general of many legions, would be defeated by the forces of so barbarous a people ?

---

[1] No special exercises are given on Paragraphs 476-483 ; the principles enunciated therein will be applied in this and subsequent exercises. The student should therefore make himself familiar with the rules for the sequence of Tenses before going any further.

[2] 481, III., 2.

[3] *May*, when it means "may possibly," is translated by "*Fieri potest ut.*"

[4] *Should, may, might,* and *would,* are here principal verbs.

12. From Athens, which has been called the light of Greece, to Rome, which is the capital of the whole world, would be a long journey.

13. Cicero, the illustrious orator, was born at Arpinum, of noble parents, in the hundred and sixth[1] year before the birth[2] of Christ, and was murdered by Anthony in the forty-third year.

14. Near the little hill on which my house is built, there is a very thick wood, in which he and I used to walk whenever we were tired of labour.

15. I, who you say had returned, was at that time forty miles away from home.

16. That which was imputed to them as a crime, not only was not a crime; it was even a most distinguished deed ; and this circumstance was of great service to all of them.

XLI.

SUBJUNCTIVE OF DESIRE OR COMMAND.

(487, 488).

1. Let us speak well of those who pardon their friends ; it is not every one who (say: "it is not the part of any one,"[3] &c.) can put a check upon his feelings.

2. May I perish of hunger, if I believe that you, who consider yourself a wise man, are trying to conceal your faults from your parents.

3. It was Titurius who, when the battle was over (say : " finished "), died[4] exhausted by his wounds. Wretched man ! his bravery cost him his life. May his countrymen remember his daring deeds !

4. As I live, I feel sorry for his sons. Although it was to his advantage that the soldiers should not obtain possession of the town, his children were accused of treachery.

5. Any one may say that he is more learned than any of his pupils, but this may not be true.

---

[1] Note that the Latins make both numerals of the ordinal form. See 171 *ff.*
[2] 530. [3] 458.
[4] For this idiom say simply : "Titurius died," emphasizing by the *order* of the words in Latin the subject which English emphasizes by a *construction* involving the use of a redundant "it."

6. Happiness, which may you never lose, seldom belongs to any of us. Would that my friend and I were happy !

7. I should say that you, such is your courage, might[1] have helped me when I resisted his sixteenth attack on the 5th of July.

8. In a short time the good, brave[2] general marched thirty miles, crossed the river, attacked the enemy's camp by night, took it as quickly as possible, and slew ten thousand men.

9. All the most learned men are sorry that you bought this book from the Sosii for thirty-five shillings ; you have done well in coming here (say : " because you have come here ").

10. As to[3] the two brothers, they love one another (say : "the one the other ") ; as to my hopes, I may have made a mistake. May I not be deceived !

11. Would that I had set out in time ![4] May I die, if the cowardly Brutus has not bespattered me with praises. Oh, if my father were here !

12. No poet[5] ever valued any one so highly as himself ; and this is not wonderful ; for most of us think more of our own virtues than of those of our friends.

XLII.

SUBJUNCTIVE OF PURPOSE, PURE AND MIXED.

(490, 493).

1. Five days afterwards he sent me to Gabii that you and I might be greatly honored[6].

2. Some live to eat, others eat to live ; but many have not enough money to buy (say : "with which they may buy ") the bread all of us need.

---

[1] "Might" here implies "ability." Be careful in translating "have helped." Note that the English *perf. inf.* after a verb denoting *possibility, duty, permission*, &c., is to be translated into Latin by the *pres. inf.*, unless the act should have been completed before the time spoken of, when it is to be translated by the *perfect*.

[2] Latin idiom " good *and* brave."   [3] "As to" = *de or quod attinet ad.*

[4] "In time " = *tempori*, when it means "punctually."

[5] "No poet" = *nemo poeta.* "No" when applied to *persons* is generally translated by *nemo*, not by *nullus.*

[6] "To be greatly honored" = *in magno honore esse, magno honore affici* and *magno honore augeri.*

3. It was he who strove with all his might to destroy the town of Corioli, which was afterwards taken by the Romans.

4. I took care to devote myself to my studies that I might not be at the mercy[1] of Titurius, by whose orders five thousand (men) were slain.[2]

5. The wise, brave general who stands high in the consuls' favour, caused his soldiers to storm the city exactly[3] thirty days after my return.

6. I exhort you to help me; for next to[4] God you are my hope, and to you I trust my daughters and my property.

7. The Senate decided to instruct the consul to preserve the city from this great danger, but, in the judgment of Servius, his rashness cost him much.

8. When the camp of the enemy had been taken, the general, relying on the courage of his men, commanded them to pitch their own camp four miles from the town of Antium.

9. I fear I shall have to compel my son to go by himself to Baiæ to-morrow; even yesterday he might have gone with his sisters.

10. I am afraid I shall not be able to promise to do a pleasure to the brothers Caius and Cassius, whom you have been the first to forget.

11. The days are an hour longer now than they were when you and your brother gave orders that no one should return from Gabii.

12. "See that you have," says he, "plans that are good and acceptable to the senate. You cannot compel them to trust a man who is ignorant of war, much less can you persuade them to send the best general they have. The [5] wiser you show yourself, the more grateful will they be."

---

[1] "At the mercy" = in manu, or in postestate alicujus.
[2] 461, 2   [3] 452, 3.   [4] "Next" = secundum.
[5] "The better one is, the happier one is" is in Latin either Quo (or Quanto) quis melior, eo or (tanto) felicior or Ut quisque optimus, ita felicissimus.

XLIII.

SUBJUNCTIVE OF RESULT, PURE AND MIXED.

(494—496).

1. Caius was a man of such gentleness that they seemed to be happiest with whom he stayed longest.

2. He makes a speech in such a way that even his enemies put a higher value on him than is right.[1]

3. He lives with his father in the country in such happiness that he has persuaded his sister to remain at home, content with his riches and trusting to his friends. May they be happy !

4. The sword of the general who reduced the Spaniards to subjection,[2] will make the Gauls yield before the seventh of July.

5. It follows that he has been long desirous[3] of death, though this was done by chance and not intentionally (say: "not by chance but," &c.).

6. It was my misfortune[4] to make a long speech without persuading (say : "and not (*neque*), however, to persuade," &c.) any of his friends to pardon him.

7. Virtue must[5] take possession of those who watch over the state ; she is of far more value than riches.

8. It would be unfair[6] for you to go and leave me here ; I am persuaded that what he says is false (say : "that he is saying false things"); it will be to the advantage of all of you to make a stand against him.

9. It is true that poets have written many things concerning women, some of which are true, some false ; but Tacitus relates that the ancient Germans considered the sayings of women prophetic.

10. The praetor, wretched man that he is, spoke too quickly to be able to speak the truth ; he is different from[7] what he once was.

11. So far from wishing to pretend, neither to buy for a little, nor to sell for much, will the good man conceal[8] any thing.

---

[1] 417, 6.　　[2] "To reduce to subjection" = *suae ditionis facere*, or *in* or *ad ditionem subigere*.

[3] "To have been long desirous" = *jamdudum optare*.

[4] "To be one's misfortune" = *accidere* ; "to be one's good fortune" = *contingere*.　[5] *Oportet*　[6] *Iniquum*.　[7] *Alius atque*.　[8] Use *dissimulo*.

12. I now fear that I may be able to make you no return,[1] except the tears which you shed[2] so abundantly (say : "which very many"), when I shed my blood for my country.

XLIV.

SUBJUNCTIVE WITH QUO, QUIN AND QUOMINUS.

(497—499).

1. It happens that there is no one but thinks that troops ought to be given to the general that he may be more powerful.
2. Which of your countrymen could see the death of Regulus, that brave man, without thinking that to die is sometimes more honorable than to live?
3. There is no one who can say that the matter is so difficult that it may not be explained : I fear, however, that he may not try to explain it.
4. He was very[3] nearly accused of theft and flogged by the very men who had said there was no doubt but he was innocent.
5. I cannot refrain[4] from thinking that you put too high a value on plans that are more pleasant than prudent.[5]
6. The too prudent consul did not hesitate to walk in this wood, though he had often been warned that there was a wolf there.
7. He who is master of himself should have no doubt that it is better to use wise counsels than arms in this matter : I have been persuaded to prefer the former to the latter.
8. What prevents a consul, endowed with valor and full of courage, from being a match for the Gauls, the too greedy enemies of our country? It is his interest to defend his wife and his children from the attacks of the wicked.
9. It was owing to your father and mother that he and I arrived on the 11th of September : I am now anxious for your sake[6].

---

1 "To make no return" = *nihil reddere.*
2 "To shed tears" = *effundere*; " to shed blood " = *profundere.*
3 "He was very nearly," &c. = *minimum abfuit quin.*
4 "To refrain " = *Temperare mihi.*   5 444, 2.
6 *Tuam vicem sollicitus sum.*

10. Caius does not refuse to receive money : he is too poor to hope to resist his foes without prior knowledge.[1]

11. A little more[2] and he would have been killed by a soldier of the name of Servilius. It is the part of a foolish man (say : "of folly") to say that he does not fear to die.

12. Pompey was disgusted at Cæsar's victories, and one[3] day being asked his opinion, he advised the senate to recall Cæsar from Gaul. Nothing could have been more hateful to Cæsar than the command he received from the senate, nor did he hesitate to declare that he would not leave the army.

XLV.

RELATIVE OF PURPOSE OR RESULT.

(500, 501).

1. Ambassadors were sent by the Gauls to inform[4] Cæsar that the Helvetii had led their forces across the river on the 6th of September.

2. He is not such a one as to forget the kindness of his master who has bestowed on him his freedom.

3. The consul stood so high in the favour of the citizens that messengers were sent to his house to tell him that he had been appointed dictator.

4. Contrary to the wishes of his parents (say : "his parents being unwilling"), he bought for ten talents a house to live in (say: "where he might live").

5. The brave Labienus having pitched his camp in the midst of the plain, near the river Rhone, sent a lieutenant to Cæsar to say that all the bravest captains were in need of troops.

6. The matter has been of such a kind that, being anxious in mind and unaccustomed to labour, the women cannot be restrained from shedding tears abundantly.

7. There are some who believe him ; but there are many who refuse to pardon his folly, and who undertake to inflict punishment upon him for his crimes.

8. The is no one, as far as I know, in Antium who does not desire to turn out worthy of being called "Father of his country."

---

[1] "Without prior knowledge" = *nisi re ante cognita.*

[2] "A little more," &c. = *haud multum abfuit quin.*   [3] 456.

[4] "To inform one" = *aliquem certiorem facere.*

9. The is no reason[1] why you should think that while
    these preparations were being made[2] (say : "while
    these things were being prepared"), Volsinii, a city
    of the Etrurians, was being burned.

10. Wisdom is the only thing, so far as I remember, to dis-
    pel sadness; I have no reason to accuse you of folly;
    there is, however, reason why you should rejoice.

11. Domestic embarrassment[3] very nearly prevented the citi-
    zens from sending to the army at Athens a general
    fit to be in command of such soldiers as the consul
    had.

12. So far is it from the truth that their losses are too great
    to be borne, that with a clear conscience,[4] I can take
    their side ;[5] I shall, at any rate,[6] strive to prove
    myself worthy of praise.

XLVI.

REVIEW EXERCISE.

1. With four legions the illustrious Cæsar was sent to Gaul
    to reduce it under the Roman power. In certain
    books called Commentaries he tells us how he dis-
    charged the mandates of the senate. His example
    has taught me to despise the cowardly.

2. He threatens[7] his own[8] mother with death ; he imputes
    my valour to me as a fault ; he has long been desirous
    of my death ; he should be ashamed of his wickedness.

3. The battle was fought (say: "it was fought"), with
    Brutus for our leader, about two o'clock[9] on the
    morning of the twenty-fifth of June (say : "on the
    25th of June, in the morning"); the slaughter was
    less than was to be expected[10] from the violence of the
    battle.

4. He stayed two days longer than his brother who arrived
    ten days ago, and brought back with him fruit which[11]
    he called grapes.

---

[1] 501, 1.   [2] 467, 4.

[3] " Domestic embarrassment " = *domestica difficultas.*

[4] " With a clear conscience " = *salvo officio, salva fide, bona mente, or bono
animo.*   [5] " To take one's side " = *in partes alicujus transgredi.*

[6] " At any rate " = *nihilominus.*

[7] " To threaten one with death " = *alicui mortem minari.*

[8] 397, 3.   [9] 711.   [10] 417, 6.   [11] 445, 4.

5. He said, for the third time, that I was not honourable ;
    you say that I was not wise ; one of you pities no
    one, even when he is innocent ; the other denied[1] it
    all, and that too in my presence.

6. Once every five years (say : " each fifth year "), somehow
    or other,[2] he set out for Africa, where there is nothing
    to prevent him from becoming rich.

7. Instead of this account being true,[3] it is not even pro-
    bable ; he opposed his enemies with too much vio-
    lence[4] to be pardoned.

8. It was Brutus who said it was not after the Roman
    fashion (say : " that it was not of the custom of the
    Romans ") to hesitate to speak well of the good.
    What was I to do ? Nothing is more difficult than
    to prevent an obstinate man from following out his
    own plans.

9. That you should have apples twice a day is unfair ; it
    greatly interests me that you should be the first to
    put a check on yourself.

10. The child hoped that the beast would[5] grow tame ; but
    his home is not the sort of place (say : " the place ;"
    indicating the force of the English by the form of the
    verb) where this can be done.

11. I am inclined to think that he is beneath your notice
    (say : " that he is baser than that you ought to be
    angry with him "), although he is at the point of
    death.[6]

12. Your account is not to the purpose (say : " is nothing
    to [ad] the matter "); for it is manifest that he has
    been brought to trial before[7] the judges. O that he
    may be acquitted !

---

[1] "To deny it all" = infitiari omnia.
[2] "Somehow or other" = nescio quomodo.   [3] 496, 3.   [4] 496, 2   [5] 544.
[6] "To be at the point of" = in eo esse ut.
[7] "To be brought to trial before " = reus fieri apud.

XLVII.

SUBJUNCTIVE OF CONDITION.

(502—506).

1. Nobody, without prior knowledge (say: "unless the thing having been known before"), would do this without blushing (say: "not blushing"). A man without honour (say: "dishonourable"), would not be a fit person for you to converse with (say: "with whom," &c.).

2. A man without sense[1] would soon be a man without money;[2] a man without a plan[3] may often act without thought;[4] you are acting as foolishly as if (say: you are "doing the same as if," &c.) you were questioning a deaf man.

3. To fight without the consuls' permission must be worse than to fight without previously taking food (abl. abs.).

4. Provided the enemy are too strong to be conquered, Athens, the light of Greece, is in safety; the danger of the city, however, does not at all trouble me (say: "moves me nothing").

5. Does any one say that he has not gone instead of my brother (say: "in the place of")? I say he has not. I could scarcely keep (say: "I with difficulty kept myself") from venting my rage on him.

6. There is no one who would do this; unless, perhaps, anxiety for distinction[5] caused him to act thoughtlessly.

7. Instead of writing,[6] you play;[7] if only industry remains, you may laugh instead of crying (say: "tears being left out").

8. If only they do not use money for wisdom, they may take possession of the town.

---

1 "Without sense" = *insulsus*.
2 "To be without money" = *carere pecunia*.
3 "Without a plan" = *expers consilii*.
4 "To act without thought" = *aliquid imprudenter facere*.
5 "Anxiety for distinction" = *hiatus præmiorum*.
6 496, 3.—We may also say: *Quum debeas scribere, &c.*
7 "To play" = *ludere* or *nugas agere*.

4

9. The elections were fixed for[1] the first of January, but
    on the previous day they voted that the games should
    be held as if they were at liberty to consult for their
    own interests.

10. No one, so far as I know, could have been more hateful
    to the Sicilians than Verres, whom the Romans made
    pro-consul of their island; you will do well to remem-
    ber (say: "if you remember"), that you should not
    become like[2] him.

11. It is expedient for us to write a letter to our friend
    Lucilius, who is now at Naples. Unless he receives
    two letters from us, I have no doubt he will remain
    there during the winter; it cannot be[3] that each of
    us has made a mistake.

12. The wise, brave general has no reason to fear that the
    enemy will attack the camp sooner than is usual[4];
    though there are some who say they are not worthy
    of being trusted.

XLVIII.

SUBJUNCTIVE OF CONDITION.

(Continued).

(507—511).

1. If relying on your courage, my soldiers, I have no
    hesitation (say: "I do not hesitate") in attacking
    the Gauls, I have no reason[5] to fear that I shall be
    defeated; but, if I be not so skilful as to conquer
    my enemies, I shall not impute the defeat as a fault
    to you.

2. Money is of little value to a state, unless it has skilful
    generals and brave soldiers. Let us persuade the
    senate not to give our Brutus orders (say: "not to
    instruct") to reduce the Gauls to subjection.

3, If you were to keep your soldiers always ready,[6] ought
    you not to hope to obtain a place in history?[7] Give
    orders that no one is to leave[8] the camp.

---

1 " For " = *in* ; if the exact time = *ad*.   2 399, 3, 2).

3 "It cannot be that " = *fieri non potest ut*.   4 417, 6.   5 501, I., 3.

6 "To keep soldiers ready " = *in procinctu milites habere*.

7 "To obtain a place in history " = *nomen famae inserere*.

8 Use *exire*.

4. It was the valiant Crassus who was afraid (say: "feared") that, if the senate unexpectedly enforced the conscription,[1] popular feeling[2] might leave nothing undone[3] to condemn him to death, or at least to send him into exile.

5. If, to cut off the enemy's retreat,[4] I have made the inhabitants the same promise (say: "promised the same things") as (I did) to my own family,[5] pardon me, O countrymen; I am now ashamed of my folly.

6. I am-inclined-to think that, if I shall not be able to do what I like (say: "what it pleases me to do") at[6] my father's, I shall, with your permission, remain here at Auxur for just ten days.

7. If I were the first to be able to undertake to finish the business to his satisfaction, I should not ask you for help. The man who purposely[7] leaves nothing undone to be of assistance to his friend, is, for the most part, really (say: "in reality") of service to the state.

8. It would have been[8] better to have given him food every time he asked[9] for it; even on earth (say: "amongst mortals," or "in this life"), one may not always do what he likes. ⟋

9. There can be no doubt (say: "it cannot be doubted," or "it is not doubtful"), that London is situated on[10] the Thames. The general had been conquered, had he made a mistake about this matter.

10. What might have been (the result) if anxiety for distinction had caused me to deny it all! May I perish, if I shall be so foolish as to refuse to obey those who desire to benefit me!

11. Instead of the son I sent the father; but the latter acted without thought, instead of taking the side of the former; he is not fit to be trusted.[11]

12. There are some who have made up their minds to give the crafty Titurius more money, that[12] he may be the more unworthy of being created prætor by the people. But, in my judgment, the more the crafty man receives, the more difficult is it to cast it up to him.[13]

---

[1] "To enforce a conscription" = *omnes sacramento adigere.*
[2] "Popular feeling" = *inclinatio animorum plebis.*
[3] "To leave nothing undone to" = *nihil praetermittere quin.*
[4] "To cut off the enemy's retreat" = *fugam hosti intercludere.*
[5] "A man's family" = *uxor cujusdam liberique,* not *familia.*
[6] Use *apud.*   [7] "purposely" = *de industria.*   [8] 475, 4, 1).
[9] 486, III., 5.   [10] "on" = *ad.*   [11] 500, III.   [12] 497.
[13] "To cast a thing up to one" = *aliquid alicui objicere* or *a. a. exprobrare.*

XLIX.

SUBJUNCTIVE OF CONDITION AND CONCESSION.

(512—516).

1. He makes a great mistake[1] who supposes that those who are mindful of the past will take this in good part.[2] Even if they are ashamed of the past, they still wish to consult for their own interests.

2. They would have thrown themselves upon the compassion of their foes,[3] had not the general warned them that they were unworthy of being trusted.

3. If anyone should remind me that I said that they did not care a straw for a man in extreme need (say : "needy of all things"), I should take it as a reproach.[4]

1. Although they are accused of theft by the consul's daughters, they hope to establish their innocence.[5]

5. And yet why do I say that he imposed on them more than they were able to bear[6]?

6. Though prudence may not belong to all men, it certainly is the part of every general to keep his soldiers ready, if he wish to have glory in war.[7]

7. However much you regret the cowardice of your soldiers, you would not be a suitable person to be in command if you took no notice of[8] it.

8. Though[9] the letter has been written with my own hand and sent by a slave to the town of Antium, still there should be nothing to prevent me from standing high in the favour of the senate.

9. They found him guilty of treachery, though he[10] said he was innocent of the charge. We must pity the condition of those who are thus condemned to death.

10. The fellow at first denied it all, though he had been the first to plunder the flag-ship[11] of his own countrymen.

---

[1] " To make a great mistake " = *longe errare.*   [2] 402, III., 3.

[3] " To throw oneself on anybody's compassion " = *ad misericordiam alicujus confugere.*   [4] " To take as a reproach " = *accipere in* or *ad contumeliam ; vertere ad contumeliam.*   [5] " To establish their innocence " = *se purgare.*   [6] 496, 2.   [7] " To have glory in war " = *militari gloria florere.*   [8] " To take no notice of " = *praeterire aliquid silentio* or *tacitum,* or simply *praeterire* or *relinquere.*   [9] Use *ut.*   [10] Use *qui.*

[11] " Flagship " = *praetoria navis.*

11. My brother is now at Cumæ, and has written a letter in which he says : "Although my slave is sick of a dangerous disease,[1] my family and I are going to return as fast as we can."

12. Two thousand and fifty-six of our soldiers were slain in that battle, and so dreadful was the slaughter of the enemy, that, although they fled by hundreds,[2] few were left to warn[3] those who had stayed at home with the women and children, to send for assistance to the neighbouring nations.

L.

THE SUBJUNCTIVE: CAUSAL CLAUSES WITH QUUM AND QUI.

(518, 519).

1. Since you are swift of foot,[4] you may overtake them in their flight,[5] if you set out at once ; but, if you delay, you will need the swiftest horse to be found.

2. Would not (the man) who should see these things, be compelled to confess that to all appearances there are gods even on earth (say : "that there seem to be," &c.) ?

3. When he saw them rather angry,[6] he accepted thirty shillings,[7] and sold his horse for less than he had bought it (at) on the 25th of March.

4. A fellow of the name of Licinius advised my friends to send their compliments to the daughters of my friend Brutus, although he should have minded his own business.[8]

5. The time will come when you will feel sorry that you held the same opinion as they did (say : "to have been of their opinion") ; for London, the city built upon the Thames, is not the sort of place in which (say : "the place which," putting the verb in the proper mood), a very poor man would gladly dwell.

---

[1] "To be sick of a dangerous disease" = ægrum esse gravi or periculoso morbo.   [2] Use distributive numeral.   [3] Use qui.

[4] 429.   [5] 578, 1.   "To overtake" = excipere, assequi or consequi.

[6] 444, 1.   [7] 431.

[8] "To mind one's own business" = nihil praeter suum negotium agere.

6. There is no doubt but there are some who say that Cæsar is not the man to declare (say : "the man who would," &c.) that he has too few soldiers for the number of the enemy.

7. There was a time when I thought wine the only thing to dispel any one's cares. May I perish, if I do not now desire to put a check upon myself.

8. He thinks highly of his father and mother, for-they, as they stood high in the practor's favour, were able to do a great deal with him.[1]

9. This being the case (say : "since which things are so "), I shall give Plancus more money that he may be more fitted to resist his enemies.

10. O wretched man, since your faults are too great to be endured.[2] The more one pities a wretch like you, the more he needs pity.

11. We have to-day seen a man who, though born[3] of humble parents, hopes that some day or other[4] he will be in command of the army, if only[5] the people are mindful of his deeds.

12. When the Lacedemonians in a severe war were pressing the Athenians, the king, laying aside his royal garb, entered the enemy's camp five days before the great battle, to throw himself on their compassion, although his daughter was sick of a dangerous disease. In doing this (say : "when he did this "), he made a great mistake.

LI.

THE SUBJUNCTIVE : CAUSAL CLAUSES WITH QUOD, QUIA, QUONIAM, AND QUANDO, AND REVIEW.

(520).

1. Since nothing prevents him from doing what he likes, nothing can be done in[5] this matter without violating the laws.[6] I fear, however, all our pains will be thrown away.[7]

---

[1] "To be able to do a great deal with a person " = *auctoritate sua multum valere.*   [2] 501, IV.   [3] 578, IV.

[4] "Some day or other " = *aliquando.*   [5] 505.

[6] "In " = *de.*   [7] "Without violating the laws " = *legibus salvis.*

[8] "To throw away one's pains " = *operam perdere.*

2. It is my duty to accuse certain of the senators of a capital crime,[1] since I have reason to believe them implicated in the matter. They are not worthy of remaining at Rome, much less of being members of the senate (say : "senators" or "men of-the-senate ").

3. It is a pleasure to me (say : "it pleases me "), that[2] you are acting a noble part (say : "are acting nobly "), in thus loving your enemies (say : "when you thus love," &c.). It would have been more equitable to punish them.

4. It is now many years since Caius has been in my debt (say : "there are many years since [*quum*] Caius is in my debt [*in aere meo*]") ; but as he had been banished on-the-ground-that he had been found guilty of extortion, I forgave him his debts.[3]

5. I congratulate you on having so much influence (say : "since you have," &c.) with[4] the enemy's leaders, not because I see clearly through your designs,[5] but because I am in great hopes (say : "great hope holds me "), that through you things will turn out well for all of us.[6]

6. I was on the point of setting out[7] to throw myself on their mercy when your name came into my head (say : "mind "). Remember that you are my only hope, since-you, with your usual courage, have always helped the miserable, even without being asked. [8]

7. You would have thought[9] that he was striving to conquer the Gauls in-such-a-way as-to bring about their destruction[10] (say : "as to effect that they might be destroyed "). May I perish, if I do not hope that he will fail in his object.[11]

8. You, on the first good opportunity,[12] will praise highly the learned Cato, since-he stands high in the favour of the people, provided that he do not go away without your perceiving (it).

---

[1] " To accuse of a capital crime " = *capitis reum facere.*   [2] 554, IV.

[3] " To forgive one his debts " = *pecunias creditas alicui condonare.*

[4] " With " = *apud.*

[5] " To see through one's design " = *consilium alicujus perspectum habere*

[6] " To turn out well " = *bene evenire, prospere procedere,* or *succedere ; alicui res fauste, feliciter, prospereque evenire.*

[7] " To be on the point of" = *in eo esse ut.*

[8] 581.   [9] 486, III., 4.   [10] 492, 1.

[11] " To fail in one's object " = *propositum non assequi.*

[12] " On the first good opportunity "= *ut primum occasio* (or *potestas*) *data est* or *erit.*

9. So far from wishing to send ambassadors to declare war, I have, so far as I know, left nothing undone to give him satisfaction (say : "to satisfy him ").

10. No food is so heavy as not[1] to be cooked in twenty-four hours (say: "in a day and a night"). There is hardly any one[2] who does not believe that in saying this, I am speaking the truth.

11. If, as he ought,[3] he set out for Rome immediately after[4] the battle with-the-Germans, his friends will not forbid his standing for the consulship (say : "seeking the consulship "). If, however, he were to delay day after day,[5] he would have to trust to chance.[6]

12. What is that to you (say : "what does that matter to you ")? When you and I are returning from the country on the 3rd of March, your father and sister, who, Heaven be praised![7] have long wished[8] to do me a kindness, will defend my interests.[9]

LII.

SUBJUNCTIVE OF TIME WITH CAUSE OR PURPOSE : DUM, DONEC, QUOAD, ANTEQUAM AND PRIUSQUAM.

(521—523).

1. It was the clever Licinius who for ten years studied under[10] Titurius, in the town of Antium, until he was wiser than any of his friends.

2. As long as his family were eminent in every kind of virtue, he envied no one, but, when his eldest son was fifteen years of age, there was hardly any one he did not envy.

3. It follows that valour has this (advantage), that[11] its possessor[12] is too[13] brave to fear death : the coward, however, so long as he is in safety, puts on the appearance of a brave man (say :"pretends that he is brave ").

---

[1] 498, 1. [2] "Hardly any one " = nemo fere.
[3] 445, 7. [4] "Immediately after " = confestim a.
[5] "Day after day " = diem ex die or diem de die.
[6] "To trust to chance " = rem in casum ancipitis fortunae committere.
[7] Deo or diis gratia. [8] "I have long wished " = jampridem cupio.
[9] "To defend one's interests " = alicujus causam defendere.
[10] "To study under a person " = aliquem audire. [11] 595, 3.
[12] 454, 2, 2. [13] 496, 2; or 501, IV.

4. Since this is the case, the general has ordered his lieutenant to supply them with food during good behaviour (say : "so long as they conduct themselves well ").

5. You are acting as foolishly as if you were now out of danger.[1] Who would believe that he would waste his time[2] while he frequented the school of the learned Ligarius.[3]

6. It is the duty of a father who is anxious for praise to do good to his children as long as he lives. Who can deny that it is my duty to obey my parents willingly ?

7. Before the battle was fought, and three days after he had returned home, he told me that he had sent the rest of the troops, under the command of a lieutenant, to the camp at Ardea a few days before. I could scarcely keep from venting my rage on him because he had not informed me of this sooner (say: "before"). I would sooner[4] die than be conquered.

8. Before trusting you I shall have to persuade my brother to receive both of us into his house. But I have no reason to fear that he will hesitate to receive us, provided you promise not to say even a word about this matter.

9. Ten days before he returned from Athens he went to see his very aged father and mother since they had sent for him. They were so much pleased to see him that at first their joy was apparently (say : "seemed ") too great for human feelings to contain.[5]

10. Before a man was found brave enough to smother the flame with his hand (say : "a man was found who might place his hand in the flame ") the whole house took fire[6] : I never saw Brutus afterwards without calling[7] him a coward.

11. He came sooner than was expected,[8] to say that there were only four in the state who[9] could be trusted with one's secret's (say : " to whom one's secrets could be trusted "); but before he went back he had a different opinion of the matter (say : " he did not think the same about the matter ").

---

1 " To be out of danger " = *jam e vadis emergere.*

2 "To waste one's time" *tempus terere.*

3 " To frequent his school " = *scholam frequentare, aliquem audire frequentem,* or *alicujus frequentem auditorem esse.*

4 Use *malo.*   5 " Contain " = *capere.*

6 " To take fire " = *ignem* or *flammam concipere.*   7 498, 3.

8 417, 6.   9 500, II.

12. There can be little doubt that, since you are greatly
    dissatisfied with the position of matters, you cannot
    think otherwise.[1] Had you observed, a few days
    before you came to visit me, the course which public
    affairs are taking,[2] you would have entertained a
    different view.[3]

LIII.

INDIRECT QUESTIONS AND ATTRACTION.

(525—527.)

1. I am in doubt whether I ought to give you this book or
   not ; for if I gave it to you you might[4] not read it,
   and in that case[5] it would do you no good.

2. I don't know whether he intends to set out to-morrow or
   the day after,[6] but this I know, that he told me that
   the army would march against the enemy who were
   posted[7] about nine miles off on a high hill which was
   close to the river called the Rhine.

3. The general asked his soldiers whether they had retreated[8] intentionally to the camp or had been driven
   back by the enemy ; "for," said he, "it would be
   the greatest dishonour for a Roman army to be
   conquered in battle by an enemy whom we have
   often defeated, and who last year were forced to
   leave their camp and return home."

4. You all know with what kindness he received you into
   his house when you were needy, and I hope that
   you will remember that I besought him to save your
   lives when you were condemned to death.

---

1 "To think otherwise" = *in alia voluntate esse.*

2 "To observe the course which public affairs are taking" = *itinera flexusque rerum publicarum videre.*

3 "To entertain a different view" = *non idem sentire.*

Observe the following idioms :—" I saw him three days before he came " = (1) *Eum vidi tribus diebus* (or *triduo*) *antequam venit;* (2) *Eum vidi tertio die antequam venit;* (3) *Eum vidi ante tres dies* (or *ante triduum*) *quam venit;* (4) *Eum vidi ante diem tertium quam venit.* "He came four years after I saw him " = (1) *Venit quatuor annis* (or *quadrennio*) *postquam eum vidi;* (2) *Venit quarto anno postquam eum vidi;* (3) *Venit quarto anno quam eum vidi;* (4) *Vidi post quattuor annos* (or *post quadrennium*) *quam eum vidi;* (5) *Venit post quartum annum quam eum vidi.*

4 See Ex. XI. 5 "In that case" = *tum.* 6 "The day after to-morrow" = *perendie.* 7 "To be posted" = *considere.* 8 "To retreat " = *se recipere.*

5. The Romans deserted[1]; it is not known for certain whether this was done under the advice of the general or not, but we know that such a thing never happened when Cæsar was commander.

6. It was a question[2] among the ancients whether Homer or Virgil was the greater poet, but there are now very few with whom this is a question,[2] since almost all to a man[3] admit[4] that Homer is not only superior[5] to Virgil, but to all poets in ancient or modern times.[6]

7. I am afraid that the question, whether Cæsar should give up his legions, will be laid before the senate[7]; and if it does, there are many who will favour the designs of Pompey, since they believe they are beneficial to the state.

8. I happened to see him yesterday at the consular elections; he said that he did not know whether his friend had returned from Gaul or had gone to Geneva, since he had not received any news from him for the last ten days.[8]

9. "Tell me," said the legate to the soldiers, "whether you will aid me or not, for if I can rely on your ✗ assistance I am determined[9] to march against the enemy and take the citadel which they have built near the hill."

10. He asked whether the general had gone to war or had sent his soldiers to winter quarters; I said I could ⟩ not tell, for I had not been in Italy since the consulship of Cicero,[10] and that was twenty years ago.

11. Without waiting for the word of command,[11] and with objurgations against their general,[12] they returned to their camp. You would have thought them conquered. This circumstance knocked the plan on the head.[13]

12. By the exertions of Crassus,[14] who did what every valiant soldier ought to do, although he was too old to fight on foot, the soldiers of the sixth legion determined to compel the enemy to fight it out.[15]

---

1 "To desert" = *signa relinquere.* 2 "To be a question" = *quæri.*
3 "Almost all to a man" = *omnes fere ad unum.* 4 "To admit" = *confiteri.* 5 To be superior" = *excellere.* 6 "Modern times" = *recentior ætas.* 7 "To lay before the Senate" = *referre ad senatum.*
8 "For the last ten days" = *his decem diebus.* 9 "I am determined" = *stat mihi sententia.* 10 "Since the consulship of Cicero" = *ex quo tempore Cicero consul.* 11 "Without the word of command" = *injussu.* 12 Uno *exsecrare.* 13 "To knock a plan on the head" = *consilium dirimere.* 14 "By the exertions of any one" = *adnitente aliquo.* 15 "To fight it out" = *depugnare.*

LIV.

OBLIQUE NARRATION.

(528—533.)

1. "I wish you would tell me," said the old man to the youth, "what object¹ you pursue in life?" The young man said that he wished to be consul of the Republic and general of the army.

2. To these things the general answered that if the consul would set out within ten days he would give up the army to him, and that he would aid him in conquering the Gauls who were near the walls of the city.

3. "Whether you are speaking the truth, or not," said the general, "it matters not; I never asked you to come to Corinth with your army to aid me; nor do I rejoice that these legions which you command are here, since I could easily take the city without your aid if I wished."

4. "If we do not look after the interests of the state,"² said Cicero, "Italy will not be safe. We ought not to hesitate at this time to choose a general to march against the enemy before they arrive at Rome; and no one, I think, will deny that we ought not to hesitate, for the enemy have been for a whole year collecting their forces."³

5. The general turning to his dejected⁴ soldiers said: "We must defeat the enemy at the first attack, and teach them that they are not fighting now with those soldiers whom they defeated last year at Cannæ. But why do you remain here when you ought to be marching against the enemy?"

6. The brave Camillus said: "Return and tell your king that Italy is not to be redeemed⁵ with money but with swords; the Romans know not what defeat is, for as soon as they are conquered one day they renew the battle⁶ on the next."

7. "Are you come," said the consul, "to say that the soldiers in the camp (say: "who are in the camp") did not often defeat the enemy at the foot of the mountain, which is only a few miles from the place where we are now encamped."

Note.—In doing this and the next exercise express each sentence in *Oratio recta* and *obliqua*.

¹ "Object" = *res.*   ² "To look after the interests of the State" = *prospicere* or *providere reipublicæ*—385, 3.   ³ "To collect forces" = *comparare copias.*   ⁴ "Dejected" = *demissus spe.*   ⁵ "To redeem" = *redimere.*   ⁶ "To renew a battle" = *instaurare, redintegrare,* or *iterare prœlium.*

8. "What are you doing there," said the king. "Do you know that the enemy are here at our very gates with a large army ; that they will soon take these hills which lie between[2] the city and the river unless some of the allies come to aid the unfortunate Romans?"

9. "Why are you retreating,"[2] said he. "Do you hope for safety in flight? Do you know that the enemy have set out from home for Rome, and that they have encamped without previously taking food? You cannot flee, for you are surrounded on both sides. On the right hand is the sea, on the left a high mountain ; here you must conquer or die."

10. "If," said the soldier, "you had seen Cæsar carrying on war in Gaul, you would never have thought that Pompey was equal[3] to him in military talent ; for, though the latter had many excellent qualities[4] which were necessary to a commander, he was not so well skilled as the latter in the art of war."

LV.

OBLIQUE NARRATION.

(Continued.)

1. "Now," said he, "nothing but pity[5] for your defeat prevents me from killing you all to a man.[6] You know that you cannot resist until your allies arrive and aid you in repelling the enemy. Whether the Romans come or not, matters little ; if you do not defeat the enemy before the legions of the consul arrive, you will all perish."

2. When the consul read the letter which was sent to the Senate, he said : "It is all over[7] with the glory of Rome unless we go to the hills and pitch our camp in a place where the enemy cannot attack us ; if we do not do this we shall be made slaves and sent under the yoke."[8]

---

[1] "To lie between" = *interjacere*. [2] "To retreat" = *vertere* or *convertere signa*. Notice the following expressions : "To engage in battle with anyone" = *conferre signa cum aliquo ;* "To desert the standards" = *relinquere signa ;* "To wheel about or retreat" = *vertere*, and *convertere signa ;* "To advance against anyone" = *inferre signa in aliquem ;* "To give the signal by a trumpet" = *signa canere.* [3] "Equal" = *par.* [4] "Quality" = *virtus.* [5] "Pity" = *misericordia.* [6] "To a man" = *ad unum.* [7] "It is all over with" = *actum est de.* [8] "To send under the yoke" = *mittere sub jugum.*

3. "Can any one not see," said he, "that it is the duty of
    a good man to aid the brave soldiers who have
    fought for their native land, and have checked[1] the
    wicked plots of this man who is the greatest enemy
    to the State and to that land which is the common
    parent of us all."

4. Cæsar replied: "Let Pompey depart to his province;
    let him give up his legions which are encamped near
    the city; let the whole State be ruled by the Senate
    and the people of Rome. But if he is unwilling to
    do so, I shall be compelled to march[2] to Italy with
    my legions and show my enemies what my uncon-
    quered soldiers can do."

5. The dictator seeing that victory was now in his hands,
    and that a very wealthy city was on the eve of being
    captured,[3] sent a letter to the Senate (representing)
    that by the kindness of the gods, through his own
    skill[4] and the endurance[5] of his soldiers Veii would
    soon be in the power of the Roman people. What
    did they think should be done with the booty?

6. Express the following sentences in *oratio obliqua*.

    (1.) *Imperator* "*misi*," *inquit*, "*servos quos habui
    fidelissimos. Veniam ipse, si potero, quamquam
    hodie ægroto: sin minus, veniet frater, qui decem
    millia passuum abest. Vincendum est nobis aut
    moriemur.*"

    (2.) "*Progredere*," *inquit*. "*Cur hic moraris? Ne
    dubites de vestra virtute aut de mea vigilantia.
    Si ignavus fuissem, vos deseruissem: urbs enim
    ut opinor, non facile capietur, neque frigoris vis
    mitescet.*"

    (3.) "*Qui sim*," *inquit*, "*scies ex hoc, quem ad te
    misi. Cura ut vir sis, et cogita in quem locum sis
    progressus: vide, quid jam tibi sit necesse, et
    cura ut omnium tibi auxilia adjungas, etiam in-
    firmorum.*"

    (4.) "*Est vero*," *inquam*, "*notum quidem signum,
    imago avi tui, clarissimi viri, qui amavit unice
    patriam et cives suos, quæ quidem te a tanto
    scelere etiam muta revocare debuit.*"

---

[1] "To check" = *prohibere*.   [2] 492, 2.   [3] Use pres. inf.   [4] "Skill"
= *consilium*.   [5] "Endurance" = *patientia*.

LVI.

IMPERATIVE.

(534—538.)

1. The father said to his son : "Practise[1] virtue, for in so doing (say : "when you do this") you will be an example to your friends ; but if you do not imitate the good, you will be a disgrace to yourself as well as to your friends. In listening to me you will be consulting your own interests. Lend me due attention."[2]

2. You shall do whatever I command, since in obeying me you are doing what a son ought to do ; a man who embezzles public money[3] is a disgrace to his father and mother who are especially anxious for his welfare.[4]

3. See that you write me daily ; for, since you left Italy I have not received any letter to inform me whether you are enjoying yourself[5] at the city of Thebes or spending the winter at Ephesus, the well known seat of Diana.

4. Don't imitate your neighbours too much.[6] In giving this advice I may say, however, that it is no harm[7] to place before our eyes the noble deeds of great men who have died for the state and have shed their blood on many a battlefield.[8]

5. Ask to-morrow the question you asked yesterday ; for the consul will then lay before the senate all the facts concerning the conspiracy[9] which has been formed against the State and the lives of the citizens.

6. Take care not to commit this mistake[10] again ; for it is not the characteristic of a wise man to injure his friends who do all they can to aid him in life.

7. Don't ask me that same question again and again, [11] for you ought to know this without my aid, since I have shown you how you can find out all the facts you desire, if only you will apply yourself[12] to the subject.

---

[1] "To practise " = colere. [2] " To lend due attention " = studium atque aures adhibere. [3] "To embezzle public money " = publicam pecuniam avertere. [4] " Welfare " = felicitas. [5] "To enjoy oneself " = se delectare. [6] "Too much " = nimium. [7] "To harm " = nocere. [8] "Battlefield " = campus. [9] "Conspiracy " = conjuratio. [10] "To commit this mistake = hoc peccare. [11] "Again and again " = iterum atque iterum ; iterum et sæpius; semel et sæpius; semel atque iterum; semel iterumve (the last two less strong = "several times, more than once"). [12] "To apply oneself " = se incumbere ad.

8. I wish that the citizens may be safe. Happy may they be, and freed from all the dangers of war and the schemes of these wicked men who are trying to cause[1] discord among us !

9. Let them dare to come forth from their camp in battle array and advance to the plain, for we shall then find[2] out what a Roman army can do against the Gauls who are inexperienced[3] in war.

10. See that you come and visit me to-morrow, for I shall then tell you how we can check the schemes of that most wicked man who has dared with the aid of the enemy to raise an army[4] against his native land.

LVII.

INFINITIVE.

(539—554.)

1. There is a tradition[5] that that tribe, enticed[6] by the hope of plunder, crossed the Alps in the reign of Numa ; but many believe that this could not have been, for there is no mention of the fact in the records[7] of the time. It does not interest us much at any rate.

2. Was ever any man so unfortunate as I am ! I am too late in coming ;[8] and, although this has happened, I do not blame either my friend or my brother for not telling me that the elections were appointed[9] for the 1st of January.

3. I desire to be merciful ;[10] I desire amid such dangers to our state not to appear negligent.[11] O, happy would our state be if only it were freed from war !

4. What grief do you suppose was in our city when that attack was made[12] on Africanus while sleeping in his own house ? Who did not grieve that he was slain at a time when the republic especially needed his aid ?

5. You ought to be diligent, for no one but the active[13] man can do good to the state. O, wretched man ! that you should be so unfortunate as to spend your time in war. You should be ashamed of your folly.

---

[1] "To cause" = *incitare*.   [2] "To find out" = *experiri*.   [3] "Inexperienced" = *imperitus*.   [4] "To raise an army" = *copias parare* or *comparare ; exercitum conficere*.   [5] "There is a tradition" = *traditur*, or *memoriae traditur*.   [6] "Enticed" = *captus*.   [7] "Records" = *annales*.   [8] "I am too late in coming" = *sero venio*.   [9] "To appoint" = *constituere*.   [10] "Merciful" = *clemens*.   [11] "Negligent" = *dissolutus*.   [12] "To make an attack" = *vim inferre*.   [13] "Active" = *industrius*.

6. I hope that it will be your good luck to see Cicero before you go to the city ; for if you do not, I am afraid that the friends of Antonius will aim at a revolution,[1] and this would be unfortunate for those who are anxious for peace.

7. After they had burst into his house,[2] they sought the king in all directions ;[3] they slew those who were sleeping and filled the whole palace with fear and tumult.

8. I despair of finding (say : "there is no hope to me that I shall find, &c.") that friend of mine with whom I carried on my wars in Asia ; I believe that he is on the point of visiting the cities of Asia, and that he intends to return some day or other to Baiæ if he regains his health.[4]

9. It is acknowledged that, during the last ten years of the reign of Augustus, the Roman empire was larger than at any other time, although the state was weakened[5] by vices, and the armies were not so brave as they had been when Cæsar was commander.

10. Since setting out from home I have not received a single letter from him, and this is more remarkable, because when I was at home I received often two or three letters a month from him.

11. In blaming him you blame me, and say that I am a traitor to my country because I allowed Catiline to go out of the city without trying to prevent him from collecting forces against the state.

LVIII.

SUBJECT AND OBJECT CLAUSES.

(556—559.)

1. I am ashamed of the audacity[6] of that man ; for, when he ought to aid the state by his wisdom and counsel, he openly[7] carries on war against it, and under these circumstances he does the greatest harm he can to his native land. On the first good opportunity I will show him that I entertain different views.

---

[1] "To aim at a revolution " = *rebus novis studere*.   [2] "To burst into a house" = *in ædes irrumpere*.   [3] "In all directions " = *passim*.   [4] "To regain one's health " = *convalescere*.   [5] "To be weakened" = *debilitari*.   [6] "Audacity " = *audacia*.   [7] "Openly " = *palam*.

5

2. It often happens [1] that the best of men make egregious mistakes, [2] although there is this difference between good and bad men that the former are sorry for their faults while the latter often boast [3] of them. Instead of taking the side of the latter, it is my duty to leave nothing undone to establish my innocence. There are some, however, who hold a different view.

3. He ordered me to ask his friend to come and see the cities of Asia, but he said that he could not come since he intended to canvass for the office of consul, [4] and that he must be in Rome on the first of January because the elections were appointed for that day. He is too wise to delay any longer.

4. Success [5] in life often renders men proud, and I am glad that this fault is not a stain [6] on your character; for, if it were, I should not be your friend.

5. I am glad that the state has been freed from the designs of wicked men, but I am very sorry that you should have incurred enmity [7] when consul, because you were the only one bold enough to drive [8] Catiline out of Rome.

6. I pray you to aid these most unfortunate men, who are in great distress on account of cold and hunger. They exhorted me to come to their aid, but you know this was impossible at that time, for I was sick. [9]

7. It was the good fortune of that man to send me timely [10] aid when I did not expect it; for, though beset [11] with many dangers, none of my friends arrived in time with the assistance they promised to bring.

8. How does it happen that you advise me to go and see the rural scenes; [12] for I have often heard you say that Rome was the most beautiful of all places with the exception of Baiæ, which all of us know surpasses all other towns.

9. The republic decreed that the consuls should see that the republic received no harm. When this was done they proceeded to the camp, collected the soldiers and determined to storm the citadel which the enemy had held for more than three years.

---

[1] "It happens" = *evenit.*   [2] "To make an egregious mistake" = *vehementer errare.*   [3] "To boast of" = *gloriari de* or *in.*   [4] "To canvass for the office of consul" = *petere consulatum.*   [5] "Success" = *res secundæ.*   [6] "Stain" = *macula.*   [7] "To incur enmity" = *invidium contrahere,* or *invidiâ affici.*   [8] 504, II.   [9] "To be sick" = *adversâ valetudine laborare,* or *morbo affici.*   [10] "Timely" = *opportunus.*   [11] "To beset" = *obsidere.*   [12] "Rural scenes" = *rura.*

10. Granting[1] that Cicero was a great orator, this does not prove that he was equal to Demosthenes, for many believe, and that too rightly, that the Romans merely imitated the best specimens[2] of Greek eloquence. How few[3] there are who equal the ancients in ability.

LIX.

GERUND AND GERUNDIVE.

(559—566.)

1. We ought to consult the interests[4] of our native land,. but there are some who think that in opposing (say : "when we oppose ") the designs of the man we are not doing what is of advantage to our fellow-citizens.

2. "What you have[5] to do, do quickly ; for we must either conquer the enemy in this battle or be sent into slavery." To carry[6] out this order the soldiers acted with haste, for they knew that the consul had to fight the enemy or be taken prisoner.[7]

3. Wherefore see that you do not hesitate ; bend[8] with all energy to the prosecution[9] of this war since the king has given up many Roman citizens to be butchered[10] and slain.

4. Can it be that I must be silent while this man is speaking ? The crimes of these men who have been condemned as guilty must be punished or else the state must be overthrown, [11]

5. If all power is to be vested[12] in one man, there is no doubt Pompey is the most suitable person to carry on the war. But there are some who say that all power should not be given to one man.

---

[1] Use *facio* 558, iv. 2.   [2] " Specimen " = *exemplar.*   [3] Use *Quotus quisque.* Note also the following idiomatic expressing : —(*a*) " All the best people " = *optimus quisque ;* (*b*) " One in ten " = *decimus quisque ;* (*c*) "One after the other " — *primus quisque ;* (*d*) " Each several "= *suus quisque ;* (*e*) " One would have thought " — *cogitares ;* (*f*) " Should one say " = *dicat quis; (g)* "One often says " — *solet dici ; (h)* " One may not " == *non licet ; (i)* " What one hopes " — *quæ speramus.*   [4] 385, 3.   [5] See Ex. 36. [6] " To carry out " *perficere.*   [7] " To be taken prisoner " = *capi.*   [8] " To bend " *incumbere.*   [9] " To prosecute " *persequi.*   [10] " To butcher " = *trucidare.*   [11] " To overthrow " = *evertere.*   [12] " To vest " = *tribuere.*

6. Conon caused the wall pulled[1] down by Lysander to be rebuilt,[2] and by carrying on successfully[3] the affairs of Athens he soon made it powerful among the states of Greece ; and even more powerful than it had been for some years before the conclusion of the war.

7. It has been said that many men who afterwards became generals were fond when young of listening to the warlike deeds of great men, and this we know for a fact that Alexander often read the poems of Homer, and was delighted when reading of the exploits[4] of Achilles.

8. The question is not whether the state is to be deserted by the good and given up to our enemies to be plundered, but how we shall best ward[5] off the swords of the enemy and defeat them in the field of battle.

9. They appointed ten men to draw up laws[6] in the year 451, B.C., but these men afterwards remained in office for two years when they gave up their magistracy[7] on account of the lust[8] of Appius Claudius, the most violent of them all.

10. Bravery is seen in undergoing[9] dangers, self-restraint[10] in giving up pleasure, prudence in the choice between good and bad, and justice in giving to each his own. For my part I[11] am of this opinion.

---

[1] "To pull down" = *diruere.*   [2] "To rebuild" = *reficere.*   [3] "Successfully" = *bene.*   [4] "Exploits" = *res gestæ.*   [5] "To ward off" = *amovere.*   [6] "To draw up laws" = *leges scribere.*   [7] "To give up a magistracy" = *se magistratu abdicare.*   [8] "Lust" = *cupido.*   [9] "To undergo a danger" = *periculum subire.*   [10] "Self-restraint" = *temperantia.* [11] Note the following idiomatic modes of translating our "for" :—1. *For* (in place of) salt they use nitre. *Pro sale utuntur nitro.* 2. *For* (on behalf of) one's country it is sweet to die. *Dulce est pro patriâ mori.* 3. *For* (considering that it is) a German town it is a fine one. *Urbs ampla ut est captus Germanorum.* 4. *For* (to the advantage of) himself, not his country, Cæsar invaded Britain. *Sibi non patriæ Cæsar Britanniam invasit.* 5. *For* (because of) joy tears leap from my eyes. *Præ lætitiâ lacrimæ prosiliunt mihi.* 6. *For* (with a view to) the games they voted the money. *Ad ludos pecuniam decreverunt.* 7. *For* a penny (price) he bought his pint of wine. *Denario sibi sextarium vini emeb t.* 8. *For* (as much as) three years she patiently waited. *Per triennium illa patiens exspectabat.* 9. The comitia was fixed *for* (date) the First of January. *Comitia in Kalendas Januarias constituta sunt.* 10. *For* (as to what concerns) aught I care you can stay. *Per me licet maneas.* 11. *For* (about) that matter we thanked God. *In eâ re gratias Deo agebamus.* 12. *For* (on account of) his learning he was much renowned. *Ex doctrinâ admodum nobilis fuit.* 13. He is too quick tempered *for* me. *Iracundior est quam ut mihi placere possit.* 14. *For* my part I am of the same opinion. *Equidem eadem censeo.* 15. You will suffer for your folly. *Ob stultitiam pœnam dabis.* 16. *For* appearance sake a few were left. *Pauci ad speciem relicti.* 17. *For* doing this you will be sorry. *Te qui hæc feceris pœnitebit.* 18. *For* skill he exceeds them all. *Peritiâ facile est princeps.* 19. He was too late *for* dinner. *Serius advenit quam ut posset e convivis esse.* 20. This is the kind of place *for* you to occupy. *Hic est locus quem teneas.* 21. *For* a cough there is no better cure. *Tussis nullum est medicamentum salubrius.*

LX.

GERUND AND GERUNDIVE.

(Continued.)

1. Man is naturally born for action : but we ought always to consider this in all our actions,[1] whether they are right or not ; for, if we do not do this, we shall often do wrong to those who are our best friends.

2. Many plans were formed[2] for checking that man ; some of these did not please the consul ; "for," he said, "I shall incur[3] envy if I carry out[4] the wishes of those men who are advising the death of the conspirators.

3. We must go to Rome in the beginning of spring and return to Athens, which is the capital of Greece, in the autumn, and then we shall be too late to see the games at Olympia, since they are held at midsummer in the plains of Elis, near the banks of the Alpheus.

4. The general employed[5] his soldiers in erecting a wall two hundred feet long and ten feet broad, and in digging[6] a ditch which extended from the river to the hill, where they had been encamped for the last six months. In doing these things he spent at least six months.

5. The Athenians charged Socrates with corrupting[7] the youths, and in condemning him they committed an act of most wanton[8] cruelty, since he alone at that time taught me the golden maxim[9] " Know thyself."

6. It is said that a man once came all the way[10] from Gades, in Spain, to Rome to see Livius the great historian, who spent many years in writing a history of Rome. This work was highly thought of in his own time, but many since have thought that the work of Polybius is in many respects[11] much more trustworthy.[12]

7. When the plebeians were not able to pay[13] their debts they either became slaves of the wealthy or were sent to prison,[14] and this often aroused their feelings to such a degree that they raised a rebellion,[15] the first of which took place 494, B.C.

---

[1] " Action " = *factum*   [2] " To form a plan " = *inire consilium*.   [3] "To incur" = *con rahere*.   [4] "To carry out " = *perficere*.   [5] " To employ" = *adhibere*.   [6] "To dig" = *effodere*.   [7] 517, II.   [8] " Wanton " = *insolitus*.   [9] "Maxim " = *dictum*.   [10] "All the way" = *usque*.   [11] "In many respects " = *multis de causis*.   [12] "Trustworthy " = *spectatæ fidei*.   [13] "To be able to pay " = *esse par solvendo*.   [14] " Prison " = *carcer*.   [15] "To raise a rebellion " = *seditionem incitare*.

8. The Roman soldiers did not wish to begin the battle until the tenth hour of the day, but the general by raising the flag [1] caused them to form in battle array and to march against the enemy without delay.

9. We can see the character of boys best while they are playing, for then they are wont to show their character, but at other times they often pretend and conceal their feelings under the assumed appearance [2] of virtue.

10. By reading the works of Demosthenes we learn a great deal, for we have placed before our eyes one of the best examples of virtue and patience that the world has ever seen, and these qualities [3] must be cultivated if we desire to gain [4] the praise of posterity and the good opinion of honorable men.

LXI.

SUPINES AND PARTICIPLES.

(567—581.)

1. By breaking [6] down the bridge over [7] the river the Romans prevented the enemy from following them, and when it was evening the Roman soldiers saw them encamped on the opposite [8] bank of the river.

2. He speaks well without persuading anybody (say : "nor does he persuade, &c.) ; for, though we think him a great man, it is hard to tell whether he is equal to his brother in justice and honour. He is going to destroy all my hopes instead of minding his own business—a thing which it is very easy to do.

3. He came back from that journey without doing anything, [9] because the general said he would condemn his friends without being heard. [10] He then sent the legate to the general, who said he still had the same opinion [11] as before.

---

[1] "To raise a flag" = *tollere vexillum.* [2] "Assumed appearance" = *simulatio.* [3] "Qualities" — *mores.* [4] "To gain" - *impetrare.* [6] Observe the following idiomatic expressions :—(a) "To get a bridge built" = *Pontem faciendum curare.* (b) "To let out execution of a work" = **Opus faciendum locare.** (c) "To give up a dead person for burial" = *Mortuum sepeliendum tradere.* (d) "To lease out a tax" *Vectigal fruendum conducere.* (e) "To be in a condition to bear a burden" - *Oneri ferendo esse.* (f) "To witness a contract" *Scribendo adesse.* [6] "To break down" - *rescindere.* [7] "Over" = *in.* [8] "Opposite" = *ulterior.* [9] "Without doing anything" - *re infecta.* [10] "Without being heard" = *inauditus.* [11] "To be of the same opinion" = *manere in eodem consilio.*

4. On his return to the city he was seized with a violent disease, and after he got well he intended to set out to see his friends whom he had left a few days before at Ephesus, a beautiful city of Asia, noted for a temple built in honour of Diana.

5. While the prætor, as being the guardian of the people, was endeavouring to drive the enemy from the town he was struck[1] on the head with a dart and conveyed back to the tent[2] which he had left in the morning when he went to meet the enemy.[3]

6. He is apparently about to go and ask the consul whether it is better to remain here with the Romans or to cross the river and engage in battle with[4] the Gauls, who have again and again seen the plains of Germany laid waste by their victorious armies.

7. Though I have seen him often I doubt whether I should recognize[5] him ; for he has greatly changed since I saw him last, when he was serving his first campaign[6] in Spain under Scipio the general.

8. It is said that Plato died while writing his work on Philosophy. He retained[7] his vigor of mind even till his death. Some say that his last works were his best; others, however, doubt this.

9. Though I have been long expecting your arrival I am not at all sorry that you did not come on the day you appointed, for I then received and read with great care a letter informing me of your mother's sickness. Besides I knew from my friend that you could not come. If nature opposes, what can mortals do ?

10. He came back because he wished to ask the consul whether he intended to delay from day to day. He had heard from some of the soldiers, without asking them, that the enemy were going to pitch their camp near the Roman lines,[8] and were hastening to avenge their injuries. What was to be done he knew not.

---

[1] "To strike" = icere. [2] "Tent" = prætorium. [3] "To go to meet the enemy " = ire obvium hostibus. [4] "To engage in battle with " = prælium committere cum. [5] "To recognize " = agnoscere. [6] "To serve a campaign " = mereri stipendium. [7] Use sum. [8] "Lines " = acies.

GENERAL EXERCISES.*

(Selected from BELCHER's *" Short Exercises," Part II.)*

———◆———

1. It is told that when an aged man entered the theatre at Athens there was no place in that large assemblage allotted to him by his fellow citizens, but on his reaching the place where some Lacedæmonian envoys sat, they all rose together to offer him a seat.— *Cic. de Senec.*

2. As ladders and men fell headlong indiscriminately, and as the boldness and courage of the foe increased in consequence of their success, the "Retire"[1] was sounded.—*Liv.*

3. Vercingetorix, immediately on hearing of Cæsar's arrival, *raised the siege*[2] and goes to meet Cæsar, who had had resolved to capture a town that lay on his route. —*Cæs. G.*

4. A good man will *make up his mind,*[3] not to admire, nor to choose, nor to *covet*[4] anything except what is honourable and becoming, nor will he *yield*[5] to any (turn of) fortune.—*Cic. Off.*

5. Let a man in *conversation*[6] first consider on what topics he is speaking ; if on grave ones, let him manifest seriousness ; if on *merry*[7] subjects, *humour.*[8]—*Id.*

6. Affairs do *not* even now seem to be in *a very bad way,*[9] and if the neglect of some people were not evident, they would be in *a highly satisfactory condition.*[10]— *Cic. Fam.*

7. *Popular feeling was*[11] more inclined to sustain the burden of an *exhausted treasury*[12] than to listen to terms of peace.—*Liv.*

8. Catiline, *crestfallen,*[13] began to plead that the fathers would not come to hasty conclusions about him ; he could get no gain from the ruin of the republic, which a *mere sojourner*[14] in the city was able to preserve.—*Sall. C.*

---

* For these Exercises an English and Latin Dictionary should be used.

[1] *Signum receptui.*   [2] *Obsidione desistere.*   [3] *Use persuadere.*   [4] *Expetere.*
[5] *Succumbere.*   [6] *Sermo communis.*   [7] *Jocosa.*   [8] *Lepor.*   [9] *Haud facillimo loco.*   [10] *Facillimo loco.*   [11] *Inclinatio animorum plebis.*
[12] *Inopia ærarii.*   [13] *Vultum demissus.*   [14] *Inquilinus.*

9. It will be most disgraceful to return from Athens *empty-handed*,[1] as one goes there, so to speak, *to traffic*[2] in the *liberal arts*.[3]—*Cic.*

10. When however the *popular government*[4] ceased to exist, then also *of course*[5] the literature of the forum and of the senate *lapsed into silence*.[6]—' *ic. de Off.*

11. After the *day grew clearer*,[7] and the Romans had fled into the citadel, the *roar of combat*[8] gradually hushed, and Hannibal ordered the Tarentines to assemble without their arms.—*Liv.*

12. Before I address myself *to the point of law involved in the case*[9] of Cornelius, it seems fitting to briefly mention a certain fact which may help in further inquiry. —*Cic. Pro Balbo.*

13. He asked the soldiers at what they were hesitating? were they not aware that their contest was with no Latin or Sabine foe, but with wild beasts who *must be exterminated?*[10]—*Liv.*

14. Cæsar explained his services to the Ædui, whom he had established on such *liberal terms*,[11] that not only had they assumed their former dignity, but had even excelled it.—*Cæs. G.*

15. The Loire was now so swollen by the (*melted*) *snow*[12] that nowhere did it seem possible to effect a crossing by a ford ; hence Cæsar judged it best to engage at once.—*Id.*

16. If I had wished to *poison you*[13] at dinner, what was *less to the purpose*[14] than to make you angry?—*Sen. N. Q.*

17. Nothing will ever move you ; if so many instances of courage do not move you, human life will never be *cheap*[15] if such slaughter has not made it so.—*Liv.*

18. I say that in all Sicily there was not a single silver *goblet*[16] which Verres had *not ferreted out*,[17] and, *on his liking*[18] it, had not confiscated.—*Cic. Verr.*

19. From which the *conclusion is*,[19] not that pleasure is not pleasure, but that it is not the chiefest good.— *Cic. Fin.*

20. He orders them to go away and leave the candelabrum. So they returned empty-handed to Antiochus. He suspected nothing. *Days pass.*[20] It was not brought back.—*Cic. in Verr.*

---

[1] *Inanis.*   [2] *Ad mercaturam.*   [3] *Bonæ artes.*   [4] *Respublica.*
[5] *Scilicet*   [6] *Conticescere.*   [7] *Lux certior.*   [8] *Tumultus.*   [9] *Jus causamque.*
[10] *Hauriendi.*   [11] *Amplitudo.*   [12] Use plural.   [13] *Veneno tollere.*
[14] *Minus aptum.*   [15] *Vilis.*   [16] *Vas.*   [17] *Conquærere.*   [18] *Quod placitum sit.*   [19] *Efficitur.*   [20] *Dies unus, alter plures.*

21. Now, although the threats of the senate were very dire, yet, *after much talking to no purpose*,[1] the envoys departed without success.—*Sall. J.*

22. Therefore must I make more strenuous efforts, that you be not *taken in*,[2] and they be without success.— *Marius ap. Sall. J.*

23. Themistocles sent the most trustworthy of his slaves to Xerxes to say that his adversaries were in flight. *The object of this was*[3] to compel the Athenians to *fight it out*.[4]—*Nep. Themist.*

24. On consulting the (oracular) books, and on the state *having satisfied the duties of religion*,[5] they nominated a dictator for the purpose of settling *the (special) holidays*.[6]—*Liv.*

25. The regular ranks of infantry alone stood *unquailing*,[7] and if the battle had been fought according to military usage, appeared by no means unlikely to prove a match for the enemy.—*Liv.*

26. In reality the place was naturally adapted for the concealment of a party in ambush ; the more because in a valley *destitute*[8] *of vegetation* no *stratagem*[9] would be apprehended.—*Id.*

27. He returns to Bocchus, and brings word that Jugurtha had frequently on previous occasions found a *compact*[10] with the Roman commanders without result.— *Sall. F.*

28. Instead of deliberating they *wasted*[11] their time in altercation while Hannibal attacked a *watering party*[12] of the Romans.—*Liv.*

29. Although by reason of the *very hard*[13] weather, the road was blocked up with snow of a very great depth, yet the troops, with *very great toil*,[14] *cut a way through the snow*[15] and arrived in Auvergne.--*Cœs. G.*

30. Although Cæsar knew that what had happened *on previous occasions*[16] would not happen, yet he arrayed his troops in front of his camp. - *Id.*

31. The Vitelliani roll-down *huge stones*[17] and *probe*[18] the testudo through and through with lances, so that the troops lay *weltering in blood*[19] upon the ground. —*Tac. H. iii.*

---

[1] *Multa oratione consumpta.* [2] *Capere.* [3] *Hoc co valebat.* [4] *Depugnare.* [5] *Plena religione esse.* [6] *Feriæ* (distinguish *imperative, stativa,* and *conceptivæ*). [7] *Impavidus.* [8] *Nudus.* [9] *Fraus* [10] *Pacem conventam.* [11] *Terere.* [12] *Aquatores.* [13] *Durus.* [14] *Summo sudore.* [15] *Discutere nivem.* [16] *Superioribus diebus.* [17] *Pondera saxorum.* [18] *Scrutari.* [19] Use adjective.

32. However much we aim at being *fluent and witty*,[1] we have to learn that influence in the *dining-room*[2] is one thing, in the public assembly another.—*Cic. Cœl.*

33. I willingly yield every one *his share*[3] of wealth, provided I may live without interruption, according to your way of life.—*Cic. Fam.*

34. Who, on being commended by the words of a man so illustrious, would not wish to help his country with all his zeal?—*Cic. Legg.*

35. "On the slope," said he, "three men could if they wished *check the advance*[4] of a multitude; but ye are Romans, and the bravest of the Romans."—*Liv.*

36. The *sutlers*[5] *perched*[6] on mules were dragging leafy boughs along the ground and thus raised a cloud of dust greater than might have been expected from their numbers.—*Liv.*

37. Jugurtha sent envoys to the senate, for he *was firmly persuaded*[7] that anything in Rome could be had for money.—*Sall. F.*

38. The *brilliancy*[8] of the sun is *greater*[8] than that of any fire; inasmuch as it illumines the whole world in *every direction.*[9]—*Cic. N. D.*

39. Nothing seems to me preferable to being able by the force of speech to *sway*[10] the minds and move the wills of men.—*Cic.*

40. Therefore being of opinion that the state was *relaxing in spirit*[11] through ease, he began to search on all sides for *a substantial reason*[12] for provoking war.

41. We have been told by the most eminent men that acquirements in other things depend on instruction, and principles, and practice, but that a poet is *a natural product.*[13]—*Cic.*

42. Every philosopher, in those very pamphlets he has written to show how glory should be condemned, *has inscribed his name on the title-page.*[14]—*Id.*

43. What painter or what poet is there who does not work for fame? Some has found fame the only reward of their toils.—*Id.*

44. If one were to indulge *their taste for drink,*[15] but supplying as much as they would like, they will be as easily overcome by their feelings as by warfare.—*Tac. Ger.*

---

[1] *Dicax facetus.* [2] *Triclinium.* [3] *Suus.* [4] *Arcere.* [5] *Calo.* [6] *Insidens.* [7] *Hærere in animo.* [8] *Candor . . . illustris.* [9] *Longe lateque.* [10] *Allicere.* [11] *Senescere.* [12] *Materia.* [13] *Natura ipsa valere.* [14] *Inscribere nomen suum.* [15] *Ebrietas.*

45. There is nothing beyond but waves and rocks ; and the Romans worse than either, whose pride one vainly tries to escape by *submission.*[1]—*Id.*

46. If these things *constitute an offence*[2] *in your eyes,* I do not think that a good action will for the future be a commendation of any man.—*Cic. Pro Balbo.*

47. There is no knowing master from slave by any refinements of education ; they grow up amid the same herds, and on the same soil.—*Tac. Germ.*

48. In talking about the ancients use the freedom of the ancients, from which, rather than from their eloquence, we have degenerated.—*Tac. de Orat.*

49. Heavy rains bagan just after midnight and drove the guards and outposts to disperse from their stations and *take shelter under cover.*[3]—*Liv.*

50. The old man rode past eleven of the lictors, when the consul bade the twelfth lictor tell him to get off his horse.—*Id.*

51. Then in the open plains the sight was horrible. These follow—those fly—are cut down—captured. Men, horses, *in complete disorder.*[4] Many on account of their wounds could neither fly *nor abstain from moving.*[5]—*Sall. J.*

52. Yet if they but *stirred*[6] they were immediately cut in pieces. Finally every place, as far as the eye could reach, was strewn thick with weapons, armour, and corpses.—*Id.*

53. And now the day *was quite spent,*[7] yet the foreigners relax no effort ; rather, thinking night in their favour, they *increase the fierceness of their attack.*[8]—*Id.*

54. Hereupon the foreigners, as their manner is, pass the greater part of the night in rejoicing, *revelling,*[9] and *loud hurras.*[9]—*Id.*

55. At the signal the foe rush down on them from all sides. They cast javelins and stones against the vallum. Our troops make a brave resistance, *being vigorous and fresh.*[10]—*Cæs. G.*

56. When day discovered the enemy's flight Marcellus resolved to follow him, so he left his wounded under guard at Numistro.—*Liv.*

57. They stated that the whole army was *in a similar plight,*[11] and that no one's strength was sufficient to *cope with*[12] the toil of the undertaking.—*Cæs. G.*

---

[1] *Obsequium.*   [2] *Obesse apud aliquem alicui.*   [3] *Suffugere in tecta.*
[4] *Afflicti.*   [5] *Nec quietm pati.*   [6] *Niti.*   [7] *Consumere.*   [8] *Acrius instari.*
[9] *Exsultare, strepere vocibus.*   [10] *Integris viribus.*   [11] *Simili inopia premi.*
[12] *Pati.*

58. Thus this storm *shattered* [1] both the men-of-war in which Cæsar had *got* [2] his army *conveyed across*, and the merchant ships lying moored at anchor.—*Cæs. G.*

59. The hand by the motion of the fingers is capable of [3] painting, modelling, graving, and producing from strings and pipes their sounds.—*Cic. N. D.*

60. We are both of us thoroughly tired, he with flogging, I of being flogged.—*Ter. Ad.*

61. As this direction was carefully observed, when any cohort charged the enemy very swiftly retreated.—*Cæs. G.*

62. Previously as often as each cohort had *advanced to the front* [4] there fell a large number of the enemy.—*Id.*

63. Even in places of intense cold they have no kind of garments except skins, of which *the supply is not plentiful.* [5]—*Id.*

64. The treason was *discovered ere it was matured,* [6] and Mago arrested them all and handed them over to his colleague to take to Carthage.—*Liv.*

65. Claudius read the captured *despatches,* [7] and then sent them on to the senate to keep them *fully informed* [8] of what was going on.—*Id.*

66. After two troopers had been sent ahead *to make a reconnaissance* [9] in the direction of the enemy's camp, word was brought back that the country was free from danger.—*Id.*

67. The consul, *by forced marching of the severest kind,* [10] hastened to his colleague while Q. Catius was left to take charge of the camp.—*Id.*

68. I make this one request that if ye consider the case *sound* [11] in itself ye allow the defendants' *distinctions* [12] to be a help rather than a hindrance to him.—*Cic. Brut.*

69. Cincinnatus, when he had prayed that in a state of things so *critical* [13] his years might be no source of [14] loss or disgrace to the common weal, was nominated dictator by the consul.—*Liv.*

70. The eminent German was of opinion that the friendship of the Romans ought to be no source [14] of weakness to him but a distinction and a protection, otherwise he would not have sought it.—*Cæs. G.*

---

[1] *Afflictare.*   [2] *Curare* with gerundive.   [3] Use *aptus ad* with the proper forms of *scalpere, fingere*, and *elicere.*   [4] *Procurrere.*   [5] *Exiguitas,* with adjective.   [6] *Patefieri,* with adjective.   [7] *Litteræ.*   [8] *Edocere.*   [9] *Speculari.*   [10] *Quantis maximis itineribus poterat.*   [11] *Stabilis.*   [12] *Ornamentum.*   [13] *Trepidus.*   [14] Use predicative dative.

71. Four military tribunes with consular power were elected,
     three of whom proceeded to Veii, where they af-
     forded[1] a *warning*,[2] how useless in war it is to have
     supreme command in the hands of more than one
     person.—*Liv.*

72. The *diminutive stature*[3] of the Italians in comparison
     with the bulk of a Gaul frequently *excited ridicule*[4]
     in the latter.—*Cæs. G.*

73. At this action the applause was *very great*,[5] and some
     remarked that the Athenians knew what was the
     proper thing to do, but would not do it.—*Cic. de
     Senec.*

74. It is an understood *principle*[6] in friendship, that we
     neither ask, nor are asked of, our friends to do what
     is dishonourable.—*Cic. de Amicit.*

75. I will, *upon my word*,[7] punish you for these sayings and
     doings of yours, to stop your *making fun*[8] of us.—
     Ter. Eun.

76. The trunks of trees are enveloped in bark that they
     may better withstand *extremes of heat and cold.*[9]—
     Cic. N. D.

77. *He remained at anchor*[10] till three o'clock, for the rest of
     the fleet to join him there.—*Cæs. G.*

78. Virginius waited to consult his colleague, and then with
     his consent he named a dictator.—*Liv.*

79. We have been expelled from our own country, and have
     come hither against our will; but if you wish by
     kindness to earn our gratitude we can be most use-
     ful friends.—*Cæs. G.*

80. The wall of the oppidum, *measured in a straight line*[11]
     from the beginning of the rise, was distant about
     1,200 paces.—*Id.*

81. They were much excited by this news, because they
     deemed it hardly credible, that a nation so mean
     and *spiritless*,[12] would dare to declare war on Rome.
     —*Cæs. B. G.*

82. On the completion of this business, Cæsar marched
     towards the oppidum Avaricum, *being sure*[13] that on
     the reduction of this oppidum *the tribe*[14] would give
     in its submission.—*Id.*

83. On their return they find the camp full of commotion
     and panic because an *unwarlike crew*[15] of women and
     children were all *confused together.*[16]—*Liv.*

---

[1] Use predicative dative.   [2] *Documentum.*   [3] *Brevitas.*   [4] Con-
temptui esse.   [6] *Multiplex.*   [6] *Lex.*   [7] *Pol.*   [8] *Pludere.*   [9] Use
plural   [10] *In ancoris stare.*   [11] Translate by a hypothetical clause : " a
straight line " = *regio recta.*   [12] *Humilis.*   [13] *Quod confidebat.*   [14] *Civitas.*
[15] *Imbellis turba.*   [16] *Permixta.*

84. As however they could find no *tracks of persons in re-treat*,[1] they brought back his corpse, asserting that he had been murdered by his fellow-countrymen.— *Liv.*

85. There are certain of our troops who took no part in the battle at all, but on the camp being captured, fell into the enemy's hands.—*Liv.*

86. What do you think the Alps are? What are they else than lofty mountains ?—*Id.*

87. He was informed that the Gauls blocked the defile only in the daytime, that at night each of them *retired*[2] to his own house.—*Id.*

88. They had taken up their accustomed posts, when they suddenly perceive their foes, some in a threatening position quite over their heads, others marching across by the road.—*Id.*

89. The confusion was very great ; there was more contest among themselves as each man *struggled selfishly*[3] to get out of peril than there was against the enemy. —*Id.*

90. When Vespasian was sacrificing on Carmel, Basilides the priest, on inspecting the entrails, said, "What-ever you are trying to gain, Vespasian, is granted to you."—*Tac. Hist.*

91. I say nothing about your possessing 400 jars of honey, furniture for fifty dining-rooms, and chandeliers in-numerable, but I want to know what you were going to do with them.—*Cic. in Verr.*

92. These entries signify that the men could pay their debts to Verres only by borrowing from somebody else. —*Id.*

93. Flaminius, although he had arrived at the lake the pre-ceding day at sunset, passed through the defiles without reconnoitring the spot. -*Liv.*

94. Considering the confusion of the moment, the consul retained considerable presence of mind, and drew up his troops as time and place permitted.—*Id.*

95 They were entrusted by the senate with the duty of strengthening the walls and towers of the city, of placing garrisons, and of breaking down bridges.—*Id.*

96. There is a kind of virtue which is honourable even *with-out*[4] being ennobled, and which, without the praise of men, would be in itself commendable.—*Cic. Off.*

---

[1] *Vestigia abeuntium.* [2] *Dilabi.* [3] *Sibi tendens* (abl.). [4] Use si non . . . tamen.

97. Without waiting for the word of command, with objurgations against their general, and full of sadness, they returned into camp. You would have thought them vanquished.—*Liv.*

98. The general, however, tried no *method of dealing*[1] with so pernicious a *precedent*,[2] so much sooner does *tact*[3] in *managing men*[4] fail persons of high ability than skill in vanquishing a foe.—*Liv.*

99. Divitiacus stated that the Sequani, because they dreaded the cruelty of Ariovistus *though absent*[5] just as much as if he were present, did not venture even to utter a complaint.—*Cæs. G.*

100. Cæsar announced that he would *strike his camp*[6] at dawn to discover, as soon as possible, whether a sense of duty or a feeling of panic prevailed among them.—*Cæs. G.*

101. Thieves, so long as there is what they can steal and carry off, reckon that they shall never be in want of anything.—*Cic. Phil.*

102. I was *doubly*[7] pleased with your despatches, both because I laughed myself and because I perceived that you can still laugh.—*Cic. ad Ter.*

103. *However*[8] useful a thing may be, if it is impossible, *discussion is out of place*.[9]—*Cic.*

104. The troops, although quite weary with fighting and marching, hold on their course to meet the foe.—*Sall. Fug.*

105. Albeit a man may attain an opulent old age, by good luck or industry, *the influence of his former life*[10] nevertheless prevails.—*Tac. A.*

106. Suppose a man sell a house; he knows it is *unhealthy*;[11] if he does not mention the fact to the purchaser, has he committed an injustice?—*Cic. Off.*

107. It may be that *fits of anxiety, of watchfulness, apprehensions*[12] day and night, and a life full of dangers and plots are good for a man. I doubt it.—*Cic. de Off.*

108. I am sure *you will be pleased*[13] to hear that your son's exploits in the late war were pre-eminent. I congratulate you thereupon: you have in him a man worthy of yourself and his grandfather.—*Sall. J.*

---

[1] *Remedium.* [2] *Exempla a.* [3] *Ars.* [4] *Regere cives.* [5] *Absensque.*
[6] *Castra movere, permovere, or proferre.* "To choose a place for a camp" = *locum idoneum castris diligere.* "To measure out a camp" = *castra metiri* or *dimetire.* "To pitch a camp" = *castra ponere, locare, collocare, constituere, tendere, or munire.* "To remove a camp" = *castra transferre.* "To take the enemy's camp" = *hostem castris exuere.* "A summer camp" = *æstiva.* "A winter camp" = *hiberna.* [7] *Dupliciter.* [8] *Quamvis.*
[9] *Deliberatio tollitur.* [10] *Prior animus.* [11] *Pestilens.* [12] *Angores, sollicitudines, metus.* [13] Use the predicative *gaudium.*

109. You are anxious to see the *records*[1] which we all know perished when the *Record Office*[2] was burnt in the Italian war.—*Cic.*

110. On perceiving this Ambiorix *issued directions*[3] for them to hurl their darts *at long range*,[4] and to retreat in any quarter where the Romans should make a direct attack. — *Cæs. G.*

111. Till nightfall, and with difficulty, they resisted ; but during the night, all to a man, *in despair*[5] committed suicide.—*Cæs. G.*

112. He sent frequent messengers to Cæsar, some of whom were captured, and in sight of the troops in camp *tortured to death*.[6]—*Id.*

113. On vanquishing their foes our generals have often in public assembly conferred on their private secretaries a gold ring.—*Cic. in Verr.*

114. These thieves have violently seized the property of Roscius and retain it in their possession.—*Cic. Pro. Rosc. A.*

115. Pompeius repaired to the legions which he had received from Cæsar and had *quartered*[7] in Apulia.—*Cæs. B.G.*

116. Alexander drew off a ring from his finger and handed it to Perdiccas, a gift causing much dispute.—*Curt.*

117. My slave says to me, "I am no thief, no runaway." "You have your reward, you do *not smart*[8] under the lash." "I am a good and *honest*[9] servant." My bailiff shakes his head to that, saying, "No ! No !" —*Hor. Ep.*

118. He used the same cruelty also towards their allies, who he heard had proceeded *to lay their grievances*[10] before Scipio, and behaved in a way *discreditable*[11] to himself and his superior.—*Liv.*

119. There are many who think their wealth, from whatever source *derived*,[12] *is highly creditable*[13] to themselves.—*Hor. S.*

120. "God speed thee, Cn. Cornelius, but take care lest the short time thou hast to escape from the enemy's hands be wasted in *fruitless commiseration*."[14]—*Id.*

---

[1] *Tabella.*   [2] *Tabellarium.*   [3] *Jubere pronuntiari.*   [4] *Procul.*   [5] Use abl. abs.   [6] *Cruciatu enecare.*   [7] *Disponere.*   [8] *Uri.*   [9] *Frugi.*   [10] *Conquirere injurias.*   [11] Use *infamia.*   [12] *Parare.*   [13] Use *magna laus.*   [14] *Frustra miserando.*

PART II.

I.

The priests are accustomed to keep aloof from war, nor do they pay taxes along with the rest; they enjoy an exemption from military service and immunity in all things.[1] Urged on by such rewards,[2] and of their own accord[2] many assemble for instruction, and are sent by their parents and relatives.[3] They are said to learn there by heart a large number of verses; accordingly some remain in training twenty years[4] each. Nor do they consider it right to commit these things to writing, though[5] in almost everything else, in public and private transactions, they make use of Greek letters.[6]

Sacerdos a bellum absum consuesco, neque tributum una cum reliquus pendo; militia vacatio omnisque res habeo immunitas. Tantus excito praemium, et suus sponte multus in disciplina convenio, et a parens propinquusque mitto. Magnus ibi numerus versus edisco dico; itaque annus nonnulli viceni in disciplina permaneo. Neque fas sum existimo, is litera mando, cum in reliquus fere res, publicus privatusque ratio, Graecus utor litera.

II.

The river takes its rise among the Leopontii who inhabit the Alps, and for a great distance[7] passes in rapid course[8] through the territory of the Germans; and, where it approaches the ocean, it divides into several branches, forming many large islands,[9] a great part of which is peopled by fierce and uncivilized tribes, (some of whom are supposed[10] to live on fish and the eggs of birds), and by many mouths it empties into the Atlantic.

Flumen orior ex Leopontius, qui Alpes incolo et longus spatium per fines Germanus cito fero; et, ubi Oceanus appropinquo, in multus diffluo pars, multus ingensque insula efficio, qui pars magnus a ferus barbarusque natio incolo, (ex qui sum qui piscis atque ovum avis vivo existimo), multusque caput in Oceanus influo.

---

[1] 393, 1   [2] 414   [3] 414, 5.   [4] 378 & 174, 2, 1)   [5] 518, I.   [6] 419, 1.
[7] 378, 2.   [8] 578, II.   [9] 431 & 440, 1.   [10] 501, I., 2.

1A

III.

In that battle seventy-four of our cavalry are killed, (and)
among these, Numa, a Spaniard, a very brave man, born
of a most distinguished family,[1] whose grand-father had held
supreme power in his own state, having received the title of
friend from our senate. When aiding[2] his brother, who was
cut off by the enemy, he rescued him from danger; he himself was thrown[3] from his wounded horse,[4] and held his
ground with very great bravery as long as[5] he was able.

*In is prœlium ex eques noster interficio quatuor et septuaginta,
in hic vir fortis, Numa, Hispanus, amplus genus nascor, qui avus
in civitas suus regnum obtineo, amicus ab senatus noster appello.
Hic cum frater intercludo ab hostis auxilium ferro, ille ex periculum eripio ; ipse, equus vulnero dejicio, quoad possum, fortiter
resisto.*

IV.

The nation of the Suevi is by far the largest and most warlike of all the Germans. They are said to possess a hundred
cantons, from each of which they lead yearly a[6] thousand
armed men beyond their confines for the purpose of making
war.[7] The rest who[8] have remained at home[9] support themselves and these. The latter again, in turn, the next year[10]
bear arms ; the former stay at home. In this way neither is
agriculture nor the art and practice of war interrupted. But
amongst them there is no[11] land (held by) private (individuals) and apart (from the state); nor are they allowed to
remain in one spot more than a year[12] for the sake of a place
of abode.[7]

*Suevi gens sum longe magnus et bellicosus Germanus omnis.
Hic centum pagus habeo dico, ex qui quotannis singuli mille
armatus bello causa ex fines educo. Reliquus, qui domus maneo,
sui atque ille alo. Hic rursus invicem annus post in arma sum ;
ille domus remaneo. Sic neque agricultura, nec ratio atque usus
bellum, intermitto. Sed privatus ac separatus ager apud is nihil
sum ; neque longe annus remaneo unus in locus incolo causa licet.*

---

[1] 425, 3.   [2] 518, II.   [3] 579.   [4] 425, 2, 2).   [5] 522, I.   [6] 174, 2, 1).
[7] 563, 1.   [8] 501, 1.   [9] 424, 2.   [10] 427.   [11] 396, III., 2, 1).   [12] 417.

V.

And[1] our soldiers, with their strength still fresh,[2] having followed[3] these burdened (with baggage) slew a large number of them ; the cavalry having eagerly pursued[3] the rest left (alive) few (of those) who had escaped from the rout. Thus at the same time[4] Caius was informed of the naval battle, and the leader, of the victory of Caius, and all the states immediately surrendered to the lieutenant. For, as the temper of the enemy is bold and ready to undertake wars,[5] so their resolution is feeble and by no means firm to undergo misfortunes.[5]

Qui impedio integer vis miles noster consequor, magnus numerus is occido ; reliquus eques consector, pauci, qui ex fuga evado, relinquo. Sic, unus tempus, et de navalis pugna Caius et de Caius victoria dux certus facio, civitasque omnis sui statim legatus dedo. Nam, ut ad bellum suscipio hostis alacer et promtus est animus, sic mollis ac parum resistens ad calamitas perfero mens is sum.

VI.

When the news[2] of this battle was carried beyond the Rhine, the enemy, who had come to the banks of the river, began to return home ;[6] and the tribes that live next[7] the Rhine, having thoroughly terrified[8] and pursued these, killed a great number of them. The general, having brought to a close two very great wars[2] in one summer,[9] led off his army to winter-quarters in[10] the country of the Sequani, a little earlier than the season of the year required. Over the winter-quarters he placed[11] his lieutenant ; he himself set out into hither Gaul to hold[12] his circuits.

Hic proelium trans Rhenus nuncio, hostis, qui ad ripa flumen venio, domus revertor coepi ; qui gens, qui proximus Rhenus incolo, perterreo insequor, magnus ex hic numerus occido. Dux, unus aestas duo magnus bellum conficio, mature paulo quam tempus annus postulo, in hiberna in Sequanus exercitus deduco. Hiberna suus legatus praepono ; ipse in citerior Gallia ad conventus ago proficiscor.

---

[1] 453.   [2] 431, 2.   [3] 465, II., 3 & 225, 1.   [4] 426.   [5] 562 & 565, 1.
[6] 379, 3, 1.   [7] 433, 1.   [8] 576.   [9] 426, 2, 2), (3).   [10] See p. 7, sent. 3 &
435, 1.   [11] 386.   [12] 562 & 565, 3.

VII.

The ambassadors said that[1] they would lay these matters before their (people), and return three days after,[2] when the question had been discussed;[3] they begged of him not[4] to move his camp in the meantime nearer[5] them.   Scipio replied that[1] even this could not be obtained from him ; for he had learned that[1] a great part of the cavalry had been sent by them, some days before,[2] across the Meuse to the allies, for the purpose of[6] plundering[7] and foraging.[7]   He thought that[1] these horsemen were being waited for, and that a delay was being made on this account.

Legatus hic sui ad suus refero dico, et, res delibero, post dies tertius revertor ; interea ne prope sui castra moveo, peto.   Ne is quidem Scipio ab sui impetro possum dico; cognosco enim, magnus pars equitatus ab is aliquot dies ante praedor frumentorque causa ad socius trans Mosa mitto.   Hic expecto eques, atque is res causa mora interpono, arbitror.

VIII.

The commander having divided his forces[8] with the lieutenant and the quaestor, and having quickly built the bridges,[8] marches against them in three divisions, burns the buildings and villages, and takes possession of[9] a large number of cattle and men.   Forced by these things, the Britons send ambassadors to him to ask for peace.[10]   Having accepted hostages,[8] he assures them that he[11] will regard them in the light[12] of enemies, if[13] they admit either the king or his legates within their territories.[12]   After the settlement of these matters, he leaves Fabius, the Campanian, with cavalry as[12] a guard among the Britons ; he himself sets out into the country of the Celts.

Imperator partio copiæ cum legatus et quaestor, celeriterque efficio pons, adeo tripartito, aedificium vicusque incendo, magnus pecus et homo numerus potior.   Qui res cogo Britanni, legatus ad is pax peto causa mitto. Ille, obses accipio hostis sui habeo numerus confirmo, si aut rex, aut is legatus, suus fines recipio.   Hic confirmo res, Fabius, Campanus, cum equitatus custos locus in Britanni relinquo ; ipse in Celtae proficiscor.

---

[1] 545. [2] 427. [3] 431,-2. [4] 490 & 492, 2. [5] 433, 1. [6] 414, 2, 3). [7] 559 & 563, 1.
[8] 431, 2. [9] 419, 1. [10] 562 & 563, 1. [11] 545. [12] 422, 1, 1). [13] 511, II.; 531 & 532, 3.

IX.

He made a requisition for hostages on other states[1]. Finally he appoints a day for this matter. He orders[2] all the cavalry, fifteen thousand[3] in number[4], to assemble here quickly. He says that he will be content[5] with the infantry he formerly had[6], and that he will not try his luck or contend in battle : but, since he has[6] a large supply of cavalry, it will be a very easy thing to do[7] to keep[8] the Romans from obtaining corn[9] and (from) foraging. After the arrangement of these matters, he levies ten thousand soldiers from the enemy who are nearest Italy[10]. To these he adds eight hundred cavalry.

Ille impero reliquus civitas obses. Denique is res constituo dies. Huc omnis eques, quindecim mille numerus, celeriter convenio jubeo. Peditatus, qui ante habeo, sui sum contentus dico, neque fortuna tento, aut in acies dimico: sed, quoniam abundo equitatus, perfacilis sum facio, frumentatio pabulatioque Romanus prohibeo. Hic constituo res, hostis qui sum finitimus Italia, decem mille pedes impero. Huc addo eques octingenti.

X.

Thus the battle was renewed and all the enemy fled, nor did they leave off fleeing until[11] they came to the river Danube about five miles[12] from that place. There a very few, either putting confidence[13] in their strength, strove to swim across, or, having come upon skiffs[14], found safety for themselves. Among the latter was the chief of the enemy, who, having lighted on a little boat tied to the bank, escaped in it. Our cavalry pursued[15] and killed all the rest. This chief[16] had two wives ; one of the Dacian nation,[17] whom he had brought with him from home ; the other of the Maesian nation, sister of the king, whom he had married in Macedonia, when sent by her brother. Both (of these) perished in the rout.

Ita proelium restituo atque omnis hostis tergum verto neque prius fugio desisto quam ad flumen Ister mille passus ex is locus circiter quinque pervenio. Ibi perpauci aut vis confido transnato contendo aut, linter invenio, sui salus reperio. In hic sum dux hostis, qui, navicula deligo ad ripa nanciscor, is profugio ; reliquus omnis consequor eques noster interficio. Duo sum hic dux uxor, unus Dacus natio, qui ab domus sui cum educo ; alter Moesicus, rex soror, qui in Macedonia duco, a frater mitto ; uterque in is fuga pereo.

---

1 384, II.   2 551, II, 1.   3 363.   4 429.   5 419, IV.   6 531, I.   7 570, 1.
8 549, 2.   9 425, 2, 2).   10 391, I.   11 523, IL   12 378.   13 385, 1.   14 431, 2.
15 579.   16 401.   17 428.

XI.

The influence of this state is far the greatest of all the countries on the sea-bord, because[1] the inhabitants have very many vessels in which they are accustomed to sail to Britain, and excel the rest in knowledge and experience of maritime affairs ; and as the violence of the sea is great and the coast exposed (lit. "in the great and exposed violence of the sea,") with (only) a few ports[2] at intervals, they have tributary (to them) almost all that are in the habit of using that sea. By them the example is set of detaining[3] the ambassadors, because[1] they were of the opinion that through them they would recover their hostages which they had given[4] to Crassus.

Hic sum civitas longe amplus auctoritas omnis ora maritimus regio is, quod et navis habeo incola multus, qui in Britannia navigo consuesco, et scientia atque usus nauticus res reliquus antecedo, et, in magnus impetus mare atque apertus, pauci portus interjicio, qui teneo ipse, omnes fere, qui is mare utor consuesco, habeo vectigalis. `Ab hic fio initium retineo legatus, quod per is suus sui obses, qui Crassus do, recupero existimo.

XII.

At day break all our (men) were carried across and the line of the enemy was distinctly seen. The lieutenant gives the signal for battle, having urged his men to bear[5] in mind their former valour and so many very successful engagements, and to consider that the commander himself, under whose leadership they had again and again defeated[4] the enemy, was there in person. At the first onset, on the right wing, where the seventh legion had taken its stand, the enemy are repulsed and put to flight ; on the left, which position the twelfth legion held, although[6] the front ranks of the enemy had fallen, pierced with javelins, still the rest held their ground very bravely, nor did any one give room for suspicion of a desire to flee.

Prior lux et noster omnis transporto et hostis acies cerno. Legatus, miles cohortor, "ut suus pristinus virtus et tot secundus proelium memoria retineo, atque ipse dux, qui ductus saepenumero hostis supero, praesens adsum existimo," do signum proelium. Prior concursus ab dexter cornu, ubi septimus legio consisto, hostis pello atque in fuga conjicio ; ab sinister, qui locus duodecimus legio teneo, cum prior ordo hostis transfigo pilum concido, tamen, acriter reliquus resisto, nec do suspicio fuga quisquam.

---

1 520, 1. 2 431, 2. 3 562 & 563. 4 531. 5 492, 2, & 481, IV. 2. 6 513, II.

XIII.

After entering on his command,[1] the chief, when[2] about thirty miles[3] distant from Gabii, having suddenly called together his soldiers, said, while weeping, "Whither do we set out, soldiers? All our cavalry, all our nobility, have perished. The leaders of our state, falsely accused[4] of treason, have been put to death by the Romans without a hearing.[1] Learn this from those who have escaped from the very slaughter: for I, since my brothers as well as my relatives have been killed, am prevented by grief from announcing[5] publicly what has been done." Those whom he had instructed as to what he wished[6] to be said are brought forward, and they set forth to the multitude the same statements which the speaker had made publicly: "that the horsemen of their friends had been slain because[7] they were said to have had a conference with the neighbours; that they had concealed themselves in the crowd of soldiers and had escaped out of the midst[8] of the massacre."

Princeps, accipio exercitus, cum mille passus circiter triginta ab Gabii absum, convoco subito miles, lacrimo, "Quo proficiscor, inquam, miles? Omnis noster equitatus, omnis nobilitas intereo: princeps civitas, insimulo proditio, ab Romanus indico causa interficio. Hic ab is cognosco, qui ex ipse cædes fugio: nam ego, frater atque omnis meus propinquus interficio, dolor prohibeo, qui gero, pronuncio." Produco is, qui ille edoceo, qui dico volo, atque idem, qui orator pronuncio, multitudo expono: "omnis eques unicus interficio, quod colloquor cum finitimus dico; ipse sui inter multitudo miles occulto atque ex medius cædes profugio."

XIV.

Meanwhile, on the arrival of the news that all their soldiers were fast in the power of the consul, they flock together to the tribune. They show that nothing has been done by the advice of the state; they order an enquiry concerning the plundered property; they confiscate the goods of the chief and his brothers; they send ambassadors to the consul for the sake of clearing themselves.[9] They do this to recover[10] their friends, but, being tainted with guilt and charmed with the gain (arising) from the plundered goods, because[11] that concerned

---

[1] 431, 2. [2] 518, II., 1. [3] 375. [4] 410, III., 2. [5] 490, 2. [6] 501, 1.
[7] 531. [8] 441, 6. [9] 563, 4. [10] 563, 1, 1). [11] 520, 1.

many, and terrified by the fear of punishment, they begin
secretly to form projects for war, and they stir up the other
states by means of embassies.

*Interim nuncius affero, omnis is miles in potestas consul teneo,
concurro ad tribunus. Nihil publicus facio consilium demonstro;
quaestio de bona diripio decerno; princeps fraterque bona
publico. Legatus ad consul sui purgo gratia mitto. Hic facio
recupero suus causa; sed, contamino facinus et capio compendium
ex diripio bona, quod is res ad multus pertineo, et timor poena
ecterreo, consilium clam de bellum ineo incipio, civitasque
reliquus legatio sollicito.*

XV.

In the meantime he is informed a few days afterwards[1] by
the Etrurians, that all the Samnites are collecting their forces
at one spot, and are ordering those tribes which are under their
sway,[2] to send[3] auxiliaries of infantry and cavalry. After this
is known, he makes arrangements for a supply of provisions;
he choses a suitable place for the camp; (and) orders the
Etrurians to drive off their cattle and collect all their property
from the country to the towns, hoping that barbarous and
ignorant men, cast down by the scarcity of provisions, could
be induced to fight on unfavourable terms. He gives (them)
instructions to send many scouts among the Samnites, and to
find out what is being done[4] among them.

*Interim pauci post dies facio ab Etruscus certus, Samnis omnis
unus in locus copiae cogo atque is natio, qui sub is sum imperium,
denuncio, uti auxilia peditatus equitatusque mitto. Hic cognosco res, res frumentarius provideo; castra idoneus locus deligo:
Etruscus impero, ut pecus deduco suusque omnis ex ager in oppidum confero, spero, barbarus atque imperitus homo inopia
cibaria affligo, ad iniquus pugno conditio possum deduco.
Mando, ut creber explorator in Samnis mitto, quique apud is
gero, cognosco.*

XVI.

About one hundred and thirty thousand men survived that
battle, and they marched all that night[5] without stopping. No
interruption to the journey having taken place during any part[6]

---

of the night (lit. "the journey having been interrupted during no part of the night"), on the fourth day[1] they came into the territory of the enemy, since[2] our men, having delayed three days,[3] both on account of the wounds of the soldiers and the burial of the slain, were not able to follow them. The general sent a letter and messengers to the Etruscans not to aid[4] them with corn or anything else; for that, if[5] they should aid (them), he would regard[6] them in the same light as (he did) the Latins. He himself, after the lapse of three days, began to follow them with all his forces.

Ex is proelium circiter mille homo centum et triginta supersum isque totus nox continenter eo. Nullus pars nox iter intermitto, in fines hostis dies quartus pervenio, cum, et propter vulnus miles, et propter sepultura occisus, noster, triduum moror, is sequor non possum. Imperator ad Etruscus litterae nunciusque mitto, ne is frumentum, neve alius res juvo ; qui si juvo, sui idem locus, qui Latinus, habeo. Ipse, triduum intermitto, cum omnis copiæ is sequor coepi.

XVII.

On the same day, having been informed by scouts that the enemy had encamped at the foot of the mountain, eight miles[7] from his camp, he sent persons to examine[8] what the nature of the mountain was,[9] and what kind of ascent (there was) by going round it. Word was brought back[10] that it (the ascent) was easy. About the third watch he orders[11] his lieutenant with praetorian power, to ascend the highest ridge of the mountain, with two legions and those as guides who had examined the road. He shows him what[12] his plan is. He himself, about the fourth watch, marches after them by the same road as[13] the enemy had taken, and sends all his cavalry ahead of him.

Idem dies ab explorator certus facio, hostis sub mons consido mille passus ab ipse castra octo, qualis sum natura mons et qualis in circuitus ascensus, qui cognosco, mitto. Renuncio, facilis sum. De tertius vigilia legatus pro praetor, cum duo legio, et is dux, qui iter cognosco, superus jugum mons ascendo jubeo ; quis suus consilium sum, ostendo. Ipse de quartus vigilia idem iter, qui hostis eo, ad is contendo, equitatusque omnis ante sui mitto.

---

[1] 426. [2] 518, II. [3] 378. [4] 492, 2. [5] 531. [6] 530, II., 1. [7] 378.
[8] 509. [9] 525. [10] 301. [11] 551, II., I. [12] 396, III., 3). [13] 414.

XVIII.

When[1] this announcement was made[2], that they were
attempting to pass through our Province, he hastens to leave
the neighbourhood of the city, and by as long marches as[3] he
can he proceeds into the country, and comes to Cremona.
He levies from the whole Province as great a number of
soldiers as he can (there was in all but one legion in farther
Gaul). The bridge which was at Cremona he orders to be
destroyed. When the enemy are informed of his approach,
they send ambassadors to him, the noblest men of the state,
of which embassy Caius and Cassius held the chief place, to
say[4] that their[5] intention was, without doing any harm to pass
through the Province, because[6] other road they had none.

*Cum is nuncio, is per Provincia noster iter facio conor,
maturo ab urbs proficiscor, et quam magnus possum iter, rus
contendo, et ad Cremona pervenio. Provincia totus quam magnus
miles numerus impero (sum omnino in Gallia ulterior legio
unus). Pons qui sum ad Cremona jubeo rescindo. Ubi de is adventus hostis certus facio, legatus ad is mitto, nobilis civitas, qui
legatio Caius et Cassius princeps locus obtineo, qui dico, sui sum
in animus, sine ullus maleficium iter per Provincia facio,
propterea quod alius iter habeo nullus.*

XIX.

Then at length the general, induced by the address of his
his friend, disclosed[7] what previously he had said nothing about.
He said:[8]—"There are some whose influence among the common
people is[9] very great, who, though private persons, have more
weight than the magistrates themselves. These by their
factions and dishonest speeches deter the populace from collecting[10] the corn which they ought to furnish. If now they
cannot hold the sovereignty, it is better to submit to the
dominion of friends than to that of enemies ; nor ought they
to doubt but that[11] if the Romans should conquer, they would
take by force their liberty from the nation as well as from
the rest of Gaul. By these same parties our plans, and whatever is done in the camp, are told to the enemy."

*Tum demum dux, oratio amicus adduco, qui antea taceo,
propono. Sum nonnulli, qui auctoritas apud plebs multum valeo :
qui privatus multum possum, quam ipse magistratus. Hic sedi-
tiosus atque improbus oratio multitudo deterreo, ne frumentum*

---

1 518, II.   2 478.   3 170, 2, 2) & 444, 3.   4 500.   5 387.   6 530, 1.
7 467, III., 1.   8 530, II., 1.   9 531.   10 499, 2.

confero, qui praesto debeo. Si jam principatus obtineo non possum, amicus quam hostis imperium perfero, satis sum ; neque dubito debeo, quin, si supero Romanus, una cum reliquus Gallia gens libertas eripio. Ab idem noster consilium, quique in castra gero, hostis enuncio.

XX.

The lieutenant, with his horse at full gallop, rides up to him. He says that the mountain which[3] he desired the soldiers. to take possession of is held by the enemy; that he has ascertained this from the arms and standards. The general leads up his own forces to the nearest hill, (and)[2] draws up his army. As orders had been given him by the general not to engage in battle, unless[3] his forces were seen near the camp of the enemy, so that an attack might be made at the same time on all sides against the enemy, the lieutenant, after taking the mountain, kept waiting[4] for our men and refraining from battle. Finally, late in the day,[5] the general learned through scouts that the mountain was in possession of his men, that the enemy had moved their camp, and that the messenger, owing to his great terror,[6] had reported to him as seen what he had not seen.

Legatus, equus admitto, ad is accurro. Dico mons qui a miles occupo volo, ab hostis teneo ; is sui ab arma atque insigne cognosco. Dux suus copiæ in propior collis subduco, acies instruo. Legatus ut is praecipio a dux, ne proelium committo, nisi ipse copiæ prope hostis castra video, ut undique unus tempus in hostis impetus facio, mons occupo noster expecto proeliumque abstineo. Multus denique dies per explorator dux cognosco, et mons a suus teneo, et hostis castra moveo, et nuntius timor perterreo, qui non video, pro visus sui renuncio.

XXI.

Having ascertained these things, the general cheered the minds of the inhabitants by his words, and promised that he would attend[7] to the matter; that he had great hope that their king, induced by his kindness and influence, would put an end to his wrong-doing. When this speech was delivered he dismissed the assembly ; and besides these

---

1 531. 2 587. 1., 6. 3 510, 487, & 503, III. 4 469, I. 5 426.
6 578, II. 7 390, I.

12   EXERCISES IN LATIN PROSE.

(statements) many things led him to think[1] that this matter
should be considered[2] and undertaken by him; especially since[3]
he saw that the nation, who had been very frequently styled
brothers and kinsmen by the senate, were being kept in
slavery and under the dominion of others, and he knew that
their hostages were with the king; this he regarded as most
disgraceful to him and the state in such an empire as the
Roman people had.

*Hic res cognosco, dux incola animus verbum confirmo, polli-
ceorque, sui is res cura sum; magnus sui habeo spes, et beneficium
suus et auctoritas adduco rex finis injuria facio. Hic oratio
habeo, concilium dimitto; et secundum is multus res is hortor,
quare sui is res cogito et suscipio puto; in primus quod natio,
frater consanguineusque saepenumero ab senatus appello, in servitus atque in ditio video alius teneo, isque obses sum apud rex
intelligo; qui in tantus imperium Populus Romanus turpis sui
et respublica sum arbitror.*

XXII.

Therefore he sends his lieutenant with the cavalry into the
territory of the nations who are next the river.   He gives him
orders to go[4] to the rest of the inhabitants and keep them in
allegiance; and to hold in check the Germans, who were said
to have been summoned to their aid, should they attempt[5] by
force to cross the river in ships.   He orders Calpurnius to set
out for the country with twelve legionary cohorts and a large
number of cavalry, lest auxiliaries should be sent to Gaul
from these nations, and so great nations should form a union.
He sends Tullius, the lieutenant with three legions to cause[6]
that force to be kept apart.[7]

*Itaque legatus in fines natio, qui propior flumen sum, cum
equitatus mitto.   Hic mando, reliquus incola adeo, atque in
officium contineo; Germanusque, qui auxilium arcesso dico, si
per vis navis flumen transeo conor, prohibeo.   Calpurnius cum
cohors legionarius duodecim, et magnus numerus equitatus, rus
proficiscor jubeo, ne ex hic natio auxilia in Gallia mitto, ac
tantus natio conjungo.   Tullius legatus cum tres legio mitto,
qui is manus distineo curo.*

---

[1] 492, 2 & 500, 1.   [2] 562 & 565.   [3] 520, I.   [4] 493, 2.   [5] 509.   [6] 500.
[7] 562 & 565.

XXIII.

The battle was fought[1] long and fiercely, since[2] the enemy, relying on their former victories, thought that the safety of all the state rested on their valour ; (while) our men moreover wished it to be seen what they could[3] do under the leader-ship of a mere youth, without their commander and without the rest of the legions. At length the enemy, weakened by wounds, fled. After a large number of them had been slain, Crassus began to besiege on his march the enemy's town. When they offered a brave resistance, he brought forward his vineae and towers. At one time having attempted a sally, at another having worked up mines to the mound and the vineae (and in this these people are by far the most skil-ful, because[4] in many places among them there are mines of copper), they sent[5] ambassadors to our general and asked[6] him to take them under his protection, when they saw that no benefit could be gained from these things in consequence of the activity of our (soldiers). After this request had been granted, when ordered to give up their arms, they did so.

Pugno diu atque acriter, cum hostis, superus victoria fretus, in suus virtus totus civitas salus pono puto ; noster autem, quis sine imperator et sine reliquus legio, adolescentulus dux, efficio possum, perspicio cupio. Tandem, conficio vulnus, hostis tergum verto. Qui magnus numerus interficio, Crassus ex iter oppidum hostis oppugno coepi. Qui fortiter resisto, vineae turrisque ago. Ille, alias eruptio tento, alias cuniculus ad agger vineaeque ago (qui res sum longe peritus hic natio, propterea quod multus locus apud is aerarius sectura sum), ubi diligentia noster nihil hic res proficio possum intelligo, legatus ad noster imperator mitto, suique in deditio ut recipio peto. Qui res impetro, arma trado jubeo, facio.

XXIV.

Almost at the same time, although[7] the summer was now nearly past, still, because[8] after the subjugation of all the other tribes, these alone[9] remained in arms, and had never sent ambassadors to him about peace, the general led his army thither, thinking that this war could be quickly finished ; these determined to carry on war in a very different manner from the other tribes. For since they knew that very great tribes who had fought in battle had been routed and beaten, and (since) they had extensive woods and marshes, they collected all their property thither. When the general had come to

---

the beginning of these woods and had begun to pitch his camp, and (when) no enemy meanwhile had shown himself, while ours were scattered at work, suddenly from all parts of the woods they rushed out and made an attack on our men.

Idem fere tempus, imperator etsi prope exiguo jam aestas sum, tamen, quod, omnis reliquus gens paco, hic supersum, qui in arma sum neque ad is unquam legatus de pax mitto, arbitror, is bellum celeriter conficio possum, eo exercitus adduco ; qui longe alius ratio, ac reliquus natio, bellum ago instituo. Nam, quod intelligo, magnus natio, qui proelium contendo, pello superoque, continensque silva ac palus habeo, eo suus omnis confero. Ad qui initium silva cum imperator pervenio, castraque munio instituo, neque hostis interim video, dispergo in opus noster, subito ex omnis pars silva evolo et in noster impetus facio.

XXV.

There was a certain Greek in the camp, Xenophon by name,[1] born of an honourable family,[2] who after the beginning of the siege had fled for refuge to Brutus, and had given him proofs of his fidelity. He persuades his slave, by the hope of liberty and by great rewards, to take a letter to Athens. He carries this fastened on his javelin, and a Greek going about without any suspicion among the Greeks, he comes to the praetor. From him information is obtained about the dangers of Brutus and the legion. After receiving the letter about the eleventh hour of the day, the praetor immediately sends a messenger to the quaestor, whose winter quarters were twenty-five miles[3] distant from him. He orders the legion to set out at midnight and to come to him quickly. Crassus set out with the messenger. He sends a second (messenger) to [4] Fabius, the lieutenant, to lead his legion into the territory of the Lacedæmonians, where he knew he[5] would have to pass.[6]

Sum unus intus Graecus, nomen Xenophon, locus nascor honestus, qui a prior obsidio ad Brutus perfugio, suusque is fides praesto. Hic servus spes libertas magnusque persuadeo praemium, ut litterae Athenae defero. Hic ille in jaculum illigo effero, et, Graecus inter Graecus sine ullus suspicio versor, ad praetor pervenio. Ab is de periculum Brutus legioque cognosco. Praetor, accipio litterae hora circiter undecimus dies, statim nuncius ad quaestor mitto, qui hiberna absum ab is mille passus viginti quinque. Jubeo medius nox legio proficiscor celeriterque ad sui venio. Exeo cum nuncius Crassus. Alter ad Fabius legatus mitto, ut in Lacedaemonii fines legio adduco, qua sui iter facio scio. ·

---

[1] 429.　　[2] 425, 3.　　[3] 378.　　[4] 384, II., 2.　　[5] 388.　　[6] 562.

XXVI.

Accordingly, when towards evening he had summoned a council,[1] having exhorted them to execute[2] with care and zeal those things which[3] he had ordered, he allots to the Roman knights, one to each, the ships which he had brought off from Naples ; and at the end of the first watch[1] he orders them to proceed silently four miles down the stream,[1] and there await him. The five cohorts which he regarded as the least reliable for battle he leaves to guard[4] the camp ; the other five of the same legion he orders to set out[5] with all their baggage about midnight up the river[1] with great commotion.

Iaque sub vesper concilium convoco, cohortor ut is, qui impero, diligenter industrieque administro, navis, qui a Neapolis deduco, singuli eques Romanus attribuo, et, prior conficio vigilia, quatuor mille passus secundus flumen silentium progredior ibique sui expecto jubeo. Quinque cohors, qui parum firmus ad dimico sum existimo, castra præsidium relinquo ; quinque idem legio reliquus de medius nox cum omnis impedimenta adversus flumen magnus tumultus proficiscor impero.

XXVII.

There were these difficulties in conducting[6] the war which we have shown above, but many things, notwithstanding, urged him on to that war ; the wrong done by retaining the knights ;[7] the renewal of the war that took place after the surrender ; the revolt, although hostages had been given ; the conspiracy of so many states ; and above everything else (this), lest, if he paid no attention to this part,[8] the other tribes might think that they[9] were at liberty to do the same. Accordingly, since he knew that almost all were anxious for change and easily and quickly stirred up to war, that all men, moreover, are naturally eager for liberty and hate a state of slavery, he thought that he ought[10] to divide his force and spread it over a larger surface, before more states entered[11] into a conspiracy.

Sum hic difficultas bellum gero, qui supra ostendo, sed multus is tamen ad is bellum incito ; injuria retineo eques ; rebellio facio post deditio ; defectio do obses ; tot civitas conjuratio ; in primus, ne, hic pars negligo, omnis fere Gallus novus res studeo, et ad bellum mobiliter celeriterque excito, omnis autem homo natura libertas studeo, et conditio servitus odi ; priusquam multus civitas conspiro, partio sui ac late distribuo exercitus puto.

XXVIII.

These instructions were carried back to the general at the same time, and ambassadors came from the Gauls and the Germans; the former, to complain[1] that the tribes who had lately been brought over into Gaul were laying waste[2] their territory; that they could not have obtained peace from the king[3] even after giving hostages : the latter, moreover, that a hundred cantons had settled near the banks of the Rhine, who were making attempts to cross the river; that two brothers were over them. Our general, being greatly alarmed at this, thought that he must make haste,[4] lest, if a new body should unite with the old forces, resistance might be less easily offered[5] to him. Accordingly, having arranged for a supply of corn as quickly as possible, he hastens against the king by forced marches.

Hic idem tempus imperator mandatum refero, et legatus a Gallus et Germanus venio; ille queror, quod gens, qui nuper in Gallia transporto, fines is populor; sui ne obses quidem do pax res redimo possum; hic autem, pagus centum ad ripa Rhenus consido, qui flumen transeo conor ; is praesum duo frater. Qui res noster imperator vehementer commoveo, maturo sui existimo, ne, si novu, manus cum vetus copiae rex sui conjungo, parum facile resisto possum. Itaque res frumentarius, quam celeriter possum, comparo, magnus iter ad rex contendo.

XXIX.

When he had advanced a three days' journey,[6] word was brought him, that the king, with all his forces, was hastening to occupy the town, and had accomplished three days' journey from his territory. Our general thought that he[7] should take great care[8] to prevent this from happening ;[9] for in the town there was the utmost abundance of everything of use for war ; and it was so fortified by the nature of the place that it afforded[10] great facilities for prolonging the war : because a river surrounds[11] almost the whole town, as if drawn round by a pair of compasses ; the rest of the space, which is not more than six hundred feet,[12] where the river breaks off, a mountain of great height occupies, so that the foot of the mountain touches the bank of the river in both directions. A wall thrown around[13] it makes a citadel of this (mountain), and

----

[1] 569.   [2] 520, II.   [3] 396, I.   [4] 232.   [5] 465, II., 2.   [6] 396, IV., 1, 2).
[7] 388.   [8] 232 & 465, II , 2.   [9] 492, 1.   [10] 494.   [11] 520, 1.   [12] 396, IV.
[13] 384, II., 1.

connects it with the town. Hither our general hastens by forced marches by day and night, and, having taken possession of the town, places a garrison in it.

Cum triduum via procedo, nuntio is, rex cum suus omnis copiæ ad occupo oppidum contendo, triduumque via a suus finis proficio. Is ne accido, magnus opus sui præcaveo noster imperator existimo; namque omnis res, qui ad bellum usus sum, superus sum in is oppidum facultas; isque natura locus sic munio, ut magnus ad duco bellum do facultas, propterea quod flumen, ut circinus circůmduco, pœne totus oppidum cingo; reliquus spatium, qui sum non amplus pes sexcenti, qua flumen intermitto, mons contineo magnus altitudo, ita ut radix is mons ex uterque pars ripa flumen contingo. Hic murus circumdo arx efficio et cum oppidum conjungo. Huc imperator magnus nocturnus diurnusque iter contendo, occupoque oppidum, ibi præsidium colloco.

XXX.

That day, after cavalry skirmishes near the water, both kept[1] on their own ground; the enemy, because[2] they were waiting for larger forces which had not yet assembled; our general, to engage[3] in front of the camp on this side of the valley, if perchance by a pretence of fear he could[4] entice the enemy to his ground; if he could not bring this about, to cross the valley and river with less risk after an exploration of the roads. At daybreak the enemy's cavalry approaches the camp and engages with our men. Our general designedly orders the horsemen to give way and retire to the camp; at the same time he gives orders that the camp should be fortified in all directions with a higher rampart, and the gates blocked up; and further, that in executing[5] these orders there should be as much running to and fro as possible,[6] and that the work should be executed with an assumed appearance of fear.

Is dies, parvulus equestris prælium ad aqua facio, uterque sui suus locus contineo; hostis, quod amplus copiæ, qui nondum convenio, expecto; noster imperator, si forte timor simulatio hostis in suus locus elicio possum, ut citra vallis pro castra prælium contendo; si is efficio non possum, ut, exploro iter, parvus cum periculum vallis rivusque transeo. Prior lux hostis equitatus ad castra accedo, prælinmque cum noster eques committo. Imperator consulto eques cedo suique in castra recipio jubeo; simul ex omnis pars castra altus vallum munio, portaque obstruo, atque in hic administro res, quam magnopere concurso et cum simulatio timor ago jubeo.

---

[1] 481, IV. [2] 520, I. [3] 491. [4] 503, III. [5] 562& 560, II. [6] 170, 2, (2).

2 A

18 EXERCISES IN LATIN PROSE.

XXXI.

In their behalf the ambassador said: "That they who before
had had[1] most influence in the state, owing both to their own
valour and the hospitality and friendship of the Roman people,
crushed by these battles and calamities, had been forced[2] to
give hostages, the noblest men in the state, and to bind the
state by an oath that they would neither ask back[3] the hostages
nor call upon the Roman people for help, nor would they refuse
to remain[4] forever under their sway and power. He was the
only one of all the state who could not be induced[1] to take[5]
the oath or give his children as hostages. For this reason
he had fled from the state, and come to the senate at Rome
to ask[6] aid, since he alone was bound neither by an oath nor
hostages. But it had turned out worse for the conquerors
than for the conquered; because the king of the Germans had
settled in their territory and taken possession of the third
part of the land which was the best in all Gaul, and was
now ordering the inhabitants to leave the other third part ;
because a few months before about twenty-four thousand men
had come to him, for whom a place and habitations were to be
got ready. In a few years all of them would be driven[7] out
of the territory, and all the Germans would cross the river."

*Pro hic loquor legatus: "Qui prælium calamitasque frango,
qui et suus virtus, et Populus Romanus hospitium atque amicitia,
multum ante in civitas possum, cogo obses do, nobilis civitas, et
jusjurandum civitas obstringo, sui neque obses repeto, neque
auxilium a Populus Romanus imploro, neque recuso, quo minus
perpetuo sub ille ditio atque imperium sum. Unus sui sum ex
omnis civitas, qui adduco non possum, ut juro, aut liberi suus
obses do. Ob is res sui ex civitas profugio et Roma ad senatus
venio, auxilium postulo, quod solus neque jusjurandum neque
obses teneo. Sed male victor quam rictus, accido ; propterea
quod rex Germanus in is fines consido, tertiusque pars ager, qui
sum bonus totus Gallia occupo, et nunc de alter pars tertius
incola decedo jubeo ; propterea quod, pauci mensis ante, mille
homo viginti quatuor ad is venio, qui locus ac sedes paro. Sum
pauci annus, uti omnes ex fines pello, atque omnis Germanus
flumen transeo."*

XXXII.

When this answer was brought back to our general, he
again sent[8] messengers to him with the following instructions :
"Whereas, (though) treated with so great kindness by him and

---

[1] 531.　[2] 530, I.　[3] 543.　[4] 499.　[5] 492, 2.　[6] 569.　[7] 544, 1.
[8] 467, III., 1.

the Roman people, he was making[1] such a return that[2] he objected when invited to come to a conference, and did not consider that it was his[3] duty to speak[4] about the common interests and to inform himself. The following were what he had to ask of him : first, no longer to bring[5] across the river into Germany a multitude of men ; in the next place, to restore the hostages he had taken from the Celts, and to let the Germans have permission to restore to them with his consent those they had ; nor to harass the Celts without cause, or wage war on them and their allies. If he did so, he and the Roman people would forever be grateful and on friendly terms with him ; if he should not obtain (what he wanted), he would not overlook the injury done the Celts,[6] since, in the consulship of Caius Titurius and Marcus Brutus, the senate had passed a resolution[7] that whoever had the government of the province should defend the Celts and the other friends of the Roman people, so far as he could do it consistently with the interest of the state."

Hic responsum ad imperator refero, iterum ad is legatus cum hic mandatum mitto: " *Quoniam tantus suus Populusque Romanus beneficio afficio, hic gratiam refero ut in colloquium venio invito gravor, neque de communis res dico sui et cognosco puto ; hic sum qui ab is postulo ; primum, ne quis homo multitudo ample trans flumen in Germania transduco ; deinde obses, qui habeo ab Celtæ, reddo, Germanusque permitto, ut, qui ille habeo, voluntas is reddo ille licet ; neve Celtæ injuria lacesso, neve hic sociusque is bellum infero. Si is ita facio, sui Populusque Romanus perpetuus gratia atque amicitia cum is sum ; si non impetro, sui, quoniam Caius Titurius Marcus Brutus consul, senatus censeo, uti, quicunque Provincia obtineo, quod commodum res publicus facio possum, Celtæ ceteraque amicus populus Romanus defendo, sui Celtæ injuriae non negligo.*"

XXXIII.

To this the king made answer : "That it was the law of war that the conquerors[8] should rule the conquered as they wished ; in like manner that the Roman people were wont to rule the conquered, not according to the dictates of another, but their own pleasure. If he did not direct the Roman people how to use their right, he ought not to be obstructed by the Roman people in the exercise of his right. The Germans had become tributary to him, since they had put the fortune of war to the test, and had fought and been overcome. The general was doing him a great injury, since by his coming he

---

[1] 531.   [2] 494.   [3] 388.   [4] 562 & 563.   [5] 492, 2.   [6] 396, II.
[7] 494, 3.   [8] 453, 2, 1).

was rendering his revenues of less value to him. He would
not restore the hostages to the Germans, nor would he make
war on them or their allies without just cause, if they stood
by what they had agreed upon, and paid the tribute yearly ;
if they did not do this, the name of brothers of the Roman
people would be of no use to them. As to the menace which
the general had employed towards him, that he would not
overlook the wrongs done to the Germans, no man had entered the lists with him without being ruined.　Let him try a
contest[1] when he pleased ; he would understand what an un-
conquered people, highly skilled in the use of arms, who had
not entered a house for fourteen years, could do[2] by valour."

*Ad hic rex respondeo: " Jus sum bellum, ut, qui vinco, is, qui
vinco, quemadmodum volo, impero ; item Populus Romanus vinco
non ad alter præscriptum, sed ad suus arbitrium impero consuesco.
Si ipse populus Romanus non præscribo, quemadmodum suus
jus utor, non oportet sui a Populus Romanus in suus jus
impedio ; Germanus sui, quoniam bella fortuna tento et arma
congredior ac supero, stipendiarius facio ; magnus imperator injuria facio, qui suus adventus vectigal sui deterior
facio. Germanus sui obses reddo non, neque, is neque is socius
injuria bellum infero, si in is maneo, qui convenio, stipendiumque
quotannis pendo ; si is non facio, longe is fraternus nomen
Populus Romanus absum. Qui sui imperator denuntio, sui
Germanus injuria non negligo ; nemo sui cum sine suus pernicies
contendo ; quum volo, congredior ; intelligo, quis invictus populus,
exercitatus in arma, qui inter annus quatuordecim tectum non
subeo, virtus possum."*

XXXIV.

There are two professions which can place men in the
highest rank of honour : one, that[3] of a general ; the other,
that of a good orator ; for by the latter the ornaments of
peace are maintained ; by the former the dangers of war are
averted.　Other virtues, however, justice, fidelity, modesty
(and)[4] temperance, are intrinsically of great importance ; and
in these, O Servius, all know that you excel.　But I am now
arguing about the pursuits that assist men in attaining honour, not about the innate worth of each.　All these pursuits
are dashed from our hands as soon as some new commotion
begins to sound forth the signal of war.　For, as an ingenious
poet and very excellent writer remarks, when battles are pro-

---

[1] 530, II.　　[2] 531 & 525.　　[3] 397, 1.　　[4] 587, I., 6.

claimed, not only is that wordy pretence of prudence that you have, but even "wisdom," that mistress herself of (all) things, "is driven away."

Duo sum ars, qui possum loco homo in amplus gradus dignitas ; unus imperator, alter orator bonus ; ab hic enim pax ornamentum retineo ; ab ille bellum periculum repello. Cetera tamen virtus ipse per sui multum valeo, justitia, fides, pudor, temperantia ; qui tu, Servius, excello omnis intelligo ; sed nunc de studium ad honor dispono, non de insitus quisque virtus disputo. Omnis iste ego studium de manus excutio, simul atque aliquis motus novus bellicum cano coepi. Etenim, ut aio ingeniosus poeta, et auctor valde bonus, proelium promulgo, "pello e medium," non solum iste vester verbosus simulatio prudentia, sed etiam ipse ille domina res, "sapientia."

XXXV.

There is the highest dignity in those who are pre-eminent in military glory ; for all things, which are in the empire and in the constitution of the state, are supposed to be defended and strengthened by them. There is also the greatest profit (in them), if, indeed, by their wisdom and danger we are able[1] to enjoy both the republic and even our own possessions. That ability in speaking is also of influence and full of dignity (and often has it[2] had weight in choosing[3] a consul), to be able,[4] (namely), to move by wise counsels and oratory the minds of the senate, of the people, and[5] of those who decide matters. A consul is needed who may check by his eloquence at times the madness of the tribunes, sway the excited people, and resist corruption.

Superus dignitas sum in is, qui militaris laus antecello ; omnis enim, qui sum in imperium, et in status civitas, ab is defendo et firmo puto. Superus etiam utilitas ; siquidem is consilium et periculum, cum res publicus, tum etiam noster res perfruor possum. Gravis etiam ille sum, et plenus dignitas, dico facultas, (qui saepe valeo in consul deligo,) possum consilium atque oratio, et senatus et populus, et is, qui res judico, mens permoveo. Quaero consul, qui dico nonnunquam comprimo tribunicius furor, qui concitatus populus flecto, qui largitio resisto.

XXXVI.

And two consuls having been sent to the[1] war with this in view, that[2] the one should pursue Mithridates, the other, guard Bithynia; the disasters of one[3] both by sea and land greatly increased both the wealth and reputation of the king; of Lucius Lucullus, indeed, the exploits were so great that neither can[4] there be mentioned a greater war, nor (one) carried on with greater wisdom and ability. For, when[5] the force of the whole war had centred against the walls of the Cyziceni, and Mithridates had thought that that city would be to him the door of Asia, on the breaking[6] down and bursting open of which, the whole province would be open[7] to him; all these things were (so) managed by Lucullus, that the city of our most faithful allies was defended, and all the king's forces wasted away in consequence of the length of the siege.

Ad qui bellum duo consul ita mitto, ut alter Mithridates per-sequor, alter Bithynia tueor; alter res et terra et mare calami-tosus vehementer et opis rex et nomen augeo; L. Lucullus vero res tantus exsisto, ut neque magnus bellum commemoro possum, neque magnus consilium et virtus gero. Nam, cum totus impetus bellum ad Cyziceni moenia consisto, isque urbs sui Mithridates Asia janua sum puto, qui effrango et revello, totus pateo pro-vincia; perficio ab Lucullus hic sum omnis, ut urbs fidelis socius defendo, et omnis copiae rex diuturnitas obsessio consumo.

XXXVII.

But we are foolish in presuming[8] to compare Drusus, Africanus, Pompey, ourselves, with P. Clodius. These (instances) were endurable; no one with equanimity can bear the death of P. Clodius. The senate laments; the order of knights grieves; the whole state is wasted away with sorrow; the municipal towns have put on mourning; the colonies are in deep distress; in a word, the very fields regret so generous, so benign, so humane a citizen! This was not the reason, O judges—it was not, indeed—why Pompey thought[9] an investi-gation should be proposed by him; but being a man of sense, and endued with a profound and almost god-like intelligence, he took many things into consideration; that the former was his foe, Milo his personal friend. If in the general exultation of all (parties), he too indulged in joyous feelings,[7] he was

----

afraid lest the sincerity of their re-established regard should seem but weakly founded.

Sed stultus sum, qui Drusus, qui Africanus, Pompeius, egomet ipse cum P. Clodius confero audeo. Tolerabilis sum ille; P. Clodius mors nemo æquus animus fero possum. Lugeo senatus, mærco equester ordo, totus civitas conficio senium, squaleo municipium, afflicto colonia, ager denique ipse tam beneficus, tam salutaris, tam mansuetus civis desidero. Non sum is causa, judex, profecto, non sum, cur sui censeo Pompeius quæstio fero; sed homo sapiens atque altus et divinus quidam mens praeditus multus video; sum ille sui inimicus, familiaris Milo; in communis omnis laetitia, si etiam ipse gaudeo, timeo, ne video infirmus fides reconcilatus gratia.

XXXVIII.

As it was evident[1] that a murder had taken place on the Appian (way), I accordingly gave it as my own opinion, not that the man in defending[2] himself had acted injuriously to the state; but, since violence and waylaying were connected with the matter, I reserved the question of guilt for trial; I recorded my reprobation of the affair. But, if the senate had been allowed[3] by that turbulent tribune to carry out its resolution[4], we should have no new commission; for it was coming to a decree that an investigation should be held in accordance with the ancient laws, only out of the regular routine. The question was voted on under its separate heads on the motion of some one,[5] for it is not necessary for me to bring to light the worthlessness of all. Thus the remaining resolution of the senate was got rid of by a hired veto. But, some say, Cn. Pompey by his bill gave his decision both concerning the fact and the question; for he brought in a bill regarding the affray which had taken place[6] on the Appian way, wherein P. Clodius had been slain.[6]

Itaque ego ipse decerno, quum caedes in Appius facio constat, non is, qui sui defendo, contra res publicus facio; sed, quum insum in res vis et insidiæ, crimen judicium reservo, res noto. Quod si per furiosus ille tribunus senatus, quis sentio, perficio licet, novus quaestio nullus habeo. Decerno enim, ut vetus lex, tantummodo extra ordo, quaero. Dividio sententia postulo nescio quis; nihil enim necesse sum omnis ego flagitium profero. Sic reliquus auctoritas senatus emo intercessio tollo. At enim Cn. Pompeius rogatio suus et de res et de causa judico; fero enim de caedes, qui in Appius via facio, in qui P. Clodius occido.

---

[1] 518, II. [2] 517, 1. [3] 510. [4] 453, 2, 1), [5] 431, 2. [6] 531.

XXXIX.

You pressed for a law about bribery, which you[1] had no need of ; for there was the Calpurnian (law) drawn up with the severest penalties attached. Regard was shown both to your wishes and your dignity. But the whole of that law would have armed your accusation, if you had[2] (one really) guilty before the court ; it has, indeed, thwarted your candidature. A penalty more severe against the people—the minds of the lower orders were alarmed—(namely) the penalty of exile against our order, was pressed for by your speech ; the senate yielded to your demand ; but with reluctance, at your suggestion, it enacted a more severe restriction against our common fortunes. A penalty was attached to an excuse of sickness. The friendly feelings of many were hurt, who[3] had to make a great effort,[4] to the detriment of their health, or else, in addition to the distress of illness, even the other enjoyments in life had to be given up.

Lex ambitus flagito, qui tu non desum; scribo enim severe Calpurnius. Gero mos et voluntas et dignitas tuus. Sed totus ille lex accusatio tuus, si habeo nocens reus, fortasse armo ; petitio vero refragor. Pœna gravis in plebs tuus vox eflagito, (commoveo animus tenuis), exilium in noster ordo ; concedo senatus postulatio tuus, sed non libenter durus fortuna communis conditio, tu auctor, constituo. Morbus excusatio poena addo ; voluntas offendo multus, qui aut contra valetudo commodum laboro, aut incommodum morbus etiam cetera vita fructus relinquo.

XL.

But, since[5] many imagine that military employments are preferable to civil, this opinion must be refuted. For many have often sought after war through a desire for glory ; and this is generally the case with men of great spirit and natural ability ; and still more, if they have an aptitude for military affairs and are fond of carrying on wars. If,[6] however, we are desirous of forming a correct judgment, there have been many instances of civil employments of greater importance and higher renown than warlike pursuits. For, though[7] Themistocles be justly praised, and his name be more illustrious than that of Solon, and though Salamis be cited as an evidence of a most brilliant victory which may be

---

preferred to that design of Solon's by which he founded the
council of the Areopagus, the latter act must not be considered
less renowned than the former ; for the former was of service
once for all, the latter will always benefit the state.   By the
latter plan the laws of the Athenians ; by the latter the
institutions of their forefathers are maintained.

*Sed cum plerique arbitror, res bellicus magnus sum quam
urbanus, minuo hic opinio.   Multus enim bellum saepe quaero
propter gloria cupiditas ; atque is in magnus animus ingeniumque
plerumque contingit, eoque magnopere, si sum ad res militaris
aptus et cupidus bellum gero, vere autem si volo judico, multus
res exsisto urbanus, magnus clarusque quam bellicus, quamvis
enim Themistocles jus laudo, et sum is nomen quam Solon illustris, citoque Salamis clarus testis victoria, qui antepono consilium
Solon is, qui prius constituo Areopagites ; non parum praeclarus
hic quam ille judico.   Ille enim semel prosum, hic semper prosum
civitas ; hic consilium lex Atheniensis, hic majores institutum
servo.*

XLI.

When C. Canius, a Roman knight, possessed of considerable talent, and very well versed in literature, had gone to
Syracuse for the purpose, not of business,[1] but of pleasure,
as he used to say, he repeatedly declared that he wished to
purchase some pleasure grounds where he might invite his
friends, and enjoy himself without intruders.   When this
remark had been repeated often, one Pythius, who carrried
on the business of banker at Syracuse, (told him) that he had
not gardens for sale indeed, but that Canius might use them
as his own ; and at the same time he invited the man to dinner in his gardens the next day.   When he had accepted the
invitation, then Pythius, who, being[2] a banker, was a man of
influence with all classes, summoned fishermen into his presence, and asked them to fish the next day before his pleasure
grounds ; and he told them what he wished[3] them to do.

*C. Canius, eques Romanus, nec infacetus et satis litteratus,
cum sui Syracusae otior, ut ipse dico soleo, non negotior causa,
confero, dictito, sui hortulus aliquis emo volo, quo invito amicus,
et ubi sui oblecto sine interpellator possum.   Qui cum percrebesco,
Pythius is quidam, qui argentaria facio Syracusae, venalis
quidem sui hortus non habeo, sed licet utor Canius, si volo, ut
suus ; et simul ad coena homo in hortus invito in posterus dies.
Cum ille promitto, tum Pythius, qui sum, ut argentarius, apud
omnis ordo gratiosus, piscator ad sui convoco, et ab hic peto, ut
ante suus hortulus postri lie piscor : dicoque, quis is facio volo.*

XLII.

To return to fables; Sol said to his son Phaethon that he
would do whatever he asked.   He asked to be taken up into
his father's car.   He was taken up: and before[1] he was settled, he was set on fire by the stroke of a thunderbolt.   How[2]
much better had it been for the father's promise not to have
been kept in this case?   What of the fact that Theseus ex-
acted a promise of Neptune?   When Neptune had given him[3]
three wishes, he asked for the death of his son Hippolytus:
and when this request had been granted, Theseus was plunged
into the greatest grief.   What?   When Agamemnon had
vowed to Diana the most beautiful thing that[4] was born in his
realm that year, he sacrificed Iphigenia, than whom that year
indeed nothing was born more beautiful.   It is better that a
promise should not be kept than that so foul a deed should
be committed.

*Sol Phaethon filius, ut redeo ad fabula, facio sui dico, quis-
quis opto.   Opto, ut in currus pater tollo.   Tollo.   Atque is
antequam consisto, ictus fulmen deflagro.   Quanto bene sum, in
hic promissum pater non servo?   Quis, quod Theseus exigo promissum a Neptunus?   Qui cum tres optatio Neptunus do, opto
interitus Hippolytus filius; qui optatum impetro, Theseus in
magnus sum luctus.   Quid?   Agamemnon cum devoveo Diana,
qui in suus regnum pulcher nascor ille annus, immolo Iphigenia,
qui nihil sum is quidem annus nascor pulcher.   Promissum
potius non facio quam tam taeter facinus admitto.*

XLIII.

Do you ask for more reliable authorities?   For it is the
characteristic of these virtues to fear nothing, to despise all
human affairs, to think that nothing that can[5] happen to man
ought to be shirked.   What then did he do?   He came into
the Senate, and he fully explained his instructions: he re-
fused to declare[6] his opinion; (he said) that he was not a
Senator, so long as he was bound[7] by an oath sworn to his
enemies.   And (O foolish man, some one may have said, and
standing in the way of his own interest!) he declared that it
was also inexpedient that the prisoners should be restored;
for that these were young and the leaders were good; that
he was worn out with old age.   And when his influence prevailed, the prisoners were retained; he himself returned to

---

[1] 523, I.   [2] 418.   [3] 453.   [4] 453, 5.   [5] 485.   [6] 499, 2.   [7] 486, III.

Carthage; neither affection for his native land nor for his friends kept him back. Nor, indeed, was he ignorant at the time that he was going to a most cruel enemy, and to refined punishment; but he thought that his oath should be kept.

Num locuples quæro auctor? Hic enim sum virtus proprius, nihil extimesco, omnis humanus despicio, nihil, qui homo accide possum, intolero puto. Itaque quis facio? In senatus venio, mandatum expono: sententia ne dico, recuso; quam diu jusjurandum hostis teneo, non sum sui senator. Atque ille etiam, (O stultus homo, dico quisquam, et repugnans utilitas suus!) reddo captivus, nego sum utilis; ille enim adolescens sum et bonus dux, sui jam conficio senectus. Qui cum valeo auctoritas, captivus retineo, ipse Carthago redeo; neque is caritas patria retineo, nec suus. Neque vero tum ignoro, sui ad crudelis hostis et ad exquisitus supplicium proficiscor: sed jusjurandum conservo puto.

XLIV.

And on account of this kind of wrong the Lacedæmonians expelled the Ephor Lysander. They put king Agis to death, a thing which[1] had never happened before among them. And after that time so great dissensions followed that tyrants arose, the leading men were expatriated, and the state founded under the most distinguished auspices fell to pieces. Not merely, however, did it fall itself, but it even overthrew the rest of Greece by infecting it with evils, which, originating with the Lacedæmonians, spread more widely. What? Did not the disturbances about the land measures ruin our Gracchi, the sons of Tiberius Gracchus, a most excellent man, the grandsons of Africanus? But truly Aratus of Sicyon is justly praised, who having left Argos for Sicyon, when his native state had been held by tyrants for fifty years, entered the city secretly and took possesson of it.

Ac propter hic injuria genus Lacedæmonius Lysander ephorus expello. Agis rex, qui nunquam antea apud is accido, neco. Exque is tempus tantus discordia sequor, ut et tyrannus exsisto et optimus extermino et præclare constituo res publicus dilabor. Nec vero ipse solum cado, sed etiam reliquus Græcia everto contagio malum, qui a Lacedæmonius proficiscor mano late. Quid? Noster Gracchus, Ti. Gracchus, superus vir, filius, Africanus nepos, nonne agrarius contentio perdo? At vero Aratus Sicyonius jus laudo, qui, cum is civitas quinquaginta annus a tyrannus teneo, proficiscor Argi Sicyon, clandestinus introitus urbs potior.

---

[1] 415, 7.

XLV.

But in these precepts about what is useful, Antipater, the Tyrian, a Stoic, who lately died at Athens, thinks that two things have been left unnoticed by Panætius (namely), the care of health and money. And these, I imagine, have been left unnoticed by that most distinguished philosopher, because[1] they are obvious; they certainly are useful. But health is maintained by the knowledge of one's own constitution, by observing what[2] usually does us either good or injury, by temperance in every mode of living and luxury, for the sake of preserving our constitution, and by giving up our pleasures; finally, by the skill of these men to whose knowledge these things belong. Our own property, moreover, ought to be acquired by means free from baseness; it should also be kept intact by care and frugality; (it ought) even to be increased by these qualities. Xenophon, the disciple of Socrates, has discussed these subjects most suitably in that work which is styled Œconomicus.

In hic autem utilitas præceptum Antipater Tyrius, Stoicus, qui Athenæ nuper morior, duo prætereo censeo a Panætius, valetudo curatio, et pecunia. Qui res a superus philosophus prætereo arbitror, quod sum facilis: sum certe utilis. Sed valetudo sustento notitia suus corpus: et observatio, qui res aut prosum soleo, aut obsum: et continentia in victus omnis atque cultus, corpus tueor causa: et prætermitto voluptas; posterius ars is, qui ad scientia hic pertineo. Res autem familiaris quæro debeo is res, a qui absum turpitudo; conservo autem diligentia et parsimonia; idem etiam res augeo. Hic res commode Xenophon Socraticus persequor in is liber, qui Œconomicus inscribo.

XLVI.

Many, moreover, have been found ready not only to throw away[1] their money but even their lives for their native land: they would also be unwilling to make even the least sacrifice of their glory, even should the state require it. As (for instance) Callicratidas, who, when he was leader of the Lacedaemonians in the Peloponnesian war, and performed many distinguished deeds, finally overturned everything, when he did not follow the advice of those who thought that the fleet should be withdrawn from Arginusæ, and that a battle should not be fought with the Athenians. His reply to them was, that the Lacedaemonians, after that fleet had been lost, were able to build another; that he could not flee without disgracing himself. And this indeed was a slight blow to the Lacedaemonians : that was fraught with ruin by which the rower of the Lacedæmonians was utterly destroyed when Cleombrotus, fearing unpopularity, rashly engaged with Epaminondas.

Invenio autem multus, qui non modo pecunia, sed etiam vita profundo pro patria sum paratus : idem gloria jactura ne parvus quidem facio volo, ne res publicus quidem postulo. Ut Callicratidas, qui cum Lacedæmonius dux sum Peloponnesiacus bellum, multusque facio egregie, verto ad extremum omnis, cum consilium non parco is, qui classis ab Arginusæ removeo, nec cum Atheniensis dimico puto. Qui ille respondeo, Lacedæmonius, classis ille amitto, alius paro possum; sui fugio sine suus dedecus non possum. Atque hic quidem Lacedæmonius plaga mediocris; ille pestifer, qui cum Cleombrotus invidia timeo temere cum Epaminondas confligo, Lacedæmonius opis corruo.

XLVII.

But, if the force of integrity is so great that we love it either in the case of persons whom we have never seen, or, what is stranger, in that even of an enemy, what wonder is it if the affections of men receive an impulse when they seem to discern clearly the virtue and goodness of those with whom they may be united in familiar intercourse? And yet love is strengthened by the receipt[1] of a friendly service, the discernment of good-will, and the addition of close familiarity ; and when these motives have been added to that first inclination of affection and love, a certain extent of kindly feeling, that may well be regarded with admiration, is kindled. But, if[2] any imagine this to spring from the weakness (of our nature), that each may have some one through whom he may obtain something of which he feels[3] the want, they leave the origin of friendship, mean indeed, and, if the expression be allowed me, far from noble, inasmuch as they will have it to be sprung from a feeling of want and poverty. For, if this were so, according as any man thought[3] there were the least resources in himself, so would he be best adapted for friendship ; and this is far from being the case.

---

¹ 503, 1, 1).   ² 508.   ³ 525.

Quod si tantus ris probitas sum ut is vel in is qui nunquam video, vel, qui magnus sum, in hostis etiam diligo, quis mirus sum si animus homo moveo, quum is qui cum usus conjungo possum virtus et bonitas perspicio video? Quamquam confirmo amor et beneficium accipio et studium perspicio et consuetudo adjungo; qui res ad ille prior motus animus et amor adhibitus admirabilis quidam exardesco benevolentia magnitudo; qui si quis puto ab imbecillitas proficiscor, ut sum per qui assequor qui quisque desidero, humilis sane relinquo et parum generosus, ut ita dico, ortus amicitia qui ex inopia atque indigentia nascor volo. Qui si ita sum, ut quisque parvus in sui sum arbitror, ita ad amicitia sum aptus: qui longe secus sum.

XLVIII.

Quintus Mucius, the augur, was in the habit of relating many anecdotes concerning his father-in-law, from memory and in a pleasing manner, and of not hesitating to call him wise whenever he spoke of him. Moreover, I had myself, on assuming the gown of manhood, been introduced by my father to Scævola, with the view that, so far as I could and was allowed, I should never quit the old man's side. Accordingly I used to commit to memory many arguments ingeniously handled by him, and many things said in a terse and apt manner, and kept zealously striving to become better informed by his (superior) knowledge. After his death I had recourse to Scævola, the pontiff, an individual whom I venture to call the first in our state in ability and integrity. But of him elsewhere. I now return to the augur. As well do I frequently call to mind many things that occurred as (in particular this) that, seated at home in his easy chair, when both I was with him and a few very intimate friends, he commenced to speak on this subject, which then was in the mouths of almost all.

Quintus Mucius augur multus narro de socer suus memoriter et jucunde soleo nec dubito ille in omnis sermo appello sapiens. Ego autem a pater ita deduco ad Scævola sumo virilis toga, ut quoad possum et licet a senex latus nunquam discedo. Itaque multus ab is prudenter disputo, multus etiam breviter et commode dico memoria mando, fioque studeo is prudentia doctus. Qui morior ego ad pontifex Scævola confero, qui unus noster civitas et ingenium et justitia præstans audeo dico. Sed de hic alias; nunc redeo ad augur. Quum sæpe multus, tum memini domus hemicyclium sedeo, ut soleo, quum et ego sum una et pauci admodum familiaris, in is sermo ille incido qui tum fere omnis sum in os.

XLIX.

If I were to assert that I was not moved with regret for
the loss of my friend, be it for the wise to consider how far I
should be right in so doing ; but I should certainly speak un-
truly. For I am grieved at being bereft of a friend, such as,
I believe, no man will be to me again ; (such) as I can confi-
dently affirm no one else at all events was ; but I require no
medicine ; I console myself, and chiefly with this consolation,
that[1] I am free from that erroneous belief by which most men
are apt to be afflicted on the departure of their friends. For
I believe that no harm has happened to my friend. Whatever has happened has happened to me ; and to be sorely
afflicted by one's own disasters is the part of a man that
loves himself, not his friend. Who indeed can deny[2] that he
ended his career splendidly ? For, unless[3] he chose to hope
for immortality, which he was far from thinking desirable,
what is there that was right for man to desire, which he has
not obtained ?

*Ego si amicus meus desiderium ego moveo nego, quam is
recte facio video sapiens ; sed certe mentior. Moveo enim talis
amicus orbo, qualis, ut arbitror, nemo unquam sum ; ut confirmo possum, nemo certe sum. Sed non egeo medicina : ego ipse
consolor et magnopere ille solatium quod is error careo qui
amicus decessus plerique ango soleo. Nihil enim malum accido
amicus meus puto ; ego accido si quis accido. Suus autem in-
commodus graviter ango non amicus sed sui ipse amans sum.
Cum ille vero quis nego ago praeclare ? Nisi enim, quod ille
parum puto, immortalitas opto volo, quis non adipiscor qui
homo fas sum opto ?*

L.

There is a fixed boundary of all times of life ; but there is
no fixed boundary of old age ; and life is conducted[4] properly
in it so long as[5] you can perform and maintain the require-
ments of your situation, and yet despise death. Whence it
happens[5] that old age is even more stout-hearted and valiant
than youth. Of this sort was that reply which was given by
Solon to Pisistratus the Tyrant, when to the former asking,
with reliance on what hope he so resolutely withstood him, it
is said that he answered, "On old age." But the best termi-

[1] 520, I.   [2] 486, XI.   [3] 511, II.   [4] 301, I.   [5] 522, II.   [6] 556, II.

nation of life is when, with the mind and the other senses un-
impaired, the same nature which cemented together takes to
pieces her own work.   As he who has built a ship or a house
likewise pulls it down with the greatest ease, so the same
nature which has glued man together takes him to pieces
best.   Now every fastening of glue, when fresh, is rent
asunder with difficulty, but easily, when hardened by time.
Thus it is that that brief remnant of life should not be either
eagerly desired, or without reason given up by old men ; and
Pythagoras forbids us to retire from the post and station of
life without the command of our general, that is, of God.

*Omnis aetas certus sum terminus : senectus autem nullus certus
sum terminus, rectoque in is vivo, quoad munus officium exsequor
et tueor possum et tamen mors contemno.   Ex qui fio ut animosus
etiam senectus sum quam adolescentia et fortis.   Hic ille sum
qui Pisistratus tyrannus a Solon respondeo, quum ille quaero, qui
tandem spes fretus sui tam audaciter obsisto, respondeo, dico,
"Senectus."   Sed vivo sum finis bonus, quum integer mens ceteraque sensus opus ipse suus idem qui coagmento natura dissolvo.
Ut navis, ut aedificium idem destruo facile qui construo, sic homo
idem bene qui conglutino natura dissolvo.   Jam omnis conglu-
tinatio recens aegre, inveteratus facile divello.   Ita fio ut ille
brevis vita reliquus nec avide appeto senex nec sine causa desero ;
vetoque Pythagoras injussu imperator, is sum, Deus, de praesidium et statio vita decedo.*

LI.

I have frequently heard from my seniors,[1] who said that
they in turn, when boys, had heard it from old men, that
C. Fabricius used to wonder at what he had heard from
Cineas the Thessalian, when he was ambassador at the court
of king Pyrrhus, that there was a certain man at Athens, who
declared himself a wise man, and that he said that every
thing we did was to be referred to pleasure ; and on hearing
him say so, that M.' Curius and T. Coruncanius were accustomed to wish that[2] that might be the conviction of the Samnites and of Pyrrhus himself, in order that[3] they might the
more readily be conquered, since they had given themselves
up to sensuality.   M.' Curius had lived with P. Decius, who
five years before the consulship of the former, had in his
fourth consulship devoted himself for the republic.   Fabricius
knew him, Coruncanius knew him, who, as well from the

course of his own life as from the exploit of him whom I
mention, Publius Decius, inferred that there was something
in its own nature lovely and glorious which was to be sought
after for its own sake, and which, despising and continuing
pleasure, all the best[1] of mankind pursued.

*Sæpe audio a senex, qui sui porro puer a senex audio dico,
miror soleo C. Fabricius qui, quum apud rex Pyrrhus legatus
sum, audio a Thesalus Cineas, sum quidam Athenæ qui sui
sapiens profiteor, isque dico omnis qui facio ad voluptas refero ;
qui ex is audio M.' Curius et T. Coruncanius opto soleo ut is
Samnis ipseque Pyrrhus persuadeo, quo facile vinco possum
quum sui voluptas do. Vivo M'. Curius cum P. Decius qui
quinquennium ante is consul sui pro res publicu quartus consulatus devoveo. Nosco idem Fabricius, nosco Coruncanius, qui
quum ex suus vita, tum ex is qui dico P. Decius factum judico
sum profecto aliquis natura pulcher atque præclarus qui suus
spontis peto, quique sperno et contemno voluptas bonus quisque
sequor.*

LII.

Do you see how in Homer, Nestor very often speaks of his
own virtues ? for he was now living in the third generation[2] of
men ; nor had he any occasion to feel apprehensive, lest[3] in
telling the truth of himself, he should seem to be either too
overbearing or too talkative. For (as Homer says) from his
tongue flowed words sweeter than honey, for which sweetness
he needed no strength of body ; and yet the illustrious chief-
tain of Greece nowhere desires to have ten men like Ajax,
but like Nestor ; and if this should have happened, he doubts
not but[4] that Troy would quickly fall. But I return to myself.
I am in my eighty-fourth year. In truth, I should like to
have it in my power to make the same boast[5] as Cyrus did :
this, however, I can say, not indeed that I have such bodily
powers[6] as I had either in the Punic war as a private, or in
the same war as quaestor, or in Spain as consul, or four years
afterwards when I fought at Thermopylae as military tribune,
in the consulship of M.' Acilius Glabrio ; yet still old age (as
you see) has not quite unnerved me, nor broken me down—
the senate house regrets not the loss of my strength, nor the
rostra, nor my friends, nor my clients, nor my guests. For I
have never given in to that old and much praised proverb,
which admonishes you to become an old man early, if you
wish to be an old man long.

---

1 458, 1.   2 378.   3 492, 4, 1).   4 498, 3, 1).   5 371, 1, 3), (2).   6 423.

3 A

Videone ut apud Homerus sæpe Nestor de virtus suus prædico? Tertius enim jam aetas homo rivo, nec sum is vereor ne verus prædico de sui nimis video aut insolens aut loquax. Elenim ut aio Homerus, ex is lingua mel dulcis fluo oratio, qui ad suavitas nullus eyeo corpus vires ; et tamen dux ille Græcia nusquam opto ut Ajax similis habeo decem ; at ut Nestor, qui si accido, non dubito quin brevis Troja pereo. Sed redeo ad ego. Quartus annus ago et octogesimus ; volo equiden idem possum glorior qui Cyrus ; sed tamen hic queo dico, non ego quidem is sum vires qui aut miles bellum Punicum aut quæstor idem bellum aut consul in Hispania sum, aut quadrennium post quum tribunus militaris depugno apud Thermopylæ M'. Acilius Glabrio consul ; sed tamen, ut tu video, non plane ego enervo nec affligo senectus ; non curia vires meus desidero, non rostrum, non amicus, non cliens, non hospes. Nec enim unquam assentior vetus ille laudatusque proverbium qui moneo, Mature fio senex, si diu volo sum senex.

LIII.

In the meantime, as soon as Clodius knew (for it was not hard to ascertain)[1] that Titus, on the twentieth of January,[2] had a stated, legally appointed and unavoidable journey (to make) to Lanuvium to nominate a flamen, because Titus was dictator at Lanuvium; he suddenly left Rome himself the day before, in order (as[3] was known by what happened) to place an ambuscade for Titus in front of his own farm. And he set out in such a way that he left behind him a tumultous assembly in which his fury was greatly missed, which was held on that very day, and which, if he had not wished to compass a time and place for the atrocious enterprise, he would never have quitted. But Titus, after having been in the senate on that day until it was adjourned,[4] came home, changed his shoes and clothes, waited for some time while his wife, as is customary, made[5] her preparations, and then set out at the time[6] when Clodius, if indeed he had intended returning to Rome that day, might have already returned.

Interim, quum scio Clodius—neque enim sum difficilis scio— iter sollennis, legitimus, necessarius ante dies XIII Kalendae Februarius Titus sum Lanuvium ad flamen prodo, quod sum dictator Lanuvium Titus, Roma subito ipse proficiscor pridie, ut ante suus fundus, qui res intelligo, Titus insidiæ colloco. Atque ita proficiscor, ut contio turbulentus, in qui is furor

---

[1] 549.   [2] 710, II.   [3] 445, 7.   [4] 522, I.   [5] 467, III., 4.   [6] 396, III., 2, 3).

*desidero, qui ille ipse dies habeo, relinquo, qui nisi abeo facinus
locus tempus volo, nunquam relinquo.   Titus autem quum in
senatus sum is dies, quoad senatus dimitto, domus venio, calceus
et vestimentum muto, paulisper, dum sui uxor, ut fio, comparo,
commoror, deinde proficiscor is tempus quum jam Clodius, si
quidem is dies Roma venio, redeo possum.*

LIV.

A decree was passed[1] that ten commisssioners should par-
tition the state, over which the king had ruled, between his
son and nephew.   Of this commission Caius Julius was the
leader, a man distinguished, and at that time of weight in
the senate, because, when consul, on the death of Marcus
Crassus and Spurius Cassius he had made a most cruel use
against the commons of the victory of the nobility.   Although
the nephew had regarded him as one of his friends at Rome,
still he received him with the most formal attention: by
liberality[2] and by lavish promises he brought it about that
he preferred the king's advantage to reputation, to honor, in
short to all his interests.   Having made advances to the other
ambassadors in the same way, he gains over very many of
them; few held honor in higher esteem than money.

*Decretum facio, uti decem legatus regnum, qui rex obtineo,
inter filius et frater filius.   Qui legatio princeps sum Caius
Julius, homo clarus et tum in senatus potens; quia consul,
Marcus Crassus et Spurius Cassius interficio, acriter victoria
nobilitas in plebs exerceo.   Is frater filius tametsi Roma in
amicus habeo, tamen accurate recipio; do et pollicitor perficio
uti fama, fides, posterius omnis suus res commodum rex antefero.
Reliquus legatus idem via adgredior, plerique capio; pauci
carus fides, quam pecunia sum.*

LV.

By frequently making[2] these (charges), and others of a
a similar nature, the tribune persuaded[1] the people that Cornelius Cinna, who was at that time prætor, should be sent to
Andriscus, and that he should bring him to Rome (the public
faith being pledged for his safety), in order that[3] the crimes
of the commander, and of the others whom they accused of

---

having received money,[1] might be proved by the evidence of
the king. While these things were going[2] on at Rome, those
who had been left by Metellus in Mysia in charge of the
army, adopting the practice of their commander, committed
very many most flagrant crimes. There were some who,
under the influence of a bribe, handed[3] over the elephants to
Andriscus ; others put up[4] the deserters for sale ; some[5] carried off booty from peaceful (states) ; such a violent attack
of avarice like some infection had taken possession of their
minds. But Cornelius Cinna sets out to go to Andriscus,
after the bill proposed by the tribune had been passed and
all the nobility defeated. He persuaded him, (now) timid
and without confidence in his own strength from a conscious-
ness of guilt, not to prefer recourse to violence to recourse to
pity, since he had given himself up to the Roman people.

*Hic atque alius hicce modus saepe dico tribunus populus
persuadeo, uti Cornelius Cinna, qui tum praetor sum, ad
Andriscus mitto, (interpono fides publicus), Roma duco ; quo
facile, indicium rex, imperator et reliquus, qui pecunia capio
arcesso, delictum patefacio. Dum hic Roma gero, qui in
Mysia relinquo a Metellus exercitus praesum, sequor mos imperator, multus et flagitiosus facinus facio. Sum qui, aurum
corrumpo, elephantus Andriscus trado ; alius perfuga vendo ;
pars ex pacatus praeda ago ; tantus vis avaritia in animus is,
veluti tabes, invado. At Cornelius Cinna, perfero rogatio a
tribunus, ac percello omnis nobilitas, ad Andriscus proficiscor ;
is timidus et ex conscientia diffido res suus persuadeo, quo sui
populus Romanus dedo, ne vis quam misericordia experior malo.*

LVI.

The state at that time was violently disturbed at Rome by
the quarrels of the tribunes. Aulus Sulpicius and Licinius
Crassus, tribunes of the commons, in opposition to the wishes
of their colleagues, were endeavouring to keep in office : and
this difference of opinion continued to delay the elections of
the whole year. In consequence of this delay, Porcius, who,
we mentioned before, had been left with praetorian power in
the camp, being led to expect either that he would finish[6] the
war or that he would exact money from the king through the
terror caused by his army, summons his troops from their
winter quarters to an expedition in the mouth of January ; and
by forced marches, though the winter was severe, he arrives
at the town of Pergamus, where the royal treasury was.
Although this (town) could be[7] neither taken nor besieged, both

---

1 410, II.   2 467, III., 4 & 522, I.   3 501, I.   4 515, 1.   5 438, 6.
6 562 & 563, 1, 1).   7 516, I.

in consequence of the severity of the weather and the advantage of its position, (for around the wall, which was built on the ledge of a rugged mountain, a muddy plain had formed a marsh owing to the winter's rains) ; still, either for the purpose of making a feint to inspire the king with terror,[1] or blinded by the desire (of its wealth), he began to bring forward[2] the *rineæ*, to throw up a breastwork (and) to hasten other things which were likely to be of use[3] for his plan.

Is tempestas Roma seditio tribunicius atrociter res publicus agito Aulus Sulpicius et Licinius Crassus. tribunus plebs, resisto collega, continuo magistratus nitor ; qui dissentio totus annus comitia impedio. Is mora in spes adduco Porcius, qui pro prætor in castra relinquo supra dico, aut conficio bellum, aut terror exercitus ab rex pecunia capio, miles mensis Januarius ex hiberna in expeditio eroco : magnus iter, hiems asper, pervenio ad oppidum Pergamus, ubi rex thesaurus sum. Qui quamquam et sævitia tempus, aut opportunitas locus, neque capio, neque obsideo possum, (nam circum murus, sino in præruptus mons extremum, planities limosus hiemalis aqua palus facio,) tamen, aut simulo gratia, quo rex formido addo, aut cupido cæcus, vineæ ago, agger jacio, alius, qui inceptum usus sum, propero.

LVII.

To this Quintus Antonius (replied): "If they wished[2] to make any request of the senate, let them lay down their arms, (and) set out for Rome as suppliants ; that the senate and the Roman people had always been distinguished for such a degree of mildness and pity, that no one ever asked aid from them in vain." But the general of the enemy wrote a letter, while on the march, to very many of consular rank, (and) besides to all the most distinguished individuals, "that beset by false charges, since he was unable to oppose the faction of his enemies, he was yielding to his fate, and was going into exile at Marseilles, not because he felt guilty of so great a crime, but that the state might be undisturbed, and that no sedition might arise out of his opposition." Lucius Scipio read aloud in the senate a letter very different from this, which he said had been given him in the name of the general. A copy of it is given below.

Ad hic Q. Antonius : "Si quis ab senatus peto volo, ab arma discedo, Roma supplex proficiscor ; is mansuetudo atque misericordia senatus populusque Romanus semper sum, ut nemo unquam ab is frustra auxilium peto." At dux hostis ex iter

---

[1] 380, 1.   [2] 545, 1.   [3] 529.

plerique consularis, prœterea bonus quisque, litteræ mitto : "*sui
falsus crimen circumvenio, quoniam factio inimicus resisto
nequeo, fortuna cedo, Massilia in exilium proficiscor ; non quo
sui tantus scelus conscius ; sed uti res publicus quietus sum, neve
ex suus contentio seditio orior.*" *Ab hic longe diversus literæ
L. Scipio in senatus recito, qui sui nomen dux reddo dico. Is
exemplum infra scribo.*

LVIII.

There were at that time some who[1] said that the conspirator, after the delivery of his speech, when he was swear-
ing[2] the accomplices of his guilt, carried[3] round in goblets
the blood of a human body mingled with wine ; that when,
after a solemn imprecation, all had tasted thereof, as is customary[4] in sacred rites, he unfolded his plan ; and that he
repeatedly declared (or, "and it was currently reported that")
he did so with this object that[5] they might be more faithful
to one another, being partners[6] with one another in so great a
crime. Some thought that these (stories), and many others
besides, were trumped up by those who believed[7] that the
hatred against the consul[8] which afterwards arose, was les-
sened by the heinousness of the crime of the men who had
been punished. This matter has been insufficiently ascertained, considering its importance. But at that meeting was
Caius Titurius, descended from a very honourable family,
(and) covered with villanies and crimes, whom the censors
had expelled from the senate on account of his infamy. The
vanity of this man was no less than his boldness. He neither
kept to himself[9] what he had heard, nor did he himself conceal his own crimes: in short, he had not the slightest regard
for what he said or did.

*Sum is tempestas, qui dico, conjuratus, oratio habeo, cum ad
jusjurandum popularis scelus suus adigo, humanus corpus
sanguis, vinum permisceo, in patera circumfero ; inde cum post
exsecratio omnis degusto, sicuti in solemnis sacrum facio consuesco, aperio consilium suus, atque eo, dictito, facio, quo inter
sui fidus magnopere sum, alius alius tantus facinus conscius.
Nonnulli fingo hic, multus prœterea, existimo, ab is, qui consul
invidia, qui postea orior, lenio credo atrocitas scelus is, qui
pœna do. Ego is res pro magnitudo parum comperio. Sed in
is conventio sum Caius Antonius, nascor haud obscurus locus,
flagitium atque facinus cooperio ; qui censor senatus, probrum
gratia, amoveo. Hic homo non parvus vanitas quam audacia ;
neque reticeo, qui audio, neque suusmet ipse scelus occulto ;
prorsus neque dico, neque facio, quisquam pensus habeo.*

---

[1] 501. 1.   [2] 529.   [3] 530, I.   [4] 531, 3.   [5] 497.   [6] 399, 2, 2).
[7] 501, 2.   [8] 396; II.   [9] 545, 1.

LIX.

When he said this, having made a slight delay, he orders the signal for battle to be given, draws up his troops, and leads them forth to even ground; then, after the horses of all had been removed, that the soldiers might have[1] greater courage when the danger was made equal, he himself on foot arranges his army in accordance with the nature of the ground and the extent of his forces. For, as there was a plain between mountains on the left, and a rugged rock on the right, he places eight cohorts in front; the other divisions he stations in closer array as a reserve force. From these he draws off to the front rank all the picked centurions and the veterans as well as all the best in arms of the common soldiers. He orders Cneius Piso to take the command on the right wing, (and) a certain Tarquinian on the left[2]; he himself takes his post along with his freedmen and the cohorts near the eagle, which it was said Caius Julius had had in the Mithridatic war. But in the other part (of the field), Aulus Gabinius, being footsore,[3] entrusts his army to his lieutenant, because he was unable[4] to take part in the battle. He (arranges) in the front rank the veteran cohorts, which he had enrolled on account of the rising; he arranges the rest of the army behind these among the reserves.

Hic ubi dico, paullulum commoror, signum cano jubeo, atque instruo ordo in locus aequus deduco: dein, removeo omnis equus, quo miles, exaequo periculum, animus amplus sum, ipse pedes exercitus, pro locus et copiae, instruo. Nam, uti planities sum inter sinister mons, et, ab dexter, rupes asper, octo cohors in frons constituo: reliquus signum in subsidium arcte colloco. Ab hic centurio omnis lectus, et evocatus, praeterea ex gregarius miles bonus quisque armatus in prior acies subduco. Cneius Piso in dexter, Tarquiniensis quidam sinister pars curo jubeo: ipse cum libertus et colonus propter aquila adsisto, qui bellum Mithridaticus Caius Julius in exercitus habeo dico. At ex alter pars Aulus Gabinius pes aeger, quod praelium adsum nequeo, legatus exercitus permitto. Ille cohors veteranus, qui tumultus causa conscribo, in frons; post is, cetera exercitus in subsidium loco.

LX.

But after the news arrived in the camp that the conspiracy had been brought to light at Rome, (and) that punishment had been inflicted upon the conspirators (whom I have men-

---

[1] 497 & 357.　　[2] 422, 1, 1).　　[3] 429.　　[4] 520, I.

tioned above), very many, whom the hope of plunder or the
desire for a revolution had induced to join in the war, slipped
away.[1] The chief conspirator led off the rest through rugged
mountains by forced marches to the territory of Etruria,
with the intention of escaping[2] by by-ways into Gaul. But
Caius Marius with three legions held the command in this
district, since he suspected that the leader of the enemy
would form this very plan, which we have before mentioned,
in consequence of the difficulty of his position. When, therefore, he learned from deserters of the direction he had taken,
he quickly moved his camp and pitched it at the very base of
the mountains, where he would descend (literally : " there
was a descent to him ") when hastening into Gaul. Still
Cornelius Sylla was not far distant, inasmuch as[3] he followed
in pursuit with a large army, encountering fewer obstacles in
a more level country. But when the conspirator saw that
he was hemmed in by mountains and by the forces of the
enemy, that matters in the city were against him and that
there was no hope of escape or assistance, he determined to
engage in battle·with Cornelius Sylla at the first opportunity,
thinking that the best course in such an emergency was to
try the fortune of war.

*Sed, postquam in castra nuntius pervenio, Roma conjuratio
patefacio, de conjuratus, qui supra memoro, supplicium sumo :
plerique, qui ad bellum spes rapina, aut novus res studium
illicio, dilabor. Reliquus dux conjuratus per mons asper, magnus iter, in ager Etruscus abduco, is consilium, uti per trames
occulte perfugio in Gallia. At Caius Marius cum tres legio in
hic locus præsideo, ex difficultas res idem ille existimo, qui supra
dico, dux hostis agito. Igitur, ubi iter is ex perfuga cognosco,
castra propere moveo, ac sub ipse radix mons consido, qua ille
descensus sum in Gallia propero. Neque tamen Cornelius
Sylla procul absum ; utpote qui magnus exercitus, locus æquus
expeditus, in fuga sequor. Sed conjuratus, postquam video
mons atque copia hostis sui claudo, in urbs res adversus, neque
fuga, neque præsidium ullus spes ; bonus factum reor in talis
res fortuna bellum tento, statuo cum Cornelius Sylla quam-
primum confligo.*

LXI.

He therefore entrusts the matter to one Lucius Scipio to
find out the deputies of the Gauls and influence them, if he
could, to join in the war, thinking that they could be easily
induced to adopt such a course, being burdened with debt as
a people and individually ; (and) further, because the nation

1 467, III., 1.   2 481, IV., 2.   3 519, 3, 1).

was[1] naturally fond of war. Scipio was well known by many of the leading men, and knew them, because he had traded[2] in Gaul. Therefore, as soon as he saw the deputies in the market place, after he had made a few enquiries about the condition of the state, and as if he lamented its lot, he began, without any delay, to ask what end they expected[3] to such misfortunes. After he saw[4] that they complained of the avarice of the magistrates; that they made accusations against the senate, because there was no assistance (for them) in it; that they awaited death as the remedy for their miseries; "but I," said he, "provided you are willing[5] to be men, shall point out a way by which you may escape such evils as you complain of." When he said this, the deputies of the Gauls, being led to form the highest expectations, began to entreat[6] Lucius Scipio to take[7] compassion on them; that there was nothing so hard or so difficult that they would not do most eagerly, provided such a course would free the state from debt. Besides he sends for Gracchus, that what he said might have more weight. In his presence, he disclosed[4] the conspiracy, and told the names of his associates; (and), in addition, those of many innocent persons of all classes, that the deputies might have more courage.

Igitur Lucius Scipio quidam negotium do, uti legatus Gallus requiro, isque, si possum impello ad societas bellum, existimo publice privatimque æs alienus opprimo, præterea, quod natura gens bellicosus sum, facile is ad talis consilium adduco possum. Scipio, quod in Gallia negotior, plerique princeps nosco atque is nosco. Itaque sine mora, ubi prius legatus in forum conspicio, percunctor pauci de status civitas, et quasi doleo is casus, requiro cœpi, "qui exitus tantus malus spero?" Postquam ille video, "queror de avaritia magistratus, accuso senatus, quod in is auxilium nihil sum; miseria suus remedium mors expecto;" "at ego," inquam, "tu, si modo vir sum volo, ratio ostendo, qui tantus iste malum effugio." Hic ubi dico, legatus Gallus, in magnus spes adduco Lucius Scipio oro, uti sui misereor; nihil tam asper, neque tam difficilis, quin cupide facio, dum is res civitas æs alienus libero. Præterea Gracchus arcesso, quo magnus auctoritas sermo insum; is præsens conjuratio aperio; nomino socius, præterea multus quisque genus innoxius, quo legatus animus amplus sum.

LXII.

He himself gives Cassius a letter for the conspirator, of which the following is a copy: "Who I am[8] you will learn

from him whom I have sent to you. Take care that[1] you
reflect how great your misfortune is, and that you be a man;
consider what your circumstances require ; seek help from
all, even from the lowest." In addition to this he gives
verbal instructions : "Since he has been declared an enemy
by the senate, with what object does he reject[2] the slaves?
that those things which he ordered were ready in the city ;
that he himself should not hesitate to come nearer." These
things having been done in this way, on the night appointed
for their setting out, the consul, having learned everything
through the deputies, orders the prætors to arrest by means
of an ambuscade the retinue of the Gauls at the Mulvian
bridge. He discloses the whole object for which they were
sent ; he gives them permission to conduct the rest of the
affair according to the necessities of the case. (Being) men
of military experience, they secretly blockade the bridge
according to instructions, having stationed the guards without any disturbance. After the deputies came to the place,
and a shout arose at that moment on both sides, the Gauls,
who soon understood the design, surrendered themselves to
the prætors without delay. At first Cassius defends himself
with a sword against the crowd, having exhorted the others
(to do so) ; afterwards, when he was deserted by the deputies, he first earnestly besought the prætor to save him
because he was known to him, (and) finally, through fear
and despairing of his life, he surrendered himself to the
prætors as to enemies.

*Ipse Cassius literæ ad conjuratus do, qui exemplum infra
scribo: "Quis sum, ex is, qui ad tu mitto, cognosco. Facio
cogito, in quantus calamitas sum, et memini tu vir ; considero,
quis tuus ratio postulo ; auxilium peto ab omnis, etiam ab
inferus." Ad hic mandatum verbum do: "Quum ab senatus
hostis judico, qui consilium servitium repudio ? in urbs paro,
qui jubeo ; ne cunctor ipse prope accedo." Hic res ita ago,
constituo nox, qui proficiscor, consul per legatus cunctus edoceo,
prætor impero, ut in pons Mulvius per insidiæ Gallus comitatus
deprehendo ; res omnis aperio, qui gratia mitto ; cetera, uti
factum opus sum, ita ago, permitto. Ille, homo militaris, sine
tumultus præsidium colloco, sicuti præcipio, occulte pons obsido.
Postquam ad is locus legatus venio, et simul utrimque clamor
exorior, Gallus, cito cognosco consilium, sine mora prætor sui
trado. Cassius prius, cohortor cetera, gladius sui a multitudo
defendo ; dein, ubi a legatus desero, multus prius de salus suus
prætor obtestor, quod is notus sum, posterius timidus ac vita
diffido velut hostis sui prætor do.*

---

[1] 493, 2.   [2] 530, II.

LXIII.

The Samnites, however, held possession of the citadel, and from it, on the following day when the Roman army in battle array had filled[1] all the ground[2] that lies between the Palatine and Capitoline hills, they no sooner came down to the plain than the Romans advanced to meet[3] them, since resentment and a desire to retake the citadel wrought upon their spirits. The chiefs on each side gave a new impulse to the battle, Aulus Postumius on the side of the Samnites and Quintus Curtius on that of the Romans. The latter, although his position was disadvantageous at the first onset, maintained the Roman cause with courage and bravery. As soon as Hostus fell, the Roman army immediately gave way, and was beaten back to the old gate of the Palatium. The Roman king himself, too, carried away amid the crowd of the fugitives, raising his arms to heaven says : "O Jupiter, under the direction of thy birds, here on the Palatine I laid the first foundations of the city. The Samnites now hold the citadel, which has been purchased by treachery. From it they are now advancing hither in arms, having already passed the intervening valley. But do thou, father of gods and men, keep back the enemy at least from here ; dispel terror from the Romans, and stop their foul flight. I vow (that I will erect) on this spot a temple to thee, Jupiter Stator, which may be[4] a memorial to posterity that the city was saved by thy timely aid." Having uttered this prayer, he says, as if he felt that his prayers were heard : "At this spot, Jupiter, supremely good (and) great, commands you to halt, and renew the fight." The Romans halted as though commanded by a voice from heaven. The king himself flies forward to the van.

Teneo tamen arx Samnis, atque inde posterus dies, cum Romanus exercitus instruo qui inter Palatinus Capitolinusque collis campus sum compleo, non prius descendo in æquus, quam ira et cupiditas recupero arx stimulo animus in adversus Romanus subeo. Princeps utrimque pugna cieo ; ab Samnis Aulus Postumius, ab Romanus Quintus Curtius. Hic res Romanus iniquus locus ad primus signum animus atque audacia sustineo. Ut Hostus cado, confestim Romanus inclino acies, fudoque ad vetus porta Palatium. Rex Romanus et ipse turba fugiens ago arma ad cælum tollo. "Jupiter, tuus" inquam "jubeo avis hic in Palatium primus urbs fundamentum jacio. Arx jam scelus emo Samnis habeo ; inde hic armatus supero medius vallis tendo. At tu, pater deus homoque, hinc saltem arceo hostis, demo terror Romanus fugaque fædus sisto. Hic ego tu templum Stator Jupiter, qui monumentum sum posterus tuus præsens opis servo urbs, moveo." Hic precor, velut si sentio audio, preces, "hinc" inquam, "Romanus, Jupiter bonus magnus resisto atque itero pugna jubeo." Resisto Romanus tanquam cælestis vox jubeo ; ipse ad primoris rex provolo.

---

¹ 518, 2. ² 396, III., 2, 3). ³ 523, I. ⁴ 500.

LXIV.

Ancus reigned twenty-four years, equal to any of the former kings both in the arts and renown of war and peace. His sons were now near the age of puberty. For this reason Tarquinius was more urgent[1] that the assembly for the election of a king should be held[2] as soon as possible. And when this was settled he sent the boys out of the way to hunt[3] on the eve (of the election). He also is said to have been the first who obsequiously sought after power and to have delivered a set speech with a view to gain over the affections of the commons: (he said), "though (he was acting thus), (or: "whilst he kept declaring that he did not aim," &c.), that he did not aim at anything unprecedented, inasmuch as he was not the first foreigner (a thing at which anyone might feel[4] indignation or wonder), but the third, who aspired[5] to sovereignty at Rome ; that Tatius, not only from being an alien, but even an enemy, was made king ; and that Numa, unacquainted with the city, without asking for it, had been, without solicitation on his part, invited by them to the throne ; that he, as soon as he was his own master, had migrated to Rome with his wife and all his goods ; that he had lived at Rome the greater part of that age in which men are employed in civil offices ; that he had learned thoroughly, at home[6] and abroad, under no mean instructor, even King Ancus himself, the Roman laws (and) Roman rites ; that he had vied with all in ready loyalty and watchful deference to the king, even with the king himself in his bounty to others." On his relating these undoubted facts, the Roman people, by general consent, elected him as king.

Regno Ancus annus quattuor et viginti: quilibet superus rex bellum paxque et ars et gloria par. Jam filius prope pubes aetas sum. Eo magnopere Tarquinius insto, ut quam primum comitia rex creo facio ; qui indico sub tempus puer renor ablego. Isque prior et peto ambitiose regnum et oratio dico habeo ad concilio plebs animus compositus ; cum sui non res novus peto, quippe qui non prior, (quod quisquam indignor mirorque possum), sed tertius Roma peregrinus regnum affecto ; et Tatius non ex peregrinus solum sed etiam ex hostis rex facio, et Numa ignarus urbs non peto in regnum ultro accio, sui, ex qui sui potens sum, Roma cum conjux ac fortuna omnis commigro : magnus pars aetas is, qui cirilis officium fungor homo, Roma sui quam in vetus patria viro ; domus militiaque sub haud pœnitendus magister, ipse Ancus rex, Romanus sui jus, Romanus ritus disco ; obsequium et observantia in rex cum omnis, benignitas erga alius cum rex ipse certo. Hic is haud falsus memoro ingens consensus populus Romanus regno jubeo.

---

1 545, 1.   2 481, IV., 2.   3 569.   4 519, 3, 1).   5 423, II., 2, & 424, 2.

LXV.

He was also preparing to surround the city with a stone wall, when a Sabine war interrupted[1] his designs. And this was so sudden, that the enemy crossed the Anio before the army of the Romans was able[2] to meet and check them. There was therefore great consternation[3] at Rome, and at first they fought without any decisive result, with great slaughter on both sides. Afterwards, the forces of the enemy having been been led back to the camp, and the Romans having got time to make[4] fresh preparations for the war, Tarquinius, thinking that his forces were especially weak in not having cavalry, determined to add other centuries to those which Romulus had enrolled, and to have them distinguished by his own name. Since Romulus had done[5] this, after consulting the auguries, Attus Navius, distinguished at that time as an augur, declared[6] that no change could be made nor any innovations introduced without the approval[7] of the birds. In consequence of this, rage was stirred up in the breast of the king, and he, as is related, said, in ridicule of the art: "Come, now then, inspired one, tell me by your auguries whether what I am now thinking of can be[8] done (or not "). When he, testing the matter by his augury, said that it certainly could. "But I was considering if you were likely to cut this whetstone with a razor; take it and do what these birds of thine portend may be done." They say that without delay he then cut the whetstone. A statue of Attius, with his head veiled was erected in the comitium on the very steps to the left of the senate house, on the spot where the transaction occurred.

Murus quoque lapideus circumdo urbs paro, cum Sabinus bellum cœptum intervenio. Adeoque is subitus res sum, ut prius Anio transeo hostis, quam obviam eo ac prohibeo exercitus Romanus possum. Itaque trepido Roma. Et primo dubius victoria magnus utrimque cædes pugno. Reduco deinde in castra hostis copiæ doque spatium Romanus ad comparo de integer bellum, Tarquinius, eques magnopere suus desum vis reor, ad is centuria, qui Romulus scribo, addo alius constituo, suusque insignis relinquo nomen. Is quia inaugurato Romulus facio, nego Attus Nævius, inclutus is tempestas augur, neque muto neque novus constituo, nisi avis addico, possum. Ex is ira rex moveo, eludoque ars ut fero, "Ago dum" inquam, "divinus tu, inauguro, facione possum, qui nunc ego meus concipio." Cum ille in augurium res experior profecto sum dico, "Atqui hic animus agito" inquam, "te novacula cos discido; capio hic et perago, qui avis tuus facio possum portendo." Tum ille haud cunctanter discido cos fero. Statua Attius caput velo, qui in locus res ago, in comitium, in gradus ipse ad lævus curia sum.

---

[1] 518, II., 3.   [2] 523, II.   [3] 465, II., 2.   [4] 562 & 565.   [5] 520, I.
[6] 545, 1.   [7] 531.   [8] 525.

LXVI.

At that time a prodigy was seen in the palace, and it was wonderful in its results. They say that the head of a boy, named Servius Tullius[1], as he lay asleep, blazed with fire in the sight of many persons ; that the royal pair, therefore, were awakened by the very great outcry that then arose in consequence of the wonderful appearance of such a thing ; that when one of the household was carrying[2] water to extinguish (the flame), he was held back by the queen ; and that after the commotion had ceased, she forbade the boy to be disturbed, until he should awake of his own accord. They say, also, that soon afterwards the flame went away with his sleep. Then the queen, taking her husband into a private place, said : "Do you see this boy whom we are bringing up in so humble a style ? We may be sure that some day or other he will be a light to our perplexed affairs and the protection of our palace when in distress. Let us, then, train up with every attention this source of great glory to our state and to our family." (They say) that after that the boy began[3] to be regarded in the light of a son, and instructed in the arts by which talents are incited to support exalted rank. It was easily accomplished, because it was[4] agreeable to the gods. The youth turned out to be of a disposition truly royal, and when a son-in-law for Tarquin was sought, none of the Roman youths could be compared to him in any accomplishment, and the king betrothed his own daughter to him.

Is tempus in regia prodigium video, eventusque mirabilis sum. Puer dormio, qui Servius Tullius sum nomen, caput ardeo fero multus in conspectus ; multus igitur clamor inde ad tantus res miraculum orior excio rex, et, quum quidam familiaris aqua ad restinguo fero, ab regina retineo, sedoque jam tumultus moveo veto puer, donec suus sponte expergiscor. Mox cum somnus et flamma abeo. Tum abduco in secretus vir regina " videone tu puer hic," inquam, "qui tam humilis cultus educo ? Scio licet hic lumen quondam res noster dubius sum præsidiumque regia afflictus ; proinde materia ingens publice privatimque decus omnis indulgentia noster nutrio." Inde puer liberi locus cœpi habeo erudioque ars, qui ingenium ad magnus fortuna cultus excito. Evenit facile, qui deus cor sum. Juvenis evado vere indoles regius, nec, quum quæro gener Tarquinius, quisquam Romanus juventus ullus ars confero possum, filiaque is suus rex despondeo.

LXVII.

When the name of Numa was mentioned, though the balance of power seemed to incline to the side of the Sabines,

---

owing to a king being chosen from them, the Roman Fathers not daring[1] to prefer to that distinguished man, either any one[2] himself or any other of his faction, or, in a word, any of the fathers or citizens, all to a man decreed that the sovereign power should be conferred on Numa. Just as Romulus, at the founding of the city, obtained the sovereignty by augury, being sent for he gave orders that the gods should be consulted in his own case also. Upon this, being led into the citadel by an augur (to whose profession this priesthood was afterwards made a public and perpetual one by way[3] of honor), he sat down, facing the south, on a stone. The augur, with his head covered, took his seat on the left, holding in his right hand a crooked stick free from knots, which they called a lituus ; then, when after taking a look towards the city and the country, he uttered[1] a prayer to the gods, and marked out the regions from east to west, he said that the parts towards the south were on the right ; those towards the north, on the left ; in front of him he mentally fixed a mark as far as his eyes could reach. Then shifting the staff to his left hand, his right being laid on the head of Numa, he uttered this prayer : "O father Jove, if it is[4] thy will that this Numa, whose head I am holding, should be king of Rome, (I beseech thee) that thou would'st manifest sure indications within the bounds which I have made." Then he enumerated the omens he wished to be sent; and, when these were sent, Numa was declared king, and came down from his place of observation.

Audio nomen Numa pater Romanus, quamquam inclino opis ad Sabinus rex inde sumo videor, tamen neque sui quisquam nec factio suus alius nec denique pater aut civis quisquam præfero ille vir audeo ad unus omnis Numa regnum defero decerno. Accio, sicut Romulus augurato urbs condo regnum adipiscor, de sui quoque deus consulo jubeo. Inde ab augur, qui deinde honor ergo publicus is perpetuusque sacerdotium sum, deduco in arx in lapis ad meridies verto consido. Augur ad lævus is caput velo sedes capio, dexter manus baculum sine nodus aduncus teneo, qui lituus appello. Inde ubi prospectus in urbs agerque capio deus precor regio ab oriens ad occasus determino, dexter ad meridies pars, lævus ad septentrio sum dico, signum contra, quoad longe conspectus oculus fero, animus finio. Tum lituus in lævus manus transfero dexter in caput Numa impono precor ita : "Jupiter pater, si sum fas hic Numa, qui ego caput teneo, rex Roma sum, uti tu signum ego certus adclaro inter is finis, qui facio." Tum perago verbum auspicium, qui mitto volo ; qui mitto declaro rex Numa de templum descendo.

---

¹ 579.   ² 401, 3.   ³ 411.   ⁴ 508.

LXVIII.

Meanwhile, at the camp, the consul Furius, after enduring[1] the siege at first without making an effort, burst forth from the Decuman gate on the enemy, who were off their guard; and though it was in his power to pursue them, he halted, through fear that some attack might be made on the camp on the other side. His impetuosity carried too far Furius, the lieutenant-general (he was brother of the consul); from his eagerness in the pursuit, he neither saw his own party retreating, nor the attack of the enemy on the rear. Being thus intercepted he fell, fighting bravely, after repeatedly making many vain attempts to force his way to the camp. And while the consul, who had turned about to renew the battle, on receiving the news that his brother had been surrounded, was rushing forward[2] into the midst of the fray with more rashness than caution, he both damped the courage of our men, and rendered the enemy more daring, owing to his having been rescued with difficulty by the bystanders when he fell wounded. The latter, being elated by the death of the lieutenant-general and by the consul's wound, could not afterwards be withstood by any force, since the Romans had been driven into the[3] camp and were being again besieged,[1] without the same expectation of success or strength; and the safety of the state would have been endangered, had not Titus Quinctius come to their relief with foreign troops from the Latin and Hernican army.

Interim, in castra, Furius consul cum primo quietus obsidio patior, in incautus hostis decumanus porta erumpo, et, quum persequor possum, metus subsisto, ne quis ex pars alter in castra vis facio. Furius legatus—frater idem consul sum—longe effero cursus, nec suus ille redeo persequor studium neque hostis ab tergum incursus video. Ita excludo multus sæpe frustra conatus capio ut via sui ad castra facio, acriter dimico cado. Et consul nuntius circumvenio frater converto ad pugna, dum sui temere magnopere quam satis caute in medius dimicatio infero, vulnus accipio ægre ab circumsto eripio. Et suus animus turbo et ferox hostis facio. Qui cædes legatus et consul vulnus accendo nullus deinde vis sustineo possum, cum compello in castra Romanus rursus obsido nec spes nec vis par, venioque in periculum summa res, ni T. Quinctius peregrinus copia, cum Latinus Hernicusque exercitus subvenio.

---

[1] 518, II.   [2] 522, I., & 467, III., 4.   [3] 579.

LXIX.

Spurius Cassius and Proculus Virginius were next made consuls. A treaty was made with the Hernici, two-thirds of their land was taken from them. Of this the consul intended to distribute[1] one-half among the allies, the other among the commons. To this donation he was adding a considerable portion of land,[2] which, although belonging to the state, he alleged was being held by private persons. This proceeding continued to alarm many senators indeed, who were themselves possessors, at the danger of their property. But there was also among the senators a source of anxiety for the public welfare, that the consul by his donation was establishing an influence dangerous to liberty. Then for the first time an agrarian law was brought forward, which from that time, down even to our own day, was never agitated without the greatest commotions in the state. The other consul was opposed to the donation, with the influence of the senators, and not against the wishes of all the commons, since they at first had felt disgust that the gift was extended from citizens to allies. They also heard the consul often afterwards in the assemblies, prophesying, as it were, "that the gift of his colleague was hurtful; that those lands were sure to bring slavery to those who received[3] them; that the way for sovereignty was being paved. Why was it that the allies and the Latin nation were thus admitted[4]? What was the object of restoring to the Hernici, enemies a short time before, a third part of the captured territory, unless that these tribes may have Cassius instead of Coriolanus as leader."

Spurius Cassius deinde et Proculus Virginius consul facio; cum Hernici fœdus ico; ager pars duo adimo. Inde dimidium socius, dimidium plebs divido consul. Adjicio hic munus ager aliquantum, qui publicus possideo a privatus criminor. Is multus quidem pater, ipse possessor, periculum res suus terreo. Sed et publicus pater sollicitudo ineo, largitio consul periculosus libertas opis struo. Tum prius lex agrarius promulgo, nunquam deinde usque ad hic memoria sine magnus motus res agito. Consul alter largitio resisto auctor pater nec omnis plebs adversor, qui prius cœpi fastidio; munus vulgo a civis in socius. Sæpe deinde et consul in contio velut vaticinor audio pestilens collega munus sum, ager ille servitus is qui accipio fero, regnum via facio. Quis ita enim adsumo socius et nomen Latinus? Quis attineo Hernicus, paulo ante hostis, capio ager pars tertius reddo, nisi ut is gens pro Cassius dux Coriolanus habeo?

---

[1] 578, V., & 573.   [2] 396, III.   [3] 530, II.   [4] 553, III., 3

4 A

LXX.

The dictator, however, as one who went[1] into battle relying rather on the courage than on the strength (of his men), began to look about and to consider in every way how he might by some artifice strike terror into the enemy. He cleverly devises a new plan, which many of our own generals and of those of foreign nations have since adopted, some indeed in our own day. He orders the burdens to be removed from the mules, and two side cloths only being left to each, he places the muleteers on them, arrayed in arms belonging partly[2] to the prisoners and partly to the sick. Having (thus) equipped nearly a thousand of these, he mixed with them[3] one hundred cavalry, and orders them to march by night to the mountains above the camp, and hide themselves in the woods, and not to stir from this place before they received[4] the signal from him. As soon as it was dawn, he began to extend his line along the base of the mountain, intending that the enemy should be placed with the mountain facing them. The means of infusing groundless terror being completed, which terror indeed was almost of more service than real strength, the leaders of the Gauls at first believed that the Romans would not come down to the place; then, when they saw that they suddenly descended, they also eager for the fray rushed to battle, and the struggle began before the signal was given[5] by their leaders.

Dictator tamen, ut qui magnopere animus quam vis fretus ad certamen descendo, omnis circumspicio atque agito cœpi, ut ars aliquis terror hostis incutio. Sollers animus res novus excogito, qui deinde multus noster atque externus imperator, noster quoque quidam œstas, utor. Mulus stratum detraho jubeo binique tantum centunculus relinquo agaso partim captivus partim œger arma orno impono. Hic fere mille efficio centum admisceo eques, et nox super castra in mons evado ac silva sui occulto jubeo neque inde ante moveo, quam ab sui accipio signum. Ipse, ubi illucesco, in radix mons extendo acies cœpi sedulo, ut adversus mons consisto hostis. Instruo vanus terror apparatus, qui quidem terror multum pœne verus vis prosum, primo credo dux Gallus non descendo in œquus Romanus; deinde, ubi digredior repente video et ipse avidus certamen in prœlium ruo, priusque pugna cœpi, quam signum ab dux do.

---

[1] 519, 3.   [2] 461, 5.   [3] 385, 5.   [4] 523, I., & 473.   [5] 523, II., 2.

LXXI.

The proposal seemed too harsh to the senate, and almost drove the commons to arms through exasperation. (They said[1]) "that they were now being attacked by famine as if they were public enemies; that they were being defrauded of food and sustenance; that foreign corn, the only main-tenance[2] which fortune unexpectedly gave[3] them, would be taken out of their mouths, unless the tribunes were given up in fetters to Caius Marcius, unless satisfaction be afforded him on the backs of the Roman commons; that he had sprung up as their new executioner, to sentence them either to death or to slavery." An assault would have been made on him as he was going out of the senate house, had not the tribunes just in time appointed[4] a day for his trial. There-upon their rage was checked. Each one saw that he him-self had become a judge; that he had become the arbiter of the life and death of his foe. At first with haughty air, Marcius listened to the threats of the tribunes. (He replied) "that the right of lending aid, not of inflicting punishment, was given to that office; that they were tribunes of the com-mons, not of the senators." But, with such hostile feelings had the commons arisen that the senators had to obtain im-munity[5] by the punishment of one. They made a stand, however, in his favour in spite of the public ill-will, and individually availed themselves both of their own strength as well as that of the entire order. And at first a trial was made whether, by posting their clients in suitable places, by deterring[6] individuals from attending cabals and meetings, they could upset the affair. Then in a body they proceeded (you would have said all[7] the senators were on their trial), earnestly entreating the commons, that if they would not pardon as innocent, they would at least, out of regard for them, pardon as guilty one citizen, one senator.

Et senatus nimis atrox videor sententia et plebs ira prope armo: "Fames sui jam sicut hostis peto, cibus victusque fraudo; peregrinus frumentum, qui solus alimentum ex insperatus fortuna do, ab os rapio, nisi Caius Marcius vincio dedo tribunus, nisi de tergum plebs Romanus satisfacio; is sui carnifex novus exorior, qui aut morior aut servio jubeo." In exeo e curia impetus facio, ni peropportune tribunus dies dico. Ibi ira supprimo; sui judex quisque, sui dominus vita nexque inimicus facio video. Contemptim primo Marcius audio minæ tribunicius: "Auxilium non pœna jus do ille potestas, plebsque non pater tribunus sum."

Sed adeo infensus coorior plebs, ut unus pœna defungor pater. Resisto tamen adversus invidia, utorque qua suus quisque, qua totus ordo vis. Ac primo tempto res, si dispono cliens absterreo singuli a coitio consiliumque disjicio res possum. Universus deinde procedo—quisquis sum pater reus dico—preces plebs exposco, unus sui civis, unus senator, si innocens absolvo nolo, pro nocens dono.

LXXII.

After the defeat of the Sabines, when the government of the king and the whole Roman state was[1] in high renown' and very flourishing, word was brought to the king and the senators that there had been a shower of stones[2] on the Alban mount. As this could scarcely be believed, on persons being sent to inquire into this prodigy, a thick shower of stones fell from heaven,[3] just as when winds pelt on the earth hail in balls. They seemed also to hear a loud voice from the grove on the hill top, (requesting) the Albans to perform, in accordance with the custom of their fathers, their religious rites, which they had consigned to oblivion, as though their gods had been abandoned together with their country ; and either they had adopted the rites of Rome, or, as usually happens, enraged at their evil destiny, had renounced the worship of the gods. A festival lasting for nine days was instituted at the public expense by the Romans[4] also, on account of the same prodigy, either in obedience to the heavenly injunction sent from the Alban mount (for that tradition is also given), or by the advice of the haruspices. At least it remained an established usage that whenever the same prodigy was announced,[5] a festival of nine days should be held. Not very long afterwards, they were afflicted[6] with a pestilence ; and though from this there arose[7] an aversion to military service, still no respite from arms was granted by the warlike king, who believed that the bodies of the youths were even healthier when on service[8] than when at home, until he himself also was seized[9] by a lingering disease.

Devinco Sabinus cum in magnus gloria magnusque opis regnum rex ac totus res Romanus sum, nuntio rex paterque in mons Albanus lapis pluo. Qui cum credo vix possum, mitto ad is viso prodigium in conspectus haud aliter, quam cum grando ventus glomero in terra ago, creber cado cælum

---

lapis. Videor etiam audio vox ingens ex superus cacumen lucus, ut patrius ritus sacrum Albanus facio, qui velut deus quoque simul cum patria relinquo oblivio do; et aut Romanus sacrum suscipio aut fortuna, ut fio, obiratus cultus relinquo deus. Romanus quoque ab idem prodigium novendialis sacrum publice suscipio, seu vox coelestis ex Albanus mons mitto (nam is quoque trado), seu aruspex monitus. Maneo certe sollemne, ut, quardoque idem prodigium nuntio, feriæ per novem dies ago. Haud ita multus post pestilentia laboro. Unde cum pigritia milito orior, nullus tamen ab arma quies do a bellicosus rex, salubris etiam credo militia quam domus juvenis corpus sum, donec ipse quoque longinquus morbo implico.

LXXIII.

They then set out to the war against the Veientians, to which auxiliaries had flocked from all parts of Etruria, roused not so much for the sake of the people of Veii as that they had come[1] to expect that the Roman state might be destroyed by internal dissension. And in the councils of all the tribes of Etruria the leading men kept asserting strongly that the Roman power was eternal, unless they were distracted[2] by seditions among themselves; that this was the only poison, this the bane, found for powerful states to render great empires mortal. This evil, a long time retarded, partly by the wisdom of the senators, partly by the forbearance of the commons, had now reached its utmost height. Two states had been formed from one: each party had its own magistrates, its own laws. Though at first they were wont to be turbulent when levies were held, still the same individuals, had been obedient to their leaders in time of war: whatever was the condition of the city, if military discipline had been maintained, order might have been established; that now the custom of disobeying their magistrates followed the Roman soldier even to the camp. In the last war, on the very field, in the very struggle, by the consent of the army, the victory was voluntarily surrendered to the vanquished Æqui; the standards were deserted; the general abandoned on the field; that the army had returned to the camp without orders. Without doubt, if they persevered, Rome could be conquered by her own soldiery. Nothing else was necessary than to declare and make a show of war: the fates and the

gods would of themselves manage the rest." This hope had
armed the Etruscans, who had been in the many vicissitudes
(of war) vanquished and victors in turns.

*Inde ad Veiens bellum proficiscor, quo undique ex Etruria
auxilium convenio, non tam Veiens gratia concito, quam
quod in spes venio discordia intestinus dissolvo res Romanus
possum.   Princepsque in omnis Etruria populus concilium
fremo " æternus opis sum Romanus, nisi inter suimet ipse
seditio sævio; is unus venenum, is labes civitas opulentus
reperio, ut magnus imperium mortalis sum.   Diu sustento
is malum partim pater consilium partim patientia plebs
jam ad exterus venio.   Duo civitas ex unus facio; suus
quisque pars magistratus, suus lex sum.   Primum in dilectus
sævio soleo, idem in bellum tamen pareo dux, qualiscumque
urbs status maneo disciplina militaris sisto possum; jam
non pareo magistratus mos in castra quoque Romanus miles
sequi.   Propior bellum in ipse acies, in ipse certamen consensus exercitus, trado ultro victoria vinco Æquus, signum
desero, imperator in acies relinquo, injussu in castra reditus.
Profecto, si insto, suus miles vinco Roma possum.   Nihil
alius opus sum quam indico ostendoque bellum, cetera suus
sponte fatum et deus gero."   Hic spes Etruscus armo multus
in vicis casus victus victorque.*

LXXIV.

Immediately after the success of this most mischievous precedent a levy is ordered; and the tribunes being now overawed,
the consuls carry out the matter without any opposition from
them. Then, indeed, the commons became enraged,[1] more
on account of the silence of the tribunes than at the power
exercised by the consuls : and they said "that there was an
end of their liberty. They had come back to the old state
of matters. The tribunician power died, and was buried
along with Genucius. Some means must be contrived and
put in execution whereby resistance may be offered to the
patricians. This, however, was the only method ; that the
commons should defend themselves since they had aid from
no other source. Twenty-four lictors attended on the consuls, and these very men were from the commons. Nothing
could be more despicable, nothing weaker, if there were only
persons to despise them. Each one in his own case magnified

---

[1] 545, 1.

these things and regarded them as dreadful." When they had stirred up one another's feelings by such words, a lictor was despatched to Volero, a man belonging to the commons, because he had stated[1] that he ought not to be a common soldier, since he had held a military command. Volero appeals to the tribunes. When no one came[2] to his aid, the consuls order the man to be stripped and the rods to be got ready. "I appeal to the people," said Volero, "since the tribunes had rather[3] see a Roman citizen scourged with rods before their eyes, than themselves butchered by you in their own beds." The more vehemently he kept crying out, the more violently did the lictor tear off his clothes and strip him.

Sub hic malus exemplum victoria dilectus edico ; paveoque tribunus, sine intercessio ullus consul res perago. Tum vero irascor plebs tribunus magnopere silentium quam consul imperium, et dico " ago de libertas suus ; rursus ad antiquus reditus ; cum Genucius una morior ac sepelio tribunicius potestas. Alius agito et cogito, quomodo resisto pater ; is autem unus consilium sum, ut sui ipse plebs, quando alius nihil auxilium habeo, defendo. Quattuor et viginti lictor appareo consul, et is ipse plebs homo. Nihil contemptus, nihil infirmus, si sum qui contemno. Sui quisque is magnus atque horrendus facio." Hic vox alius alius cum incito, Volero, de plebs homo, quia, quod ordo duco, nego ad sui miles facio debeo, lictor mitto a consul. Volero appello tribunus. Quum auxilium nemo sum, consul spolio homo et virga expedio jubeo, "provoco" inquam, " ad populum," Volero, "quoniam tribunus civis Romanus in conspectus suus virga cædo malo quam ipse in lectus suus a tu trucido." Quo ferociter clamito, eo infeste circumscindo et spolio lictor.

LXXV.

Then the dictator, having sent criers through the streets, and having summoned the alarmed citizens to an assembly, began to chide them : "That they had allowed[4] their minds to be influenced by so slight changes of fortune, as that on meeting with a trifling loss, which itself was sustained not through the bravery of the enemy, nor the cowardice of the Roman army, but through the discord of the commanders, they now dreaded the Veientian enemy though six times vanquished, and Fidenae which had been almost oftener taken than attacked;

[1] 520, II.　　[2] 518, II.　　[3] 520, I.　　[4] 529.

that both the Romans and the enemies were the same, as they
had been for so many ages; that they retained the same
courage the same bodily strength, the same arms. He himself
also was the same dictator, who had formerly defeated the
armies of the Veientians and Fidenatians, with the additional
support of the Faliscans, at Nomentum; and his master of the
horse would be[1] the same in the field, who, as military tribune
in the former war had slain the king of the Veientians in the
sight of both armies, and brought the *spolia opima* into the
temple of Jupiter Feretrius. Wherefore, let them take up[2]
arms, mindful that with them were triumphs, with them spoils,
with them victory; while with the enemy rested the guilt of
murdering ambassadors contrary to the law of nations, the
massacre of colonists in time of peace, the infraction of
truces, and a seventh unsuccessful revolt. As soon as they
brought their camp near them, he was fully confident that
the joy of these most impious enemies at the disgrace of the
Roman army would not be of long continuance; and that
the Roman people would be convinced how much better those
persons deserved of the state, who had nominated him to the
dictatorship for the third time, than those who, in consequence
of his abolishing the despotism of the censorship, would cast
a slur on his second dictatorship."

*Tum trepidus civitas præco per vicus dimitto dictator ad
contio advoco increpo, quod animus ex tam levis momentum
fortuna suspendo gero, ut parvus jactura accipio, qui ipse
non virtus hostis nec ignavia Romanus exercitus sed discordia imperator accipio, Veiens hostis sexiens vinco per-
timesco Fidenæque prope sæpe capio quam oppugno. Idem
et Romanus et hostis sum, qui per tot sæculum sum; idem
animus, idem corpus vis, idem arma gero. Sui quoque
idem dictator sum, qui antea Veiens Fidenasque adjungo
Faliscus ad Nomentum exercitus fundo, et magister eques
idem in acies sum, qui prior bellum tribunus miles rex
Veiens in conspectus duo exercitus occido spolium opimus
Jupiter Feretrius templum infero. Proinde memor sui cum
triumphus, sui cum spolia, sui cum victoria sum; cum hostis
scelus legatus contra jus gens interficio, cædes in par colonus,
indutiæ rumpo, septimus infelix defectio, arma capio. Simul
castra conjungo, satis confido nec sceleratus hostis diturnus
ex ignominia exercitus Rom mus gaudium sum, et populus
Romanus intelligo, quanto bene de res publicus mereor, qui
sui dictator tertius dico, quam is qui ob cripio censura
regnum labes secundus dictatura suus impono.*

---

[1] 544, 1·3.　　　[2] 52) & 530, II.

LXXVI.

And when both had proceeded[1], free from any apprehension, although unarmed, to a considerable distance from their friends, the young Roman, having the superiority in strength, seized the feeble old man, before the eyes of all, and carried him off to his own friends, although the Etruscans made an ineffectual disturbance. And when he, being led before the commander, was afterwards sent to the senate at Rome, on their asking him what that was' which he had told[3] them about the Alban lake, he said : that "certainly the gods had been incensed against the Veientian nation on the day when they had prompted[4] him to disclose the ruin of his country which had been decreed by the fates. Therefore, what he then prophesied under the influence of divine inspiration, he could not now recall so as to render it unsaid ; and perhaps the guilt of impiety might be contracted in as high a degree, by concealing what it was the will of the immortal gods should be published, as by publishing what ought to be concealed. Thus, therefore, was it recorded by tradition in the books of the fates, and in the Etruscan doctrine, that whenever the Alban water should rise to an unusual height, if the Romans should then let it out in a proper manner, victory would be granted to them over the Veientians; but until that should be done the gods would never abandon the walls of Veii." He then gave directions with respect to the proper method of draining it ; but the senate, deeming his authority of but little weight, and not to be entirely relied on in a case of such importance, resolved to wait for the deputies and replies of the Delphic oracle.

Cumque progredior ambo a suus longe inermis sine ullus metus, prævalens juvenis Romanus senex infirmus in conspectus omnis rapio nequidquam tumultuo Etruscus ad suus transfero. Qui cum perduco ad imperator, inde Roma ad senatus mitto, sciscito, quisnam is sum, qui de locus Albanus doceo, respondeo profecto iratus deus Veiens populus ille sum dies, qui sui is mens objicio, ut excidium patria fatalis prodo. Itaque qui tum cano dirinus spiritus instinctus, is sui nec ut indictus sum revoco possum, et taceo forsitan, qui deus immortalis vulgo volo, haud parum quam celo effor nefas contraho. Sic igitur liber fatalis, sic disciplina Etruscus trado, ut quando aqua Albanus abundo, tum, si is Romanus rite emitto, victoria de Veiens do: antequam is facio, deus mœnia Veiens desero non. Exsequor inde, qui sollemnis derivatio sum : sed auctor levis nec satis fidus super tantus res pater reor decerno legatus sorsque oraculum Pythicus experto.

---

[1] 518, II.   [2] 525, 1.   [3] 501, 1.   [4] 529.

LXXVII.

Then, in the consulship of Marcus Minucius and Aulus
Sempronius, a great quantity of corn was brought from Sicily,
and the question was discussed in the senate at what rate[1] it
should be given[2] to the commons. Many were of the opinion
that the time had come for checking[3] the commons, and for
recovering[4] the rights which had been wrung[5] from the
patricians by secession and violence. In particular, Marcius
Coriolanus, a foe to the tribunician power, says : "If they
desire[6] the old rate, let them restore to the patricians their
former rights ; why, therefore, do I, after being sent under
the yoke, why, after being, as it were, rescued from robbers,
do I behold plebian magistrates, (and) Sicinius invested
with power? am I to endure[7] these insults longer than is
necessary? am I, when I have not put up with[8] king Tarquinius,
to put up with Sicinius ? let him now secede ; let him call away
the commons. The road lies open to the Sacred Mount and
to the other hills ; let them carry off the corn from our lands
just as they did three years ago. Let them benefit by that
dearness of provisions which they by their mad acts have
caused. I venture to assert that, brought to submission by
these sufferings, they themselves will become tillers of the
lands rather than prevent them from being tilled by taking
up arms and seceding." It is not so easy to say[9] whether it
should have been done,[10] although I think it could have been
brought about that the senators, on condition of lowering
the price of corn, could have rid themselves of both the
tribunician power and all the restraints imposed on them
against their will.

M. Minucius deinde et A. Sempronius consul magnus vis
frumentum ex Sicilia adveho, agitoque in senatus, quantus plebs
do. Multus venio tempus premo plebs puto recuperoque jus, qui
extorqueo secessio ac vis pater. In primus Marcius Coriolanus,
hostis tribunicius potestas, "si annona" inquam " vetus volo,
jus pristinus reddo pater. Cur ego plebeius magistratus, cur
Sicinius potens video, sub jugum mitto, tamquam ab latro
redimo ? Egone hic indignitas diu patior quam necesse sum?
Tarquinius rex qui non fero. Sicinius fero? Secedo nunc,
avoco plebs ; pateo via in Sacer Mons aliusque collis. Rapio
frumentum ex ager, qui ad modus tertius annus rapio. Fruor
annona, qui furor suus facio. Audeo dico hic malum domo
ipse potius cultor ager sum, quam ut armatus per secessio collis
prohibeo." Haud tam facilis dico sum, facioque sum, quam
possum arbitror facio, ut conditio laxo annona et tribunicius
potestas et omnis invitus jus impono pater demo sui.

---

[1] 402, III., 2, 2).   [2] 545.   [3] 562 & 563, 1, 1).   [4] 559 & 563, 1,#1).
[5] 531.   [6] 508, 2.   [7] 486, II.   [8] 517, I.   [9] 570.   [10] 525 & 562.

LXXVIII.

Cicero to Ligarius : Be assured[1] that I am employing all my labour, (my) whole pains, care, and zeal, in procuring your safety; for, as I have always felt the greatest attachment for you, so the singular filial affection and love of your brothers, for whom, as well as for yourself, I have always possessed the utmost esteem, never suffer me to neglect any opportunity of doing my duty and a service to you. But what I am doing,[2] or have done in your behalf, I would have you learn from their letters rather than from mine. But as to what I hope or believe and consider certain in regard to your safety, that I desire to tell you. For if any man is[3] timorous in great and dangerous affairs, and always fearing the worst instead of hoping the best, I am he ; and, if this is a fault, I confess that I am not free from it ; yet, on the 27th of November,[4] when, at the desire of your brother, I had come[5] early to Cæsar, and gone through all the trouble and indignity of getting access[6] to, and of having an audience with, him ; when your brothers and relations had thrown themselves at his feet and I had stated what your cause and circumstances demanded ; not only from the discourse of Cæsar, which was mild and generous, but from his eyes and looks and many other signs besides, which I could better observe than describe, I came away with this idea, that there was no doubt in my mind of your safety ; wherefore see[7] that you be of good courage and stout heart ; and as you have borne the most perplexed state of matters wisely, bear this calmer one cheerfully. I, however, shall take part in your affairs, as if there were the greatest difficulty in them, and I shall most gladly supplicate in your behalf, as I have hitherto done, not only Cæsar, but even all his friends, whom I have ever found most affectionate to me. Adieu.

Cicero Ligarius. Ego scio omnis meus labor, omnis opera, cura, studium in tuus salus consumo : nam quum tu semper

---

[1] 537, I.   [2] 525, I,   [3] 508.   [4] 708, III., 2, 3, 4, & 710, II.   [5] 518, II.   [6] 562 & 563, 1.   [7] 535, 1, 1).

NOTE.—The Romans began their letters with the *address*, giving first the name of the writer, and then the name of the person to whom the letter was sent. We often find, besides, abbreviations, such as S. or S. D. or S. P. D., which mean respectively *Salutem, Salutem dicit,* or *Salutem plurinam dicit* = "Greeting," or "Gives a hearty greeting." If either party held any civil or military office, it was usual to express it thus : *P. Serv. Rullus, trib. pl. X. vir. Pompeio, consuli* = "P. Servius Rullus, tribune of the commons, one of the decemviri to Pompey the consul." When the person addressed was an intimate friend, such epithets as *humanissimus, optimus, suavissimus,* or frequently *suus,* were added. Sometimes the address was as follows : S. V. B. E. V., *si vales, bene est,* or *valeo;* or S. V. G. E. V., *si vales, gaudeo, ego valeo.* The latter ended generally with *vale,* sometimes with *ave* or *salve.* The date and place were frequently placed at the end.

*magnopere diligo, tum frater tuus, qui æque atque tu superus
benevolentia complector, singularis pietas amorque fraternus
nullus ego patior officium erga tu studiumque munus aut tempus
prætermitto. Sed qui facio facioque pro tu ex ille tu litteræ
quam ex meus malo cognosco. Quis autem spero aut confido et
exploro habeo de salus tuus, is tu a ego declaro volo. Nam si
quisquam sum timidus in magnus periculosusque res semperque
magnopere adversus res exitus metuo quam spero secundus, is
ego sum, et si hic vitium sum, is ego non careo confiteor. Ego
idem tamen quum a. d. V. Kal. intercalaris prior rogatus
frater tuus venio mane ad Cæsar atque omnis adeo et convenio
ille indignitas et molestia perfero, quum frater et propinquus
suus facio ad pes et ego loquor, qui causa, qui tuus tempus postulo, non solum ex oratio Cæsar, qui sane mollis et liberalis
sum, sed etiam ex oculus et vultus, ex multus præterea signum,
qui facile perspicio possum quam scribo, hic opinio discedo, ut
ego tuus salus dubius non sum. Qui ob res facio animus magnus fortisque sum, et, si turbidus sapienter fero, tranquillus læte
fero. Ego tamen tuus res sic adsum ut difficilis, neque Cæsar
solum, sed etiam amicus is omnis, qui ego amicus sum cognosco,
pro tu, sicut adhuc facio, libenter supplico. Valeo.*

LXXIX.

Cicero to Cassius, greeting : With what zeal I have defended[1] your reputation, both in the senate and before the
people, I would have you learn rather from your (other) friends
than from me. And that opinion which I expressed would
easily have prevailed in the senate, had not Pansa violently
opposed it.[2] After that opinion was voted on I was brought
before the assembly of the people by Servilius, the tribune.
I said everything I could of you with a strength of voice that
filled the forum, and with such clamour and approbation on
the part of the people that I never saw anything equal to it.
I should like[3] that you would pardon[4] me for this, which I
have done contrary to the will of your mother-in-law. The
timid woman was afraid that the feelings of Pansa would be
hurt. Pansa, indeed, in the assembly said that both your
mother and brother were opposed to the opinion expressed
by me ; but that did not move me : I had other considerations
more at heart. I had a regard both for the state, for which
I have always had a regard, and for your reputation as well
as glory. Moreover, as to what I both enlarged upon in
fuller terms in the senate and said in the assembly, on this
I would like[3] that you would make[4] my words good. For I
held out the hope, and almost assured them, that you neither

---

[1] 525, 1.   [2] 570.   [3] 486, III., 3.   [4] 493, 2.

had waited, nor would wait, for our decrees ; but that you
would defend the state yourself in your own way ; and
though we had heard nothing, as to where you were[1] or
what forces you had,[1] still I took it for granted that all the
resources and troops which were in these parts were yours ;
and I had confidence that by you the province of Asia had
been gained over to the side of the republic. See[2] that you
even surpass[3] yourself in advancing your glory. Farewell.

*Cicero Cassius S.: Quantus studium dignitas tuus et in senatus
et ad populus defendo ex tuus tu malo quam ex ego cognosco.
Qui meus sententia in senatus facile valeo, nisi Pansa vehementer
obsisto. Is sententia dico produco in contio a tribunus Servilius. Dico de tu qui possum tantus contentio, quantus forum
sum, tantus clamor consensusque populus, ut nihil unquam
similis video. Is volo ego ignosco qui invitus socrus tuus facio.
Mulier timidus vereor ne Pansa animus offendo. In contio
quidem Pansa dico mater quoque tuus et frater ille a ego
sententia nolo dico. Sed ego hic non moveo; alius malo.
Faveo et res publicus, qui semper faveo, et dignitas ac gloria
tuus. Qui autem et in senatus multus verbum dissero et dico in
contio, in is volo fides meus libero; promitto enim et prope confirmo tu non exspecto nec exspecto decretum noster, sed tu ipse
tuus mos res publicus defendo. Et quamquam nihildum audio,
nec ubi sum nec qui copiæ habeo, tamen sic statuo, omnis, qui
in iste pars sum opis copiæque, tuus sum, per tuque Asia provincia confido jam res publicus recipero. Tu facio in augeo
gloria tu ipse vinco. Valeo.*

LXXX.

Plancus to Cicero : As soon as I had learned this, I did not
hesitate : I thought that Lepidus ought to be supported in
carrying out his good intentions. I saw what advantage my
joining him would be,[4] since I was able[5] to pursue and destroy Antony's horse with mine, or to correct and restrain by
the presence of my army that part of the army of Lepidus,
which was corrupt and alienated from the republic. Having
made a bridge, therefore, in one day over the Isere, a very
large river in the territory of the Allobroges, I led across my
army on the 12th of May[6] ; but when word was brought back
that Lucius Antonius, who was sent forward with the cavalry
and cohorts, had arrived at Forum Julii, I sent forward my
brother on the 11th of May, with four thousand cavalry to
meet him ; I myself, by as long marches as I could, followed
with four legions, without heavy baggage, and with the

[1] 525, 1.   [5] 535, 1, 1).   [3] 493, 2.   [4] 525.   [6] 520, II.
[6] 708, III., 1-4 & 710, II.

rest of the horse. If only ordinary good luck for the republic aid[1] us, we shall here put an end to the audacity of the desperate, and to all our trouble. But if the robber, upon hearing of my arrival, begin[1] to return again to Italy, it will be Brutus's part to meet him there, and in his case I know neither wisdom nor courage will be wanting. Still, should this happen,[1] I shall send my brother with the cavalry to follow and to preserve Italy from being ravaged by him. Take[2] care of your health,[3] and love me as I do you.

Plancus Cicero : Qui res ego cognosco cunctor non ; in cursus bonus consilium Lepidus adjuvo puto. Adventus meus quis proficio video, vel quod equitatus meus persequor atque opprimo equitatus Antonius possum vel quod exercitus Lepidus is pars, qui corruptus sum et ab res publicus alienatus, et corrigo et coerceo præsentia meus exercitus possum. Itaque in Isara, flumen magnus, qui in fines Allobrox, pons unus dies facio, exercitus a.d. IV. Idus Maius traduco. Quum vero ego nuntio L. Antonius præmitto cum eques et cohors ad Forum Julii venio, frater cum eques quatuor mille, ut occuro is, mitto a.d. V. Idus Maius ; ipse magnus iter cum quattuor legio expeditus et reliquus equitatus subsequor. Si ego mediocris modo fortuna res publica adjuvo, et audacia perditus et noster sollicitudo hic finis reperio. Quod si latro præcognosco noster adventus rursus in Italia sui recipio cœpi, Brutus sum officium occurro is ; qui scio nec consilium nec animus desum. Ego tamen, si is accido, frater cum, equitatus mitto qui sequor, Italia a vastatio defendo. Facio, valeo, eyoque mutuo diligo.

LXXXI.

On the third day after, when I was intending[4] to set out from Athens, his friend, Publius Postumius, came to me about the tenth hour of the night, and informed me that Marcus Marcellus, my colleague, after supper time had been stabbed with a dagger by Publius Magius Chilo, his friend, and had received two wounds, one in his stomach, the other in his head near the ear ; still he expected that he might possibly live ; that Magius after this killed himself ; that he had been sent by Marcellus to me to bring[5] this news, and to request me to bring physicians to him. I brought some together, and I instantly set out thither at daybreak. But when I was not far distant from the Piracus, Acidinus's boy met me with a note, which contained the news that Marcellus died a little before day. Thus a most distinguished man was murdered in the foulest manner by a most despicable villain ;

---

[1] 508 & 473, 1.   [2] 535, 1, 1).   [3] 493, 2.   [4] 518, II.   [5] 500.

and he, whom his enemies had spared on account of his
dignity, was found the friend of him who caused his death.
I went forward, however, to his tent. I found two freedmen
and a few slaves; they said that the rest had fled terror-
stricken, because their master had been slain[1] in front of
their tent. I was forced to carry back his body to the city
in that same litter in which I was brought, and by my own
servants, and there I took care that his burial rites should
be performed as magnificently as the means at our disposal
at Athens would permit. 1 was unable to obtain from the
Athenians my request to grant[2] him a burial place within
the city, since (they alleged) they were hindered by their
religious scruples, and they had granted this to no one before.
They allowed us, what was most desirable in the next place, to
bury[3] him in the grounds of whichever of their public schools
we wished.[4] I chose a spot—the school of the academy, the
most celebrated in the universe—and there I burnt him; and
I afterwards gave orders that the Athenians should provide a
marble monument for him in the same place. Thus I have
faithfully performed to him both living and dead every duty
which our partnership in office and my relationship required.
Adieu. The thirty-first of May. Athens.

*Post dies tertius is dies, quum ad Athenæ proficiscor in animus
habeo, circiter hora decimus nox, P. Postumius, familiaris
is, ad ego venio, et ego nuntio M. Marcellus, collega noster, post
cœna tempus a P. Magius Chilo, familiaris is, pugio percutio et
duo vulnus accipio, unus in stomachus, alter in caput secundum
auris, spero tamen is vivo possum; Magius sui ipse interficio
postea; sui a Marcellus ad ego mitto qui hic nuntio et rogo, uti
medicus cogo. Cogo et e vestigium eo proficiscor prior lux.
Quum non longe a Piræus absum, puer Acidinus obviam ego
venio cum codicillus, in qui scribo, paullo ante lux Marcellus
dies suus obeo. Ita vir clarus ab homo deterior acerbus mors
afficio, et, qui inimicus propter dignitas parco, invenio amicus
qui is mors offero. Ego tamen ad tabernaculum is pergo.
Invenio duo libertus et pauculus servus; reliquus aio profugio
metus perterreo, quod dominus is ante tabernaculum interficio.
Cogo in idem ille lectica, qui ipse defero, meusque lecticarius in
urbs is refero, ibique pro is copia, qui Athenæ sum funus is satis
amplus facio curo. Ab Atheniensis, locus sepultura intra urbs
ut do, impetro non possum, quod relligio se impedio dico, neque
tamen is antea quisquam concedo. Qui propior sum, uti in qui
volo gymnasium is sepelio, ego permitto. Ego in nobilis orbis
terra gymnasium Academia locus deligo ibique is comburo,
posteaque curo, ut idem Atheniensis in idem locus monumentum
is marmoreus facio loco. Ita, qui noster officium sum, pro
collegium et propinquitas et vivus et mortuus omnis is præsto.
Valeo. D. pr. Kal. Jun. Athenæ.*

---

[1] 520, II.   [2] 492, 2.   [3] 493, 2.   [4] 525.

PASS PAPERS IN LATIN PROSE

OF THE

UNIVERSITY OF TORONTO.

—◆—

ALL THE YEARS: 1864.

I have assisted your commanders with naval forces, so that not one of your allies can equal me : I have furnished supplies by land and by sea : I have been present at all the naval battles that have taken place : I have nowhere spared my labor, or my risk. I have suffered that which is most wretched in war, a siege, having been shut in at Pergamus with the utmost danger at once of my life and of my kingdom. Afterwards, having been freed from the siege, I met your consul with my whole fleet at the Hellespont, that I might assist him in getting his army over. After your army had crossed into Asia, I never departed from the consul ; no Roman soldier was more regular in your camp than I and my brother. No expedition, no cavalry engagement took place without me.

Navalis copia, ut nemo vester socius ego æquiparo possum, imperator vester adjuvo ; commeatus terra mareque suppedito ; navalis prælium, qui fio, omnis adsum ; nec labor meus, nec periculum usquam parco. Qui miser sum in bellum, obsidio patior, Pergamus includo cum discrimen ultra simul vita regnumque. Libero deinde obsidio, totus classis ad Hellespontus consul vester occurro, ut is in trajicio exercitus adjuvo ; postquam in Asia exercitus vester transgredior, nunquam a consul abscedo ; nemo miles Romanus magis assiduus in castra vester sum, quam ego fraterque meus. Nullus expeditio, nullus equestris prælium sine ego fio.

———

JUNIOR MATRICULATION : 1864.

When Xenophon was performing a customary sacrifice, he learned that the elder[2] of his two sons, by name Gryllus, had fallen in battle at Mantinea ; nor did he think that the commenced worship of the gods should be stopped on that account, but he was satisfied merely to lay down the crown. Having enquired in what manner he had fallen, when he heard that he had died fighting very bravely, he replaced the crown on his head, having called the deities, to whom he was sacrificing, to witness, that he felt greater pleasure from the valour of his son than pain at his death.

Xenophon cum sollemnis sacrificium perago, e duo filius magnus natus, nomen Gryllus, apud Mantinea in prœlium cado cognosco ; nec ideo instituo deus cultus omitto puto, sed tantum-modo corona depono contineo. Perconctor quisnam modus occido, ut audio fortiter pugno intereo, corona caput repono, numen, qui sacrifico, testor magnus sui ex virtus filius voluptas quam ex mors amaritudo sentio.

ALL THE YEARS : 1865.

When the consul had demanded from the senate a triumph on account of these achievements, rather from regard to usage than from hope of obtaining it, and when he saw that some, because he had rather been tardy in taking his depar-ture from the city, others, because he had passed from Sam-nium into Etruria without the order of the senate, partly his own enemies, partly the friends of his colleague, were refus-ing the triumph, he says: "Conscript fathers, I shall not be so far mindful of your dignity as to forget that I am consul. By the same right of office by which I conducted the wars, those wars being brought to a happy conclusion, Samnium and Etruria being subdued, victory and peace being obtained, I shall now triumph."

Ob hicce res gero consul quum triumphus ab senatus, mos causa magis quam spes impetro, peto, videoque alius, quod tarde ab urbs exeo, alius, quod, injussus senatus ex Samnium in Etruria transeo, partim suus inimicus, partim collega amicus, triumphus nego, non ita, inquam, "Pater conscribo, vester majestas memini, ut ego consul sum obliviscor. Idem jus im-perium, qui bellum gero, bellum feliciter gero, Samnium atque Etruria subigo, victoria et pax pario, triumpho."

JUNIOR MATRICULATION : 1865.

Hanno was the commander of the Carthaginians, but they placed their whole dependence on Mutines and the Numidians. He, roaming through all Sicily, carried off spoils from the allies of the Romans, and could not be shut out from Agri-gentum by force or any art, nor prevented from sallying

5 A

forth, whenever he wished. This reputation of his, because it was now obscuring the fame even of the commander, finally turned to envy, so that not even successful actions now were sufficiently agreeable to Hanno on account of the author, on account of which things he finally gave the command to his own son.

Hanno sum imperator Carthaginiensis, sed omnis in Mutines Numidaque spes repono habeo. Per totus Sicilia vagus præda ago ex socius Romanus ; neque intercludo ab Agrigentum vis aut ars ullus, nec, quin erumpo, ubi volo, prohibeo possum. Hic is gloria, quia jam imperator quoque fama officio, postremo in invidia verto ; ut ne bene gero quidem res jam Hanno propter auctor satis lætus sum, propter qui postremo præfectura is filius suus do.

ALL THE YEARS : 1866.

Both consuls proceed to the province, and because they are successful there, a thanksgiving for one day was decreed. About two thousand Spaniards came to the boundary of the province, where Sabinus was encamped, praying that they might be received. Sabinus, having ordered the Spaniards to wait in the same place, consulted the senate by letter. The senate ordered the prætor to write in reply to Sabinus : that it was more reasonable that the consuls, whose province it was, should decide what was to be the advantage to the republic. Accordingly the consuls received them, and they, having given hostages, surrendered. After the army retired, forgetting the hostages, they began again to collect their forces.

Consul ambo in provincia proficiscor, et quia prospere ibi res gero, supplicatio in unus dies decerno. Hispanus duo mille fere ad extremus fines provincia, ubi castra Sabinus habeo, venio, uti recipio, oro. Sabinus, opperior idem locus Hispanus jubeo, senatus per litterae consulo. Senatus rescribo prætor Sabinus jubeo ; verus sum, consul, qui provincia sum, quam sui, quis e respublica sum, decerno. Itaque consul is recipio, atque ille, obses do, sui dedo ; postquam exercitus recedo, obliviscor obses, rursus copiæ cogo cœpi.

JUNIOR MATRICULATION : 1866.

There was a marsh of inconsiderable extent between our army and that of the enemy. The enemy were waiting to see if our forces should cross this : but our men were ready under arms to attack them in disorder if they should begin to cross. Meanwhile a cavalry engagement took place between the two lines. When neither side made a commencement of crossing, the battle of the cavalry proving more favourable to our men, Cæsar withdrew his troops into the camp. Presently the foe marched from that position to our river Axona, which, as I said before, was to the rear of the camp. There, having discovered the fords, they attempted to lead across part of their forces with the intention, if possible, of storming the fort commanded by Quintus Titurius, and cutting down the bridge ; or, if they could not accomplish this, of devastating the fields of the Remi (who were of great service to us in carrying on the war), and of preventing our men from foraging.

Palus sum non magnus inter noster atque hostis exercitus. Hic si noster transeo, hostis expecto ; noster antem, si ab ille initium transeo fio, ut impeditus aggredior, paratus in arma sum. Interim prælium equestris inter duo acies contendo. Ubi neuter transeo initium facio, secundus. Eques prælium noster, Cæsar suus in castra reduco. Hostis protinus ex is locus ad flumen Axona contendo, qui sum post noster castra demonstro. Ibi vadum reperio, pars suus copiæ transduco conor, is consilium, ut, si possum, castellum, qui præsum Quintus Titurius, expugno, ponsque interscindo ; si minus possum, ager Remi populor, qui magnus ego usus ad bellum gero sum, commeatusque noster prohibeo.

ALL THE YEARS : 1867.

At first the matter seemed so incredible that the messenger was regarded not only as false but also as scarcely sound in mind. Then as one came after another, all asserting the same thing, at length credit was given : and before they sufficiently knew that he was approaching the city, all pour forth to the sight, freedmen and slaves together, also boys with women. Those who were leading the prætor were able with difficulty by putting aside those in the way to enter the gate, and a dense crowd had stopped the rest of their course, and as the greatest portion had been shut out from the sight, they suddenly filled the theatre, which was close to the road, and all with one voice demand that he should be taken into it for the view of the people.

Primum adeo incredibilis videor res, ut non pro vanus modo, sed vix pro sanus nuncius audio. Deinde ut super alius alius idem omnis affirmo venio, tandem fio fides ; et priusquam appropinquo urbs satis scio, ad spectaculum omnis, simul liberi et servus, puer quoque cum femina, effundo. Aegre submoveo obvius intro porta, qui adduco prœtor, possum, atque turba confercio iter reliquus claudo, et quum pars magnus excludo a spectaculum, theatrum repente, qui via propinquus sum, compleo, et, ut eo in conspectus populus adduco, unus vox omnis exposco.

JUNIOR MATRICULATION : 1867.

In this man there was the greatest force of intellect and ability ; no art was wanting to him of managing either public or private affairs.   He was equally well versed in matter re-lating to the city and the country.   The knowledge of law has raised some to the highest honors ; eloquence others ; military glory others.   He had ability, so equally applicable to all things, that you would say that he was naturally fitted for that one thing whatever he was doing.   In war he was most brave and distinguished in many remarkable battles.   The same, after he came to great honors, was a consummate general : the same in peace ; if you were to consult him on law, most learned ; if a cause was to be pleaded, most eloquent.

In hic vir summus vis animus ingeniumque sum.   Nullus ars, neque privatus, neque publicus res gero, is desum.   Urbanus rusticusque res pariter calleo.   Ad summus honor alius scientia jus, alius eloquentia, alius gloria militaris proveho ; hic versatilis ingenium sic pariter ad omnis sum, ut nascor ad is unus dico, quicunque ago.   In bellum fortis, multusque insignis clarus pugna ; idem, postquam ad magnus honor pervenio, summus imperator ; idem in pax, si de jus consulo, peritus ; si causa oro, eloquens.

ALL THE YEARS : 1868.

This is their manner of fighting from chariots : First they ride about in every direction and cast javelins, and they generally throw the lines into confusion by sheer fear of their horses and the noise of the chariots.   So when they have introduced themselves among the bands of cavalry, they leap from their chariots and fight on foot.   Meanwhile the charioteers gradually draw off from the contest, and so dis-pose their vehicles that if these (the warriors) are hard pressed by the overpowering numbers of the foe, they have a retreat to their friends open to them.   So in battles they combine the rapid movements of cavalry with the firmness of infantry, and, by daily drill and practice, they become so efficient, that, in a sloping and steep locality, they are accustomed to check their horses running at full speed, to rein them in and turn quickly, to run along the pole and thence very swiftly return into their chariots.

Genus hic sum ex esseda pugna. Primo per omnis pars perequito et telum conjicio atque ipse terror equus, et strepitus rota ordo plerumque perturbo et cum sui inter eques turma insinuo, ex esseda desilio et pes prælior. Auriga interim paulatim ex prælium excedo atque ita currus colloco, ut si ille a multitudo hostis premo, expeditus ad suus receptus habeo. Ita mobilitas eques, stabilitas pedes in prælium præsto; ac tantum usus quotidianus et exercitatio efficio, uti in declivis ac præceps locus incitatus equus sustineo et brevis moderor ac flecto et per temo percurro et sui inde in currus cito recipio consuesco.

JUNIOR MATRICULATION : 1868.

I ordered Lucius Catiline, plotting, not darkly but openly, the slaughter of the senate, the ruin of the city, to depart from the city, so that we might be able to be protected by walls from him, from whom we were not able by laws. I wrested the weapons aimed, in the last month of my consulship, at the throat of the city, from the wicked hands of conspirators ; I seized, produced, put out the torches already kindled for the burning of this city. This most distinguished man, Lucius Gellius, who is sitting near you, said, in their hearing, that a civic crown was owed to me by the republic.

Ego L. Catilina cædes senatus, interitus urbs, non obscure sed palam molior, egredior ex urbs jubeo, ut, a qui lex non possum, mœnia tutus sum possum. Ego telum, extremus mensis consulatus meus, intendo jugulum civitas, de conjuro nefarius manus extorqueo. Ego fax jam accendo ad hic urbs incendium comprehendo, profero, exstinguo. Ego hic vir clarus, propter tu sedeo, L. Gellius, hic audio, civicus corona debeo a respublica dico.

JUNIOR MATRICULATION : 1869.

Dionysius, although he had received from his father, in the shape of an inheritance, the sovereignty of the Syracusans and of nearly all Sicily, the lord of great wealth, the general of armies, the commander of fleets, the master of cavalry, taught little boys letters at Corinth on account of poverty, and at the same time by so great a change having become master of a school from a tyrant, he warned the older that no one should trust too much to fortune.

Dionysius cum hæreditas nomen a pater Syracusanus, ac pœne totus Sicilia tyrannis accipio, magnus opes dominus, exercitus dux, rector classis, equitatus (pl.) potens, propter inopia littera puerulus Corinthus doceo. Idemque tempus tantus mutatio, magnus natus, ne quis nimis fortuna credo magister ludus fio tyrannus moneo.

ALL THE YEARS: 1869.

What ardor for study do you suppose must have been in Archimedes, who was so occupied in drawing some mathematical figures in the sand, that he was not aware that his city was |taken? And what a mighty genius was that of Aristoxenus which, we see, was devoted to music? What fondness too for study must have inspired Aristophanes to dedicate his whole life to literature? What shall we say of Pythagoras? Why should I speak of Plato and of Democritus, by whom we see that the most distant countries were travelled over, on account of their desire for learning? And those who are blind to this never loved anything worthy of being known; and here I may say that those who say that those studies which I have mentioned are cultivated for the sake of the pleasures of the mind, do not understand that they are desirable for their own sakes, because the mind is delighted by them without the interruption of any ideas of utility, and rejoices in the mere fact of knowledge, even though it may possibly produce inconvenience.

Quis enim ardor studium censeo sum in Archimedes, qui dum in pulvis quidam describo attentus ne patria quidem capio sentio? Quantum Aristoxenus ingenium consumo video in musicus? Quis studium Aristophanes puto ætas in litteræ duco? Quis de Pythagoras? Quis de Plato aut Democritus loquor a qui propter disco cupiditas video ultimus terra sum peragratus? Quis qui non video nihil unquam magnus cognitio dignus amo, atque hic locus, qui propter animus voluptas colo dico is studium qui dico non intelligo idcirco sum propter sui expetendus, quod, nullus utilitas objicio delecto animus atque ipse scientia etiamsi incommodum do, gaudeo.

ALL THE YEARS : 1870.

We call gods and men to witness, general, that we have neither taken up arms against our country, nor to endanger any individual, but to preserve our persons secure from injury. Wretched and needy, many of us are deprived of our country, all of our fair fame and fortune, by the violence and cruelty of usurers ; nor can any of us avail himself of the laws as in former times, nor enjoy his personal freedom after the loss of his patrimony, so powerful is the persecution of the usurer and the praetor. Often have our ancestors, from compassion to the people of Rome, aided the indigent by their decrees ; and very lately in our own remembrance, on account of the extent of the debt, and with the approbation of all good men, obligations contracted in silver were paid in brass. Often have the people, urged by love of power, or the arrogance of the magistrate, separated in arms from the senators ; but our object is neither dominion, nor riches, the sources of all the wars and contests among men, but simply liberty, which no honourable man ever parts with but with his life.

Deus homoque testor, imperator, ego arma neque contra patria capio, neque quo periculum alius facio sed uti corpus noster ab injuria tutus sum qui miser egeo violentia atque crudelitas fœnerator plerique patria sed omnis fama atque fortuna expers sum neque quisquam ego licet mos majores lex utor neque amitto patrimonium liber corpus habeo tantus sævitia fœnerator atque prætor sum. Sæpe majores tu miscreor plebs Romanus decretum suus inopia opitulor ; ac nuper memoria noster, propter magnitudo aes alienus, volo omnis bonus, argentum aes solvo. Sæpe ipse plebs aut dominor studium permoveo, aut superbia magistratus, amatus a pater secedo ; at ego non imperium neque divitiæ peto, qui res causa bellum atque certamen omnis inter mortalis sum, sed libertas qui nemo bonus nisi cum anima simul amitto.

JUNIOR MATRICULATION : 1870.

The elder Hannibal, having been conquered in a naval battle by Duilius the consul, and fearing to suffer punishment for having lost the fleet, wonderfully turned aside injury by craft ; for before a message of the disaster reached home, he sent one of his friends to Carthage, who, after he had entered the senate house of that city, said : "Hannibal consults you, when the Roman chief, leading with him great naval forces, shall have come, whether he ought to fight with him." The

whole senate cried out: "There was no doubt that he ought."
"He has fought," he says, "and was overcome." Thus he
did not leave it free for them to condemn that deed which
they themselves had pronounced ought to have been done.

*Superus Hannibal, a Duilius consul navalis prælium vinco,
timeoque classis amitto pæno do, offensa astutia mire averto;
nam priusquam clades nuntius domus pervenio, quidam ex
amicus Carthago mitto, qui postquam civitas is curia intro:
"Consulo," inquam, "in Hannibal, quum dux Romanus
magnus sui cum maritimus traho copia advenio, an cum is confligo debeo." Acclamo universus senatus, "non sum dubius
quin oportet." "Confligo," inquam, "et supero." Ita liber
non relinquo is fio damno, qui ipse fio debeo judico.*

ALL THE YEARS : 1871.

Whilst these things are going on in Spain, Petelia, in
the Brutii, was taken by Himilco, Hannibal's prefect, some
months after it had begun to be attacked. This victory cost
the Carthaginians much blood and wounds. After this the
Carthaginian leads his forces to Consentia, which, being less
obstinately defended, he received within a few days to surrender. Almost at the same time the army of the Brutii also
surrounded Crotone, a Greek city, formerly rich in arms and
men, then now so reduced by many and great disasters that
less than twenty thousand citizens of every age survived.

*Dum hic in Hispania gero, Petelia in Brutii, aliquot post
mensis quam cæpi oppugno, ab Himilco, præfectus Hannibal,
expugno. Multus sanguis ac vulnus is Pænus victoria sto.
Deinde Pænus ad Consentia copiæ traduco, qui minus pertina-
citer defendo, intra pauci dies in deditio accipio. Idem ferme
dies et Brutii exercitus Crotone, Græcus urbs, circumsedeo,
opulentus quondam arma virque, tum jam adeo multus magnusque clades affligo, ut omnis atas minus viginti mille civis
supersum.*

JUNIOR MATRICULATION : 1871.

The authority of the ancients has more weight with me.
Either that of our own ancestors, who paid such sacred
honors to the dead, which surely they would not have done if
they thought these honors did in no way affect them; or that
of those who once lived in this country, and Magna Græcia,
which is now indeed destroyed, but then was flourishing,
enlightened by their institutions and instructions; or of

him who was pronounced by the oracle of Apollo to be the wisest of men, who did not first say one thing and then another, as is generally done, but always the same : namely, that the souls of men are divine, and that when they have departed from the body a return to heaven is opened to them, and the speediest to the most virtuous and just.

Multum apud ego antiquus auctoritas valeo, vel noster majores, qui mortuus tam religiosus jus tribuo ; quod non facio profecto, si nihil ad is pertineo arbitror ; vel is, qui in hic terra sum, Magnusque Græcia, qui nunc quidem deleo ; tunc floreo, institutum et præceptum suus erudio ; vel is, qui Apollo oraculum sapiens sumjudico ; qui non tum hic, tum ille, ut in plerique, sed idem semper, animus homo divinus sum, isque, cum e corpus excedo, reditus in cœlum pateo, bonusque et justus quisque expeditus.

ALL THE YEARS : 1872.

The Roman fortifications were, as has been previously related, at three points, all of which simultaneously and with the greatest violence the Ætolians attacked. They advanced, some with burning torches, others bringing tow and pitch and fire-darts, their whole line blazing with flame. At the first onslaught they overpowered many of the guards ; then, after the shouting and commotion reached the camp, and the signal was given by the consul, they seize their arms and rush out of all the gates to lend assistance. At one point the engagement was carried on with fire and sword. There, in different quarters, the two generals were cheering on the combatants and retaining them by the almost certain prospect that Nicander would soon arrive, according to arrangement, and attack the enemy's rear. After they received, however, no signal from their friends, and perceived that the number of the enemy was increasing, they were driven flying into the city, part of their fortification having been set on fire, and about ten thousand men were slain.

Tres locus, sicut ante dico, opus Romanus sum ; qui omnis simul superusque vis Ætolus aggredior. Alius cum ardeo fax, alius stuppa pixque et malleolus fero, totus colluceo flamma acies, advenio. Multus primus impetus custos opprimo. Deinde postquam clamor tumultusque in castra perfero doque a consul signum, arma capio, et omnis porta ad opis fero effundo. Unus locus ferrum ignisque gero res. Ibi diversus pars duo dux pugno hortor et prope certus foveo spes, jam Nicander compono adsum tergum hostis invado. Ceterum postquam nullus signum a suus accipio et cresco numerus hostis cerno, fugio in urbs compello, pars opus incendo et ad duo mille homo interficio.

JUNIOR MATRICULATION : 1872.

But, with regard to the overthrowing and spoiling of cities, it is to be gravely considered that nothing is done in a cruel manner, and that it is the part of a great man, when circumstances are disturbed, to punish the guilty, to preserve the multitude, to retain in every fortune things right and honourable. For as there are those who, as I have already mentioned, prefer warlike things to refined things, so may you find many to whom dangerous and crafty counsels seem both more splendid and greater than thoughtful (counsels). Never in flight from danger is the mistake to be committed that we seem unwarlike and cowardly ; but that also must be avoided that we do not present ourselves to dangers without cause, than which nothing can be more foolish. Wherefore in approaching dangers the custom of medical men must be imitated who cure by simple means those who are slightly ill, but are compelled to apply to more dangerous diseases dangerous and doubtful remedies. Therefore we ought to be more ready with regard to our own dangers than with regard to dangers of common importance, and to contend with greater preparation for honor and glory than for other advantages.

De everto autem diripioque urbs valde considero sum ne quis crudeliter, isque sum vir magnus, res agito, punio sons, multitudo conservo, in omnis fortuna rectus atque honestus retineo. Ut enim sum, quemadmodum supra dico, qui urbanus res bellicus antepono ; sic reperio multus qui periculosus et callidus consilium quietus et cogitatus et splendidus et magnus video. Nunquam periculum fuga committo sum, ut imbellis timidusque video ; sed fugio etiam ille, ne offero periculum sine causa qui nihil possum esse stultus. Quapropter in adeo periculum consuetudo imitor medicus sum qui leviter ægroto leniter curo ; gravis autem morbus periculosus curatio et anceps adhibeo cogo. Promptus igitur debeo sum ad noster periculum quam ad communis dimicoque paratus honor et gloria quam de cetera commodus.

ALL THE YEARS : 1873.

I could wish that the immortal gods had caused us to return thanks for the living Sulpicius, rather than seek honor for the dead. Nor do I doubt that, if that man could have been able to give an account of his embassy, his return would both be grateful to you and healthful for the state ; not that L. Philippus and L. Piso have been wanting either in zeal or attention. in so important a duty and so great a service ; but, since Sulpicius excelled them in age, (excelled) all in wisdom, he, having been suddenly removed from the business, has left the entire embassy destitute and weakened. Others who have died during their embassy set out without any fear of death ; Sulpicius set out with some hope of coming to M. Antony, with no hope of returning. He did not hesitate even with his last breath to try if he could bring any assistance to the state. But when he perceived that he would be unlike himself if he did not obey your authority, but, that if he obeyed, that service undertaken by him for the state would be the end of his life : he chose, during a very great crisis, to die rather than appear to have done less good to the state than he was able.

Volo deus immortalis facio ut vivus potius Sulpicius gratiæ ago quam honor mortuus quæro. Nec dubito quin, si ille vir legatio renuntio possum, reditus is et tu gratus sum et res publicus salutaris, non quo L. Philippus et L. Piso aut studium aut cura desum in tantus officium tantusque munus, sed quum Sulpicius ætas ille anteo, sapientia omnis, subito eripio e causa, totus legatio orbus et debilitatus relinquo. Cetera qui in legatio mors obeo, sine ullus mors metus proficiscor, Sulpicius cum aliquis pervenio ad M. Antonius spes proficiscor, nullus revertor, non recuso quo parum vel exterus spiritus si qui opis res publicus fero possum, experior. At ille quum video si vester auctoritas non pareo, dissimilis sum sui ; sin pareo, munus sui ille pro res publicus suscipio vita finis forem, malo in magnus discrimen emorior, quam parum quam possum video res publicus prosum.

JUNIOR MATRICULATION : 1873.

But what you assumed, as by a law of your own, in the last part of your speech, that an orator is able to speak very fluently in the discussion of every subject, we should not have tolerated, if we were not here in your domain. We would head many who would either contend with you by an interdict, or summon you to contend with them at law, because you had so rashly invaded the possessions of others. For, in the first place, all the Pythagoreans would institute a suit against you ; men who are elegant and powerful speakers, with whom you could not contend on equal terms. Bands of philosophers would assail you besides, even down from Socrates, the illustrious fountain and head, and convince you that you had learned nothing about the good things, nothing about the evil (things) in life, nothing about the passions of the mind, nothing about the names of men, nothing about the proper course of life. When they had made an attack on you altogether, then separate sects would bring an action

against you.   The Academy would be urgent to compel yc .
to deny what ever you might have asserted.

Qui vero in exterus oratio quasi tuus jus sumo, orator in
omnis sermo disputatio copiose possum versor, is nisi hic in tuus
regnum sum, non fero.   Multus præsum qui aut interdictum tu
cum contendo aut tu ex jus manus consero voco, quod in alienus
possessio tam temere irruo.   Ago enim tu cum lex primum
Pythagoreus omnis, ornatus homo in dico et gravis, quicum in
justus sacramentum contendo non licet.   Urgeo præterea philoso-
phus grex jam ab ille fons et caput Socrates, et nihil tu de bonus
res in vita, nihil de malus, nihil de animus permotio, nihil de
homo mos, nihil de ratio vita disco.   Quum universus in tu
impetus facio, tum singulis familia lis tu intendo.   Insto
Academia, qui quisquis dico, is tu ipse nego cogo.

ALL THE YEARS : 1874.

When the Athenians were utterly powerless to withstand
the invasion of the Persians, and were deciding to take to
their ships, and do battle for the liberty of Greece with the
fleet, (having previously left the city, and placed their wives
and children under charge at Trœzen), they stoned to death
one Cyrsilus, who advised them to remain in the city and
admit Xerxes.   Now, he appeared to be consulting expedi-
ency; but this was of no account when honour forbade.
Themistocles, after the successful issue of that war with the
Persians, said, before the assembly, that he had a project
advantageous to the state, but that it must not be known.
He asked the people to give him a person to whom he might
impart it.   Aristides was given.   To him Themistocles said,
that the fleet of the Lacedæmonians, which had been drawn
up on shore at Gytheum, could be secretly set on fire ; that
by this means the power of the Lacedaemonians must needs
be destroyed.   Aristides, upon hearing this, came before the
assembly, that was eagerly awaiting him, and said, that the
scheme which Themistocles recommended was very advantageous, but extremely dishonorable.

Atheniensis quum Persae impetus nullus modus possum sus-
tineo, statuoque, ut, urbs relinquo, coniux et liberi Troezen
depono, naris conscendo, libertasque Græcia classis defendo,
Cyrsilus quidam suadeo ut in urbs maneo Xerxesque recipio,
lapis coöperio.   Atque ille utilitas sequor video ; sed is nullus
sum, repugno honestas.   Themistocles post victoria is bellum
qui cum Persae sum, dico in concio, sui habeo consilium respub-
lica salutaris, sed· is scio non opus sum : postulo ut aliquis
populus do 'qui cum communico.   Do Aristides.   Hic ille, classis

Lacedæmonius qui subduco ad Gytheum, clam incendo possum; qui facio frango Lacedæmonius opis necesse sum. Qui Aristides quum audio, in concio magnus expectatio venio dicoque perutilis sum consilium qui Themistocles affero, sed parum honestus.

JUNIOR MATRICULATION : 1874.

For my part, I, a youth, was as fond of old Quintus Maximus (the one who recovered Tarentum), as if he had been of my own age. For in that man dignity was tempered with courtesy, and his years had not changed his manners, although I began to seek his friendship when he was, not a very old man, but still already well advanced in life. For the year after I was born he was consul for the first time ; and in his fourth consulship, I, a youthful soldier, went with him to Capua, and, five years afterwards, to Tarentum. Then, four years after, I became quæstor, an office which I held in the consulship of Tuditanus and Cethegus. Truly, with what vigilance, with what prudence did he recover Tarentum ! On which occasion, when Salinator (who had fled into the citadel upon the loss of the town) was boasting in my hearing, and saying: "You regained Tarentum through me, Fabius." "Undoubtedly," he replied to him, laughing ; "for, had you not lost it, I had never regained it."

Ego Q. Maximus, is qui Tarentum recipio, adolescens ita diligo senex, ut æqualis. Sum enim in ille vir comitas condio gravitas, nec senectus mos muto; quamquam is colo cœpi non admodum grandis natus, sed tamen jam ætas proveho. Annus enim post consul primum sum, quam ego nascor; cumque is quartum consul adolescentulus miles Capua proficiscor quintus-que annus post Tarentum. Quæstor deinde quadriennium post fio; qui magistratus gero consul Tuditanus et Cethegus. Tarentum vero qui vigilantia, qui consilium recipio! Quum quidem ego audio, Salinator, qui, amitto oppidum, fugio in arx glorior atque ita dico: Meus opera, Q. Fabius, Tarentum recipio: Certe, inquam, rideo, nam nisi tu amitto, nunquam recipio.

ALL THE YEAR: 1875.

Let this, therefore, be laid down as the first law of friendship, that we seek honorable things from our friends, and that we do honorable things for the sake of our friends. Let us not even wait until we are asked. Let zeal be always ready, and let delay be absent. Let us rejoice to give advice freely. Above all, in friendship, let the authority of friends,

who are giving good advice, have weight; and let it (the
authority) be applied both to advising not only openly but
sharply, if the affair will demand (such a thing); and let it
be obeyed when it is applied. For I am of opinion, that
certain wonderful things gave pleasure to certain persons
who, I hear, were reckoned wise men in Greece,—that ex-
cessive friendships are to be avoided; that everyone has
enough, and more than enough of his own affairs, and that it
is troublesome to be too much involved in the affairs of others.

*Hic igitur primus lex amicitia sancio. ut ab amicus honestus
peto, et amicus causa honestus facio. Ne exspecto quidem dum
rogo. Studium semper adsum, et cunctatio absum. Consilium do gaudeo libere. Plurimum in amicitia amicus bene
suadeo valeo auctoritas, isque et adhibeo ad moneo non modo
aperte, sed etiam acriter, si res postulo, et adhibitus pareo. Nam
quidam, qui audio sapiens habitus in Græcia, placeo opinor
mirabilis quidam, fugio sum nimius amicitia, satis superque
sum suus quisque res, et alienus nimis implico molestus sum.*

JUNIOR MATRICULATION : 1875.

This is the language of the people; mine indeed, Laterensis,
this : "That the jury ought not to enquire why you have
been beaten, provided that you have not been beaten by
bribery. For if, as often as a man shall have been passed
over, who ought not to have been passed over, so often it
shall behoove him, who shall have been elected, to be condemned; there is no longer any reason why the people should
be appealed to, no reason why the distribution of tickets
and the returning of votes, should be awaited. At once,
when I see who have announced themselves (as candidates), I
shall say : 'This man is of consular family, that man of prætorian ; the remaining candidates, I see, are from the equestrian order ; they are all without stain, they are all equally
good and upright men ; but degrees of rank must needs be
observed ! let the prætorian class give way to the consular,
nor let the equestrian position vie with the prætorian.' "

*Hic populus oratio sum ; meus vero, Laterensis, hic : Quare
vinco non debeo judex quæro, modo ne largitio vinco. Nam si,
quotiescumque prætereo is qui non debeo prætereo, toties oportet
is qui facio condemno, nihil jam sum qui populus supplico, nihil
qui diribitio, nihil qui renuntiatio suffragium expecto ; simul ut
qui profiteor video, dico : Hic familia consularis sum, ille prætorius : reliqui video sum ex equestris locus : sum omnis sine
macula, sum omnis æque bonus vir atque integer ; sed servo
necesse sum .gradus ; cedo consularis genus prætorius, nec contendo cum prætorius equester locus.*

ALL THE YEARS : 1876.

By this time battle had been joined, by the whole of the fleets simultaneously, on both sides. On the part of the Romans eighty ships were engaged, of which two and twenty were Rhodians. The enemy's fleet consisted of eighty-nine ships ; they had also some of the largest size, three with six banks of oars, and two with seven. In the strength of their vessels, and the valour of their men, the Roman forces were far superior to those of the king: the Rhodian ships were superior in their power of manœuvring, and in the tactics of their captains as well as the skill of the rowers. The greatest cause of terror, however, to the enemy were those ships which bore fire in front of them; and that circumstance, which had alone proved their salvation when surrounded at Panormus, was, on this occasion, the principal cause which led to their victory. For when, through fear of the fire in front, the king's ships had swerved in order that they might not meet prow to prow, they were both themselves unable to strike the enemy with their rams, and of their own accord offered themselves obliquely to his shock. And if any ship had directly encountered the shock, it was overwhelmed with a shower of fire ; and they were more alarmed at the flames than at the fighting.

Jam totus simul classis ab omnis pars pugna consero. Ab Romanus octoginta navis pugno, ex qui Rhodius duo et viginti sum. Hostis classis undenonaginta navis sum et maximus forma navis tres hexeris habeo, duo hepteris. Robur navis et virtus miles Romanus longe regius præsto : Rhodius navis agilitas et ars gubernator et scientia remex. Maximus tamen hostis terror sum, qui ignis præ sui porto ; et, qui unus is ad Panormus circumventus salus sum, is tum maximus momentum ad victoria sum. Nam metus ignis adversus regius navis, ne prora concurro, quum declino, neque ipse ferio rostrum hostis possum, et obliquus sui ipse ad ictus præbeo ; et si quis concurro, obruo infusus ignis, magisque ad incendium, quam ad prælium trepido.

JUNIOR MATRICULATION : 1876.

The following story also is in the Greek history of Silenus, whom Caelius follows: "Hannibal, when he had captured Saguntum, seemed in his sleep to be summoned by Jupiter into an assembly of the gods ; and when he was come there, Jupiter commanded him to carry war into Italy ; and one of the assembly was given to him as a guide ; employing whom he began to advance with his army. Then that guide charged him not to look behind. But that he could do no longer ;

and, carried away by curiosity, looked back. Then it seemed that a huge and terrible monster, girt with the coils of serpents, was utterly destroying all the plantations, shrubs and dwellings, wherever he went. And he being amazed, inquired of the god, what that portentous monster might be, and the god answered that it was the desolation of Italy, and charged him to go right on, and not to trouble himself about what was being done behind him, and in his rear."

Hic idem, in Silenus qui Cælius sequor Græcus historia sum. Hannibal quum capio Saguntum videor in somnus a Jupiter in deus concilium voco ; quo quum venio Jupiter impero ut Italia bellum infero, duxque is unus e concilium do ; qui ille utor cum exercitus progredior cæpi ; tum is dux ille præcipio ne respicio ; ille autem is diu facio non possum elatusque cupiditas respicio ; tum videor bellua vastus et immanis circumplicatus serpens quicumque incedo, omnis arbustum, virgultum, tectum perverto ; et is admiror quæro de deus quisnam ille sum talis monstrum ; et deus respondeo vastitas sum Italia, præcipioque ut pergo protinus ; quis retro atque a tergum facio, ne laboro.

ALL THE YEARS: 1877.

When the Spaniards saw the two columns of the Romans in motion on their side of the river, suddenly pouring out from their camp, they advanced to battle at a run, with the intention of falling upon them before that they could unite and take up a position. The struggle was obstinate at the commencement, the Spaniards being flushed with their recent victory and the Roman soldiers infuriated by their unwonted disgrace. In the centre, the two strongest legions sustained the fight with the greatest spirit ; and when the enemy perceived that they could not be dislodged in any other way, he renewed the assault with a column formed like a wedge, and with constantly greater numbers and closer ranks, began to press the centre hard. Thereupon Calpurnius, the praetor, when he saw that his line was in difficulties, hastily despatched T. Quinctilius Varus and L. Juventius Thalna, the lieutenants, to encourage the respective legions, and bade them to remind and warn them that "upon them depended all hope of victory and of preserving Spain. Should they give ground, not a man of this army would ever see, not merely Italy, but even the other bank of the Tagus." He himself with the cavalry of the two legions, having made a slight detour, charged on its flank the column of the enemy which was pressing his centre.

Hispanus, postquam in citerior ripa duo Romanus agmen conspicio, ut priusquam sui jungo atque instruo possum, occupo is castra repente effundo cursus ad pugna tendo. Atrox in principium prœlium sum, et Hispanus recens victoria ferox, et insuetus ignominia miles Romanus accendo. Acriter medius acies, duo fortis legio, dimico, qui quum aliter moveo locus non possum hostis cerno, cuneus insto pugno, et usque plus confertusque medius urgeo. Ibi postquam laboro acies Calpurnius, prœtor, video, T. Quinctilius Varus, et L. Juventius Thulna legatus ad singuli legio adhortor propere mitto. Doceo et moneo jubeo, " in ille spes omnis vinco et retineo Hispania sum. Si ille locus cedo nemo hic exercitus non modo Italia, sed ne Tagus quidem ulterior ripa, unquam video." Ipse, cum eques duo legio paullulum circumveho, in cuneus hostis, qui medius urgeo acies, ab latus incurro.

JUNIOR MATRICULATION : 1877.

Manius Curius, who has business at Patræ, is esteemed by me for many and great reasons : for I both have a friendship of long standing with him, which commenced when first he attended the forum, and at Patræ, both on several occasions previously, and especially on the last, in this most unhappy war, all his house has been open to me, and if there had been need I would have used it as my own. But the greatest bond between us is one, as it were, of a more hallowed kind of friendship, namely, that he is a most intimate friend of our Atticus, and respects and loves him above all other men. Now, if by chance you have already become acquainted with him, I think that I am too late in doing what I now do. For he is a man of such politeness and courtesy that I think he has already been recommended to you on his own account. But still, if this be so, I urgently beg of you that, if you have shown any inclination towards him before this letter of mine, there may afterwards accrue to it as great an accumulation as possible, through my recommendation.

M.' Curius, qui Patrae negotior, multus et magnus de causa a ego diligo. Nam et amicitia pervetus ego cum is sum, ut primum in forum venio, institutus; et Patrae quum aliquoties anteo, tum proxime hic miser bellum domus is totus ego pateo; qui si opus sum, tam utor, quam meus. Magnus autem ego vinculum cum is sum quasi sanctus quidem necessitudo, quod sum Atticus noster familiaris isque unus praeter cæteri observo ac diligo. Qui si tu jam forte cognosco, puto ego hic, qui facio, facio sero. Is sum enim humanitas et observantia, ut is tu jam ipse per sui commendo puto. Qui tamen si ita sum magnopere a tu quæso, ut ad is voluntas, si qui in ille ante hic meus litterae confero, quam magnus postea commendatio cumulus accedo.

6 A

SENIOR MATRICULATION & SUPPLEMENTAL: 1877.

When the quæstor was selling the Africans, on learning
that a well-grown boy among them of remarkable beauty,
was of royal family, he sent him to Scipio. When Scipio
questioned him, "who he was, of what country, and why, at
that age, he had been in the camp?" the boy answered, "that
he was a Numidian, that his countrymen called him Massiva.
Left an orphan by his father he had been brought up in the
house of his maternal grandfather, Gala, king of the Numidians ; he had crossed over to Spain along with his uncle
Masinissa, who had lately come with cavalry to reinforce
the Carthaginians. Restrained on account of his age by
Masinissa he had never before gone into battle. On the day
on which the battle had been fought with the Romans, having
secretly taken a horse and armour without his uncle's knowledge, he had gone out into the lines : there, his horse having
fallen, he had been thrown headlong and captured by the
Romans." Scipio, after giving orders that the Numidian
should be kept in safe custody, despatched the business
which had to be transacted in the tribunal. Afterwards,
when he had retired to the general's tent, having summoned
the boy, he asks him whether he would wish to return to
Masinissa. When, shedding tears of joy, he said "he would
indeed ;" then he presented the boy with a gold ring, a tunic
with a broad stripe, together with a Spanish cloak and a gold
buckle, also a horse richly caparisoned ; and, having ordered
cavalry to escort him as far as he wished, dismissed him.

*Quum Afer vendo quæstor puer adultus inter is forma insignis
quum audio regius genus sum ad Scipio mitto. Qui quum
percunctor Scipio, quis et cujas et cur id ætas in castra sum.
Numida sum aio, Massiva popularis roco. Orbus a pater
relinquo apud maternus avus Gala rex Numida educo cum
avunculus Masinissa qui nuper cum equitatus subsidium
Carthaginiensis venio in Hispania trajicio. Prohibeo propter
ætas a Masinissa nunquam ante prælium ineo. Is dies qui
pugno cum Romanus inscius avunculus clam arma equusque
sumo in acies exeo : ibi prolabor equus effundo in præceps capio
ab Romanus. Scipio quum asservo Numida jubeo qui pro
tribunalis ago perago. Inde quum sui in prætorium recipio
roco is interrogo volone ad Masinissa revertor. Quum effundo
gaudium lacrima cupio vero dico : tum puer annulus aureus
tunica latus clarus, cum Hispanus sagulum et aureus fibula
equusque ornatus dono jubeoque prosequor quoad volo eques
dimitto.*

JUNIOR MATRICULATION; 1878.

When Cneius Lentulus, a military tribune, riding by saw the consul sitting on a stone covered with blood, he said : " Do you, Lucius Æmilius—whom alone guiltless of blame for to-day's disaster, the gods ought to regard—take this horse while you have some strength left, and I, as your companion, can support and protect you. Do not shroud this battle in gloom by the death of a consul. Even without this we have enough of tears and mourning." To this the consul replied : " Blessings on your manhood! Cneius Cornelius, but take care that you do not waste in useless compassion the scanty time for escaping from the hands of the enemy. Go ! Carry word, on the public behalf—to the senate, that they fortify the city of Rome before the arrival of the victorious foe ; and—on my private behalf—to Quintus Fabius, that Æmilius has both lived up to this day and dies mindful of his precepts. As for me, suffer me to expire amid the carnage of my soldiers, lest I should either be again impeached after my consulship, or stand forth as the accuser of my colleague in order to protect my own innocence by the accusation of another." While they were debating this, first a crowd of flying citizens, and then the enemy came upon them. The consul they overwhelmed with missiles, not knowing who he was. Lentulus his horse carried off in the confusion. Then only the Romans flee indiscriminately.

Cn. Lentulus, tribunus miles, cum praeterveho equus sedeo in saxum cruor oppleo consul rideo. " L. Æmilius," inquam, "qui unus, insons culpa clades hodiernus deus respicio debeo, capio hic equus, dum et tu eis aliquis supersum et comes ego tu tollo possum ac protego. Ne funestus hic pugna mors consul facio : etiam sine hic lacrima satis luctusque sum." Ad is consul : " Tu quidem, Cn. Cornelius, mactus virtus sum ; sed caveo frustra misereor exiguus tempus e manus hostis evado absumo. Abeo, nuntio publice pater, urbs Romanus munio ac priusquam hostis victor advenio praesidium firmo ; privatim Q. Fabius Æmilius praeceptum is memor et vivo adhuc et morior. Egomet in hic strages miles meus patior expiro, ne aut reus iterum e consulatus sum, aut accusator collega existo, ut alienus crimen innocentia meus protego." Hic ego prius turba fugio civis, deinde hostis opprimo : consul, ignoro quis sum, obruo telum ; Lentulus inter tumultus abripio equus. Tum demum effuse fugio.

SENIOR MATRICULATION & SUPPLEMENTAL : 1878.

Having prayed thus, he ordered his lictors to go to **Titus
Manlius** and give timely warning to his colleague that he had
devoted himself on behalf of the army. He himself, girded
with the Cinctus Gabinus, fully armed, mounted his horse
and plunged into the midst of the enemy ; a mark for the
gaze of either host, far more majestic in appearance than a
man, sent, as it were, from heaven as a propitiation of all the
the wrath of the gods, to avert destruction from his countrymen and to carry it against their enemies. Thus all terror
and panic borne along with him, threw them into confusion.
first the van of the Latins, and then penetrated the heart of
their host. This was very manifest, that wherever he charged.
there the enemy, as if smitten by a baleful star, were seized
with panic : but, indeed, when he fell overwhelmed with
darts, immediately from that spot the cohorts of the Latins.
unmistakeably dismayed, spread flight and havoc far and
wide. At the same time the Romans, their minds relieved
from religious fears, rushing on together, as if then for the
first time the signal had been given, began the battle afresh.

*Hic ita precor lictor eo ad T. Manlius jubeo, matureque col-
lega sui devoveo pro exercitus nuntio. Ipse incingo Cinctus
Gabinus armo in equus insilio, ac sui in medius hostis immitto ;
conspicio ab uterque acies aliquanto augustus humanus risus
sicut coelum mitto piaculum omnis deus ira, qui pestis ab suus
averto in hostis fero : ita omnis terror parorque cum ille fero
signum primo Latini turbo, deinde in totus penitus acies per-
vado. Evidens is sum, quod quicumque equus inveho, ibi haud
secus quam pestifer sidus ictus paveo : ubi vero corruo obruo
telum, inde jam haud dubie consterno cohors Latini fuga ac
vastitas late facio. Simul et Romani exsolvo religio animus.
relut tum primum signum do coorior, pugna integer edo.*

ALL THE YEARS : 1878.

Marcus Regulus, when he had broken the maritime strength
of the Carthaginians, at length, through an adverse change of
fortune, fell into the enemies' hands. Sent as an ambassador
to Rome, in reference to an exchange of prisoners, an oath
having been given him that if he should not effect it he would
return to Africa, he advised against the proposition in the
senate. Then, having returned to Carthage, he was tortured
with the most cruel punishments. For, his eyelids having
been cut off, he was kept for some time in a dark place ; then.
being suddenly brought out when the sun was most ardent,
he was forced to gaze on the sky. At last he was cast into a

chest bristling with spikes turned inwards, and so narrow
that he was forced to remain constantly upright; and, whilst
his wearied body, wherever it might lean, was pierced with
iron points, he was killed by torture and want of sleep.

Marcus Regulus, quum maritimus Poenus ris frango, tandem
adversus fortuna mutatio in hostis manus venio. Legatus de
permuto captivus Roma mitto, do jusjurandum ut si non im-
petro, in Africa redeo, in senatus conditio dissuadeo. Tum
ille Carthago revertor, atrox supplicium vexo. Palpebra enim
reseco aliquando in locus tenebricosus habeo; deinde quum sol
sum ardens repente educo, intueor coelum cogo. Postremo con-
jicio in area clavus introrsus verto horrens atque ita angustus
ut erectus perpetuo maneo cogo, dumque fessus corpus quocum-
que inclino ferreus stimulus confodio, cruciatus et rigilia (pl.)
interimo.

JUNIOR MATRICULATION: 1879.

As soon as they are come on Roman soil, the consuls advance to meet the enemy. Valerius leads on the infantry in
battle array; Brutus moved in advance with the cavalry to
reconnoitre. In like manner the cavalry of the enemy led
the van: Aruns Tarquinius, the king's son, commanded;
the king in person followed with the legions. Aruns, when
he at a distance recognized that it was a consul by the lictors,
soon after nearer and more certain from his face, that it was
also Brutus, overcome with rage, cried out, "That is the
man who drove us exiles from our own country. See, the
fellow rides in pomp himself, decked out in our robes. Ye
gods, avengers of kings, help me." He puts spurs to his
horse and madly charges upon the consul himself. Brutus
perceived that the attack was made on him. It was honourable in those days for the commanders to engage in person;
he accordingly eagerly presents himself for the combat. And
so with infuriated feelings they met, neither, so long as he
might wound his enemy, mindful of guarding his own body,
so that, each one pierced by his adversary's blow through
the buckler, sticking fast to the two spears, they fell dead
from their horses.

Postquam in ager Romanus venio, obviam hostis consul eo.
Valerius quadratus agmen pedes duco; Brutus ad exploro cum
equitatus antecedo. Idem modus primus eques hostis agmen
sum; praesum Aruns Tarquinius, filius rex; rex ipse cum legio
sequor. Aruns, ubi ex lictor procul consul sum, deinde jam
prope ac certe facies quoque Brutus, cognosco, inflammo ira,
"Ille sum vir," inquam, "qui ego extorris expello patria.
Ipse, en ille, noster decoro insigne, magnifice incedo. Deus, rex
ultor, adsum." Concito calcar equus, atque in ipse infestus

consul dirigo. Sentio in sui eo Brutus. Decorus sum tum ipse capesso pugna dux; avide itaque sui certamen offero. Adeoque infestus animus concurro, neuter, dum hostis vulnero, suus protego corpus memor, ut contrarius ictus per parma uterque transfigo, duo hæreo hasta moribundus ex equus labor.'

SENIOR MATRICULATION & SUPPLEMENTAL : 1879.

Next day Vercingetorix, having assembled a council, represents to them that he had undertaken this war not because of his own interests, but for the sake of the general liberty, and that, as they must yield to fortune, he offers himself to them for either fate, whether they prefer to appease the Romans by his death, or to deliver him up alive. Envoys are despatched to Cæsar to treat concerning these points. He insists that their arms be surrendered and their chiefs delivered up. He himself took his seat before the camp, and the chiefs are brought out thither, Vercingetorix is delivered up, and their arms are thrown away. Reserving the Ædni and the Averni, of the rest of the prisoners, he distributed throughout the whole of the army one apiece.

Posterus dies Vercingetorix, concilium convoco, is sui bellum suscipio non suus necessitas sed communis libertas causa demonstro, et, quoniam sum fortuna cedo, ad uterque res sui ille offero, seu mors suus Romanus satisfacio, seu vivus transdo volo. Mitto de hic res ad Cæsar legatus. Jubeo arma transdo, et princeps produco. Ipse pro castrum consido, et eo dux produco. Vercingetorix dedo, et arma projicio. Reservo Æduus atque Avernus, ex reliquus captivus totus exercitus caput singuli distribuo.

ALL THE YEARS : 1879.

But on the following day, when those who were older had sufficiently rested, he told me that then Scaevola, having taken two or three turns, said : " Why do we not, Crassus, imitate Socrates in the Phædrus of Plato ? For this plane-tree of yours has put me in mind of it, which with its wide-spread boughs shades this spot no less than that whose covert Socrates sought, and which seems to me to have grown not so much from the rivulet which is described as from the language of Plato ; and what he with the hardest of feet did, namely throw himself on the grass, is certainly with more justice to be allowed to my feet."

Posterus autem dies cum ille magnus natus satis quiesco, dico tum, Scaevola, duo spatium tresve facio, dico : " Cur non imitor,

Crassus, Socrates ille qui sum in Phædrus Plato? Nam ego hic tuus platanus admoneo, qui non minus opaco hic locus patuus ramus quam ille qui umbra sequor Socrates, qui ego video non tam ipse aquula qui describo quum Pluto oratio cresco; et qui ille durus pes facio, ut sui abjicio in herba, is meus pes certe concedo sum æquus.

ALL THE YEARS: 1880.

When Sylla had arrived from Asia, he retained Pomponius with him as long as he remained there, charmed at once with the good breeding and the erudition of the young man. For he spoke Greek so well that he seemed a native of Athens, while at the same time he displayed such grace of Latin style that it seemed to possess a certain charm, native and not acquired. Whence it came that Sylla never was willing to dismiss him, but desired to take him along. When he tried to dissuade him. "Do not. I pray you," said Pomponius, "desire to lead me against those in whose company I quitted Italy, in order that I might not bear arms against you."

Ex Asia Sylla decedo cum venio, quamdiu ibi sum cum sui habeo Pomponius, capio adolescens et humanitas et doctrina. Sic enim Græce loquor ut Athenæ nascor video, tantus autem suavitas sum sermo Latinus ut appareo in is nativus quidam lepor sum, non ascisco. Qui res facio ut Sylla nusquam is ab sui dimitto, cupioque cum sui deduco. Qui cum persuadeo tento. "Nolo, oro tu," inquam Pomponius, "adversum is ego volo duco, cum qui re contra tu arma fero Italia relinquo."

JUNIOR MATRICULATION : 1880.

Cæsar, having sent messengers to the state of the Ædui to shew them that those had been preserved by his kindness whom he would have been able to put to death by right of war, and having given three hours of the night to the army to rest, moved his camp towards Gergovia. Almost in the middle of the march, horsemen, sent by Fabius, explain in how much danger the matter was ; they point out that the camp had been attacked by very great forces, since fresh men were frequently taking the place of those who had been wearied out and wore tiring out our men by constant toil, of whom on account of the size of the camp, the same men had to run to continually on the rampart ; that many had been wounded by the great number of arrows, and of every kind of weapons ; that the engines had been of great use for withstanding these difficulties ; that Fabius, at their departure, having abandoned two gates, was blocking up the rest, and was adding breastworks to the rampart, and preparing himself for a similar fortune for the following day. Having learned these things, Cæsar, with very great zeal on the part of the soldiers, arrived at the camp before sunrise.

Cæsar, nuncius ad civitas Ædui mitto, qui suus beneficium conservo doceo, qui jus bellum interficio possum, tresque hora nox exercitus ad quies do, castra ad Gergovia moveo. Medius fere iter eques a Fabius mitto, quantus res in periculum sum, expono: "Superus copia castra oppugno," demonstro: "quum crebro integer defetiscor succedo, nosterque assiduus labor defatigo, qui, propter magnitudo castra, perpetuo idem in vallum permaneo; multitudo sagitta atque omnis genus telum multus vulnero; ad hic sustineo magnus usus sum tormentum: Fabius, discessus is, duo relinquo porta, obstruo cæteri, plutensque vallum addo, et sui in posterus dies similis ad casus paro." Is res cognosco, Cæsar superus studium miles, ante ortus sol in castra pervenio.

SENIOR MATRICULATION & SUPPLEMENTAL: 1880.

The whole nation of the Gauls is very much given up to superstitions, and, for this reason, those who are engaged in battles and dangers, either sacrifice human beings as victims, or vow that they will sacrifice them; and they use the Druids as ministers for these sacrifices; because they think that the divine wrath of the immortal gods cannot be appeased otherwise unless human life is given for human life; and they have sacrifices of the same kind publicly established. Others have images of immense size, whose limbs woven with osiers they fill with living men: and when these are set on fire, the men, surrounded by the flame, are killed. They think that the punishment of those who are caught in theft, or robbery, or any crime, is more acceptable to the immortal gods; but when a supply of that sort is wanting, they have recourse even to sacrifices of innocent people.

Natio sum omnis Gallus admodum dedo religio, atque ob is causa, qui sum affectus gravis morbus, quique in prælium periculamque versor, aut pro victima homo immolo, aut sui immolo voveo, administerque ad is sacrificium Druides utor: quod, pro ritu homo nisi vita homo reddo, non possum aliter deus immortalis numen placo arbitror: publicque idem genus habeo instituo sacrificium. Alius immanis magnitudo simulacrum habeo, qui contexo vimen membrum virus homo compleo, qui succendo, circumvenio flamma examino homo. Supplicium is, qui in furtum, aut in latrocinium, aut aliqui noxa comprehendo, gratus deus immortalis sum arbitror; sed quum is genus copia deficio, etiam ad innocens supplicium descendo.

PART III.

PAPERS IN LATIN GRAMMAR.

I.

FIRST AND SECOND DECLENSIONS.

1. Give rules for the genders of the first and second declensions.

2. What are the principal exceptions to the rules for genders in the first and second declensions?

3. Decline the following words: *Ala, servus, mensa, arvum, ager, gener, aper, consilium, Tenedos, Penelope, Androgeos, Aeneas, Anchises.*

3. What old forms for the genitive singular of the first declension?

5. What nouns in the first and second declensions have the genitive plural in *-um?*

6. What is the form of the locative in the first declension? what in the second?

7. Decline the following words: *Dea, filius, filia, Pompeius, talentum, pelagus, deus, Panthus, genius, socer, equa,* and *epitome.*

5. What peculiarities in the gender of the following: *Humus, vulgus, Hadria, vannus, papyrus, pelagus, talpa,* and *carbasus?*

9. What is meant by a stem? what by a root?

II.

THIRD DECLENSION.

1. Give rules for the gender of the third declension.

2. Decline: *Trabs, sus, nubes, stirps, lex, nex, suppellex, Apollo, sitis, bos, nix, senex, vis, mare, caro, flos, corpus, opus,* and *caput.*

3. What classes of nouns have the genitive in *-ium?*

1 *

4. What words have acc. sing. always in *-im?* What words have acc. sing. in *-im* or *-em?* What other irregularity in the declension of such words?

5. Give gender and genitive of the following words: *Vas,* (surety), *cos, fons, leo, virgo, tussis, trames, cor, cinis, senex, frons* (leaf), *frons* (forehead), *radix, fax, tellus, arbor, aequor, os* (mouth), *os* (bone), *Quiris, aes, heres, obses, latus, pectus, Dido, praedo, seges, as, thorax, dens, nectar,* and *jecur.*

6. Decline: *Orpheus, Pericles, Paris, Dido, lampas, Phryx, heros,* and *Jupiter.*

7. Give abl. sing. and plural of the following words: *Ars, homo, vulnus, sedes, exul, mulier, finis, ordo, comes, virtus, scelus, animal, eques, miles, laus, sors, consul,* and *clavis.*

III.

FOURTH AND FIFTH DECLENSIONS, AND REVIEW.

1. Give rules for the genders of the fourth and fifth declensions, with the chief exceptions.

2. Decline: *Manus, cornu, res, dies,* and *spes.*

3. Indicate the gender of the following words: *Dies, res, fluctus, acus, colus, secus, tribus, specus, meridies.*

4. What irregularity in the declension of: *Arcus, domus,* and *ficus?*

5. Decline the following words: *Respublica, jusjurandum,* and *paterfamilias.*

6. What nouns are (1) heteroclitic, (2) heterogeneous, (3) wanting in the plural, (4) wanting in the singular, (5) of different meaning in the singular and plural, and (6) defective in case?

7. Mention any peculiarities with reference to the foregoing question that the following may have: *Domus, aedes, opis, aurum, arma, fas, littera, epos, moenia, ver, castrum, dapis, specimen, secus, auxilium, frugis, mos, posteri, hortus, coelum, fasti, laurus, gratia, vesper, frenum, jocus, fides, locus, rastrum, materies, epulum, opera, ficus, gratia, juventus, ancile,* and *vas* (vessel).

8. Decline: *Jugerum, vas* (vessel), *ancile, coelum, carbasus, ostrea, senatus, Saturnalia, frenum, locus, pelagus, rostrum, margarita, clipeus.*

IV.

ON THE ADJECTIVE.

1. Decline: *Parvus, tener, niger, celer, felix, audax, audacior, prudens, arans, vetus, memor, alter, alius,* and *solus.*
2. What adjectives have the genitive singular in *-ius?*
3. What irregularities in the following adjectives: *Frugi, cetera, pauci,* and *hilaris?*
4. Give the rules, with exceptions, for forming comparatives and superlatives of adjectives.
5. Write out the comparative and superlative of the folowing : *similis, ingens, pauper, alacer, dives, superus-magnus, acer, imbecillus, mirificus, bonus, frugi, bene, volus, posterus, similis, inferus, multus, adolescens, magnus,* and *senex.*
6. What adjectives have two forms for the superlative, and what is the difference in meaning between these forms ?
7. What adjectives are (1) without comparatives, (2) without superlatives, and (3) without terminational comparison ?
8. How are adverbs formed from adjectives ?
9. What adverbs are used with the positive to express the comparative and superlative ?
10. Compare : *Meritus, diversus, mortalis, capitalis, invitus, vetus, albus, propinquus, caecus, paternus, juvenis, noxius, lassus.*

V.

GENERAL EXERCISE.

1. Correct (when necessary): *Pelagus magnus ; quercus altus ; lauri celsi ; opus difficilis ; acus acer ; domus lauta ; idus proximus ; acies instructa ; eques celeres ; mons infimus ; arbor densus ; aequor ventosus ; fagus patulus ; humus uvidus ; vulnus gravis ; papaver mollis ; mulier prudens ; mare tumultuosum ; princeps magnanima ; urbs celsus.*
2. Decline in combination : *Caesar, dux victor ; miles fortis Valerius ; eques acer Gallus ; Ariovistus princeps Germanus ; legio invicta ; animal ferox leo ; lupus celer.*

3. Explain the form of the following words : *Duum virum ; nummum decem millia ; profectus socium, magnanimum generator equorum ; deum magnorum dux ; Dardanidum rex ; triumvirum unus.*

4. Decline in combination : *Vas sincerum ; locus amoenus ; domus celsa ; deus magnus ; auriga ignavus ; coelum altum ; eques acer ; quercus ferax ; dies felix ; res angusta ; acies adversa ; spes alta.*

5. Give nominative plural (if any) of : *Veteri ; arcubus, impuberis ; nullius ; desidis ; dono ; fraude ; remige ; equabus ; ditis ; iduum ; pari ; viribus ; suppellectilem ; frenos ; coelos ; opera ; furem ; nomine ; edaci ; nequam ; nigris ; quercubus ; jugerum ; vas* (surety); *vas* (vessel); *deabus ; muribus ; kalendis ; genu ; dierum ; hortus ;* and *equitatus.*

VI.

ON THE NUMERALS.

1. Write out the first twenty numerals, (1) ordinal, (2) cardinal, and (3) distributive.

2. Express in Latin : Eighteen ships ; ninety-nine boys ; fifty-five horses ; two hundred and seventy men.

3. What cardinal numerals are declined ?

4. Decline : *Unus, duo, ambo, tres, mille.*

5. When is *mille* an adjective and when a noun ? Translate into Latin : a thousand men ; ten thousand horses.

6. Give some rule for the order in which Latin numerals in combination stand and illustrate from the following numbers : 653, 235, 19, 48, 2374, 561.

7. When are distributive numerals used ? Distinguish : *Binae litterae* and *duae litterae ; duo scyphi* and *bini scyphi ; decem denarios dedit,* and *denos denarios dedit.*

8. Explain the origin of I., V., X., L., M., C., D.

9. Express the following by symbols or words : 2,357 ; 35,000 ; 2,000,000 ; 1,500 ; 90.

10. Distinguish : *Bis et vicies,* and *bis vicies.*

11. Decline : *Unus consul ; duo praemia ; binae coronae ; singulae uxores.*

VII.

ON THE PRONOUNS.

1. Decline in full: *Ego, tu, sui, hic, ille, is, idem, quis,* and *qui.*
2. Distinguish in use, *is, ille, iste, ipse,* and *hic.*
3. Decline in combination : *Quis artifex callidus ; eadem respublica incolumis ; quid jusjurandum ; ille semivir ; unusquisque homo ineptus.*
4. Decline : *Quisquis, alteruter, neuter, meus,* and *ecquis.*
5. What pronouns have double forms ?
6. Explain with what pronouns the following endings are found : *-pte, -met, -ce, -pse, -pte, -met, -ce,* and *-pse.*
7. Explain the forms: *Eccum, eccos. eccam, ellam, ollus, illuc, quā, quis, quoi, quicum.*
8. Decline in combination : *Ego uxor infelix ; neuter paterfamilias diligens : tu lepida soror ; plerique equites acerrimi ; quaedam mulier formosa.*
9. To what forms is *-cum* appended ?

VIII.

ON THE VERB.

1. What are (1) the principal tenses of a verb, (2) what the historical ?
2. How many conjugations in Latin ? How do you distinguish them ?
3. Conjugate fully : *Sum, amo, moneo, rego,* and *audio.*
4. Parse the following parts: *Amare, ameris, amaris, amere, amaverunt, amatur, amator, amavit, amatu, amatus, monere, monearis, monentor, monentur, monitus, monuerunt, monebere, monitus ero, monueris, regere, regēris, regēris, regaris, rectus, regens, regent, regunt, regat, regit, reget, rexeris, audiris, audieris, audiaris, audiantor,* and *audito.*
5. What different parts may the following be : *Fueris, es, amare, monere, regere,* and *audire ?*
6. Conjugate *capio,* and parse *capere, capiare, capiēre, capito, capto, capi, ceperitis, captum iri,* and *cepi.*
7. What is a deponent verb, and into what classes are they usually divided ?

8. Conjugate : *Hortor, vereor, sequor, blandior,* and *patior.*
9. Parse : *Hortator, hortabĕre, hortatu, hortatus, pati, patiĕris, patĕris, sequaris, blandiĕris, blandīris,* and *blandiar.*

IX.

ON THE VERB.

(Continued.)

1. What is meant by the term PERIPHRASTIC conjugation? How many are there?
2. Conjugate (by periphrastic conjugation) : *Amo, moneo, rego,* and *audio.*
3. Explain the forms : *Amasti, amaram, amasse, nesti, nerunt, audisti, audissem, nosti, audieram, scripsti,* and *dixe.*
4. What two endings for pf. indic. act. 3rd pl. ; for the 2nd pers. sing. of pres. impf. and fut. pass. in indic. ; or 2nd pers. sing. of pres. and impf. subj. pass. ?
5. What four verbs have irregular imperative 2nd sing. act. ?
6. Explain the forms: *Scibam, servibo, edam, duim, faxo, faxim, ausim, levasso, prohibesso, capso, axo, jusso, occisit, taxis, amarier, regier, viderier.*
7. What is meant by a present, a perfect, and a supine stem?
8. What different ways of forming a perfect stem, and give examples of each class?
9. What are the pres. pf. and supine stems of *carpo, sto, ago. doceo, viso, curro, do, spondeo, rego, audio,* and *moneo?*

X.

ON THE VERB.

(Continued.)

1. Conjugate the following : *veto, sto, lavo, cubo, do, tono, plico, juvo, censeo, miscceo, haereo, suadeo, teneo, jubeo, maneo, mordeo, caveo, sedeo, video,* and *liqueo.*
2. What verbs of the 1st conjugation form the perfect by reduplication? what verbs of the 2nd conjugation?

3. What are semi-deponent verbs? Give a list of them. *

4. Conjugate *duco, cedo, quatio, premo, mitto, flecto, evado, vivo, uro, gero, demo, traho, figo, cano, tango, tollo, vendo, cado, caedo, fallo, pello, pendo, emo, facio, frango, fugio, jacio, lego, edo, prehendo, verto, pando, defendo, accendo, volvo, alo, sero, rapio, meto* and *necto*.

5. What compounds of *sto* are of the first conjugation? what of the third? what compounds of *sto* have perfect in *-steti?* what in *-stiti?*

6. What compounds of *facio* have *ficio?* what, *facio*, ?

7. Distinguish: *Vēnit, vēnit; lēgit, lēgit; sēvi, sērui; cecīdit, cecĭdit; ēmit, ēmit; fūgit, fūgit; vīsit, vĭdit..*

8. What compounds of *lego* have *lēgi?* what *lexi* in the perfect?

XI.

ON THE VERB.

(*Continued.*)

1. Conjugate: *Pasco, sterno, inveterasco, sero, cerno, cresco, quiesco, suesco, sperno, cupio, lino, sapio,* and *revivesco*.

2. To what verbs may the following be referred: *cretum; crevi; victum; scivi; tentum; sustuli,* and *oblitus?*

3. Conjugate: *Amplector, apiscor, fatiscor, fruor, fungor, gradior, irascor, labor, loquor, morior, nanciscor, nascor, nitor, obliviscor, paciscor, pascor, proficiscor, queror, sequor, tueor, ulciscor, fido, aperio, amicio, salio, fulcio, vincio, sentio, reperio, ordior, orior, opperior, experior, sortior, assentior, potior,* and *molior*.

4. What are the two irregular compounds of *sum* and give rules for their conjugation?

5. Conjugate the pres., perf., and fut. of indic. and the pres. and impf. of subj., of *possum* and *prosum*.

6. What parts are the foll.:—*Potuerit, possint, possunt, possent, prosit, prosunt, profuerit?*

7. Give a rule for the correspondence of the parts of *edo* with those of *sum*. Distinguish *ĕs, ēs; ĕdit, ēdit; ĕdis, ēdis; cŏlo, cōlo; dīco, dico;* and *praedīco, praedico*.

XII.

GENERAL EXERCISE.

1. Give the genitive case and gender of: *caro, obses, jecur, fel, auceps, anceps, pollis, salix, suppellex, phalanx, heros, later* and *apex.*

2. State any peculiarity in gender, declension, or both, in *laurus, tellus, ordo, arcus, materies, Tartarus, spes, justitia, vas* (a vessel), *juventus, locus, jussu, respublica, filia, Mercurius, jugerum* and *Bacchanalia.*

3. Give the leading irregularities in the comparison of adjectives.

4. Mention the exceptions to the rule that neuters in *e, al,* and *ar,* have their ablative singular in -*i.*

5. Give the imperative mood of *patior, profiteor* and *facio,* in full; also the perfect tense and supine of *adimo, cieo, gigno, pario* and *fulcio.*

6. Decline in combination: *Remex alacer ; brevis epitome ; locuples' Dido.*

7. What difference in meaning attends difference in quantity in: *Refert, educat, sedes, fide, fere, modo, velis, rado, finis, amare, flave, flore, novi,* and *vere ?*

8. What classes of words in third declension have the genitive plural in -*ium ?*

9. What words in fourth declension have the dat. and abl. plural in -*ubus ?*

XIII.

ON THE VERB.

(Continued.)

1. Write out fully the pres. pf. and future tenses of indic., and the pres. and impf. subj. of *fero, feror, nolo, malo, volo,* and *fio.*

2. What is the derivation of *possum, nolo,* and *malo ?*

3. Parse the following : *fer, ferre, ferto, ferat, fertor, fertur, ferreris, nolit, nollet, malet, mallet, malam, nonvis, nolebatis, fi, fieris, tulere, nolito, malis, poterit, potuerit, posset, fiunt, fiant, fiemus,* and *fite.*

4. Compound *fero* with *ab, ad, con, dis, ex, in, ob, sub,* conjugating the verbs in their principal parts.

5. Conjugate *eo* in the pres., fut., and pf. indic., and the pres. and impf. subjunctive.
6. Parse : *Eundus, eunt, eant, euntes, ibit, iisti, ito, itur, itum,* and *iri.*
7. What is the active form of : *veneo, fio,* and *vapulo.*
8. Parse *abstuli, attuli, collatum, distulerint, sustuleritis, obtulisset,* and *collaturus.*

XIV.

ON THE VERB.

(Continued.)

1. Conjugate in the pf. indic. act. and the pf. subjunctive : *Coepi, odi,* and *memini.*
2. Write out the parts in use of : *Aio, inquam, fari, ave, salve, cĕdo,* and *apage.*
3. Parse : *Fatur, inquit, aiunt, foret, quaeso, defiat, coeptus sum, oderis, fare,* and *infit.*
4. Give a list of the chief impersonal verbs in Latin ?
5. What verbs can be used only impersonally in the passive ?
6. Correct any mistake in the following : *Credor, tu scribendus es, luditur mihi.*
7. Parse the following : *Cretum, stravit, moriturus, oblitus, nexui, genuerunt, altum, surrexit, volutus, victum, scissum, tenturus, concĭdit, concīdit, fregerant, pēgi, concussit, aspexerat,* and *visum.*
8. Conjugate : *Lavo, abdo, laedo, sisto, attollo, verto, fodio, jacio, ĕdo, ēdo, scindo, pendeo, pendo, cupio, meto, rapio, salio, ulciscor, expergiscor, loquor, reperio,* and *assentior.*

XV.

ON THE PARTICLES.

1. Give the different methods of forming the comparative and superlative of adverbs.
2. Compare the following adverbs : *bene, nove, prudenter, male, nuper, diu, saepe, egregie, satius, magnopere, parum,* and *multum.*

3. What adverbs have no forms of comparison?
4. What are the inseparable prepositions?
5. What prepositions govern the ablative?
6. What prepositions govern the acc. or abl.? Give a general rule for the use of such prepositions.
7. Explain the force of the prefix in: *ambieo, reddo, divello, vecors,* and *insanus.*
8. Decline in combination : *provida filia familias.*
9. What nouns are of irregular gender in the first, second, third, fourth, and fifth declensions?
10. Write out the pres. indic. and pf. subjunctive, active and passive, of *sterno.*

XVI.

ON THE FORMATION OF WORDS.

1. What are the endings of diminutives? What is the rule for the gender of diminutives?
2. What are patronymic nouns, and shew how they are formed?
3. What endings designate *place?*
4. What are the endings of abstract nouns formed from adjectives?
5. What are the endings of verbal nouns?
6. What endings of adjectives express (1) fulness, (2) material, and (3) characteristic?
7. Explain the force of the endings in the following: *docilis, longulus, forensis, ·Cannensis, maritimus, faginus, animosus, amator, amor, stabulum, ovile, quercetum, ocellus, Tantalides, filiola, Neptunine, servitium, senatus, aureus, loquax, verecundus, Fidenas,* and *urbanus.*
8. Into what classes are derivative verbs divided? Explain the force of the endings in the following : *gelasco, cantillo, esurio, canto, duresco.*
9. How are adverbs formed from adjectives?
10. Compound : *capio, eo, fero, ago,* with *ad, ante, e, in, sub,* and *re.*

XVII.
GENERAL EXERCISE.

1. Correct, if necessary, any mistakes in the following adverbial forms: *Nuperius, satissime, faciliter, grave, potissime, summiter, dulciter, benevolenter, caro, quindecime, noviper,* and *magnificenter.*
2. Compare : *Mirifice, velociter, dulce,* and *sero.*
3. Form substantives from the following : *Gigno, adolesco, foveo, ferveo, traho, veho, fundo, queror,* and *verto.*
4. What is meant by *nomina gentilicia ?*
5. What are the four classes of verbs derived from verbs?
6. Give rules for the formation of comparatives and superlatives of adverbs and adjectives.
7. Decline in combination : *Ille vir Atheniensis ; hic infelix nauta ; iste Atlas ; ego civis Romanus.*
8. Distinguish : *Pŏpulus, pōpulus ; rĕfert, rēfert ; cŏma, cōma ; ĭdem, īdem ; manŭs, manūs ; rĕgis, rēgis ; dŭcis, dūcis ; sĕdes, sēdes ; mānes, mănes ; pălus, pālus ; mălus, mālus ; procĕrum, procērum ; plăga, plāga ; sĕcuris, sēcuris* (deriving each) ; *irrĭta, irrīta ; mănet, mānet ; oblĭtus, oblītus ; artĭs, artīs ; cănet, cānet.*

XVIII.
GENERAL EXERCISE.

1. Decline throughout *quisquam, quisquis,* and *alius.*
2. Decline and give gender of : *Miles, hostis, agmen, collis, castrum, locus, spes, salus, corpus, cadaver, flumen, iter, ver, nox, dies, caro, dos, palus, vis, vir,* and *mos.*
3. What are the other degrees of comparison of the following : *Extremus, proximus, prope, latissimus, pessimus, facilior, creber, arduus, dives, frugalior, nequissimus, benevolus, posterior, egenus,* and *inferior.*
4. Write out imperative mood active and passive of : *Fero, capio, facio, vendo,* and *ferio.*
5. Write out perfect indicative, active and passive (when used) of. *Sterno, cumbo, scindo, tero, jubeo, gradior, mitto, cado, caedo, cedo, frango, emo, veho, oblino, figo,* and *fingo.*
6. Mention (1) nouns used only in the plural ; (2) nouns which change their meaning in the plural.
7. Decline fully : *Domus, mare, vas* (a vessel), *saturnalia, alter,* and *senex.*

XIX.

GENERAL EXERCISE.

1. Write down the dative singular of : *Cinis, hepar, ebur, mus, merx, obses, pecus,* and *unus;* and the genitive plural of : *aper, artus, canis, carcer, crus, deus, iter, mons, os* (bone), *os* (mouth), *vigil, virgo* and *vis.*

2. Give the pres. infinitive, perfect indicative, and the present imperative of : *Nolo, eo, fero, fio, caedo, occido, cado, quaero, obliviscor,* and *comminiscor.*

3. Explain the meaning of *duae litterae* and *binae litterae.*

4. Give the supines of the following : *Aduro, deleo, fulcio, gigno, haurio, injicio, juvo, lino, necto, meto, offero, quatio, rumpo, saepio, sero, voveo,* and *veto.*

5. Distinguish : *quis, uter, uterque, utervis, quisque, quisquam, quisquis, unusquisque.*

6. Give the supines of: *curro, decurro, cano, recurro, pello, compello, cado, recido, recido, fugio, veneo, venio, vello, vivo, vincio ;* and the perfects of : *nascor, nanciscor, mentior, metior, paciscor.*

XX.

GENERAL EXERCISE.

1. Decline : *Chlamys, thorax, lis, cometes, crater,* and *pecten.*

/ 2. Point out any peculiarities in the inflection of the following : *species, instar, moenia, jocus, bos, pelagus, senatus, vicis, jecur, plebs, pecus, dea, portus, idus, nefas* and *domus.*

✓ 3. Decline in combination : *Uterque prudens senex ; civis quidam Capenas.*

✓ 4. Give the perfect tense and supine of : *Sarcio, differo, ferio, torreo, redimo, condio, resisto, condo, comprimo, poto, mico, lavo, fluo, caedo, fundo, faveo, sono, cedo, sero, lino, necto, tero,* and *suffero.*

5. Distinguish between : *rĕgis, rēgis ; lĕgis, lēgis ; sĕdes, sēdes ; ambĭtum, ambītum ; dŭcis, dūces ; fĭdes, fīdes, mălus, mālus ; sŏlum, sōlum ; nē, nĕ ; modŏ, modō ; Ăsia, Āsia ; decĭdo, decīdo.*

6. Explain the forms *nutribam, scibo, edim, perduim.*

7. What is the third person singular, in all the tenses and moods, of *queo, fio, aio, inquam?*

✓ 8. Explain the composition of the following: *parsimonia, velum, acriter, superstitio, maxilla, jumentum, anceps,* and *funditus.*

9. Decline: *virus, vellus, bes, acus, Tempe, Thales,* and *Trapezus.*

SYNTAX.

XXI.

ON THE NOMINATIVE AND ACCUSATIVE CASES.

1. Explain what is meant by the predicate nominative and appositive nominative.

2. With what verbs may the predicate nominative be used?

3. What are the different uses of the accusative?

4. What prepositions compounded with intransitive verbs make them transitive?

5. What is meant by the cognate accusative? Give examples.

6. What verbs govern two accusatives (1) of the same person or thing, and (2) of person and thing.

7. What is meant by the accusative of specification? What other name is applied to it?

8. Translate the following, explaining the syntax:
(1) *Cicero Romam venit.* (2) *Britanni maximam partem lacte vescuntur.* (3) *O me miserum! frater meus mortem turpissimam mortuus est.* (4) *Totam hiemem in Italiâ mansit.* (5) *Milites quinque millia passuum ambulaverunt.* (6) *Populus eum consulem creavit.* (7) *Ille primus sententiam ab consule rogatus est.* (8) *Adiit multas terras.* (9) *Mortem sui patris dolet.* (10) *Adversum femur ictus est.*

9. Translate and express in the passive form the following:
(1) *Quis eum eloquentiam docuit?* (2) *Senatus eum dictatorem nominavit.* (3) *Cæsar frumentum Aeduos flagitavit.* (4) *Philosophum ferunt in Siciliam adiisse.*

10. Correct or justify the following:
(1) *Hic oratio olei redolet.* (2) *In Romam ivit.* (3) *Cicero militibus Antoni occisus est.* (4) *Reductus est in domum Cæsar.* (5) *Jupiter multam pluviam terris misit* (6) *Trans Rhenum copias trajecit.* (7) *Hoc mei poscit.* (8) *Consul longo veste indutus castra pervenit.*

XXII.

ON THE DATIVE CASE.

1. What are the general uses of the dative case ?
2. With what verbs is it used ?
3. What is meant by the Ethical dative ?
4. What verbs govern two datives ?
5. What adjectives take the dative after them ?
6. What adjectives may be used with the dative or genitive ?
7. Translate, and explain the syntax of, the following :
   (1) *Haec cohors ab Caesare praesidio castris relicta est.*
   (2) *Hoc bellum populo Romano gerendum est totam aestatem.*
   (3) *Non mihi bonus homo es.*
   (4) *Haec pecunia militibus data est.*
   (5) *Nonne canis similis lupo est ?*
   (6) *Hoc consilium imperatori defuit.*
8. Correct or justify the following :
   (1) *Ego Mario juvabo.* (2) *Illa virum nupsit.* (3) *Iste homo sapientiae confidit.* (4) *Ille puer urbi profectus est.* (5) *Ejus vicinum pecuniam invidet.* (6) *Meam culpam me ignoscit.* (7) *Ejus nomen est Scipio.*
9. What different constructions may be used with : *Prospicio, moderor, tempero, comitor, differo, misceo, natus, similis, propior, alienus, timeo, adulor, circumdo,* and *proprius ?*

XXIII.

ON GENITIVE.

1. Explain the meaning of (1) subjective, (2) objective, and (3) partitive genitives.
2. What is meant by (1) genitive of characteristic and (2) genitive of specification ?
3. What adjectives govern the genitive ? What verbs ?
4. Translate, and explain the syntax of, the following sentences :
   (1) *Vir consilii magni ab Atheniensibus capitis damnatus est.* (2) *Accusatio Ciceronis ab juris perito homine instituta est.* (3) *Quis vestrum curarum expers est ?* (4) *Homo est rationis particeps.* (5) *Odium regum in defensores libertatis exercetur.* (6) *Venit in meam mentem Platonis.* (7) *Taedet me hujus libri.* (8) *Populum omnem timoris implevit.* (9) *Reipublicae multum interest hoc bellum gerere.* (10) *Senatus salutem civitatis nihili facit.*

5. Correct or justify the following :

(1) *Nemo vestri puero jussit.*   (2) *Hannibal puer annorum novem natus aram adductus est.*   (3) *Omnes hominum huic homini fidunt.*   (4) *Caesaris ad pedes projecit.*   (5) *Ille homo peritus in bello multa bella gessit.*   (6) *Nusquam terra tantum pecuniae erat.*   (7) *Bellum Romanum una aestate confectum est.*   (8) *Domus mei ab igne deflagratus est.*   (9) *Hi manus caedis avidi sunt.*   (10) *Ille insula fertilis in omnibus est.*

6. What verbs govern the accusative and genitive ?

XXIV.

ON THE ABLATIVE.

1. Give the general uses of the ablative.

2. Give a list of verbs and adjectives that govern the ablative.

3. What are the rules as to words expressing (1) place, (2) time ?

4. What prepositions govern (1) ablative, (2) accusative or ablative ?

✓5. Translate and explain the syntax of the following :

(1) *Multi gloria belli moventur.*   (2) *Multis horis diem aestate quam hieme esse longiorem scimus.*   (3) *Fretus sua innocentia in hostium castra adit.*   (4) *Tibure natus est, sed Romae decem annos vixit.*   (5) *Opus est nobis tua arte.*   (6) *Patriam meam multo pretio aestimavi.*   (7) *Hercules, Jove natus, multa miracula confecit.*   (8) *Juvenis summâ virtute abhinc annis novem mortuus est.*   (9) *Paucis post diebus in Galliam iter suo exercitu contendit.*   (10) *Regibus exactis consules creati sunt.*   (11) *His diebus hoc fecit.*

6. Correct or justify the following :

(1) *Hic homo ab virtute laudatur.*   (2) *Cum ejus judicio laetus eram.*   (3) *Spartanis cum lapide interfectus est.*   (4) *Pater domum plure aestimat.*   (5) *Plus annis quatuor Tarento vixit.*   (6) *Dignus patris nobilis est.*   (7) *In montibus Alpium sunt multi pecudes.*   (8) *Scholam in Neapoli properavit.*   (9) *In rus primo die post adventum consulis fugit.*   (10) *Ille lapis coelo cecidit nonis Aprilis.*

XXV.

GENERAL EXERCISE.

1. Give the various endings of diminutive nouns; and explain the termination in such derivatives as *quercetum, ovile, Thesides, senatus, ludio, aerarium, Neptunine.*

2. State the uses of the ablative. In what circumstances can other cases be used for the ablative?

3. Give the syntax of the following :
   (1) *Ille est oblitus sui regni.* (2) *Navis est nuda remigio.* (3) *Se consulatu abdicavit.* (4) *Opus est imperitare equis.* (5) *Illi nomen Vitellio erat.* (6) *Dis mea pietas et musa cordi est.* (7) *Agrum illi dono dedit.* (8) *Urbem quam statuo vestra est.* (9) *Parvi arma sunt foris nisi est consilium domi.* (10) *Illis persuasum est.* (11) *Coelo clamor it.*

4. Mention any irregularities of inflexion in *pecus, frugi, hepar, semis, tigris, equa, vis, sol, jugerum, Dido, nequam, solus, Tempe, plus, Orpheus* and *instar.*

5. Give the gender and genitive of *seges, senio, bidens, aer, tibicen, far, carcer, domus, avis, iter, puer, grex, remex, anceps,* and *salix.*

6. Define and explain the formation of : desiderative, frequentative, inceptive and diminutive verbs. Give examples of frequentatives formed from frequentatives.

XXVI.

GENERAL EXERCISE.

1. Decline *gelu, tonitrus, veru, penus, vulgus, humus, pecus, specus ;* giving only the forms actually in use. Write down the gender of each, with any varieties of gender or inflection that they may have.

2. Explain the following : *Quid refert mea ? quin facis hoc ? haud secus ac ; nescio quis discit ; vereor ut faciat ; vereor ne faciat.*

3. Distinguish between *supremus* and *summus ; infimus* and *imus ; postremus* and *postumus ; extremus* and *extimus.* Give the positive and comparative of each.

4. Give examples of verbs in -sco, -urio, -sso, -to or -ito, -illo, and shew the force of these terminations.

5. Give instances of adjectives in -rnus, -osus, -icius, -icus, -bundus; -itus, -inus; and specify their several meanings.

6. What different constructions may the following have : *Alienus, potior, adjaceo, tempero, prospicio, caveo, moderor, circumdo, peto*, and *dubito* ?

7. Distinguish between *alius, alter; illic, illuc, illinc; quando, aliquando, quandoque ; inde, istinc ; quattuor, quater, quaternus, quartus, quartanus, quadrimus.*

8. Give the diminutive of the following nouns : *Ager, codex, corona, dies, flos, frater, ignis, lapis, liber, labrum, pars,* and *signum,*

XXVII.

ON THE ADJECTIVE, PRONOUN AND VERB.

1. Explain the uses of the adjectives in the following :
   (1) *Triste lupus stabulis,* (?) *Laetus officium confecit.* (3) *Frater et soror erant parati.* (4) *Pars militum interfecti sunt.* (5) *Prior puerorum.* (6) *Primus puerorum.* (7) *Nihil boni fecit.* (8) *Labor et otium inter se contraria sunt.* (9) *Primus me juvit.* (10) *Eloquentior quam sapientior fuit.*

2. Explain the uses of *hic, iste, ille, is, idem,* and *ipse.*

3. Distinguish between the uses of *aliquis, quis, qui, quispiam ; quivis, quilibet, quisquam, ullus ; alius, alter ; uter, utervis, uterque.*

4. Distinguish between (1) *doctior quam gratior est ; doctus quam gratus est ;* (2) *Nostrum ; nostri ;* (3) *Me rogavit ut sibi legatus sim ; me rogavit ut ei legatus essem.* (4) *primum abiit ; primus abiit.*

5. What is the rule for the sequence of tenses ?

6. In what instances may the ordinary rule be violated ?

7. Explain the syntax of the following:
   (1) *Spero fore ut adsis.* (2) *Caesar jubet ut Helvetii veni-rent.* (3) *Hic homo erat tam carus civibus ut pater patriae appellatus esset.* (4) *Tibi dedit hunc librum ut legas.*

2 *

XXVIII.

ON THE VERB.

(Continued).

1. What particles are used to express (1) purpose, (2) result?
2. Explain the uses of *ut, ne, quo, quin, quominus.*
3. Explain fully the use of *qui* with the subjunctive.
4. What particles are used with the Subjunctive of condition?
5. What are the different forms of hypothetical sentences and the chief rules for their construction?
6. Explain the syntax of the following:
   (1) *Si quid habet, dat.* (2) *Civitas manet, modo cives sint fortes.* (3) *Non est quod filio imperes.* (4) *Haud recusavit quominus puero succurreret.* (5) *Quis non dubitat quin Europa minor Asia sit?* (6) *Plus quam facere posset, fecit.* (7) *Sol efficit ut omnia lucida sint.* (8) *Vereor ut veniat.* (9) *Vereor ne veniat.* (10) *Hortabor puerum ut studeat.* (11) *Sunt qui putent.* (12) *Dignus est qui ametur.*
7. Distinguish between *si non* and *nisi*; *quin* with indicative, subjunctive and imperative; *sunt qui amant* and *sunt qui ament.*

XXIX.

ON THE VERB.

(Continued).

1. With what particles is the Subjunctive of concession used?
2. What different usages were observed by the Latins in the use of *quamvis?*
3. Explain the use of *quum, quod, qui,* with subjunctive and with the indicative.
4. State the principal rules for the use of *donec, quoad; priusquam, antequam,* with indicative and with the subjunctive.
5. What is meant by an indirect question?
6. What particles are used with double questions?

7. What is meant by the attraction of the subjunctive?
8. Explain the syntax of the following :
   (1) *Dubito an illi credam necne.* (2) *Quid pater faciat, nescio.* (3) *Priusquam in urbem venissent, rus volavi.* (4) *Pugnent dum sibi placeat.* (5) *Sine ut vires illis sint.* (6) *Donec pons in flumine faceretur, fugiebant.* (7) *Non stilus mihi erat, quo scriberem.*
9. Explain the difference between *nescio quis scripsit, nescio quis scripserit; necne, annon; narrabo quod sentio, narrabo quid sentiam.*

XXX.

ON THE VERB.

(Continued).

1. Give the principal rules for the use of the moods and tenses in *oratio obliqua*.
2. With what verbs is the infinitive used as the object of a proposition?
3. Explain the use of the gerund, and of the gerundive.
4. What is the use of the supine in *-um?* What of the supine in *-u?*
5. Translate and explain the syntax of the following :
   (1) *Dicit se intra muros includere eos ; quia per agros vagari.* (2) *Cæsari responsum est, si obsides det, pacem futuram esse.* (3) *Scribit legato cum legione veniat.* (4) *Quum pugnam videris, ad castra fuge.* (5) *Eum visum iri a me puto.* (6) *Patricio tribuno plebis fieri mihi non licebat.* (7) *Mene incepto desistere victam ?* (8) *Mihi neglegenti esse non licet.* (9) *Dignus est qui ametur.* (10) *Quo factum est ut plus quam collegae Miltiades valuerit.*
6. Correct, where necessary ;
   (1) *Venit videre montem.* (2) *Multum interest inter dare et accipere.* (3) *Te legere decet.* (4) *Volo te breviter respondere.* (5) *Platonem audivisse dicitur.* (6) *Ego Phidias esse malo.* (7) *Censes eum gavisurum esse, si scivit te in Roma manere ?*

XXXI.

GENERAL EXERCISE.

1. What is the locative case? Give the endings of the locative in the different declensions.
2. How is the absence of the simple future in the Latin subjunctive supplied?
3. Distinguish carefully between the Gerund and Gerundive in Latin.
4. What is the construction of—*cavere, consulere, constat, jubere, eniti, sperare, prospicere, abesse,* and *gaudere?*
5. Write out the imperfect and pluperfect subjunctive (1st person sing. only) of—*orior, ordior, potior, aggredior, tono, faveo, rapio, profiteor, allicio, sentio, veho,* and *eo.*
6. Correct where necessary the following :
   (1) *Nocte ultima quam Athenis egit.* (2) *Gratulatus est me quia hanc honorem adeptus sum.* (3) *Socius ad auxilium venit.* (4) *Marcus persuasus est istum dolorem patienter esse ferendum.* (5) *Milites sub jugo missi sunt.*
7. Explain and distinguish carefully between the following uses of *quin :*
   (1) *Haud dubium est quin veniat.* (2) *Eum videre non potuit quin lacrimaret.* (3) *Quin veni.* (4) *Quin ad navem venimus?*

XXXII.

GENERAL EXERCISE.

1. Give the future and perfect indicative (3rd person plural), of —*accumbo, excieo, torqueo, negligo, colligo, pango, collido, relino, retego, tero, coquo, stringo, experior,* and *tendo.*
2. Distinguish between—*Odi hominem qui hoc fecit* and *Odi hominem qui hoc fecerit.*
3. Mention verbs that are transitive in English, while their Latin equivalents govern another case than the accusative.

4. Correct where necessary, the following :
   (1) *Nescio quid malum fecit.* (2) *Ei habentes divitias debent alios opitulari.* (3) *Nisi aliquod de te sciret, non loqueretur.* (4) *Nemo fuit qui magis pravus mihi visus est.*

5. Explain what is meant by Ethical Dative, Ablative Absolute, Cognate Accusative, and Accusative of Specification.

6. When is *any* to be translated by *quisquam,* or *ullus,* when by *quivis* or *quilibet,* and when by *quis?*

7. Give the comparative and superlative (when used) of : *gracilis, intra, honorificus, maturus, sero, novus, utilis, uber, vetus, male* and *parum.*

XXXIII.

GENERAL EXERCISE.

1. Decline—*ambo, uter, duo,* and *unus.*

2. Give the perfect indicative, 1st person singular, of— *percello, decurro, dedisco, veneo, prodo, jaceo, jacio, peto, scisco,* and *perdo.*

3. What is the construction of—*indigeo, careo, invideo, ulciscor, minor, precor, indulgeo, blandior, carus, alienus, celo,* and *affinis.*

4. Correct the following where necessary :
   (1) *Dicebat nihil esse quod facere poterat melius.* (2) *Quid facinus fecisti occidendo inimico tuo?* (3) *Rogo te quantam pecuniam tibi datam iri expectas, pro perficiendo mihi hoc opere.*

5. Explain the syntax of *si,* based on the following expressions :
   (1) *Si quid cogitat, loquitur.* (2) *Si quid cogitet, loquetur.* (3) *Si quid cogitaret, loqueretur.* (4) *Si quid cogitasset, locutus esset.*

6. Explain the use of the accusatives in the following sentences :
   (1) *Sedet aeternumque sedebit.* (2) *Cyclopa saltabat histrio.* (3) *Os humerosque deo similis.* (4) *Induitur faciem Dianae.* (5) *Pro deum fidem! pedes tumet.* (6) *En Ascanium, ille mansit apud Romam totam hiemem.* (7) *Haud trecentos pedes distat.*

XXXIV.

GENERAL EXERCISE.

1. What is meant by a deponent verb? Notice anything special in the use of the participles of these verbs. Give examples of the Middle Voice in Latin.

2. Correct where necessary, the following sentences :

   (1) *Paenitet mei talia verba uti.* (2) *Interest patri diligenter me studere linguam Latinam.* (3) *Speculatores nuntiabant quod hostes non longe abessent.* (4) *Operam dabo ut epistolam meam postridie acciperes.* (5) *Non oportet tibi tot dies consumere in legendo libros.*

3. Explain fully the following constructions :

   (1) *Permagni nostra interest.* (2) *Auctoritate tua tibi opus est.* (3) *Quod parato opus est, para.* (4) *Postridie ejus diei iter contendit.* (5) *Cur otio pecuniam mutas ?*

4. What are the differences between : *Patēre, patĕre; oblitus, oblitus ; cōmes, cōmes ; dīcat, dĭcat ; diffĭdit, diffĭdit ; frētum, frĕtum ; lābor, lăbor ; nītēre, nĭtĕre ; pālus, pălus ; plācet, plăcet; condĭtus, condītus ; lābatur, lăbatur ; nōtis, nŏtis ; rādis, rădis ; mānes, mănes ?*

5. What construction attends the use of *vescor, similis, alienus, implere, pudet, pasci, dare, metus, libet, oportet,* and *consulo ?*

6. Explain what is meant by *Dativus Commodi ?*

VOCABULARY.*

ABLE . . . . posse, *irreg.*
ABOUT . . . . i. *around,* circa, circum, *with acc.* ii. *concerning,* de, *with abl.*
ACCEPT . . . . accipere, recipere, 3.
ACCOUNT, AN . . narratio, onis, 3, f.
ACCOUNT, TO . . habere, 2.
ACCEPTABLE . . gratus, acceptus (*both with dat.*).
ACHILLES . . . Achilles, Achillei, and Achillis, 3, m.
ACCUSE . . . i. accusare, 1, ii. reum facere (*person in acc., charge in gen.*).
ACCUSER . . . accusator, criminator, oris, 3.
ACROSS . . . trans (*with acc.*).
ACQUIT . . . absolvere, 3.
ADD . . . . addere, 3 ; subjicere, 3.
ADMINISTER . . administrare, 1.
ADMIRE . . . admirari, 1, *dep.*
ADMONISH . . . admonere, 2.
ADVANTAGE . . commodum, i, 2, n.
ADVANTAGEOUS . utilis, e.
AFFECTING . . luctuosus.
AFFORD : . . præbere, 2.
AFTER . . . . post, *with acc.*; *also an adv. of time. After that,* postquam.
AFTERWARDS . . postea.
AGAINST . . . i. contra, *with acc.* ii. in, *with acc. especially after verbs of attacking.*
AGE . . . . ætas, ætatis, 3, f. Saeculum, i, 2, n.
AGED, VERY . . admodum senex.
AGO . . . . abhinc.
AGREEABLE . . gratus, acceptus, *both with dat.*; conveniens = "in accordance with."
AGRICOLA . . . Agricola, æ, 1, m.
AID, TO . . . auxiliari, opitulari, 1, *dep.*
ALESIA . . . . Alesia, æ, 1, f.
ALL . . . . . i. omnis, e. ii. totus, totius. iii. universus. iv. cunctus.
ALTHOUGH . . etsi, etiamsi, licet.
ALWAYS . . . semper.
AM . . . . . esse, *irreg.*
AMBASSADOR . . legatus, i, 2, m.
AMIABLE . . . suavis, e. ; amabilis, e.

* For irregular forms and principal parts of verbs, &c., consult Grammar and Dictionary.

AMONG . . . . . inter, per, apud.
ANCIENT . . . antiquus (*what has ceased to exist*) ; vetus (*what still exists*).
AND . . . . . et, que (*enclitic*).
ANDROMACHE . Andromache, es, 1, f.
ANGER . . . . ira, 1, f.
ANGRY . . . . iratus, iracundus ; *to be angry*, irasci, *dep.* 3.
ANIMAL . . . animal, is, 3, n. ; *a wild animal*, fera, æ, 1, f.
ANNOUNCE . . *to convey news*, perferre, *irreg.* ; *also* nun- tiare, 1.
ANOTHER . . . i. *with reference to a second person only*, alter. ii. *generally*, alius.
ANSWER . . . i. *verb*, respondere, 2. ii. *subst.*, respon- sum, i., 2, n.
ANTONIUS . . . Antonius, i., 2, n.
ANXIOUS FOR, TO BE studere, 2.
ANXIOUS . . . anxius.
ANXUR . . . Anxur, ūris, 3, n.
ANY—ANY ONE .. quis, qui (*used as adjective*); quivis (*any one at all*); quisquam (*any particular person*).
APPLE . . . . malum, i., 2, n.
APPOINT . . . constituere, 3.
APPROACH . . . aditus, 4, m.
APULEIUS . . . Apuleius, i., 2, m.
APULIA . . . Apulia, æ, 1, f.
ARABIAN . . . Arabs, is, 3, c.
ARIOVISTUS . . Ariovistus, i., 2, m.
ARMINIUS . . . Arminius, i., 2, m.
ARMS . . . . arma, orum, 2, n.
ARMY . . . . agmen, inis, 3, m. (*army on the march*); exercitus, us, 4, m. (*army encamped*); acies, ei, 5, f. (*line of battle*).
ARRIVAL . . . adventus, us, 4, m.
ARRIVE . . . advenire, 4 ; pervenire, 4, (*to reach the end of a journey*).
ART . . . . ars, artis, 3, f.
ASCEND . . . ascendere, 3.
AS FAST AS POS-
SIBLE . . . . quam celerrime (*adverbial phrase*).
ASHAMED, TO BE . pudet, impers, 2.
ASK . . . . rogare, 1 ; petere, 3.
ASSERT . . . aio, 3, *defect.* ; affirmare, 1 ; asseverare, 1.
ASSIST . . . . juvare, 1, *with acc.* ; subvenire, 3, *with dat.*
ASSISTANCE . . auxilium, 2 n.
AT . . . . . i. ad. *with acc.* ii. *meaning near*, apud, *with acc.* At *is also a sign of location* : e.g. *at* Capua = Capu-æ.
ATILIUS . . . Atilius, i., 2, m.

AT HAND, TO BE . adesse. *Irreg.*
ATHENIANS . . Athenienses, ium, 3, c.
ATHENS . . . Athenæ, arum, 1, f.
ATTACK, TO . . aggredi, 3, *dep.*
ATTACK, AN . . impetus, us, 4, m.
ATTENDANT . . minister, i., 2, m.; famulus, 1., 2, m.
ATTICUS . . . Atticus, i., 2, m.
ATTRIBUTE . . vertere, 3 ; dare, 1 ; tribuere, 3.
ATTRIBUTE BLAME vertere alicui culpam.
AUGUSTUS . . . Augustus, i., 2, m.
AVARICE . . . avaritia, 1, f.
AWAY, TO BE . . abesse. *Irreg.*

BACK, TO COME . redire, 4 ; revenire, 4.
BACULUS . . . Baculus, i, 2, m.
BAD . . . . malus, improbus.
BAIÆ . . . . Baiæ, arum, 1, f.
BAND . . . . manus, 4, f.
BANISH . . . ex urbe *or* ex civitate pellere.
BANK . . . . ripa, æ, 1, f.
BASE . . . . turpis.
BARBARIAN . . barbarus.
BATTLE . . . pugna, æ, 1, f. ; prælium, i., 2, n.
BE (TO) . . . . esse. *Irreg.*
BEAST . . . bellua, æ, 1, f.; *wild beast,* fera, æ, 1, f.
BEAUTIFUL . . pulcher, formosus.
BECAUSE . . . quia (*emphatic, usually with indicative*) ;
               quod (*less emphatic*).
BECOME, TO . . fieri.
BEGIN . . . . cœpisse, *defective,* incipere, 3.
BEHEAD . . . securi percutere.
BELIEVE . . . credere, 3.
BENEFIT . . . prodesse. *Irreg. (with dat.*).
BENEFIT . . . beneficium, i.. 2, n. ; *confer benefits,* bene-
               ficere, 3, *with dat.*
BENEVOLENT . . benevolus, beneficus.
BESEECH . . . orare, 1 ; obsecrare, 1.
BESIEGE . . . obsidere, 2.
BESPATTER . . aspergere, 3.
BESTOW . . . dare ; donare.
BITTER . . . amarus, asper.
BITTERLY . . . aspere, acerbe ; *bitterly-hostile,* infestus.
BLAME . . . . culpa, æ, 1, f.
BLIND . . . . cæcus.
BLOCK . . . . præcludere.
BLOOD . . . . sanguis, inis, 3, m.
BLUSH . . . . erubescere, 3.
BODUOGNATUS . Boduognatus, i., 2, m.
BODY . . . . corpus, oris, 3, n.
BODY, OF TROOPS . præsidium, i, 2, n.

BOOK . . . . liber, bri, 2, m.
BOOKSELLER . . librarius, i., 2, m.
BOOTY . . . . præda, æ, 1, f.
BORN . . . . nasci, 3, *dep.* natus, nata = *a son, a daughter.*
BOTH . . . . ambo (*both together*) ; uterque (*both separately*).
BOTH-AND . . . et . . et.
BOY . . . . puer, i., 2, m.
BRAVE . . . . fortis, e.
BRAVELY . . . fortiter.
BREAD . . . panis, is, 3, m.
BREAST . . . . pectus, oris, 3, n.
BRIBERY . . . ambitus, us, 4, m.
BRING-BACK . . referre, *irreg.*, reportare, 1.
BRITAIN . . . Britannia, æ, 1, f.
BROAD . . . . latus.
BRONZE . . . . æs, ris, 3, n.
BROTHER . . . frater, tris, 3, m.
BRUNDUSIUM . . Brundisium, i., 2, n.
BUILD . . . `. ædificare, 1 ; condere, 3.
BUILDING . . . ædificium, 2, n.
BURIAL . . . . sepultura, æ, 1, f.
BURN . . . . incendere, 3.
BURY . . . . sepelire, 4.
BUSINESS . . . i. *one's affairs*, negotium, i., 2, n. ; res, ei, 5, f. ii. *trade*, ars, artis, 3, f.
BUSHEL . . . medimnus, i., 2, m.
BUT . . . . . sed (*comes first in a sentence*); autem (*second in a sentence*) ; nisi (*after negatives*).
BUY . . . . . emere, 3.
BY . . . . . ab, a (*used with abl. of agent*); per, acc. (*used of secondary agent*).

CÆSAR . . . Cæsar, ris, 3, m.
CALL . . . . vocare, 1 ; *call out*, clamare, 1, = *name*, appellare ; nominare.
CAMP . . . . castra, orum, 2, n.
CAPITAL . . . caput, capitis, 3, n.
CAPTAIN . . . centurio, onis, 3, m.
CAPTIVE . . . captivus, i., 2, m.
CAPUA . . . . Capua, æ, 1, f.
CARE . . . . cura, æ, 1, f.
CARE, TO TAKE . cavere, 2 ; curare, 1.
CAREFULLY . . diligenter, caute.
CARRY ON A WAR bellum gerere.
CARTHAGE . . . Carthago, ginis, 3, f.
CARTHAGINIAN . Carthaginiensis, e., Pœnus, i., 2, m.
CAST . . . . . projicere, 3.
CASTLE . : . . castellum, i., 2, n.
CATCH . . . . capere, 3.

CATILINE . . .	Catilina, æ, 1, m.
CATIUS	Catius, i., 2, m.
CAVALRY, THE .	equitatus, us, 4, m.
CAVE	antrum, i., 2, n.; specus, us, 4, m.
CECILIA . . .	Cecilia, æ, 1, f.
CENTURION . .	centurio, onis, 3, m.
CERTAIN . . .	i. *fixed, sure*, certus. ii. *a particular person*, quidam.
CERTAINLY . .	certe.
CHANCE . . .	casus, 4, m.
CHARGE . . .	crimen, 3, n ; nomen, 3, n.
CHARGE, TO . .	prædicere, 3.
CHEERFUL . . .	lætus.
CHECK ON, TO PUT	moderare, 1 ; temperare, 1.
CHIEFLY . . .	præcipue, maxime.
CHIEF POST . .	principatus, 4, m.
CHILDREN . . .	i. liberi, orum, 2, m. ii. *child*, puer, 2, m.
CHOOSE	legere, 3 ; deligere, 3.
CHRISTIAN . .	Christianus, *adj.*
CICERO	Cicero, onis, 3, m.
CIRCUMSTANCE .	res, rei, 5, f.
CITIZEN . . .	civis, is, 3, c.
CITY	urbs, urbis, 3, f.
CLAD	vestitus, 4, m. ; indutus, 4, m.
CLEAR, IT IS . .	constat. *Impers.*, 1.
CLEVER	callidus, sollers.
CLIMATE, CLIME .	cœlum, i., 2, n.
CLOAK	pallium, i., 2, n.; pœnula, 1, f.
CLOSE TO . . .	prope (*with acc.*) ; juxta (*with acc.*).
COAT	tunica, æ, 1, f. ; vestimentum, 2, n.
COAT, A GREAT .	pœnula, œ, 1, f.
COHORT . . .	cohors, 3, f.
COLOUR. . . .	color, oris, 3, m.
COME	venire, 4 ; pervenire.
COMMAND . . .	i. *verb*, imperare, 1 (*followed by dative, and* ut *with subj.*); jubere (*with acc. and infinitive*), *to be in command*, præesse. ii. *subst. a command*, jussum, i.
COMMIT A CRIME.	admittere scelus ; commitere scelus.
COMMON . . .	communis, e.
COMPANION . .	socius, 2, m.
COMPARE . , .	confere, 3 . . . *with*=cum.
COMPEL, TO . .	cogere, 3.
COMPLIMENTS, TO SEND	salutem dicere, 3.
CONCEAL, TO . .	celare, 1.
CONCERNS, IT . .	interest. *Impers. with acc. and gen.*
CONCLUSION . .	finis, is, 3, m.
CONDEMN TO DEATH	capitis damnare.
CONDITION . .	conditio, 3, f.

Conduct oneself   se gerere, 3.
Confer   . . .   tribuere, 3 ; *confer benefits*, beneficere, 3
                  (*with dat*).
Confess   . . .   confiteri, fateri, 2, *dep.*
Congratulate .   gratulari, 1, *dep.*
Conqueor . . .   vincere, 3 ; superare, 1.
Conscious . . .   conscius.
Consider . . .   cogitare, 1 ; æstimare, 1.
Consist   . . .   constare, 1 ; consistere, 3.
Conspiracy . .   conjuratio, 3, f.
Construct   . .   construere, 3 ; facere, 3.
Consul   . . .   consul, is, 3, m.
Consulsiiip .   consulatus, us, 4, m.
Consult for .   consulere (see 385, 3).
Content . . .   contentus (*with abl.*), *contentedly*, con-
                  tentus sorte.
Convenient . .   opportunus.
Cook   . . . .   coquere, 3.
Corinth   . . .   Corinthus, i., 2, f.
Corn   . . . .   frumentum, 2, n.
Cost. . . . .   stare, 1 ; constare, 1.
Counsel   . . .   consilium, i., 2, n.
Countenance   .   facies, ci, 5, f.; vultus, us, 4, m.; *to
                  give one's countenance to*, favere, 2
                  (*with dat.*).
Country . . .   rus, ruris, 3, n.; ora, 1, f.; terra, 1, f.
Countryman . .   civis, 3, m.; popularis, 3, m.
Courage   . . .   virtus, tutis, 3, f.
Courtesy . . .   humanitas, tis, 3, f.
Coward   . . .   ignavus, *adj.*
Cowardice   . .   ignavia, æ, 1, f.
Crafty   . . .   astutus, dolosus, callidus.
Create, to   . .   creare, 1 ; facere. 3.
Crime . . . .   flagitium, i., 2, n.; scelus, eris, 3, n.
Crœsus   . . .   Crœsus, i., 2, m.
Crown . . . .   corona, æ, 1, f.
Cross . . . .   transire, 4 ; trajicere (*with two accusatives*).
Cruelty . . .   crudelitas, atis, 3, f.
Cubit . . . .   cubitum, i, 2, n.
Cumæ . . . .   Cumæ, arum, 1, f.
Custom. . . .   mos, moris, 3, m.; consuetudo, inis, 3, f.

DAILY   . . .   i. diurnus, quotidianus, *adj.* ii. quotidie,
                  adv.
Danger   . . .   periculum, i, 2, n.; discrimen, is, 3, n.
Dangerous   . .   periculosus.
Dart   . . . .   telum, i, 1, 2, n. ; jaculum, i, 2, n.
Daughter   . .   filia, æ, 1, f.
Day . . . · .   dies, ei, 4, m. and f.
Day before . .   pridie. *Day after*, postridie.

DAY, TO· . . . hodie.
DEAF . . . . surdus.
DEAR . . . . carus.
DEATH . . . . mors, tis, 3, f.
DEBT . . . . æs alienum, æs, æris.
DECEIVE, . . . fallere, 3.
DECLARE . . . declarare, 1 : edicere, 3.
DECLARE WAR . bellum indicere.
DECREE . . . decernere, 3.
DEED . . . . factum, i, 2, n.; gestum, i, 2, n. (daring
            deed); facinus, oris, 3, n.
DEFEAT. . . . i. verb, superare, 1. ii. subst. clades, is, 3, f.
DEFENCE . . . præsidium, i, 2, n.
DEFEND . . . defendere, 3 ; propugnare, 1.
DEFENDER. . . defensor, oris, 3, m.
DELIGHTFUL . . amœnus (delightful to see); jucundus (de-
            lightful in any way).
DELIGHTS, IT . . delectat ; juvat, 1, impers.
DEMAND . . . postulare, 1.
DENY . . . . negare, 1. (Nego is used to translate :
            say . . . not, e.g., he says he will not
            come = negat se venturum).
DEPART . . . abire, 4; proficisci, dep. 3 ; discedere, 3.
DEPARTURE . . discessus, us, 4, m.; profectio, onis, 3, f.
DESCENDED . . oriundus.
DESIRE . . . . cupiditas, atis, 3, f.
DESIRE . . . . cupere, 3 (= ask), quære (of = ex.).
DESIROUS . . . avidus, cupidus.
DESIST . . . . desistere, 3.
DESPISE . . . contemnere, 3 ; spernere, 3.
DESTROY . . . delere, 2 ; consumere, 3.
DESTRUCTION . . exitium, i., 2, n. ; excidium, i., 2, n.
DETAIN . . . . remorari, 1, dep.
DEVOTE. . . . studere, 2 ; incumbere, 3.
DEVOTE ONESELF TO studere (with dat.).
DICTATOR . . . dictator. toris, 3, m.
DIE . . . . . mori, dep., 3.
DIFFICULT . . . difficilis, e.
DISAGREEABLE . molestus, injucundus.
DISCHARGE . . i. discharge one's duty, fungi, dep., 3.
            ii. discharge weapons, tela conjicere.
DISCOVER . . . reperire, 4 ; invenire, 4 ; intelligere, 3, &c.
DISCREET . . . prudens, providus.
DISGRACE . . . dedecus, oris, 3, n.
DISGRACEFUL . . turpis, e, inhonestus.
DISHONOUR . . dedecus, oris, 3, n.
DISPEL . . . . pellere, 3.
DISPOSITION . . i. natural turn of mind, indoles, is, 3, f,
            ii. arrangement, dispositio, onis, 3,
            f., 3 ; collocatio, onis, 3, f.

DISSATISFIED
GREATLY, TO BE   pœnitet, 2. *Imper.*
DISTANCE, AT A   eminus, *adv.*
DISTANT . . .   i. *to be distant*, abesse. ii. *far off, adj.*
                disjunctus ; *adv.* procul.
DITCH . . . .   fossa, æ, 1, f.
DO . . . . .   facere, 3 ; agere, 3 ; *do with one,* facere
                (*with* the abl.)
DIVIDE . . . .   dividere, 3.
DIVINE . . . .   divinus.
DOUBLE, TO . .   duplicare, 1.
DOUBT . . . .   dubitare, 1.
DRACHMA . . .   drachma, æ, 1, f.
DREADFUL . . .   terribilis, e ; horribilis.
DREAM . . . .   somniare, 1 ; *a dream,* somnium.
DRINK . . . .   bibere, 3 ; potare, 1.
DUE . . . . .   debitum, i, 2, n. ; suum.
DURING . . .   per *with acc.,* inter, *with acc.; also by abl.*
                absol., e.g. *during the consulship of*
                Cæsar=Cæsare consule.
DUTY . . . .   ' i. officium, i. 2, n.; ii. *a particular duty,*
                munus, eris, 3, n., 1, *also sign of the*
                genitive, e.g., *it is the duty of the king*
                =est regis.
DWELL . . . .   habitare, 1.

EACH . . . .   uterque, *of two*; quisque, *generally.*
EASY . . . .   facilis, e.
EAT . . . . .   edere, 3.
EGG . . . . .   ovum, i, 2, n.
EIGHT . . . .   octo, *indecl. adj.*
ELDER FAMILIES .   (applied to senate) majores gentes.
ELECTIONS . . .   comitia, orum, 2, n.
ELOQUENT . . .   eloquens, facundus.
ELSE . . . . .   *taken with some other word* (e.g. *some*
                one else), alius.
EMINENT, TO BE .   eminere, 2.
EMPEROR . . .   imperator, oris, 3, m.
EMPEROR, TO BE .   imperare, 1.
EMPIRE . . . .   imperium, i, 2, n.
EMPTY, TO . . .   se effundere, 3.
ENCAMP . . .   castra ponere, 3 ; castra locare, 1.
END . . . . .   i. *subst.,* finis, is, 3, m.; summum. ii. *verb,*
                finire, 4 ; conficere.
ENDEAVOR . . .   conari, 1, *dep.*
ENDOWED . . . ⎫
ENDUED . . . ⎬ præditus (*with abl.*)
ENEMY . . . .   hostis, is, 3, c ; inimicus, i, 2, m.
ENJOY . . . .   frui, 3, *dep.;* gaudere, 2.
ENOUGH . . .   satis.

ENTER . . . . intrare, 1.
ENTRUST . . . credere, 3, (*with dat. of person and acc. of thing*).
ENUMERATE, TO . persequi, 3, *dep.*
EQUESTRIAN . . equestris, e.
EQUITABLE . . æquus.
ESTEEM . . . æstimare, 1 (*with* maximi, pluris, magni, &c.); facere, 3, *with same.*
EVEN . . . . *adv.* etiam, *but when there is a negative,* quidem, *e.g.* ne . . . quidem.
EVENING . . . vesper, 3, m.
EVER . . . . unquam, *and after* si, *use* quando, e.g. *if* ever=si . . . *quando.*
EVERY.. . . . quisque (*taken singly*), omnis, e (*taken in the aggregate*).
EVERY ONE . . quisque.
EVERYTHING . . quidque, omnia (*plural=all things*).
EVERY TIME . . quotus; ubi.
EVIL . . . . malum, i, 2, n.
EXAMPLE . . . exemplum, i, 2, n.
EXASPERATE . . exasperare ; *exasperated,* infensus, iratus.
EXCEL . . . . antecellere, 3.
EXCELLENT . . egregius, præstans.
EXCHANGE . . mutare, 1.
EXCLAIM . . . clamare, 1 ; exclamare, 1.
EXHAUSTED . . confectus (*participle*).
EXHORT . . . hortari, 1.
EXILE . . . . pellere, 3 ; *also* exterminare, 1 ; ejicere, 3.
EXPECTING, NOT . inopinans.
EXPEDIENT, IT IS. expedit, 4, *impers.*
EXPEL . . . . expellere, 3; *also* ejicere, 3.
EXPERIENCE . . usus rerum.
EXPLAIN . . . explicare, 1 ; exponere, 3 ; demonstrare, 1.
EYE . . . . . oculus, 2, m.

FABIUS . . . Fabius, *a man's name,* 2, m.
FAITHFUL . . . fidelis.
FALL . . . . cadere, 3.
FAR, BY . . . multo; longe.
FATAL . . . . funestus, fatalis, c.
FAULT . . . . culpa, æ, 1, f.; peccatum, i, 2, n.
FAUSTUS . . . Faustus, i, *a man's name,* 2, m.
FEAR . . . . metus, us, 4, m.; timor, oris, 3, m.
FEAR, TO . . . timere, 2; metuere, 3; formidare, 1 ; vereri, 2, *dep.*
FEED ON . . . vesci, 3, *dep.* (*the feeding of men*); pascere, (trans) pasci, *dep.* (intrans), 3 (*the feeding of animals*).
FEEL . . . . sentire, 4.
FEELINGS . . . animus, i, 2, m.

FELLOW . . .	homo, inis, 3, m.
FERTILITY . . .	fertilitas, atis, 3, f.
FEW	paucus, rarus.
FIELD	ager, agri, 2, m.; arvum, i, 2, n.
FIFTEEN . . .	quindecim, *indecl. adj.*
FIFTY	quinquaginta, *indecl. adj.*
FIGHT	pugnare, 1; prælium committere, 3; dimicare, 1.
FINE	tenuis, e (*fine in texture*); pulcher.
FINISH	conficere, 3; finire, 4.
FIRST	primi; primus; (adv.) primum; *at first*, primo *and* primum.
FISH	i. *subst.* piscis, is, 3, m. ii. *verb*, piscare, 1, *dep.*
FITTED	idoneus, aptus (*with dat.*).
FIVE	quinque, *indecl. adj.*
FIX	constituere, 3.
FLEE	fugere, 3, f.
FLEET	classis, is, 3.
FLESH	caro, carnis, 3, f.
FLIGHT	fuga, æ, 1, f.
FLOG	cædere virgis; (*beat*) verberare, 1.
FLOWER . . .	flos, floris, 3, m.
FLY (*snbst.*) . .	musca, æ, 1, f.
FOE	hostis, is, 3, c; inimicus, i, 2, m.
FOLLY	stultitia, æ, 1, f.
FOND	amans.
FOOD	cibus, i, 2, m.
FOOLISH . . .	stultus, fatuus.
FOOT	pes, pedis, 3, m.
FOR	pro, *with abl.* (see Part I.), propter; (*for this reason*) propter eam causam); nam, enim, *conj.*
FORBID	prohibere, 2; vetare, 1.
FORCED MARCHES.	magna itinera.
FORCES	copiæ, copiarum, 1, f.
FOREIGN TO . .	alienus, a.
FORGET, TO . .	oblivisci, 3, *dep.*
FORMER; LATTER.	ille; hic.
FORTIFICATION .	munitio, onis, 3, f.
FORTIFY . . .	munire, 4.
FORTUNE . . .	Fortuna, æ, 1, f.
FORTY	quadriginta, *indecl. adj.*
FORUM	forum, i, 2, n.
FORWARD, TO SEND	præmittere, 3.
FOUR	quatuor, *indecl. adj.*
FOUR HUNDRED .	quadringenti.
FREEDOM . . .	libertas, tis, 3, f.
FREE, TO . . .	liberare, 1.
FRIEND	amicus, i, 2, n.

FRIENDSHIP . . amicitia, æ, 1, f.
FROM . . . . a, ab, de, *with abl.*
FULL . . . . plenus.
FURTHEST, AT THE summum.

GABII . . . . Gabii, orum, 2, m.
GAME . . . . ludus, i, 2, m.
GARB . . . . vestis, is, 3, f.
GARDEN . . . hortus, i, 2, m.; *pleasure gardens,* horti.
GATE . . . . porta, æ, 1 f.
GAUL . . . . Gallia, æ, 1, f., *a Gaul,* Gallus.
GELLIUS . . . Gellius, i, 2, m.
GENERAL . . . imperator, oris, 3, m.; dux, ducis, 3, m.
GENTLENESS . . mansuetudo, 3, f.
GERMANS . . . Germani, orum, 2, m.
GIRL . . . . puella, æ, 1, f.
GIVE . . . . dare, 1 ; *(as a present)* donare, 1.
GIVE UP . . . tradere, 3 ; dedere, 3.
GLAD . . . . lætus.
GO . . . . . ire, 4; proficisci, 3; *go on,* pergere, 3;
          go away, discedere, 3 ; *go back,*
          reverti, 3, *dep.;* redire, 4.
GOD . . . . . Deus, i. 2, m. *Irreg.*
GODDESS . . . dea, æ, 1, f. *Dat. and abl. plur.* deabus.
GOLD . . . . aurum, i, 2, n.
GOOD . . . . bonus; *to do good,* prodesse.
GOVERN . . . imperare, 1; moderari, 1, *dep.*
GOVERNOR . . . proconsul, ulis, 3, m.; procurator, oris,
          3, m.
GRANT . . . . concedere, 3 ; tribuere, 3.
GRAPE . . . . uva, æ, 1, f.
GRATEFUL . . . gratus, jucundus.
GREAT . . . . magnus; *spacious,* amplus; *so great,*
          tantus.
GREAT-DEAL, A . multum, multa, *adj.*
GREAT DEAL OF, TO
  THINK A . . magni æstimare.
GREEDINESS . . avaritia, æ, 1, f.
GREEKS . . . Græci, orum, 2, m.
GRIEF . . . . dolor, oris, 3, m.
GRIEVOUS . . . gravis, e.
GROUND . . . humus, i, 2, f. ; *on the ground.* humi.
GROW . . . . gignere, 3 ; gnasci, 3, *dep.*
GUARD . . . . præsidium, i, 2, n.
GUILTY, TO FIND . damnare, 1.

HAND . . . manus, us, 4, f. ; *close-to-hand, hand to*
          hand, cominus.
HANNIBAL . . . Hannibal, is, 3, m.
HAPPINESS . . felicitas, tis, 3, f.; vita beata.

3 *

HAPPY . . . . felix, cis ; beatus.
HARD . . . . i. *hard to touch*, durus. ii. *hard to do*, difficilis, c.
HARM . . . . nocere, 2, *with dat.*, lædere, 3.
HARVEST . . . messis, is, 3, f.
HAT . . . . petasus, i., 2, m.
HATE . . . . odisse, 3, *defect.* ; *hated*, invisus, *adj.*
HATEFUL . . . odiosus ; invisus.
HAVE . . . . habere, 2.
HE . . . . . *usually translated by a verbal inflection ; emphatic*, ipse, ille, iste ; *general*, is ; *reflexive, acc. case*, se.
HEAD . . . . caput, itis, 3, n.
HEALTH . . . valetudo, inis, 3, f. ; sanitas, tatis, 3, f. ; *to be in good health*, bene valere.
HEALTHY . . . salubris.
HEAR . . . . audire, 4.
HEAVY . . . . gravis, e.
HECTOR . . . Hector, oris, 3, m.
HEIGHT . . . altitudo, inis, 3, f. ; *heights*, loca superiora.
HELMET . . . cassis, idis, 3, f. ; galea, æ, 1, f.
HELP . . . . auxilium, i., 2, n., opis, *defect.* ; subsidium, 2, n.
HER . . . . illa, ipsa, ista, ca ; *possessive adj.*, suus.
HERE. . . . . hic, *adv.*
HESITATE . . . dubitare, 1.
HIDE . . . . celare, 1.
HIGH . . . . altus.
HIGHLY, TO
   THINK OF . . magni æstimari, *with acc.*
HILL . . . . collis, is, 3, m.
HIMSELF, HERSELF,
   ITSELF . . . se, *reflexive ;* ipse, a, um, *in agreement subject ; by himself* = solus,
HIS, HERS, ITS . suus, *reflexive ;* ejus, *generally.*
HOLD . . . . tenere, 2.
HISTORY . . . historia, æ, 1, f.
HOLY . . . . sanctus.
HOME . . . . domus, us, *irreg. ; at home*, domi ; *homewards*, or (*to*) *home*, domum.
HONEY . . . . mel, lis, 3, n.
HONOR . . . . honor, oris, 3, m.
HONOURABLE . . honestus.
HONOURABLY . . honeste.
HOPE . . . . i. *verb*, sperare, 1. ii. *subst.* spes, 5, f. *You are my hope*, in te spem pono.
HORACE . . . }
HORATIUS . . . } Horatius, i., 2, m.
HORSE . . . . equus, i, 2, m. ; caballus, i, 2, m. ; *horseback on*, ex equo.

HOSTILE . . . inimicus, *bitterly hostile ;* infestus.
HOUR . . . . hora, æ, 2, f.
HOWEVER . . . tamen ; veruntamen.
HUMBLE . . . humilis.
HUNDRED . . . centum, *indecl. adj.*
HUNGER . . . fames, is, 3, f.
HURTFUL . . . noxius, nocens.
HUSBAND . . . maritus, i., 2, m. ; vir, viri, 2, m.
HOW . . . . quam (*adv.*).

I . . . . . . *usually translated by verbal inflection ; emphatic,* ego.
IDLENESS . . . ignavia, æ, 1, f.
IF . . . . . si, *with indic. if something is merely assumed : with subj. if something is represented as only likely to happen.*
IGNORANT . . . ignarus (*with gen.*).
ILL, TO SPEAK OF maledicere,, 3, *with dat.*
ILLUSTRIOUS . . clarus.
IMMEDIATELY . . statim.
IMMORTAL . . . immortalis.
IMPLICATED . . affinis.
IMPUTE . . . dare, 1 ; vertere, 3 ; tribuere, 3.
IN . . . . . in, *with acc. after verbs of motion : with abl. signifying rest* (*during*) per.
INDEED . . . vero.
INDUSTRIOUS . . industrius, strenuus, diligens.
INFLUENCE WITH,
  TO HAVE . . . valere apud.
INFORM . . . certiorem facere, 3 ; nuntiare, 1.
INHABITANT . . incola, æ, 1, c.
INJURIOUS . . . noxius, nocens ; gravis, e.
INNOCENT . . . innoxius, *not guilty ;* insons.
INSTRUCT . . . erudire, 4 ; (*command*) mandare, 1.
INSTRUCTOR . . magister, i, 2, m., &c. ; a., 1, f.
INTELLECT . . . mens, tis, 3, f.
INTENTIONALLY . de industria ; volenter.
INTEREST OF, IT
  IS THE . . . interest, *used with* meū, tuū, suū, &c., *and* the *gen. of subst.* (*See Grammar*).
INTO . . . . in, *with acc.*
IRON . . . . ferrum, i., 2, n.
ISLAND . . . . insula, æ, 1, f.
IT . . . . . is, ea, id : *our English impersonal* it *is translated by a verbal inflexion.*
ITALY . . . . Italia, æ, *name of a country,* f.
ITS . . . . . suus, sua, suum, *reflexive ;* ejus, *generally.*

JANUS . . . Janus, i. *name of a mythological personage,* 2, m.

JOURNEY . . . . iter, itneris, 3, n.; *to finish a journey*, iter
conficere.
JOVE . . . . . Jupiter, Jovis, *name of a mythological per-
sonage*, 3, m.
JUDGE . . . . judex, icis, 3, c.
JUDGMENT. . . judicium, i, 2, n.; *opinion*, sententia, æ,
1, f.
JULIA . . . . Julia, æ, *a woman's name*, 1, f.
JULIUS . . . . Julius, i., *a man's name*, 2, m.
JUST . . . . justus, æquus (*exactly, with numerals*) ipse.
JUSTICE . . . justitia, æ, 1, f.; *also by neut. of* justus,
æquus.

KEEP FROM . . continere, 2.
KEEP IGNORANT OF celare, 1.
KILL . . . . interficere, 3 ; necare, 1 ; occidere, 3.
KIND . . . . benignus, beneficus, benevolus (*of this
kind*), hujusmodo.
KIND-HEARTED . benignus.
KINDNESS . . . i. *feeling of kindness*, benignitas, atis, 3, f.
ii. *act of kindness*, beneficium, 2, n.
KING . . . . rex, regis, 3, m.
KNOW . . . . (*of a fact*) scire, 4, *followed by acc. with
infin.*; (*of a person*) cognoscere, 3.
KNOWLEDGE . . scientia, æ, 1, f.
KNOWLEDGE OF,
WITHOUT THE . clam, *with abj. ; sometimes with acc.*

LABIENUS . . Labienus, i., *a man's name*, 2, m.
LABOUR . . . i. *verb*, laborare, 1. ii. *subst.* labor, oris,
3, m. ; opus, 3, n.
LAKE . . . . lacus, us, 4, m.
LAME . . . . claudus.
LAMB . . . . agnus, 1, 2, m.
LARGE . . . . grandis, c. : magnus ; *a large house*, domus
ampla.
LAST . . . . postremus.
LAUGH & LAUGH AT ridere, 2.
LAW . . . . lex, legis, 3, f.
LAY ASIDE . . . deponere, 3.
LEAD ACROSS . . trajicere, 3.
LEADERSHIP . . *Use* dux, cis, 3, m. in *abl. absol.*, e.g.,
under my leadership = me duce.
LEARN . . . . discere.
LEARNED . . . doctus.
LEARNING . . . doctrina, æ, 1, f.
LEAVE . . . . i. relinquere, 3. ii. *to go away*, discedere,
leave out, omittere, 3.
LEFT . . . . sinister.
LEGION . . . . legio, onis, 3, f.

LENGTH . . . *In a phrase such as,* three feet in length, *use adj.* longus.
LETTER. . . . epistola, æ, 1, f.; litteræ, arum, 1, f.; *a letter of the alphabet,* littera.
LIFE . . . . vita, æ, 1, f.; also = *lifetime.*
LIGHT . . . . lumen, inis, 3, n.
LIKE (*verb*) . . amare, 1; juvare, 1.
LIEUTENANT . . legatus, i, 2, m.
LIKE . . . . *adj.* similis, *with gen. or dat.*
LIKE . . . . *adv.* similiter, *followed by* acc.; ceu, quasi, velut, haud aliter ac.
LION . . . . leo, nis, 3, m.
LISTEN . . . . auscultare, 1; audire, 4; obedire, 4.
LITTER (*a vehicle*) lectica, æ, 1, f.; *to be carried in a litter,* lectica ferri.
LIVE . . . . vivere, 3; *live on,* vesci, 3; *dwell in,* or *at,* habitare, 1.
LONDON . . . Londinium, i, *name of a town,* 2, n.
LONG . . . . longus, *when measure is specified followed by* acc.
LORD . . . . dominus, i, 2, m.
LORD, OF HIMSELF. sibi imperiosus.
LOSE . . . . perdere, 3; amittere, 3.
LOSS . . . . damnum, 2, n.
LOT . . . . . sors, tis, 3, f.
LOVE . . . . amor, oris, 3, m.; (*filial*) pietas, tis, 3, f.
LOVE, TO . . . amare, 1; diligere, 3.
LOVING . . . . amans.
LUCILIUS . . . Lucilius, i, 2, m.
LUCULLUS . . . Lucullus, i, 2, m.
LYONS . . . . Lugdunum, i, 2, n.

MAKE. . . . facere, 3.
MAN . . . . homo, inis, 3, m.; vir, viri, 2, m.
MANDATE . . . mandatum, i, 2, n.
MANLIUS . . . Manlius, i, 2, m.
MANY . . . . multi, plerique; *how many?* = quot.
MANY, A GOOD . complures; plerique.
MARCELLUS . . Marcellus, i, 2, m.
MARCH, ON THE,
  TO BE. . . . iter facere, 3; in itinere esse.
MARCH . . . . contendere, 3; iter facere, 3.
MARCUS . . . Marcus, i, 2, m.
MARIUS . . . Marius, i, 2, m.
MARRY . . . . i. *of the man,* ducere, *and* ducere in matrimonium, 3. ii. *of the woman,* nubere, *with dat.*
MARSEILLES . . Massilia, æ, 1, f.

MASTER . . . dominus, i, 2, m.; *to be master of one's-self*, sibi temperare.

MASTER OF, TO BE   potiri, 4, *dep.*

MATCH FOR, TO BE   par esse; *no match for*, impar, *with dat.*

MATTER . . . i. *subst. affair*, res, rei, 5, f. ii. *imp. verb*, *it matters*, refert.

MEANS . . . . *when used in a phrase*, by means of, *translate by* a, ab, or (*if secondary or agent*) per; *generally*, modus, i, 2, m.

MESSAGE . . . nuntius, i, 2, m.

MESSENGER . . nuntius, i, 2, m.

METELLUS . . . Metellus, i, 2, m.

MIGHT . . . . ops., *with all one's might*, summa ope.

MILETUS . . . Miletus, i, 2, f.

MILK . . . . lac, tis, 3, n.

MINA . . . . mina, æ, 1, f, *a Roman coin: in silver, worth about £3 15s. sterling; in gold, about £17 15s.*

MINDFUL . . . memor.

MISERABLE . . miser.

MISERY. . . . miseria, 1, f.

MISFORTUNE . . res adversæ; *also* adversa (*adj.*)

MISTAKE, TO . . errorem facere.

MISTRESS . . . domina, æ, 1, f.

MONEY . . . . pecunia, æ, 1, f.: *a piece of money*, numus, 2.

MONTH . . . . mensis, is, 3, m.

MORE . . . . plus, pluris, *used as a sub. in sing.*; *adv.*, magis; *also translated by the inflexion of the comparative.*

MORNING, IN THE   mane, *adv.; very early*, diluculo.

MORROW, TO- . cras, *adv.; crastino die.*

MOST . . . . plurimus, plerique, *most people; adv.* maxime; *also translated by the inflexion of superlative.*

MOUNTAIN . . mons 3, m.

MOVE . . . . movere, 2.

MOTHER . . . mater, tris, 3, f.

MUCH LESS . . nedum.

MULTITUDE . . multitudo, inis, 3, f.

MURDER . . . necare, 1; trucidare, 1.

MUSIC . . . . musica, æ, *or* musice, es, 1, f.

MY, MINE . . . meus.

NAME . . . i. *verb*, nominare, 1. ii. *subst.*, nomen, inis, 3, n.; *in the name of*, &c. = Pro fidem!

NAPLES. . . . Neapolis, is, 3, f.

NARRATE . . . narrare, 1.

NARROWNESS . . augustiæ, 1, f.

NATION . . . . gens, tis, 3, f.; natio, 3, f.
NEAR . . . . prope, juxta, *adv.*, *both with acc.*
NEARLY . . . fere, præne, *adv.*
NECESSARY, IT IS. oportet; also = "I must."
NEED . . . . i. *subst.*, opus. ii. *verb*, egere.
NEIGHBOURING . vicinus, propinquus.
NERVII . . . . Nervii, iorum, 2, n.
NET . . . . . rete, is, 3, n.; *a spider's net or web*, telæ,
          arum, 1, f.
NEVER . . . . nunquam.
NEW . . . . i. *adj.* novus, recens. ii. *subst. news*,
          nuntii.
NEXT . . . . proximus, *with dat.*; juxta, *with acc.*
NINE . . . . novem, *indecl. adj.*
NINETY. . . . nonaginta, *indecl. adj.*
NISMES . . . . Nemausus, i, 2, f.
NO . . . . . i. nullus. ii. *particle of negation*, haud
          vero, minime quidem.
NOBLE . . . . nobilis; clarus.
NOBLY . . . . præclare.
NO-ONE . . . nemo, inis, 3; nullus; *that no one*, ne quis.
NOR . . . . . neque, nec, neu.
NOT . . . . . non, haud, nē, *with imperat.; not even*,
          ne . . . quidem; *not at all*, nihil.
NOT ONLY . . . non solum.
NOTHING . . . nihil, nil; *nothing but*, nihil aliud nisi.
NOURISH . . . alere, 3.
NOW . . . . nunc; *more emphatic*, jam.
NUMBER . . . i. *verb*, numerare, 1. ii. *subst.* numerus,
          i, 2, m.

O ! . . . . . O ! *vocative;* ohē.
OBEDIENCE . . obedientia, æ, 1, f.; obtemperatio, onis,
          3, f.
OBEY . . . . parere, 2.
OBSCURE . . . obscurus; humilis, e.
OBSTINATE. . . pervicax, pertinax.
OCCUR . . . . incidere, 3 ; occidere, 3.
OF . . . . . *sign of genitive; after certain verbs use* ex,
          generally, de.
OFTEN . . . . sæpe; crebro.
OLD . . . . . senex, senis, 3, m.; vetus, antiquus, pris-
          tinus.
OLD-AGE . . . senectus, tutis, 3, f.
ON . . . . . in (*with abl.*) ; super (*with abl.*); *also, a
          sign of the abl.*
ON ACCOUNT OF . propter.
ONCE . . . . semel, *numeral adv.;* simul, *once upon a
          time*, aliquando; quodam tempore.
ONCE, AT . . . statim.

ONE . . . . . unus; *one at a time,* singuli, æ, a; *the one . . . the other;* alter . . . alter; alius . . . alius; *one of two*=alter.

ONE'S . . . . } *any one,* quivis; *oneself,* ipse; *when the sub-*
ONE-SELF . . . } *ject, use cases of* tu, *or the reflexive,* se.

ONLY . . . . solum, tantum; *not only,* non solum.

OPINION . . . sententia, æ, 1, f., judicium; *in my opinion,* me judice, *abl. abs.*

OPPOSE . . . . opponere, 3, *with dat.*

OPPRESS . . . premere, 3.

OPULENT . . . opulentus.

ORATION . . . oratio, onis, 3, f.

ORATOR . . . orator, oris, 3, m.

ORDER . . . . i. *verb,* imperare, 1, *with dat.;* jubere, 2, *with acc.* ii. *subst. an order,* jussum, 2, n.; imperatum, 2, n.

ORIGINAL . . . pristinus.

OSTIA . . . . Ostia, æ, 1, f.

OTHER . . . . alter, *other of two;* alius, *other, when not the same as any before-mentioned.*

OUR . . . . . noster.

OUT OF . . . . e, ex, de, *with abl.;* extra, *with acc.*

OUTSIDE . . . extra, *with acc.*

OVID . . . . Ovidius, i., *a man's name,* 2, m.

OWN . . . . *my own,* meus; *his own,* suus, &c.

PAIN . . . . dolor, oris, 3, m.

PANSA . . . . Pansa, æ, *a man's name,* 1, m.

PARDON . . . *(of a superior)* veni dare, *(of an equal)* ignoscere, 3.

PARENT . . . parens, tis, 3, c.

PASSIONS . . . animus, 2, m.

PAST (=PAST THINGS) . . . præterita, *pl. adj.*

PATIENCE . . . patientia, æ, 1, f.

PAY . . . . . solvere, 3; pendere, 3.

PEACE . . . . pax, pacis, 3, f.

PEOPLE . . . . populus, i., 2, m.; plebs, bis, 3, f., *the lower orders.*

PERHAPS . . . fortasse; *less emphatic,* forsitan.

PERISH . . . perire, 4.

PERMISSION, TO GIVE . . . } permittere, 3; *without permission,* invitus, injussu; *without my permission,* me invito; *with your permission,* pace tua; *I am permitted = I may =* licet mihi.
PERMIT . . .

PERSUADE . . . persuadere, 2, *with dat.*

PICTURE . . . tabula, picta, æ, 1, f.

PITCH A CAMP . castra, ponere, 3; munire, 3; and locare, 1.

PITY, TO . . . miserere, 2; miseresci, 3, *dep. and* miseret,
2. *Impers. Noun,* misericordia.
PLACE . . . . locus, i.; *plural,* loci, and loca, 2, *hetereo-geneous.*
PLAIN . . . . planities. 5, f.
PLAN . . . . concilium, i., 2, n.; *to form a plan,* concilium capere.
PLANCUS . . . Plancus, i., *a man's name,* 2, m.
PLANT . . . . serere, 3.
PLEASURE . . . voluptas, tis, 3, f.
PLEASANT . . . jucundus; *pleasant to look on,* amœnus.
PLEASE . . . . placere, 2, *it pleases me (I like)* =me libet.
PLEASED . . . lætus.
PLEASURE, TO GIVE *to do a pleasure to anyone,* gratum facere alicui.
PLENTY . . . copia, æ, 1, f.; copiæ, *forces, or troops.*
PLUNDER, TO . . diripere, 3.
POEM . . . . carmen, inis, 3, n.
POET . . . . poeta, æ, 1, m.
POND . . . . stagnum, i., 2, n.
POOR . . . . pauper, eris; egens.
POSITION (of affairs) rerum status.
POSSESSION OF, TO TAKE . . . ⎫ i. *verb,* potiri, *dep.,* 4; *with abl. or gen.*
POSSESS . . . ⎬ ii. ii. *subst.,* bona, *possessions.*
POST, CHIEF . . principatus, 4, m.
POWER . . . . vis, 3, f.; potestas, tatis. 3, f.; *in our power,* penes nos; *with all his power.* summis viribus, summa ope.
POWERFUL . . potens, validus.
PRACTISE . . . colere, 3.
PRÆTOR . . . prætor, oris, 3, m.
PRAISE. . . . i. *verb,* laudare, 1. ii. *subst.* laus, laudis, 3, f.
PRAY . . . . orare, 1; precari, 1, *dep.*
PRECEDE . . . antecedere, 3.
PREEMINENT . . præstans, insignis.
PREFER . . . malle, i. *Irreg.* Anteponere, 3, *with dat. and acc.;* posthabere, 2.
PRESENT . . . donum, 2, n.; munus, 3, n.
PRESENT AT, TO BE PRESENT, TO BE . ⎬ adesse. *Irreg.*
PRESENT, TO . . donare, 1.
PRESERVE . . . servare, 1; conservare, 1.
PREVENT . . . prohibere, 2; obstare, 1, *followed by quo minus and subj.*
PREVIOUSLY TO . ante . . . quam; prius . . . quam.
PRICE . . . . pretium, 2, n.
PROCONSUL . . pro-consul, ulis, 3, m.

PROMISE, A . . promissum, 2, n.; fides, ei, 5, f.
PROMISE, TO . . promittere, 3; polliceri, 2, *dep.*
PROPHETIC . . divinus; fatidicus.
PROPRÆTOR . . proprætor.
PROUD . . . . superbus; *to be proud*, superbire, 4.
PROVE . . . . probare, 1; docere, 2. *Prove oneself*, se
             præstare, præbere.
PRUDENCE. . . prudentia, æ, 1, f.; consilium, 2, n.;
             without prudence, expers, consilii.
PUBLIUS . . . Publius, i., *a man's name*, 2, m.
PUNISH . . .) punire, 4; pœnas sumere, 3; *to be punished*,
PUNISHMENT . .)   pœnas dare; *punishment*, pœna, 1, f.
PUPIL . . . . discipulus, i., 2, n.
PUT ON . . . inducre, 3.
PURSUE . . . sequi, 3, *dep.*; persequi, 3, *dep.*

QUEEN . . . regina, æ, 1, f.
QUESTION . . . interrogare, 1.
QUICK . . . . celer, citus; velox; *quickly*, celeriter.
QUINTUS . . . Quintus, i., *a man's name*, 2, m.

RAGE . . . . ira, æ, i., .; furor, 3, m.
RAMPART . . . vallum, i., 2, n.
RANK . . . . ordo, inis, 3, m.; *of noble rank*, haud ob-
             scuro loco natus.
RAPID . . . . celer; rapidus.
RASH . . . . præceps, temerarius.
RATHER . . . potius; *to have rather*, malle. *Irreg.*
REACH . . . . attingere, 3; pervenire, ni.
READ . . . . legere, 3; *read through*, perlegere, 3.
REALITY . . . res vera; *in reality*, re vera.
REASON . . . i. *subst.*, consilium, ratio, mens; =*cause*=
             causa. ii. *phrase: for what reason*,
             cur, quare, quamobrem.
RECALL . . . revocare, 1.
RECEIVE . . . accipere, 3; recipere, 3.
RECKON . . . i. *to value*, æstimare, 1. ii. *to count*,
             numerare, 1.
RECORD . . . referre, 3; tradere, 3.
REDUCE . . . i. *to bring to any condition*, redigere, 3.
             ii. *to conquer*, vincere, 3; subigere, 3.
REFUSE. . . . recusare, 1.
REGULUS . . . Regulus, i., *a man's name*, 2, m.
REJOICE . . . gaudere, *semi dep.*, 2; lætari, *dep.*, 1.
RELATE . . . exponere, 3; referre, 3.
RELYING . . . fretus, *with abl.*
REMAIN . . . manere, 2.
REMEMBER . . recordor, 1, *dep.*; memini, reminisci,
           . 3, *dep.*
REMIND .' . . monere, 3; admonere, 2.

RENDER . . . reddere, 3 ; præbere, 2.
RENOWNED . . præclarus.
REPAY . . . . adæquare.
REPENT . . . pœnitet, 2 ; *impers.*
REPLY . . . . i. *verb*, respondere, 2. ii. *subst.*, respon-
       sum, 2, m.
REPORT . . . renuntiare, 1 ; referre, 3 ; *to a letter*, re-
       scribere.
REQUIRE . . . (*ask*) poscere, 3.
RESIDE IN . . . (*to be placed*) poni, 3.
RESIST . . . . resistere, 3 ; obstare, 1 ; repugnare, 1.
RESTRAIN . . . retinere, 2.
RETURN . . . i. *verb*, *give back*, reddere ; *come back*,
       redire, 4 ; regredi, 3, *dep.* (*give back*)
       =reddere, 3. ii. *subst.*, reditus, us,
       4, m.
REVILE . . . . maledicere, 3, *with dat.*
REVOLUTION . . res novæ.
RHEIMS . . . . Remi, orum, 2, m.
RHODES . . . . Rhodos, i., *an island of the Ægean*, 2, f.
RHONE . . . . Rhodanus, i., *a river of Gaul*, 2, m.
RHINE . . . . Rhenus, i., *a river of Germany*, 2, n.
RICH . . . . dives, itis ; opulentus.
RICHES . . . . divitiæ, arum, 1, f. ; opes, opum, 3, f.
RIGHT . . . . justus.
RISE . . . . incrementum, 2, n.
RIVER . . . . flumen, inis, 3, n. ; amnis, is, 3, m. ; flu-
       vius, i, 2, m.
ROAD . . . . iter, itineris, 3, n. ; via, æ, 1, f.
ROB . . . . . spoliare, 1.
ROBBER . . . . latro, onis, 3, n.
ROMAN . . . . Romanus, i., *an inhabitant of Rome*, 2, m. ;
       of-Rome, Romanus, *adj.*
ROME . . . . Roma, æ, *the chief city of Italy*, 1, f.
ROOMY . . . . amplus, capax (*latter with gen.*)
ROYAL . . . . regalis.
RUBICON . . . Rubico, onis, *a river of Italy*, 3, m.
RULE . . . . regere, 3 ; imperare, 1 ; dominari, 1, *dep.*

SACRED . . . sanctus ; sacer ; religiosus.
SAFE . . . }
SAFETY, IN . . } incolumis, tutus.
SAFETY . . . . salus, 3, f.
SALUTE . . . . salutare, 1 ; salutem dicere, 3.
SAME . . . . idem.
SARDIS . . . . Sardes, ium, 3, f.
SATISFACTION, TO
 ONE'S . . . ex sententia.
SATISFY . . . satisfacere, 3.
SAY, TO . . . dicere, 3.

SAY TO, NOT . . negare, 1.
SCARCE . . . . rarus; *a scarce bird*, rara avis; *a scarce kind of friend*, rarum genus amicorum.
SEA . . . . . mare, is, 3, n.
SECOND . . . . secundus.
SECRET . . . . secretus, occultus.
SEE . . . . . videre, 2, cernere, 3; aspicere. 3.
SEEM . . . . videri, 2.
SELDOM . . . . raro.
SELL . . . . vendere, 3; *to sell at*, vendere, *with abl.*
SENATE . . . . senatus, us, 4, m.; patres, 3, m.
SEND . . . . mittere, 3; *send forward*, præmittere, 3; *to send for*, arcessere, 3.
SENECA . . . . Seneca, æ, 1. m.
SERVANT . . . servus, i, 2, m.; famulus, i, 2, m.; minister, tri, 2, m.
SERVE . . . . servire, 4.
SERVICE, TO BE OF prodesse.
SERVICE, MILITARY militia, 1, f.; *at service*, militiæ.
SET OUT . . . proficisci, *dep.* 3; abire, 4, *irreg.*
SEVEN . . . .` septem, *indecl. adj.*
SEVENTH . . . septimus.
SEVERE . . . . gravis.
SEVERELY . . . graviter; aspere.
SHEEP . . . . ovis, is, 3, f.
SHEPHERD . . . pastor, oris, 3, m.
SHIELD . . . . scutum, i, 2, n.; clipeus. i, 2, m.
SHILLING . . . solidus, i, 2, m.
SHORT . . . . brevis. e.
SHOW . . . . monstrare, 1; ostendere, 3.
SHUT . . . . claudere, 3.
SICILIAN . . . Siculus, i, 2, m.
SICILY . . . . Sicilia, æ, 1, f.
SIDE OF, ON THIS. citra, *with acc.; on the other side of*, trans, ultra, *with acc.*
SILENCE . . . i. *subst.*, silentium, i, 2, n. ii. *to keep silence (to say nothing)*, tacere, 2; *(to make no noise)*, silere.
SISTER . . . . soror, oris, 3, f.
SITUATED . . . situs.
SIT . . . . . sedere, 2; *with in, and the abl.*
SIX . . . . . sex, *indecl. adj.*
SIXTEENTH . . sextus decimus.
SIZE . . . . . magnitudo, inis, 3, f.
SKILFUL . . . peritus; callidus; sollers.
SKIN . . . . pellis, is, 3, f.
SLAVE . . . . servus, i, 2, m.
SLAY . . . . interficere.
SLENDER . . . tenuis.

So . . . . . . sic, ita, ut; *so many*, tot, *so* . . . . *as*,
     tam . . . quam, adeo . . . ut; *so*
     much . . . tantus.
Sober . . . . . sobrius.
Socrates . . . Socrates, is, *a man's name*, 3, m.
Soldier . . . miles, itis, 3, m.
Some . . . . . i. *adj.*, aliqui, aliqua, aliquod. ii. *subst.*
     aliquis, aliquid; *some one or a certain*
     person, quidam; *some* . . . . *some*,
     some . . . . *others*, alii . . . . alii;
     some people often = some.
Sometimes . . . interdum (*with notion of seldom*), non-nun-
     quam (*often*).
Soon. . . . emphatic, mox, jam; *less emphatic*, brevi
     tempore; *as soon as possible*, quam
     primum.
Sorrow . . . dolor, 3, m.
Sosii . . . . Sosii, orum, 2, m.
Soul . . . . animus, 2, m.
Sound . . . . i. *subst.* sonitus, us, 4, m. ii. *verb*, so-
     nare, 1.
Sow . . . . . serere, 3.
Spain . . . . Hispania, æ, 1, f.
Spaniards . . Hispani, orum, 2, m.
Speak . . . . loqui, 3, *dep.*; dicere, 3.
Speak well of . benedicere, 3, *with dat.*
Spear . . . . hasta, æ, 1, f.
Speech, a . . . oratio, onis, 3, f.
Speech, to make a orationem habere, 2.
Speed, at full . (*of a horse*) equo admisso.
Spider . . . . aranea, æ, 1, f.
Stand . . . . stare, 1; *to make a stand*, resistere; *to*
     stand high in one's favor, esse in gratia,
     or favore apud aliquem ; *stand round*,
     circumsistere, 3.
Start . . . . proficisci, 3, *dep.*
State . . . . prædicere, 3; narrare, 1.
State, the . . res publica, rei publicæ, f.
Station . . . i. *rank*, ordo, inis, 3, m. ii. *a place occu-*
     pied, locus, 2, *heterogeneous*.
Statue . . . . statua, 1, f.
Stay . . . . commorari, 1, *dep.* ; moraris, 1, *dep.*
Stick, a . . . baculum *and* baculus, i, 2, n.
Still . . . . tamen.
Stone . . . . lapis, idis, 3, m.; saxum, i, 2, n.
Storm, to . . oppugnare.
Storm, to take by expugnare.
Strait . . . . discrimen, inis, 3, n.
Strive . . . . niti, 3, *dep.;* eniti.
Strong . . . . fortis, e; validus, potens, robustus.

SUBDUE	domare, 1 ; (*thoroughly*) perdomare.
SUCCESS . . .	res prosperæ ; res secundæ.
SUCH	(*quality*) talis ; (*quantity*) tantus.
SUCCOUR . . .	succurrere, 3.
SUITABLE . . .	aptus, idoneus.
SULLA	Sulla, æ, *a man's name*, 2, m.
SULMO	Sulmo, onis, *an Italian town*. 3. m.
SUM	i. *an amount*, summa. ii. *a large sum of money*, grandis pecunia; *at a small sum*, parvi pretii.
SUMMER . . .	æstas, 3, f.
SUPPLY	suppeditare aliquid alicui.
SURPRISING . .	mirus.
SURRENDER . .	deditio. 3, f.
SURROUND . . .	circumdare, 3; cingere, 3.
SWAY	imperium, 2, n.
SWEET	dulcis, e.
SWIM	nare, 1; *swim across*, tranare, 1.
SWORD	gladius, i, 2, m.
SYRACUSE . . .	Syracusæ, arum, 1, f.
TACITUS . . .	Tacitus, i, *a man's name*, 2, m.
TAKE, TO . . .	capere, 3; sumere, 3 ; *to take in good part*, boni consulere, in bonem partem accipere, boni *or* æqui bonique facere.
TAKE CARE, TO .	cavere, 2; curare, 1.
TEACH, TO . . .	docere, 2.
TEACHER . . .	magister, tri, 2, m.
TEAR	lacrima ; *in tears*, lacrimans.
TEDIOUS . . .	longus.
TELL	narrare; dicere, 3.
TEMPESTUOUS . .	procellosus.
TEMPLE . . .	templum, i, 2, n.; ædes, 3, f.; pl. *a house*.
TEMPT	tentare, 1 ; sollicitare, 1.
TEN	decem.
TENEDOS . . .	Tenedos, 1, f.
TENTH	decimus.
TERMS	conditiones, 3, f.
TERRITORY . .	fines, 3, f.
TERROR . . .	terror, 3, f.
THAMES . . .	Tamesis, is, 3, m.
THAN	quam, *also translated by abl. after comparatives*.
THAT	i. *pron.* ille, iste, is, *relat.* qui. ii. *conj.* ut, quod.
THEFT	furtum, i, 2, n.
THEIR	i. *reflexive*, suus. ii. *non-reflexive*, eorum.
THEMSELVES . .	se; *they themselves*, ipsi.
THEN	tum.
THERE	illic, ibi.

THERE IS . . .	There *is used as an introductory expletive;* hence *"there is"*=est.
THEREFOR . . .	igitur.
THICK	densus.
THING	res, negotium; things *is often translated by neut. plur. of adjectives, e.g. many things*=multa.
THINK	putare, 1; censere, 2; *think highly of* or *a deal of,* magni æstimare.
THIRD	tertius.
THIS	hic, hæc, hoc.
THITHER . . .	illuc.
THREE	tres, *indecl. adj.; three days*=biduum.
THROUGH . . .	per, *with acc., or when it signifies* by means of, *translate by abl.*
THROW	jacere, 3; *to throw at one's feet,* alicui ad pedes projicere.
TIBER	Tiberis, Tybris, Tibris, is, *or* idis, 3, m.
TIBUR	Tibur, uris, 3, m.
TIME	tempus, 3, n.; *for the first time,* primum; *for the second,* iterum; *for the third,* tertium, &c.
TIME	tempus, oris, 3, n.; *age,* ætas, 3, f.
TIRED	fessus, defessus; *I am tired,* me tædet.
TITUS	Titus, i, 2, m.
TO	i. *after verbs of motion towards small towns and islands, translated by acc.* ii. *generally,* ad, in.
TO-DAY	hodie.
TOGETHER . . .	simul, una, *often followed by* cum.
TOMB	tumulus, i., 2, m.
TOMI	Tomi, orum, 2, f.; *also* Tomis, is, 3, f.
TO-MORROW . .	cras; crastino die.
TONGUE . . .	lingua, æ, 1, f.
TOP	*translate by* summus, *in agreement with subst., e.g.,* summo monte, summa voce, summis aquis.
TOWARDS . . .	erga; *(of time)* sub.
TOWN	oppidum, i. 2, n.; urbs, is, 3, f.
TRAVEL. . . .	iter facere, 3.
TREACHERY . .	proditio, onis, 3, f. (*meaning* act of treachery).
TREE	arbor, oris, 3, f.
TRIBUNE . . .	tribunus, 2, m.
TRIUMVIR . . .	triumvir, ri, g, m.; *also* tresviri, *pl.*
TROOPS	copiæ, arum, 1, f.; milites, 3, m.
TROY	Troja, æ. 1, f.
TRUMPET . . .	tuba, æ, 1, f.
TRUST	fidere, confidere, 3.
TULLIA	Tullia, æ, 1, f.

Turn . . . flectere, 3 ; vertere, 3 ; *turn back,* re-
vertere, 3.
Turn out . . . (*become*) evadere, 3.
Twelve . . . duodecim, *indecl. adj.*
Twenty . . . viginti, *indecl. adj.*
Twice . . . . vis. *Twice a day=twice in a day.*
Two . . . . duo, æ, o.

UNACQUAINTED ignarus, *with gen.,* or *used in the abl.
absolute.*
Unaccustomed . insuetus.
Under . . . . sub, *with abl., but after verbs of motion
with acc.*
Understanding. ingenium, i., 2, n. ; mens, 3, f.
Undertake . . excipere, 3.
Undertaking . inceptum, i., 2, n. ; cœptum, 2 ; con-
silium, 2.
Unexpectedly . de improviso.
Unfair . . . iniquus.
Unfortunate .. infelix, infaustus.
Unto . . . . ad, in, *with acc.: same in force as to.*
Untrue . . . falsus.
Unwilling, to be nolle. *Irreg.*
Unworthy . . indignus, *with abl.*
Use . . . . . uti, 3, *dep. with abl. ; it is of use,* juvat.
Useful . . . utilis, e. ; aptus.
Useless . . . inutilis, e. ; irritus.
Utterly . . . funditus.

VALIANT . . fortis, acer, audax.
Valour . . . virtus, utis, 3, f.
Value . . . . æstimare, 1 ; *constructed with* magni,
pluris, maximi, &c.
Value . . . . pretium, 2, n.
Value, of more. pluris (pretii, *understood*).
Varus . . . . Varus, i., 2, m.
Veil. . . . . velare, 1.
Vent . . . . evomere, 3.
Venusia . . . Venusia, æ, 1, f.
Verres . . . Verres, is, 3, m.
Verse . . . . carmen, inis, 3, n. ; *one line of verse,*
versus, 4.
Very . . . . admodum.
Victory . . . victoria, æ, 1, f.
Vigor . . . . vigor, 3, m.
Violence . . . vis, vim, vi ; *with the greatest violence,*
summa, vi ; *plur.,* vires, 3, f., *strength.*
Virtue . . . . virtus, utis, 3, f. ; probitas, 3, f.
Visit . . . . . i. visere, 3. *To visit one,* aliquem con-
venire.

VOICE . . . . vox, vocis, 3, f.; *at-the-top-of-his-voice*, summa voce.

VOTE . . . . deceruere, 3.

WALK . . . ambulare, 1.

WALL . . . . murus, i., 2, m.; *walls fortified*, mœnia, ium, 3, n.

WANT . . . . egere, 2; indigere, 2.

WAR . . . . bellum, 2, n.

WARLIKE . . . bellicosus.

WARD OFF . . depellere, 3; arcere, 2.

WATCH . . . i. *verb*, vigilare., *watch over*, cavere alicui. ii. *subst.*, vigilia, æ, 1, f.; *at the first watch*, prima vigilia.

WAY . . . . i. *a road*, via, æ, 1, f.; iter, itineris, 3, n. ii. *a manner of action*, modus; cf. *in the same way*, eodem modo.

WEALTH . . . divitiæ, arum, 1, f.; opes, opum, 3, f.

WEALTHY . . . dives, itis; opulentus.

WEAPONS . . . arma, orum, 2, n.; *a weapon*, telum, 2, n.

WEARY . . . } defessus, defatigatus; *he is wearied*, eum

WEARIED . . . } tædet.

WEB . . . . *of a spider*, telæ, arum, 1, f.

WEIGHT . . . pondus, eris, 3, n.; *a pound weight*, libra pondo.

WELL, TO BE . . valere, 2; bene se habere, 2; *to get well*, convalescere.

WHAT . . . . i. *interrog.* quid? ii. *relat.* quod; *what (things))* quæ.

WHEN , . . . quum, ubi; *interrog.* quando?

WHENCE . . . unde.

WHERE . . . . i. *interrog.* ubi; ubinam? ii. *relat.* quā ubi.

WHETHER . . . utrum . . . . an; utrum . . . . ne.

WHICH . . . . i. *interrog. which of two?* uter; *which of many?* quis, qui. ii. *relat.* qui.

WHITE . . . . albus (*opposed to* ater); candidus (*opposed to* niger).

WHITHER . . . i. *interrog.* quo? ii. *relat.* quo.

WHO . . . . i. *interrog.* quis? ii. *relat.* qui.

WHOLE . . . . totus, omnis; cunctus, universus.

WHOSE . . . . cujus; *also* cujus, cuja, cujum. Cf. *cujum pecus?*

WHY . . . . cur; quare, quamobrem.

WICKED . . . scelestus, flagitiosus, improbus.

WIFE . . . . uxor, oris, 3, f.; conjux, 3, c.

WILL . . . . i. *verb.* velle. ii. *subst.* voluntas, atis, 3, f.

WILLING . . . libens.

WING . . . . ala, æ, 1, f.

WINE . . . . vinum, i, 2, n.

4 *

WINTER . . . . hiems, is, 3, f.; *winter-quarters*, hiberna.
WISDOM . . . sapientia, æ, 1, f.
WISE . . . . . sapiens, callidus.
WISE, TO BE . . sapere, 3.
WISH . . . . i. *verb*, velle. ii. *subst.* voluntas, i, 3, f.
WITH . . . . cum, *with abl.; also abl. alone.*
WITHIN . . . intra.
WOLF . . . . lupus, i. '   m
WOMAN . . . femina, æ, 1, f.; mulier, is, 3, f.
WONDERFUL . . mirabilis, e; mirus.
WOOD . . . . silva, æ, 1, f.
WORD . . . . verbum, i, 2. n.; dictum, 2, n.; *to send word*, certiorem facere; *to have a good word for, to speak well of*, bene-dicere.
WORK . . . . i. *subst.* opus, eris, 3, n.; opera, æ, 1, f.
                    ii. *verb.* laborare, 1.
WORLD . . . . mundus, i, 2, m.; orbis, 3, m.; terræ, arum, f.; orbis terræ *and* orbis terrarum.
WORTHY . . . dignus.
WOULD THAT . . utinam.
WOUND . . . i. *verb*, vulnerare, sauciare. , 1. ii. *subst.* vulnus, eris, 3, n.
WRETCHED . . miser; infelix.
WRITE . . . . scribere, 3.

YIELD . . concedere, 3.
YOUNG MAN . adolescens ; (*grown up*), juvenis.

www.ingramcontent.com/pod-product-compliance
Lightning Source LLC
Chambersburg PA
CBHW030114030726
47498CB00007B/2385